Thomas,

I'm so glad you're putting your writing on Facebook again. You have some serious literary chops my friend. We'll definitely be hanging out in the near future. Keep doing your thing: you do it well.

The Yukon Glory

Jake Ziemba

By Jake Ziemba
Edited by Steve Ziemba
Cover and Art Direction by Evan Hume
Back Cover Text by Nate Waggoner

Wordclay
1663 Liberty Drive, Suite 200
Bloomington, IN 47403
www.wordclay.com

First published by Wordclay on 4/14/2008.

ISBN: 978-1-6048-1112-4 (sc)

Library of Congress Control Number: 2008927053

Printed in the United States of America.

This book is printed on acid-free paper.

~For David Heyer, Sarah Fletcher,
and Mom and Dad~

Table of Contents

"If you want to stay healthy in America, don't get sick."
- Unattributed

"The fields are ruined, the ground is dried up,
The grain is destroyed, the new wine is dried up,
The oil fails."
-Joel 1:10

"What is the meaning of this voyage to New York?
What kind of sordid business are you on?
I mean man, whither goest thou?
Whither goest thou, America, in thy shiny car in the night?"
-Jack Kerouac, On The Road

Chapter 1: Waking up

"I am interested in what happens to people when they must adapt to a new world."

-Jean Renoir

The roof of the boxcar kept the sunlight out well enough, but it could not hold off the rain. Fat drops of water raced each other single-file down all four walls, soon to be replaced by yet more runners in a constant relay. It was late October. The day was young, and sodden, and so was I. The man in the corner to my right looked maybe five years older than myself, early thirties, perhaps, and was equally soaked. He was wearing a prison jumper, its original orange once faded and mildewed, now restored to its former glory by the moisture. Perhaps his all-but-certain background should have alarmed me, but it did not. I was no stranger to unsavory characters, but the worst people I've known rarely, if ever, had done time.

He appeared awake and cognizant of his surroundings, but was content to lean the lower half of his face into his clasped hands, cloaking his expression. His brow was slightly furrowed from the gears apparently turning in his mind. A thinker, this one. I traced his line of vision to the corner opposite him, to my left. It was occupied by another man.

My other neighbor was wearing a tie, impeccably knotted, which clung damply to his chest like a drowned snake. The emblem of formality disturbed me far more than the other man's prison uniform. People who wore ties and worked for the man in tall, faceless skyscrapers were crazy enough; what kind of man would put on a tie to go rail-hopping? *Were* we rail-hopping? For the first time I questioned exactly what it was I was doing in a dripping boxcar with two strangers. I could not recall anything that would have prompted me to come here. I couldn't recall much of anything, actually. The issue of where I was, and what had brought me here, would have to wait until I could rid myself of the throbbing headache that, come to think of it, had been plaguing me since I awoke. That question, which no doubt held a convoluted answer, would have to wait. At the moment, I only wanted to figure out if it was safe to sleep, and hopefully do just that.

Although he appeared alert on the surface, I did not fear the Jail Bird, the nickname I had given him inside my head. The word "ESCAPEE" was practically written on his forehead, and such people were usually in dire need of friends. He didn't seem crazy, and I doubted he'd kill any potential benefactors without good reason. I determined not to give him one. The other man, whom I dubbed Mr. Tie, was not so easy to figure out. Just as surely as Jail Bird did not emanate malice, Mr. Tie gave off no overtly threatening signals. He struck me as an annoying creature, a mosquito who might get lucky and pass along some sort of pernicious disease with his bite, but was far more likely to simply be swatted. On top of that, he was asleep, curled fetal, and whimpering like a dog having a bad dream. It was not a good look for him. Thick, no-nonsense glasses hung limply from his nose.

Sleep cried out to me louder than ever, the perfect all-natural solution to my headache. The corroded iron floor of the boxcar was no mattress, but in a pinch it could be used as such. The cursed rain had not let up, and over a quarter-inch of standing murky water had aggregated on the floor. Slowly I rose, without sudden movement, and made my way to the wide door of the boxcar. Just before my hand alighted on the rusty handle to open it, I was stopped by a voice behind me.

"I'm thinkin' you don't wann' do that."

In the corner directly opposite mine, hidden in plain sight, reclined a man with stringy black hair to his shoulders. He wore a leather jacket, wrinkled and clinging to the contours of his torso. Hiking boots, partially submerged in the muck, covered his feet. He was wearing blue jeans, more accurately grey jeans, that looked older than I was. His smile held a note of cruelty.

"On second thought, go ahead, open it up. Yer not scared, are ya?" he drawled.

"Who are you?"

"I think once you quit jabbering and open the door, we'll all learn quite a bit about who we is, and who we is not."

I know intelligent conversation is a lot to ask from a stranger in a boxcar, but Jesus. The door handle remained firmly in place on my first attempt to move it. The never-ending rain kept sloshing down from the roof to my hands, stealing my grip. Attempt Number Two was slightly more successful, and the handle creaked in protest. Number Three, oft purported to be a charm, was anything but, and my right hand flew off the handle and caught on a rusted nail jutting from the car's side. Impaled beneath the right index knuckle, I fought back a scream, not of pain, but surprise. There was hardly any pain. I had to reach over with my left hand to dislodge the right, but still, I barely felt it. The only evidence was a thin scrape where my hand had raked along the edge as I freed it, and a paltry trickle of blood. I didn't understand. Maybe I should've been emboldened by the lack of pain, but I wasn't. The list of things I couldn't account for was piling up. Propelled this time by anger, not mere curiosity, I took hold of the handle with both hands and wrenched with my entire body, flinging the door open and flooding the boxcar's innards with light.

A brilliant scythe of sun chopped me in the face, and I fell to the floor with a scream. I instinctively rolled back to my corner, as far out of the light as I could get, water running out of the boxcar, over my face and into my nostrils. The rusty water filled my sinuses and I sneezed, but it was inaudible over the screaming and laughter that filled the car. My left hand reached out for the door, the light frying the bones of my fingers, and I threw the door shut with one clumsy shove. With the soft darkness restored I was able to think again, but someone was still screaming. Leatherman, who'd dared me to do that in the first place, and Jail Bird were silent, their respective corners having gone untouched by the sun. It was Mr. Tie, flopping about in what little water remained on the floor, screaming to end creation. The man in the leather jacket extended a booted heel and kicked him in the back of the head. The screams died away into a whimper, and I fell limply back to the wall of the car, with no sound but the shallow heaving breaths of Mr. Tie to disturb me. Jail Bird remained silent, with his face into his fists, watching it all transpire.

No one spoke. The man in the jacket had adopted a pose similar to the Jail Bird's, but his thick, veiny hands could not hide the giddy smile peaking at the corners of his mouth. It was the smile of a child who has just inflicted cruelty on an organism too weak to defend itself. I had been five the first time I saw it. My older brother and his friends had caught a frog in the swamp behind our house, and had pulled its legs off. One of the boys was using his eyeglasses and the harsh mid-afternoon sun to cook it. I came out of the house, hoping that the older boys would let me tag along with them when they rode their bikes to the junkyard, to do whatever mysterious things that cool older brothers did when out of the watchful sight of parents. When I got close enough to see what they were doing, I screamed and turned to run back into the house, but it was too late. They chased me down, tackled me, and made me eat what was left of the frog. The smiles they'd worn when torturing the frog and torturing me were identical. My brother was hit and killed by a train a week and a half later. I can't say I was all that sad to see him go.

The man in the leather jacket was clearly relishing the unspoken panic and confusion that hung in the air. Jail Bird still hadn't moved, or betrayed any signs of fear or uncertainty. I admired him for that. Provided he wasn't some sort of lunatic with remarkable self control (something I still couldn't rule out), he would be a good friend to make. My left hand was twitching involuntarily, and I could see layers of flesh burned away, chunks floating like little white rafts in the pool that had collected in my corner. The hand itself resembled a crude glove fashioned from hamburger. God only knows what my face must have looked like. My right hand, by contrast, bore no signs of the rusted nail that had breached it minutes earlier. A full-on puncture had done no harm, but mere seconds in the sunlight had gravely disfigured me. I wanted some goddamn answers, but Mr. Tie beat me to it.

"What did you do to us?" he croaked, still lying face down. He had caught the sunburst a lot worse than I had, and I was glad I couldn't see what it had done to him.

Leatherman just laughed. His frog had been burnt to a crisp, and he was enjoying every vicious moment. "You mean you can't figure it out? Shame on you son, you smelled like a smart one. Just calm down and think a-"

"Vampires," interjected the Jail Bird. "We're vampires, just like you."

He finally dropped his hands from his face. His lips and chin were smeared with dried blood.

"That's good son, that's real good. You stank like jail when I found you, but I spent time in a few jails myself, an' there's always few fellas with brains got locked up by mistake. If yer as smart as I think y'are, you'll learn real quick it's a bad idea to interrupt me."

Jail Bird chewed his upper lip and nodded absently. With his close-cropped hair and blood smearing his face and neck, he looked haggard, but strong, like a marathon runner who just finished a race but could do another mile or two if necessary.

"You're lying." It was Mr. Tie, still panting face-down on the floor. "There's no such...thing as...vampires."

"You want me to open that door on ya one more time? You wanna check how sharp your teeth are? You wanna check yer shirt for some poor old homeless bastard's blood?" Each taunting question was accompanied by a playfully truculent boot to the head. He was too weak to fight back.

"Cut that shit out," I barked. "I don't care if he's wearing a tie, he doesn't need to be treated like that."

"That's mighty big talk coming from a junkie I found on his knees behind a tool shed, paying for his next hit with his mouth-"

Right away I went for my gun, but came up empty. My hand was still at my fruitless hip when Leatherman cocked my pistol in my face.

"Listen, fag. A bullet in yer brain won't kill ya, but it'll ruin what's left of yer cocksukin' face, and hurt pretty goddamn bad on top of that. Watch yerself."

The steady rumble of the train was pierced by an awful screeching. A bump in the tracks caught us off guard and threw my head back into the wall. Any trace of external light snuffed out as the squealing grew louder and the train slowed to a crawl. Leatherman lumbered to his feet and brushed his stringy hair from his eyes.

"We got's us a train to catch fellas. Stay close if you wanna see tomorrow."

With the confident, if not slightly bored manner of one performing a simple daily chore, he opened the gate and hopped out of the car. The Jail Bird was right behind him, the picture of silent obedience. When I got up to follow, I noticed that Mr. Tie was still lying prone on the floor. A blend of kindness and curiosity prompted me to help him back to his feet. His skin was still raw, but the intensity of the burns had faded to the degree of only a bad sunburn. My left hand had healed significantly as well. I silently hoped my face was making a similar recovery.

"C'mon buddy, we gotta move," I told him, with an arm around his back to prop him up. "Find out what the next stop on the freak show is."

He grunted in sullen affirmation.

"Can you walk?"

"My feet really hurt, but yeah, I suppose so." His voice was thin and nasal, a surprisingly accurate reflection of his physical form.

"Alright then, let's go figure out where the hell we are."

I hopped out of the boxcar and into total darkness. There was no light of any sort, and yet I could *see,* see clearly, more clearly than I'd ever seen in the brightest daylight with my glasses. A sort of hazy, ethereal green skirted the margins of my peripheral vision, but everything else in sight was lit up and detailed with remarkable clarity. We appeared to be in some sort of train depot, a cavernous warehouse the size of a cathedral. It was really nothing special. What was special was the box on a shelf 200 yards away with **Vancouver BC** scrawled in chicken scratch on the lower left-hand corner. What was special was the enormous overhead light handing above us, its bulb smashed out long ago but the fixture still clearly visible in utter darkness. What was special was the minute scratch above the mouse hole on the other side of the room, and the moldy breadcrumbs in front of it. The mouse was burrowed a few feet back into the drywall, sleeping dreamlessly. I could smell its rudimentary animal contentment. The stench of gasoline and old rags slowly but irrefutably going to dust dominated the air. I turned around to smell the train. It was rust and rain, fire and steel, but further down, pollen, and…corn? Yes, fresh corn. In some distant past, who knows how long ago, this car had been filled with corn, on its way from the Midwest to some far away market. I was literally smelling the past, smelling through time. It felt like I had been born again, an infant waking up to the sensations and secrets of a world he's lived in, but never truly understood. Whatever I had lost in becoming whatever I currently was didn't even feel worthy of missing.

Eager to try out another sense, I reached out and placed my fingertips on the side of the car. It was coarse and weathered, as I could have determined before my change, but now I could actually *feel* its age. Almost 40 years of exposure to the elements. I have no idea how I knew this, but I put my other hand on the siding, searching for the details of a story buried under a dense layer of pure time. I pressed my ear to the wall, hoping the car would just give up and whisper its story, when I heard a woman scream.

My newfound hypersensitivity pinpointed the screamer's location right away. She was behind a dumpster about 120 yards away. I abandoned the boxcar and its library of trivia and sprinted to the sound. Seconds after I took off running I was smashed in the forehead with a brick. It sent me sliding across the floor into a shopping cart filled with spare engine parts, which clattered all about the floor and set the world ringing. The surprise blow had rattled me, but I was still able to get back to my feet, when two men promptly jumped on my back. Gloved fists rained down on my face, my head. One of them had their hands around my neck, and I was brought down again. The fists stopped for a moment, and I was able to get a clear look at one of my attackers. He had stringy hair, pallid skin, and bore quite a resemblance to Leatherman, but he had a certain simian quality that was all his own. There was no exposed skin on his body, except for his face, peeking out from beneath a hooded sweatshirt. He opened his mouth wide and I saw a pair of curved, elongated fangs poking out from behind his lip. *Another vampire?* In light of recent events, it wasn't as surprising as it could have been, but it was enough to take away the last bit of breath that hadn't been choked from me. I gasped, and he saw into my mouth, made a face that was puzzled, then terrified. Recoiling in fear, he leapt off of me and hastily threw off the gloves he'd been wearing. "Watch their blood!" he yelled to the others. "Watch their blood!"

I scurried to my feet as quickly as I could. Our attackers were now giving us a wide berth. Jail Bird and Leatherman's adversaries had relented as well. The three of us formed a tight circle, back to back to back, leaving no angle uncovered. We were massively outnumbered, but the other vampires were hesitant to attack us, even touch us.

"We're sorry," said the vampire in the hooded sweatshirt, bafflingly. "We didn't know. Now leave. There's no place for you here."

"We're just passing through," Leatherman growled. "You could've warned us."

"You didn't," he replied. It was very obvious they both wanted to harm each other, but they were restraining themselves. Why? Was there some vampire code of conduct I wasn't aware of?

On the other side of the room, a rusty door squeaked open, letting in a beam of sunlight that formed a barrier between the others and ourselves. A lone security guard waddled in, smelling like a ham sandwich.

"What the fuck is going on in here?!" he shouted, shutting the door behind him and switching on his flashlight. In doing so, he signed his death certificate, as dozens of vampires, all of them rail-thin, leapt from every available hiding place and hurled themselves upon him. The guard didn't even have a chance to scream before he went down in the shifting swarm of starved vampires.

"Fuckin' shit," muttered Leatherman, helping Jail Bird to his feet. "They're desperate.We gotta get outta here. Fast."

"We can't leave yet," I shouted back, over the moans and snarls of the feeding horde. There's no way that one man could feed them all, and they pushed and shoved each other out of the way to get to him. "There's a girl in here. I heard her scream before they jumped us."

"Uh…that was me, actually." Mr. Tie came tip-toeing out from behind an oil drum. Leatherman gave a look of shocked disgust the hair hanging over his face couldn't hide.

"I'll deal with you two later. Right now, we gotta catch a train. Follow me. No fucking around this time."

Leatherman shoved aside an oil drum, revealing a cramped but useable side door. He ducked inside, and we followed, leaving the depot vampires to their apparently long overdue meal. We came out in a long narrow hallway with more fluorescent lamps hung from the ceiling, but these still worked. The light made the skin on my arms and neck tingle unpleasantly, but not enough to be anything more than a distraction. Only a few feet in front of us sat an iron giant, dilapidated enough to make our old boxcar seem luxurious. Rust and grime dangled from its sides like icicles. Duct tape had been liberally applied to the windows of the conductor's quarters to patch their cracks. The hulking train looked like a junk stalagmite that had conveniently coalesced up from the bowels of the Earth over a set of equally crusty railroad tracks. Beneath the bronze whistle packed with cobwebs and behind the cracked headlight, the name of the beast was inlaid in filthy ivory: **THE YUKON GLORY**. The four of us looked her up and down in reverent silence, awestruck that an object so mercilessly abandoned could continue to exist and hold its shape. This train had withstood not only all the terrible wounds time and nature could inflict, but the rejection and neglect of those who had created her. Yet she continued to stand, and did so with a quiet, immutable majesty.

We heard the footsteps of the engineers long before we saw them, and thus were able to find adequate hiding behind yet another rusted out oil drum. They smelled like gin and lack of sleep, and they made me very hungry. Not for rest or alcohol, though I would have welcomed either, but for *them,* and for the blood they so miserly kept locked away in their veins. I could tell we all shared the same thoughts, but Leatherman did not move, so neither did we. Whatever crazy game we were playing, he was the only one who seemed to know the rules. Their voices bounced lazily off the concrete walls as they approached us and the train.

"So you're actually gonna try and move the Yukon?"

"Yeah, can't do much else with it. None of the museums wanted anything to do with her. I'll take it to New York and sell it for scrap before this place gets shut down."

"You an' me both know the Mountie was fulla shit. He's been saying 'One more disappearance and you guys are gone' for so long he doesn't know how to do anything else."

"He's starting to think its Americans, using this place to sneak in. If Canadian Border Patrol sets foot in this place, we're all screwed. I'd just as soon ride this out of here into New York, assuming its still there, of course. I won't get much for it, but it should be enough to sail to England, and that's good enough for me."

"That's a hell of a dangerous trip to make. Nobody's even trying to track the Locusts anymore. They could be anywhere. You heard about what they did to the last news crew that got close enough to film them? It's some ghastly shit."

"No, and I'd rather not know, thank you very much. I have the last three months of intel on their movement; assuming they stay consistent, I can use that to figure out where they're at. Besides, I just want to ride past them, not take their picture. They can't hurt me if they can't catch me."

There was a lapse in the conversation. When one of the men spoke up again, there was a slight tremor in his voice.

"Zack, don't do it. This is stupid as hell. You're gonna get killed for a few hundred dollars."

"A few hundred dollars is a lot when you're broke. The Canadian government won't let me move this thing; they think it's a health hazard or bad luck or some other excuse. If I want to sell this train, I have to take it through America. If I want to eat, and believe me, I do, I have to sell this train. It's as simple as that."

"I'm gonna miss you Zack."

"Oh, don't start with that. You're being morbid."

"I didn't mean it like that. I meant when you get to Europe."

"Yeah, yeah, sure. Trust me, I can do this. I should be the one worrying about you. You don't move your ass since you quit our baseball league. You don't start exercising again, you'll be dead before I am."

"Whatever you say, old man."

"I'm being serious. Death can't catch you if you keep moving."

The two men shook hands and parted ways. Zack, the older of the two, climbed into the Yukon, lit the furnace, and moved to the conductor's cab. The other went through a door leading back into the warehouse we'd just left. Judging by the twin aromas of blood and happiness that soon clouded the air, today was nothing short of a feast for the vampires on the other side.

Leatherman waited until the sounds of the engine had filled the corridor before motioning us to follow him. We left the oil drum and ran down the rails, looking for another boxcar linked to the Yukon that hadn't been locked shut. We finally found one roughly halfway down the line of rusted out carts and trailers. By this time the train had begun moving, albeit slowly, and we had to jog to keep up with our car.

We hopped onto the outside platform and Leatherman threw the latch and opened the door. Two more vampires were waiting for us inside.

"Son-of-a-BITCH!" he hollered, immediately jumping on the one closest to the door. Jail Bird and I took the other, who was lying on a crate and couldn't do much more than blink at our arrival. They were even more emaciated than the vampires in the depot, probably planning a last-ditch escape before starvation became a grim reality. We threw them off the train easily, but the shock at finding them was not as easy to shake. The three of us had countless questions, to which Leatherman almost assuredly held the answers, but we were rolling away from a nest of starvation and collapse, and that was good enough. Sleep had at long last presented itself, and we took it with greed.

"Get up." Leatherman was giving us our wake-up calls. I was hungry, pissed off, and somehow still tired. I was in no mood to deal with him.

"Get up. Get up. *NOW*." He was kicking Mr. Tie, still mumbling and sweating in the wake of some profoundly unpleasant dream. He seemed to hate Mr. Tie more than the rest of us, but whether this hatred stemmed from his physical weakness or formal attire I didn't know. I briefly entertained the thought of killing them both, but not seriously. I was too antsy to commit to any real action, much less something as drastic as that. My hands were shaking. My senses had grown stronger. Whatever was happening to me, I didn't like it. It made me feel self-conscious, and angry.

At long last Mr. Tie was on his feet, shaking sweat from his hair and cobwebs from his mind. Jail Bird was already up, dispassionately watching the proceedings from his corner. His hair was longer, his eyes were greener. I wanted to kiss him. I wanted to kill him.

What the fuck was wrong with me?

"I hate you," sobbed Mr. Tie, wearing his filthy dress shirt and slacks and yet somehow completely naked. "All of you. You're all a bunch of assholes, that's what you are. Kill you all myself, so help me God, that's what I'm gonna do-"

"Save it," cawed the Leatherman. "I've never seen a bunch of children like you all go to shit so badly at your first blood lust." His over-the-top southern accent was completely gone, and he spoke with an air of dignity that did not match his sully appearance. "I know you're all feeling a bit…strange. It manifests itself differently in each individual. Our friend in the tie is having a tantrum, whereas another one of you is looking at the gentleman in the prison jumper with bedroom eyes."

Hot, red anger. When I got the chance, he would be the first to go.

"It's quite educational to be around another vampire during a blood lust. As the senses sharpen in the search for food, certain…undesirable tendencies one may try to suppress are unearthed as well. You learn a lot about what motivates a vampire, be it petulance, love…" he eyed Jail Bird coyly. "…Or anger."

"But it matters not that which drives you," he continued, with an eloquence I would never have suspected of him. "What does matter is how you fulfill it. As men, you no doubt sought many different outlets for these primal urges you could never quite satiate. Now that you've changed, there's but one, albeit highly effective way to find some peace. It lies beyond this door, and I do believe you'll know it when you see it." As he spoke, he made his way to the door, insouciantly throwing the latch and grasping the handle.

"Gentlemen, welcome to the first night of the rest of your lives." Leatherman threw the door open and jumped out.

The three of us remained, leaning against the walls of the car, trying to size each other up without making eye contact.

Mr. Tie broke the silence. "We're not really vampires…are we?"

"I don't know what we are," I replied. "But I suppose we ought to find out." And with that I too began to make my way across the car to the door.

"We have to get the police. They'll know what to do. We'll tell them he drugged us. Hell, I bet he *did* drug us! That would explain everything!"

"**No one,** is getting the police." The gravity in Jail Bird's voice stopped Mr. Tie's manic pattering in its tracks. He turned to face me. "You want to find out what's out there?"

"Yeah."

"Alright then, let's go. And whatever *you* decide to do," he stared Mr. Tie right in eyes. He promptly turned away. "Is your own business.

But I swear to God if you get the cops involved in this at all, I will end you. Your life, your call. C'mon." The two of us left him stricken and blank as we exited the car.

Our train had come to a stop at an old rail yard. The stain of neglect was just as prominent as at the station we'd come from, but this one was outdoors. Overhead, the moon barely shone, but provided ample light for our sharpened eyes. A salty sea breeze blew through the humid air, bringing with it more smells than I could interpret. As time rolled forward, my senses continued sharpening, to the point of sensory overload. I felt like a first grader, having just successfully navigated his first chapter book, seated before an open dictionary and asked to make sense of it all. Hoping to stymie the flood of information, I closed my eyes and plugged my ears. My nose immediately took up the slack

(BLOOD) behind the tool shed (humans) four of them ***(HEROIN)*** inside

"You alright?" Jail Bird asked.

"Food," I panted. "People...at the tool shed. Blood...food... people..." I had the shakes. Horribly. Not since my first trip to rehab had it been this bad. I had to eat. *NOW.* I was gonna die if I didn't, just die if I didn't...

"I smell it too. C'mon." Jail Bird was very obviously salivatin0067, but he could at least keep his wits about him. I began to follow him up the tracks, over the sandy dirt, and what little moonlight there was backlit a tool shed less than a mile away, a tool shed housing four very unlucky people.

The nearer we drew to the shed, the greater two very opposing forces pulled at me: hunger and dread. I had to feed. Soon. This was non-negotiable. In order to feed, I would have to kill somebody. There was no alternative, no compromise. In elementary school, my class went on a field trip past the city limits onto a nearby farm. A friendly old man, quite grandfatherly, took us into his fields and showed us the corn and wheat he would be harvesting in the next week, and the machines he would do it with. It was all very interesting, certainly more so than another day indoors behind a desk. However, he saved the best for last. Our final stop was a trip inside the barn, the big red barn, bigger than our whole school. Inside there were goats and pigs and sheep and all other manner of typical barnyard creatures. It was just like an indoor petting zoo. More than anything else, I remember the cows. Cows by the dozen, lined up against a wall, staring that dumb stare that indicates awareness of one's surroundings on only the most basic of levels. I had seen that very same look on every one of my classmates, at one time or another, usually during something boring like math, and had no doubt worn it myself on several occasions. A kid at the back of the crowd, Jeremy, I think his name was, asked the old farmer if cows were really made of hamburgers. This set the whole group into peals of laughter, but Jeremy didn't flinch. He had asked a question, and he wanted an answer. Never in my life have I known a person less afraid to ask a question than Jeremy. We all thought he was the dumbest kid in school, but I can't help thinking that wherever he is now, he turned out smarter than any of us.

Only after the teacher had successfully shushed the class (and the farmer had swallowed his good-natured grin), did he tell Jeremy that he was correct after all, just a little bit backwards. Apparently the fact that meat came from once-living things was common knowledge to everyone but Jeremy and myself. I personally had not made the distinction between meats and fruits and vegetables and other edible things. It was all just food to me, regardless of where it came from. Sickness welled up inside me as I gradually realized that living things had died so that I could live. Earlier that year I had done a science project on parasites, and that was exactly what I felt like at that moment, looking at a bunch of dumb kids and a bunch of dumb cows trying to figure out what gave one the right to eat the other. When I got home that night I told my parents I was becoming a vegetarian. Being only 11 years old at the time I had a hard time verbalizing my reasoning to them, and they laughed the whole thing off the way parents do when you announce your plans to dig a hole to China in the backyard. They tolerated my fussy eating for three days before they got tired of the nuisance, and Dad grilled me a big, red steak for dinner. Mom conveniently "forgot" to make my salad. I sat down to dinner, and my newfound ideologies came face to face with my biological needs.

Do you know what I am? I'm food. GOOD food. Right here in front of you. You need me to live, right? How can you say "No" to what you need? How on Earth could you refuse what millions of people die for want of every day?

I ate the whole steak in less than five minutes, and the primal satisfaction it gave me was eclipsed only by the guilt that came with it. Meat has been a regular part of my diet ever since. Now I was about to take my next step on the carnivorous path. I was going to slaughter my own meal. Would this make me a cannibal? That answer lied within a bigger question. Was I still human?

"I don't want to kill anyone, man," I blurted out. We were now less than five feet from the tool shed.

"Me neither," replied Jail Bird. "But I don't think we really have a choice. The only choice we do have is us or them. I choose them."

"Yeah." I remembered something my Dad used to say. 'There's no use arguing facts.' At this point, I just wanted whatever was going to happen to happen, the sooner the better. "You take the two on the other side. I'll take the two inside."

He nodded. He went around left, I went around right.

"Hey-" *Crack.* *CRACK.*

I peeked around the corner. Two drifters lay dead on the dirt, necks bent sideways, legs still twitching. Jail Bird was hunched over one of their throats. Whoever he was, he was efficient. The sound of soft flesh puncturing coupled with frenzied sucking told me dinner had begun. Now it was my turn.

There was no lock on the tool shed, and the door opened with ease. The smell of heroin overwhelmed me, and any remorse for the murders I was about to commit faded away into its musk. Both of the sheds inhabitants were lying on coils of moldy garden hose, spent needles at their sides. I was too late. They had already used. Anger briefly surged within me, but my humane side decided this was for the best. At least now they wouldn't feel what I was about to do to them. Up until tonight I would have told you that the hardest thing I ever did was take the first bite of that damn steak all those years ago. Turns out it's a lot harder when the steak has eyes to watch you eat it.

I drained both of them dry to the bone in less than a minute. It only took the heroin in their blood a few seconds longer to hit me. Unquestionably, it was the greatest high of my life. Their blood amplified its potency, and my hands now trembled with joy rather than deprivation. I stepped out of the shed, feeling better than I'd felt since waking up in that boxcar God knows how many days ago. Jail Bird was waiting for me. We looked at each other in silence, saw the blood on our chins, the fangs curling out from under our lips, and realized we had become brothers in some strange and violent family that neither of us truly understood yet. But we were beginning to.

Leatherman strolled out from behind the shed, his mouth just as gory as ours. "Excellent work, the both of you. I like fast learners. How'd you like to learn a little bit more?"

We both nodded in unison. There was something regal about him, when he wasn't slurring his vowels like an inbred yokel. Wherever he led, I would follow. Between the blood and the drugs I had never felt so alive, and I was anxious to see what I was now capable of.

"You smell that?" asked the Leatherman. I almost certainly did, but could no more have told him what "that" was than identify a single stone from a mosaic a mile away. Now that I had fed, my senses were coming back down from overdrive, but were still too powerful to read clearly.

"That's the smell of failure. Cheap people drinking cheap whiskey to escape their cheap lives. Disillusionment at the bottom of the bottle of a man neck deep in both personal and professional mediocrity. They're killing themselves, slowly. I suppose the humane thing to do would be to help them on their way?" Far off in the distance, a tavern light shone like a beacon. When the wind blew a certain way, it carried the sound of glasses clinking to our perch upon the hill.

"I interpret your silence as consent. Follow me."

Already the rush of the heroin was beginning to wane. As strongly as it had come on was as quickly as it had left me, but there were no symptoms of withdrawal. I was too strong for that now. Never again would I be pestered by that great thorn of heroin's rose, and that made me feel stronger than all the blood, all the drugs in the world. Minutes ago I had murdered twice; never before had I felt so perfect and whole. I began to wonder why I had not been born like this in the first place, the confusion and woe it would have saved me over the years. Guilt is little more than a handicap to getting what you need.

We walked soundlessly through the no-man's land that divided the rail-station and the town. Our thoughts did not require vocal manifestation. We were killers, and we were kings. Kings of the nighttime, kings of the vagrants, kings of an ancient train whose usefulness had all but expired. But we were kings of *something;* how many men could make such a claim?

Still, I had questions. "So, we're definitely vampires?" It had not sounded so feeble in my head, but there it was, already asked.

"Did you not just kill a man, and take life from his blood?" replied Leatherman. "Yes, we are vampires. We shall remain so until death."

The little boy who'd gone to church every Sunday until age 12 was the next voice within me to speak up. "Do we still have souls?"

Leatherman only chuckled. "What makes you so sure we had them to begin with? Do you know what a vampire is, brother? A vampire is *honesty.* There is no living thing on the face of this Earth that does not survive but by feeding off of some other source. We are natural selection incarnate; we simply choose not to hide it. You ought to be proud of yourself, and deep inside, I think you are. You are a murderer, yes? Then why does your conscience not pang you? Because you are *honest.* You kill and you eat and you feel no shame. What man could find himself in your position and not count himself blessed?"

Jail Bird was next to speak. "What happened to the fourth guy, with the tie and the glasses?"

"I expect he's run off somewhere to lick his psychological wounds. I had reservations about turning him, you know; the smell of his weakness nearly eclipsed the smell of his blood. Of course, I was in a tough spot when I found you all, and in no position to be choosy. He'll either kill himself or starve to death when he refuses to feed. It won't be the first or the last time it happens. Some people are simply too frail to function when the blinders come off and they have to face who they are. We call them the Noble Cowards. They are either too noble to kill others to sustain themselves, or too cowardly to take another life. Either choice amounts to the same result, and that result is death. But he is no concern of ours right now. Eventually, we will find a new fourth, but we are strong enough as a trio tonight. Ah, the party draws near."

Sure enough, we were now mere feet from the doors of the tavern. Hastily, Leatherman changed course and walked to the side of the building. He turned on a spigot, produced a rag from his pocket, wetted it, wiped the crusted blood from his face, and bade us to do the same. "We've got to look presentable, boys."

Once we were all cleaned up, we returned to the front door. In an almost comical gesture, Leatherman creased the collar on his filthy jacket. He tossed his head about his shoulders left and right, popping his neck each time. "Big smiles everybody. And don't start the killing until I do. It's my 210th birthday tonight, as a matter of fact, and I intend to have a little fun first." Armed with a Cheshire cat grin and two-inch fangs, he kicked the door open and walked into the bar.

Chapter 2: Into Town, and Out Again

"This self-obsessed sinner,
I hear he loves to drink.
This self-obsessed sinner,
I hear he loves a fight."
-Bloc Party, *<u>Cain Said to Able</u>*

From inside the bar, the din was positively deafening. Jailbird and I fought the urge to plug up our ears. Leatherman appeared unaffected, and continued to grin just as dashingly as ever. Our arrival was subject to little more than half-hearted glances of the bored and the drunk. Their eyes bore the same lack of cognition that the cows had worn, but they had chosen to be like this. They had three-pound brains latticed with trillions upon trillions of connecting neurons, and they'd contemptuously cast the use of this blessing into a bottle of hops and grains. Skynard was on the jukebox. It was here that my anger began to percolate.

"Evening, ladies and gentleman!" boomed the Leatherman, like a sideshow barker amidst a sea of easy marks. "Quite a night for a celebration, isn't it? Drink up, everybody!" His toast was met with more of the same blank and banal stares. "Goddamn if I'm not thirsty! Who's gonna drink with me, eh? Who?" He pulled a chair from a nearby table, twirled it about on its leg, caught it with a flourish, and sat down in the middle of the room. Thus far I'd seen Leatherman the hick and Leatherman the philosopher; now I was seeing Leatherman the showman; and I'll be damned if he wasn't a likeable son of a bitch. Apparently, a gentleman at the bar begged to disagree.

"Listen up, queer." The Neanderthal lumbering out of his spot at the bar was instantly recognizable, even if I'd never met this particular model before. He had the musclebound look of a man who's spent countless hours in the gym, almost as many as he's spent convincing himself he goes there for the weights and not the other men lifting them. A greasy veneer coated his hair and his face in equal measure. His high school ring still had a special place on his right hand, despite the fact that he'd graduated over a decade ago. For him, high school had been five years of hot girls and cold beers, and having peaked at the age of 19, he couldn't bear to leave the only place he'd ever belonged behind. Shock of all shocks, he was wearing a Skynard T-shirt. Most telling, however, was the high school football jacket. It had been meticulously cared for during its life, and just barely stayed in one piece when wrapped around this guy's steroid enhanced figure. His face was bright red, and he had to waddle with his arms to the side to keep from splitting the spotless straightjacket that reminded him of glory days gone by. Conversely, Leatherman's jacket was filthy, fraying, and fit his body like a glove. "You an' yer faggit-ass friends oughta get yer cocksuckin' asses out of here, if they know what's good for em'." His voice was shockingly similar to that of the old Leatherman.

"C'mon old chap, no need for that language here. Let's just have a drink, huh?"

The man in the football jacket was bearing down on him, all but leaving a trail of liquid courage and latent homosexuality in his wake, and still Leatherman didn't bat an eye. Seconds before he pounced, Leatherman leapt up from the chair, grabbed the man's outstretched arms by the wrists, and ripped them off of his body. They hit the floor with a meaty thunk, spurting blood all over his brand new boots. They looked into each others eyes briefly, the football player sporting the confused, slightly worried stare not uncommon to the unexpected amputee, Leatherman still grinning chummily, only now permitting his fangs to become fully visible. Seconds later, he lunged forward and bit out his throat before a scream could escape it.

When a crowd of people witnesses the hitherto unplanned dissection of a live human being, there are many different ways in which they tend to react. However, there is almost always one common trait that manifests itself, and that trait is panic. But the masses in whatever shithole bar located in whatever shithole state we found ourselves in couldn't even muster that. They just gazed on absentmindedly, cows who've watched another of their lot queue up for the slaughterhouse. Where once stood a man now stood a bloodless stump, and most of them were too drunk or apathetic to even drop their drinks and run. It was at this point I jettisoned any empathy I had once harbored for them. I didn't even wait for the wink Leatherman surreptitiously shot a slack-jawed Jailbird to say, in a manner of speaking, "Go nuts." With a running start I leapt high-jump style over Leatherman's chair, landed back-first amidst a table of four, and started biting anything flesh colored. I suppose it was a little garish of me, but the three of us had already fed, and as far I was concerned, this was just a chance to let loose and kill a bunch of people who deserved it. And that's exactly what we did. We wiped out the entire bar in under 10 minutes. It was bloody, violent work, and we did it well.

Standing up from the side of my last kill, I saw Jail Bird and Leatherman standing behind the bar. They were intently perusing the bottom shelf, carelessly casting bottles onto the floor. Some broke, and some didn't. "Look for it in the very back, they always keep the good stuff behind everything else." At long last Leatherman stood up and triumphantly produced an unopened bottle of Jack Daniel's Old #7. He set it on the bar, bent over, and hoisted the limp body of the bartender, placing it on the bar in much the same fashion as the bottle. His throat was still intact, until Leatherman gently, almost scientifically removed it, catching the red warmth it contained in a nearby mug. He opened the Jack Daniels and began mixing it with the blood. "An old friend showed me how to do this," he quipped, almost to himself, stirring the dark juice. "It's good stuff. *Damned* good stuff." Having decided it was sufficiently mixed, he produced three glasses from beneath the bar and filled them. With an inviting sweep of his hand, we partook. It was smooth and syrupy, with a somewhat metallic aftertaste. I had the childlike feeling that I had just discovered some new, delicious dessert, one that I would enjoy whenever possible for the rest of my life. Sure enough, it remains a favorite of mine to this day.

When the blood and whiskey was finished, we left the bar, strolling casually out the door past pale bodies wearing wide-eyed death masks. The alcohol from Leatherman's drink and our victims' blood sat warmly in our chests. There was an eerie quiet and lack of activity. For a moment I wondered if the town was abandoned, then I remembered: We had killed everyone. A few houses over I saw a light on in an upstairs room, casting the silhouette of an old woman rocking a child to sleep. Though they were the exception to the rule, there were a few other houses where the living still clearly dwelled. We had not killed everyone, after all. There was still the matter of the young and the elderly. I asked Leatherman "What's gonna happen to the rest of these people? The ones who weren't at the bar?"

"I'd imagine those remaining are either too young to get into the bar, or old enough to not want to go. Seeing as how this town is surrounded by desert, the young ones will probably get smart and hop a train out of here. The old ones will probably starve." His nonchalance at their impending starvation sickened me, until I recalled that I was the one who had just killed their meal tickets. I found it didn't bother me nearly as much as it probably should have. Leatherman stopped walking abruptly: his eyes, ears, and nostrils flared. Anger washed over his face and he turned left, and began half-marching, half-jogging down the street. We had little choice, and so we followed him. Having seen his face when he smelled whatever he'd smelled, I did not think now would be a good time to ask questions. We had followed him nearly across town when he ducked into a tiny alley we both would have missed, pulled a man off the ground, and threw him against the wall by his shirt. It was Mr. Tie. Blood ran viscously down his face, onto his shirt and trademark tie. "You sick bastard," he hissed. "You shame us." Leatherman grabbed him by the shirt and pitched him down the alley with remarkable strength, and he landed jarringly on a pile of garbage cans. "The train leaves in half an hour. I'll be sorry if you're on it." He turned about smartly and left. I was going to ask him what had upset him so when I saw what Mr. Tie had been feeding on. It was a young girl, perhaps no more than eight years old. Her eyes had been plucked out. Blood ran thinly from the vacant, gaping holes, down her cheeks and onto the filthy ground. It was positively obscene. She was young. She was so…*young.* There was a more than decent chance that I had killed at least one of her parents minutes ago, but it hadn't been like this. This was just perverse. There was too much shock and disgust and outright incredulity for me to hate Mr. Tie for doing this. He was just a body amongst the other garbage. This was far worse. It was the transformation of innocence to abomination in the blink of some terrible eye. I pulled a handkerchief from my pocket, wiped her off as best I could, and laid it over the remains of her face. It was just wrong, that's all. The whole thing was just wrong.

Leatherman and Jail Bird looked on as I performed this strange semblance of the Last Rites. When I was finished, they nodded approvingly, and we began making our way back across town. Jail Bird was the first to speak of what had happened. "You could've killed him, you know." His voice began to quiver, but he steadied it. "I think I would've. He deserved it."

"He does indeed deserve it. Deserves far worse, in fact. But we cannot kill our own kind. Someday soon I'll tell you why. But for now we must return to the train. It leaves shortly."

The sun, though still hidden, was beginning to make its way back to the horizon. Whether or not it was attributable to the brightening light, or the somber silence in which we walked, I could see the town much more clearly this time through. When we passed by the bar a final time, I was stopped breathless by the building across the street. It was an art supply store, not terribly large, or well furnished, but an art supply store nonetheless. Right dead center in this shitbrick town, where drinking, fighting and fucking were considered the three ingredients of a good time, was an art supply store. It's shit like that that really gets to me. It's like catching a snowflake on your tongue in the middle of April. Technically, it's possible, but it's so rare that when it happens you just need to stop and say "Thanks," whether or not anyone's out there listening. "Wait here," I told the guys, and walked up to front door. It was dead bolted, of course, made of a beautiful thick maple, with a flowing arabesque carved in the middle. The large bronze knocker bore an inscription in equally fluid lettering:

**BRING TO LIFE THAT WHICH IS GREATER
THAN OURSELVES**

I was grinning like a goofball. This wasn't the kind of stuff you got after sending four easy payments of $9.95 to the clowns advertising in the back of Parade magazine. There was craftsmanship here, *real,* honest to God craftsmanship, and it had come out of a place like this. Fucking unreal, but in the best way possible.

Breaking the door down would be pretty small potatoes after what went down in the bar, but somehow hurting it felt more wrong than hurting a person. There was a small glass window next to it, little more than a display case, holding a sketch book and a few pencils (previously sharpened, fortunately). It had been a long time since I'd worked in pencil, lately I preferred acrylics, but I had taken a sketching class at school a few years ago and hadn't been all that bad. A quick flick of the knuckles and an explosion of glass heralded the arrival of Early Christmas. I dropped the pencils in my pants pocket, tucked the book under my arm, and rejoined the others.

"What's that?" Leatherman asked, squinting at my new acquisition.

"Sketchbook," I replied, taking it out to show him. "150 pages." He furrowed his brow, shrugged softly, and once more headed for the train. A breeze blew in the darkness, ruffling the pages. I let them ruffle. It was a good sound. When we finally arrived at the train, the sun had not risen, but would shortly. We climbed into our car, and Leatherman slid the giant door shut behind him. Still clutching the sketchbook under my arm, I lay down on the floor. The others followed suit, and we entered the peace of dreamless hibernation in unity.

There are many sounds it can be pleasant to awaken to. The sound of metal screeching against metal is not one of them. Leatherman was sitting up in his corner, absent-mindedly dragging some sort of blade across the wall of the boxcar, slicing long, thin ruts in the siding. Every so often he paused to lick the blade, check the angle of its cutting edge, and resume its sharpening. "What the hell is that?" I asked.

"One-armed scissor," he drawled proudly. His endearing accent was back at full strength. He grinned as he twirled it around his finger by its one remaining loop. "She's a good friend of mine. Unlike some people." Scowling, he threw a kick at the body sleeping next to him. It squealed and groggily raised its head. Mr. Tie had apparently made it back to the train after all. He groaned, "What was that for?" The dried blood of last night's meal still caked his chin.

"For sucking at life," he said, and he kicked him again. With a whimper, Mr. Tie retreated to his corner.

Jail Bird was now awake as well. "What's your name?" he asked.

"Me?" Leatherman replied, and Jail Bird nodded. "I couldn't tell you how long we've been living together, time seems a little fuzzy these days, but I don't believe we even know each others names." He raised his hand to his chin, and began to absently stroke it. 'Leatherman, the great thinker,' I thought with a smirk. At long last he replied.

"Chuck. Chuck Leroy Garrett." He extended his hand to Jail Bird. "And yours?"

"Thomas Vicker." They shook, and Chuck put on a smile and said "Pleased to make your acquaintance, Thomas," and just a hint of that urbane charm he'd worn so clearly the other night bubbled to the surface.

"*You're* Chuck Garrett? The serial killer from Georgia?" Mr. Tie was aghast, wide-eyed with shock and horror at the thought of being in the same room as a murderer, conveniently forgetting all about the crimson stains blotting his once white shirt. "How did you get all the way across the country so fast?"

"A man moves fast when he needs to," he said, addressing Mr. Tie without subsequently kicking him for the first time this morning. Though he barely showed it, he seemed faintly pleased at the recognition. "You seem to be somewhat familiar with me already. And just who are you?"

"Barry Maguire." He looked up expectantly for a handshake, but none was offered. His gaze shifted away, concealing his disappointment.

All eyes were now on me. I was the only unknown, the last bastion of mystery in our strange new family. There was a certain power in it, and I was loathe to give it up. "Ethan Patrick."

"It's good to meet you, Ethan," called Thomas from the other side of the car.

"Thanks, you too."

"Yeah, sure is," grunted Chuck who didn't sound all that convincing. Barry almost tripped over himself leaning over to offer his hand. I was going to shake it, until I saw the bloodstain beneath his thumb and remembered how it got there. I turned him a cold shoulder, and he quietly slunk back into his corner with the silent, sullen grace of a man who's had no shortage of practice with rejection.

"Hey Chuck," said Thomas. It took Chuck a moment to realize he was being addressed. I got the impression it was the first time anyone had called him by that name for a long time. News bulletins were rare these days, and I rarely watched them, but a few days before that last fateful trip out to the train yard there'd been a story on a man named Chuck who'd been seen tearing a body apart in some backwoods nowhere town in Georgia, one of the few southeast states still improbably clinging to societal norms. He had fled town, and a search of his property had turned up the pieces of 21 different people, with not a drop of blood left in any of them. It was a little unbelievable that he'd made it from Georgia to California in four days without gasoline, but life itself had been pretty unbelievable lately.

"You said something last night about how it was your 200-something odd birthday. Were you being serious?"

"Hell yeah I was being serious! What reason would I have to lie?"

"Do all vampires live that long?"

Apparently Chuck found this question rather funny. "Hahahaha, that's a good one son. Nah, most vampire's is lucky to last 30 years or so after The Change. Only the smart ones hang around longer."

"What's the longest a vampire *can* live, though?"

"Nobody knows for sure. I ain't never heard of a vampire died of old age, neither have any others I've known."

"How old's the oldest vampire you know of?"

"Well, he's been dead for a while, but Adolf Hitler was 1,100-something years old when they got him."

"Bullshit!" I blurted out. "No way was Hitler a vampire!"

"I think I'd know a little bit more about the subject than you would," he shot back. "There's a lot of stories about Hitler. I ain't saying they're true, nobody can say for sure, but I'll tell you what I've been told.

"Hitler got changed at a very young age. He was born in Germany, which was at that time a part of the Roman Empire, at a time when there was a lot of vampire activity. In that area, around that time, vampires would dismember the bodies of those they fed on, to keep them from coming back and increasing their competition. One of these vampires killed Hitler and his family when Hitler was about 5 years old, and tore them apart. Supposedly, Hitler grew a new body from his severed head. Not saying it's true, just saying this is how the story goes. So little vampire Hitler grew up and lived the typical vampire life, traveling around Europe, feeding and staying on the move. He kept a very low profile, which is prob'ly how he stayed alive for so long.

"Around 1920, something big happened. Nobody knows for sure, but somehow Hitler supposedly found out the vampire who'd Changed him had been Jewish. Personally, I think this part of the story's bullshit. No vampire would try to feed off of a Jew. You know what they say, Jews only bleed coins"

Chuck laughed uproariously at his own joke. Thomas looked a little disgusted. Barry also looked displeased. I couldn't imagine the Chuck of last night telling such a tasteless joke.

"Anyways, something happened and Hitler got it into his head that being a vampire was a Jewish disease by nature. Something happened, and he killed a whole mess of vampires, which put The Stain on him real bad. Hitler needed some protection, so he came back to Germany and started the Nazi party. Everybody hated the Jews back then, and Hitler was smart enough to use that. So Hitler comes to power and starts the Holocaust, because he believes getting rid of the Jews will get rid of vampirism. You won't read about this in any of the history books, but Hitler had a conscience. He hated having to lead his life by killing other people. He absolutely hated being a vampire. While Hitler was killing the Jews, and, in his own mind, ending vampirism, he did something no other vampire had ever done. He tried to cure himself. All the bizarre experimental drugs his personal physicians were feeding him weren't to make him a better public speaker or keep him awake for days at a time, they were to cure him of his vampirism. Those were all just side effects. There was lots of trial and error involved, but eventually, they got it right. They somehow, someway, turned Hitler from a vampire back into a human being. That was two weeks before World War II swung the other way and he went into his bunker and had all of his top advisors and scientists and physicians killed along with him. When they died, the cure died with them. However, rumor has it one of his physicians switched his cyanide pill with a sugar pill, then played dead until the others had passed out, and took the recipe for the cure and ran off to France. His name was Deutchner, and he's still alive. He's been moving around the world, in hiding and under a variety of names, ever since. Word is he's in New York right now. That's where this train is going. When it stops there, I'm going to find him. Y'all are welcome to come along if you'd like."

"How do you expect us to get into New York?" asked Barry. "The quarantine is still in effect. Since New England seceded, it's practically a Canadian Territory. Border Patrol will kill us on sight."

Chuck shrugged. "I know a guy."

"Quarantine? What quarantine?" barked Thomas.

"Yukon Flu," replied Barry. "How long have you been in jail?"

"What's Yukon Flu?"

"You seriously have no idea? You must've been in jail for over a decade!"

Thomas was becoming livid. "If you don't start talking about this Yukon Flu bullshit right now I'm going to make you very much wish you had." Chuck smiled proudly from the sidelines, pleased that at least one of his new friends had the gift of coercion.

"Well, the Second Gold Rush happened in the late 60's. Some miners stumbled on a practically bottomless virgin gold mine in the northern Yukon. They made $8.5 million dollars in the first month alone. Of course, word got out about the mine, and soon everybody in North America was packing up and heading north to make some fast money. The first two years everything was great, people were making money hand over fist. Halfway through the second year, they hit the bottom of the mine. People were sad that the money had run out, of course, but all things considered, the Second Gold Rush has been nothing but a success for all parties involved. Until the Yukon Flu showed up, of course. Turns out there was an underground lake at the bottom of the mine, untouched for millions of years. The stream was home to a previously undiscovered species of mosquito, which transmitted an extremely virulent disease through its bite. This disease came to be known as the Yukon Flu. All of the miners who had been in the mine when they reached the stream became infected. With the gold rush over, everybody came home, and spread the virus, which could also be transmitted through the air, all over Canada and America.

"By the time symptoms started showing, it was too late. Half a million people died in the first *week.* The Canadian government acted fast, established a national quarantine, and got to work on a vaccine. Final death toll was over 5 million, about 20% of the population, but within 6 months they'd stopped the outbreak. America didn't handle it so well. They also set up a national quarantine, but were never able to develop a vaccine. When Canada created its vaccine, they offered to send it to America, but our quarantine was still in effect, and the government couldn't decide if it was safe to reopen our borders. Congress got locked up in a yearlong debate, while Canadians continued to get well and Americans continued to die. The best estimates we have now claim that 168 million Americans died in all, about 80% of the population. The population fell from 210 million to 42 million in a few years. How many of those 42 million are still around, nobody knows. It was about 5 years ago when Nixon went on TV and said that in an effort to slow the spread of the Yukon Flu, he was cutting off the nation's gas supply, which didn't sit very well with all the survivors trying to flee the country. People knew something was up right away. There had been no new outbreaks in three months; the population had become too thin for the outbreak to continue spreading. Newsweek did some investigating, and found out the real reason the gas supply had been cut off; it had run out. That's when things really got bad.

"Pittsburgh was the first city to get hit by the riots. The bad riots, anyway. It burned down within two weeks. The rioters blew through the city and made their way down the coast. Eventually the riots made their way down to Washington D.C. No one really knows for sure what happened there, but-"

"Bullshit!" crowed Chuck. "I know what happened cause I was there! There's nothing vampires love more than a riot, so I started moving north from Georgia. I was scared the Big Riot would've gone through before I got there, but as I said before, a man moves fast when he needs to. We burned the city to the ground in *one day.* The White House went up like a candle. I was in the group that ran down Nixon. That was the real reason I'd gone up there, ya see. How many vampires get to drink a President's blood? We chased him and his guards through the streets for four hours until they took a wrong turn and wound up on MLK Boulevard. Imagine that, Nixon making a run for it and ending up on MLK Boulevard. I was at the back of the crowd when they caught him, unfortunately. By the time I got t'the front of the crowd, all that was left of him was a stain on the sidewalk. It wasn't a total loss though. I ate very well that night. All of us did."

Thomas was dumbstruck. Barry continued, "Well, yes, Nixon did die in the riots, along with his cabinet. In the weeks following the D.C. riot, a different Congressman would get on the TV at night and declare himself the new President, and the next morning you'd read about his death in the newspaper. The newspapers were still running at that point, but not for too much longer. Then the major TV networks started shutting down. It's hard to tell whether the operators fled, or got killed. You can still pick up the occasional local broadcast, especially out here in the West, where the rioters haven't come through yet, but depending on who you ask, it won't be too long now..."

"What about the military?" asked Thomas. "They never stepped in to try and stop the riots?"

"The military was smart enough to sit on the sidelines and wait. Now they have control of all the nation's weapons, and sell them, along with their protective services and tactical info, to the highest bidders. There's no executive branch left to tell them not to. In what's left of America, the wealthy are the top rung of society, with the military one rung below them."

"And what's below the military?"

"The rioters. They have some weapons, but most of their strength comes from numbers. Nobody knows how many of them there are now. Anybody who gets close enough to report on them never comes back. More than enough burned out husks of buildings in which to live. If they run out of something, they just find other people who have it and take it, but they lead a fairly low-maintenance life style. Below them are the few law abiding citizens left alive, mostly subsistence farmers. Below them, the dead. 80% of America's population. The biggest piece of the pie chart by far."

"And below the dead," Chuck smirked, twirling the one-armed scissor on his index finger, "Is us."

After that we slept, not necessarily out of need but to pass the time between stops. I awoke three times, twice during the day, once at night. Each time Barry and Chuck were curled up in their respective corners, sleeping deeply, drawing strength for the nights and the killings to come. But Thomas did not. He sat upright, back to the wall with his face held in his hands. Hiding his face. The second time I asked him if he had been sleeping at all. He muttered that he had been. I rolled over and lay down my head. Seconds later, he asked if it was true. If what was true? If everything was true. The disease, the death, the riots, the chaos, the utter and irrevocable collapse of the world he'd been born into and pined to return to throughout his captivity. I told him it was. He asked how I could live with it so easily. I told him I guessed that life has a way of sneaking up on you, having its way with you, and as long as it comes on slowly enough and as long as you aren't paying enough attention it can do just about any damn thing it likes to you and you don't notice until its too late to go back. I just chose not to pay it any attention at all. That way it was never an issue. He was quiet again, and just when I thought he had drifted off to sleep he told me that he still didn't believe me. I told him to get some rest, and he said that sounded like a good idea. But when I woke up the third time he was still awake, staring silently over his knuckles, looking for an explanation in the dark.

Chapter 3: The Hospital

"How many valiant men, how many fair ladies,
breakfast with their kinfolk and the same night
supped with their ancestors in the next world!
The condition of the people was pitiable to behold.
They sickened by the thousands daily, and died
unattended and without help."

~ Giovanni Boccaccio

Two nights later the train stopped and we woke up. The brakes squealed as they ground the wheels to a stop and our bones and tendons popped and cracked as we woke up and stretched. The Yukon Glory was going to stop and rest awhile, while we were about to do some traveling of our own. Shift change.

We were far from the West Coast. We could no longer smell the ocean, or feel that intangible sense of freedom that comes with standing at a continent's end. There was a chill in the wind, the smell of impending snow. I briefly envied Chuck for his jacket, then came to my senses. Forced to guess, I would say we were somewhere in Colorado. Myself and my new friends had left Washington State as humans and traveled nearly a fourth of the way across America under what I shall euphemistically call "Unique circumstances." We lumbered out of the car, into the protection of the night. This particular rail station, and the adjacent town less than a mile away, bore no signs of violence or destruction. Only neglect. Our noses turned to the sky, searching for any nearby people, but all we smelled were chill and atmosphere.

"I can't smell a damn thing," I said to no one in particular. "We might as well go search the town on foot." Chuck grunted his approval, and set off alone, for the homes and apartments on the left side. He probably wouldn't have minded us following him, but I for one had no desire to go tagging along like a child. I did, however, want to go hunting with Thomas again. The shameful thoughts and feelings that plagued me during the heights of a blood lust were not taken into consideration. He was pragmatic, and skilled, and the little I knew of him personally, I liked. In a time of great fear and loneliness, he was a friend. Silently, he strode up behind me and stopped.

"We did alright for ourselves last time. Shall we hunt together again?" Joy and acceptance welled up in silence, and I smiled and nodded. He smiled back, then turned to Barry, who was absent-mindedly fixing the knot in his tie by the car, shivering when a gust of wind blew past. "Mind what you kill tonight, and especially how you kill it." The warmth and fraternity in his voice had evaporated in an instant, blown away by the mountain winds and replaced by something equally cold and sharp. "We'll be watching you." Barry shivered again, nodding profusely, babbling his agreement. It stunned me how a voice could steal the heat from a man's soul more quickly than the cold itself. Thomas turned, and against the austere backlight of the moon I saw his frayed prison uniform dangling from his muscled frame, the twin green lights of his eyes cast upon the town where he would kill tonight, not out of evil but of necessity, and I knew he would lead us once Chuck was gone. Where exactly Chuck was to go, and who would get rid of him, and how, I did not know. But Chuck was old, and mad, and unfit to lead as long as there was a man like Thomas around. He walked into town, and I followed him gladly.

Two hours later, it finally began to snow. We were cold, and exhausted, and starving, and now, it had begun to snow. All night we searched, at first clinging to the shadows, before brazenly walking the streets, making no attempt to conceal our presence. Not once had we seen anything to indicate the presence of human life, or any life. The town was entirely deserted. Thomas and I walked side by side in silence. Neither of us wanted to admit it, but we both knew there would be no food tonight. And yet we kept walking, through the snow and the wind, too stubborn or too desperate to admit defeat.

The street we had been walking opened into a courtyard, and at its end was a large hospital. Normally there would be nothing remarkable about this, but there were lights on in at least half the windows. It was the only building we'd seen that night that still had power. All of the lights began to flicker briefly, then went back to normal. This hospital was probably running on an old generator, nearing the end of its usefulness. Once more the lights flickered, and this time the automatic doors opened and closed. When the doors opened, they released a pungent smell into the air. It was the smell of decayed flesh, and lots of it.

"You smell that?" Thomas asked.

"Yeah. What do you make of it?"

"I'm not totally sure. I'd rather not have to scavenge, but this could be our only chance to eat tonight. Let's check it out."

In another world, the room we walked into had been a lobby, but now it served as a morgue. Bodies were stacked on top of each other like cadaverous lumber. Corpses sat in chairs, on sofas, behind the main desk. They were spread across the floor, a gruesome carpet. Several bodies sat slumped on the stairs. I imagined the other floors of the hospital were probably in a similar condition, if not worse. Each body was in its own unique place in the decomposition process, although it was very obvious that they'd all been here for years. I was so taken aback by the sheer volume of death I temporarily forgot my appetite. "Jesus Christ, Thomas, it looks like...Thomas?" Thomas was hunched over, staring intently at a newspaper vending box next to the door, totally oblivious to the macabre scene we'd waded into. "Thomas, what are you looking at?" Behind the glass, the paper had turned a pale yellow, and was beginning to crumble at the edges. The headline screamed **"SUPERFLU REACHES MIDWEST"** and beneath it read "HOSPITALS STRUGGLE TO MANAGE PATIENT OVERFLOW". There was a photograph showing a line of people running around the block, trying to get into this very hospital. The date in the upper-left corner showed the paper was nearly five years old. Thomas' face was completely blank.

"It happened," he mumbled to no one in particular. "It really happened. It really, really-"

"C'mon man, that's enough." I tried to pull him away from the paper, but he was frozen in place. I decided it was best to leave him alone for the time being. I wanted to do some exploring.

Having left Thomas alone with the paper and his troubled thoughts, I began making my way back to the information desk, gingerly stepping over bodies, moving around the larger piles of them. What I was looking for couldn't be found on top of the desk, so I had to get on the other side and check the drawers. They were all locked. Fortunately, there was a fireman's axe hanging on the wall above the desk, behind a thin plate of glass that offered little resistance. Axe in hand, I set about chopping the desk up. It was well made, of a particularly hard wood, and consequently it took nearly half an hour to destroy it. It was well worth the time and effort, though, because in the bottom right-hand drawer I found what I had been searching for: A hospital map, and a ring of keys. The blood bank was located on the first floor basement. Jackpot.

I shouted to Thomas where I was going, to see if he wanted to come along, but he was still lost in that old newspaper. Once again I carefully danced around the nameless dead strewn about the floor, finally making it to the stairs. The keys hadn't been necessary after all, as the door was unlocked.

The blood bank was cold, damp, dark, and no surprise, also filled with dead bodies. Overhead, the dangling lights were covered with some sort of earthy moss. Those bodies which had been fortunate enough to be dumped here were in significantly better condition than the ones in the lobby. A few of them even looked like I could feed on them if I so desired. I made a mental note of their location, in case the blood bank turned out to be a bust. At last I found it, tucked away in the back corner furthest from the door. It was a huge, stainless steel industrial refrigerator, almost eight feet tall. I tugged at the door, and with a subtle *psshhhhh* and a gasp of carbon, it came open. Inside there were nine two-and-a-half liter pouches of blood, dangling from a rack. All of the other racks were empty. Given the size of the refrigerator, the relatively small haul was a smidge disappointing, but it was far better than sucking coagulated nuggets out of a long dead corpse's neck. I yanked the entire rack out of the fridge, slung it over my shoulder, and returned to the lobby. Thomas was no longer crouched in front of the newspaper vendor. In fact, I didn't see him anywhere. A gust of panic blew through me, and I ran to the door, hoping he'd just stepped out for some air. He hadn't. Where had he run off to, and why? I stepped back into the lobby to collect my thoughts, and saw Thomas sitting on the floor, his back leaned against the wall. He did an alarmingly good job of blending in with the dead. "Thomas?" I called gently, hoping not to alarm him

He looked up at me from the floor. "Yes?"

"I've...I've got blood." I held up the rack with the dangling pouches. He looked very surprised.

"Where'd you find that?"

"Raided the blood bank." He smiled, and chuckled a little.

"You are a genius, you know that?"

"I do what I can."

Thomas grabbed a chair and pulled himself up from the floor. "Let's go eat that outside. Too many dead people in here."

"Honestly." We both turned around and walked back out through the automatic door, sitting down on the curb. It was cold, but bearable. At least the snow had stopped. I yanked one of the pouches of the rack, sank my fangs into it, and began draining it. It was essentially flavorless, unlike the blood from a live human, but was just as nourishing. I handed the rack to Thomas, and he pulled off a pouch for himself.

"Hey Thomas."

"Yeah?"

"Are you gonna be alright man?"

"Yeah." He flashed what at least looked like a legitimate smile. "I think so. Thanks." He drained his pouch quickly. "It's just...It's just wild, you know? None of the guys in the whole prison had any idea the world was falling apart. Up until right before I escaped-"

"Escaped from what?"

Chuck came walking around the corner of the hospital, jacket flapping in the breeze. I didn't even have to look at him to know he was ravenous. It was on his scent. "Prison," Thomas said, tearing another pouch off of the rack and holding it up to Chuck. "Blood?" Chuck was utterly stunned.

"Where did you find that?"

"The hospital had a blood bank. It doesn't have a whole lot of flavor to it, but it's very filling. Go on, have some." Chuck took the pouch from his hand.

"Why thank you, Thomas." I could feel the scorn of his glare even with the hair covering his eyes. "It's good to know at least *one* of you is resourceful, as well as benevolent." He held the pouch to his face and opened his mouth wide. I leapt up from the curb and swatted the bag of blood out of his hands. It hit the cold pavement with a squishy *thud.*

"No," I snarled through my teeth, inches from Chuck's face. "You thank *me. I* chopped up the desk, *I* found the map, *I* got the blood. Now, I'm willing to share it with you, God only knows why, but you've got to thank *me* first. And if you *ever* look at me like that again I'll be the last thing you see on this Earth, do you understand?" Chuck had pulled out his damned one armed scissor again, and was holding it inches from my throat.

"Thomas," he said, never taking his eyes off of me, "Is what he has so impudently said, the truth?"

"Yes, Thomas replied. "He found the blood."

"Well, in that case... *Thank you.*" I had never heard those words spoken with such an absolute dearth of gratitude, but he had indeed thanked me, and so I kept my word.

"*You're welcome,*" I said with an equal amount of frost. "You may eat."

He turned around wordlessly, and scooped the pouch up from the ground. He drank it hungrily. "Not bad," he mumbled to no one in particular, and dropped the empty pouch down a nearby storm drain.

Thomas asked, "Chuck, have you seen Barry at all tonight?"

"Last I saw of him was about two hours ago. He was swimming in a dumpster, looking for rats," he replied. "It was very...appropriate." Thomas smiled.

"It's getting late," Chuck continued. "We oughta head back to the train." That Southern slur was already creeping back into his parlance. Why does that always happen after he feeds? I asked myself. "Follow me. Make sure you bring that extra blood along with you. It'll be handy if there's another night like tonight." It began snowing again, heavily. Chuck accelerated from a walk to a light jog, as did Thomas and myself. Visibility was getting poor, and the longer it took us to get back to the train, the greater our chances were of getting lost. We were less than five minutes from the train when we heard someone shout "Hey, wait up!" It was Barry, crawling out of a dumpster. We slowed down briefly, and he fell in line behind Thomas and myself. "Catch anything good tonight, Barry?" he asked. "I...I don't know what you're talking about" he said, making an effort to sound dignified. "Shut up and eat this." Thomas threw a blood pouch back to Barry, who caught it and drank it even quicker than Chuck had.

Over two inches of snow had already fallen when we reached the Yukon Glory. It was getting late, but there was no telltale smoke billowing out of the engine room.

"Are we early?" I asked. Chuck, the keeper of time, pulled his rusted pocket watch out of his coat and checked it.

"No, we're fine. Conductor prob'ly fell asleep or something."

He walked to the boxcar and slid open the door. It was less than halfway open when a shotgun barrel slid out of the darkness and pressed itself up against his forehead. Chuck's hands automatically flew up on either side of his head, gesturing surrender, and he began to slowly back up. With each backward step of Chuck's, the man holding the gun took an equal step forward, keeping the barrel of the gun firmly planted between Chuck's eyes. Once he was fully out of the boxcar, we could clearly see he was an old white man, nearly 70 years old, with deeply set wrinkles and a hunched posture to match. He wore a fearsome sneer on his face, but his hands shook violently, from a combination of fear and arthritis. His tattered overalls and distinctive blue-grey cap instantly identified him as Zack, the conductor of the Yukon Glory. "I knew I heard you bastards back here," he snarled in a thin, reedy voice. "Trying to get a free ride, huh?" He thrust the gun harder into Chuck's head for punctuation. "The free ride ends here, ya dirty bastards, ends right-" In the middle of the conductor's sentence, Chuck swung his hands around to his forehead and slapped the barrel of the shotgun upwards with lightning speed. The conductor's feeble old hands were no match for Chuck's strength, and the gun flew out of his grasp and up into the air. With his left hand, Chuck grabbed the old man by his shirt and slammed him into the side of the boxcar. He reached out with his right hand and caught the shotgun by the barrel as it fell back towards the Earth. It was a remarkably nimble maneuver, something I never would've expected Chuck capable of. I resolved then and there to stop being surprised by anything Chuck did.

Chuck dropped the shotgun silently into the snow, as the conductor looked on in horror. With no visible effort he then lifted the conductor off the ground, holding him up at eye level. He insouciantly licked his lips, then opened his mouth, revealing his two-inch fangs. The conductor gasped wordlessly. I hoped Chuck would have the good sense not to kill him. If he did, who would drive the train?

"It's been a long night, my friend," a hint of exasperation creeping into his words. His southern twang was back in full effect. "And I'm hungry *somethin' awful.*" The old man squirmed in Chuck's grasp like a worm on a hook. "You're a good deal older than I like my food. Hell, you're positively stale. It's a good thing, too. For your sake at least." Despite the frigid temperature, large beads of sweat were collecting on Zack's forehead. His breathing was small and shallow. Chuck had better hurry up and get to the point before the poor guy had a heart attack, or else it wouldn't even matter. "Now, just because I don't want to eat you doesn't mean I won't kill you. If you want to stay alive, here's what you're gonna do. You're gonna drive this train to New York City, just like you planned. You'll continue to make regular stops, at night, as you've been doing. Most importantly, you will never, ever, *ever* come back to this particular boxcar again, day or night, rain or shine, or else you won't live to regret it. Do you understand?" The old man nodded frantically. "Good." Chuck dropped him, and he tumbled down into the snow. He pulled himself up slowly, shaking from head to toe. When he finally got to his feet, he looked up at Chuck again.

"I…I've seen you on the news bulletin. You're the guy who killed all those people. You're…you're Chuck Lee Garrett!" Chuck grinned, once again flattered by the recognition. "Right you are, my friend.

Right you are." He casually reached down, picked up the dropped shotgun, and pointed it squarely at the old man. "So you know I mean it." Scampering as quickly as his tiny old legs could carry him, the old man ran off into the engine room, and began setting the fire to power the train. Chuck examined the shotgun in his hands, opening and closing the action. It must not have impressed him, as he dropped it in the snow and climbed into the boxcar. The rest of us followed suit, taking our usual positions, lying down in anticipation of several days sleep. There was a burst of warm air as the fire in the engine room came to life in the next car. Minutes later, the Yukon Glory was beginning to move again, and on the cusp of sleep, I closed my weary eyes.

Chapter 4: Negotiations

"I had the right to remain silent... but I didn't have the ability."

~Ron "Tater Salad" White

"You are surrounded by Kansas State Police! If you cooperate with us, nobody will get hurt! Do you understand?!"

"Shit! Shit shit shit!" I opened my eyes, startled from my sleep. Chuck was livid, pacing back and forth inside the box car. Again I heard the voice from outside the train, amplified by a mega phone.

"We are in no mood for games! If you do not respond, we're sending in the SWAT Team! This is your last chance to respond!"

"I hear ya, I hear ya!" Chuck hollered at the door. "Don't come in, if you know what's good for ya!"

"Chuck, what's going on?" I asked, wiping sleep crust from my eyes.

"He stopped the train!" Chuck whispered hoarsely, clearly antagonized. "The old bastard stopped the train, and now there's cops outside! He stopped in Kansas, of all places! This is just fan-fucking-tastic!!"

"We make the rules Chuck, not you! If you want to survive, you'll do what we tell you!"

"Shit!" He pounded his fist into his hands. Even though my eyes were now clean, I threw my hands back over them. Why was it so bright in here? I looked back at my corner of the boxcar, at the small hole rusted away in the floor, and saw sunshine beaming through it. Just *looking* at it stung. It suddenly dawned on me that we were trapped in a rusty boxcar, surrounded by police, in broad daylight. Now I knew why Chuck was so upset.

"We understand that there are at least two other men in there with you, Chuck! Exactly how many men are with you?

"Two!" He shouted. Through the cracks in my fingers, I saw a smile light up his face. "Two men, and a lady!" He spun around and whispered to Barry, who was also sitting in his corner with his hands over his face. Chuck kicked him in the leg, and whispered "Scream! Like a woman! Do it!"

"Eeeeeeeeee! Don't hurt me!" He squealed. Chuck put his ear to the door. No further commands came over the megaphone. From inside the car, we could hear the police conferring outside. Minutes later, they were back on the megaphone.

"Don't hurt the lady, Chuck. Let's work out a deal." It was subtle, but there was a change in the man's voice. There was less authority, the decisive edge dulled. Chuck suppressed a laugh, his smile now stretched from one ear to the other. Clearly, he was proud, if not surprised, that his long-shot scheme had paid off. To be honest, I was too.

"OK, here's the deal. We promise not to hurt the girl, you promise to give us a little space for 10 minutes. How's that sound?"

Silence on the other end.

"You give your word?"

"Do you?"

With one improbable bluff, Chuck had decisively shifted the balance of power. I had the feeling this wasn't the first time he'd negotiated with police.

"We do. You've got ten minutes." Silence on the outside. Suspiciously silent, actually. I asked Chuck "You really think they'll keep their word?"

"They've got to. It's in the book," he said matter-of-factly. My eyes had finally adjusted to the searing light, and I was able to take my hands from my face. Chuck was once again sitting in his corner. "Good job there, Barry," he offered pleasantly. "You really saved our asses."

"Uh, uh…uh…thanks," Barry replied, as awkwardly as humanely possible. It struck me that Barry probably didn't have much experience with positive feedback. I felt a twinge of sympathy, and even more so, gratitude. If he hadn't given us that inch of bargaining power, they almost certainly would've rushed the car. "Yeah, good work Barry," I volunteered.

"Thank you," he said, with considerably more grace and authority. On the other side of the boxcar, Thomas sat up and rubbed his eyes. "What's going on…Augh!" He opened his eyes, and stung by the secondhand daylight inside the car, immediately threw his hands back in front of his face. "Why've we stopped in the daytime? Guys?" The three of us stared at him slack-jawed. How could he have possibly slept through that?

"We're in trouble," said Chuck, furiously massaging his temples. "The old bastard stopped the train early, in Kansas, and now we're surrounded by cops."

"Cops? COPS?! No way, no fucking way, there can't be-"

"Trust us. And the only reason they aren't beating the door down right now is because they think Barry's a woman."

"*What?!*"

"There's really no time to explain, we've only got ten minutes before they come back."

"Well, what're we gonna do?!" The panic in his voice was unmistakable, although if I was wearing a prison jumper, I'm pretty sure I wouldn't want anything to do with law enforcement either.

"I'm *trying* to figure that out." Chuck inhaled deeply, and sighed, eyes closed, still furiously rubbing his temples, like a man trying to crank-start the engine of his mind.

"As long as they think Barry's a woman, we can keep them at bay until nightfall. Then, we'll have to go quietly, and spend the night in jail-"

"No. NO." Thomas, the poster boy for unflappability, was unraveling before our eyes. "I'm NEVER setting foot in jail again. We can fight them, can't we?"

"We could," Chuck said, "But not in the daylight. We wouldn't last two minutes. We need to wait till the sun goes down. We'll only be in jail for a few hours. Believe me, I've been breaking out of jails since before your great-grandparents were born. I've done right by you so far. You just need to have a little faith in me, alright?"

Thomas closed his eyes and swallowed hard. "OK…OK. Only a few hours, right?"

"Only a few hours."

There was stirring outside the car. The sound of approaching footsteps. With a hiss, the megaphone came back to life. "Time's up. We've got some more talking to do, Chuck."

"OK," Chuck hollered back, leaning against the door. "We've done some thinking, and we're willing to come out quietly. But we're not coming out until nighttime, OK?"

"That's over five hours away Chuck. We don't have that kind of time."

"Fine by me," Chuck replied solicitously. "First we kill the girl, then come out with our hands up. How'zat sound, Officer?"

"Goddamnit Chuck, you're a real pain in the ass, you know that?"

"That's a very judgmental statement to make, Officer," he said, feigning offense, his Southern drawl especially pronounced. Clearly he was enjoying this, sticking it to The Man while he still could. An involuntary smile spread across my face. 'How the hell did I end up stuck in a train with a nutcase like this?' The thought was unintentionally sobering. Seriously, how had I ended in my present situation? I could not recall a single detail about my last night as a human. It puzzled me that the circumstances behind such a profound vicissitude could be so totally unknown. Then I had another sobering thought: Perhaps it's for the better that I didn't know the truth. I was pulled out of my introspection by Chuck's ongoing negotiations. "You haven't even heard our list of demands yet!"

"Demands?!" The man behind the megaphone was incredulous. "Goddamn you!"

"What's that Officer? You want me to rape the poor girl before I kill her? You sure drive a hard bargain, sir, but I'm sure I can work something out-"

"You…bastard." I'd never heard anybody's voice sound so small through a megaphone. "What the Hell is it that you want?"

"Scotch. *Good* scotch. The worse the scotch is, the worse shape the girl will be in when we give her up tonight."

"OK, scotch, got it. Anything else?"

"Anything else?" Chuck whispered to Thomas. "Go crazy, it's on the house, but be quick about it." Thomas hardly had to think at all.

"Two cheese pizzas," he whispered back.

"And two cheese pizzas, extra large!" Chuck shouted. "Ethan, you're up." I didn't have to think either.

"20 Snickers bars."

"25 Snickers bars!" He shouted. "Barry?" Barry also knew exactly what he wanted.

"A bar of soap, and two gallons of water." Chuck looked confused, but placed the order anyway.

"And a bar of soap and two gallons of water for the lady!"

There was a brief pause, and the man with the megaphone replied "OK, got it. Just stay cool, and we should have everything within the hour. How should we give it to you?"

"There's a small latched opening in the roof. Send up one man, *one-man* to make the drop. Any more and they'll certainly wish they'd come alone. Got that?"

"Got it. Just sit tight, we'll let you know when everything's ready."

"Pleasure doing business with you Officer."

Chuck sat back down in his corner, looking exhausted but satisfied.

"What do we do now?" Barry asked.

"We wait, Barry. At this point, all we can do is wait."

Though our eyes had somewhat adjusted to the daylight, the rest of our bodies were not so adaptive. Sweat poured off our foreheads and into our eyes. Our muscles throbbed, our joints ached, and stifling misery descended on us like a blanket. The toxic sunlight was seeping in through every pore, draining the life from us. "Chuck," I asked, straining to push the words from my parched tongue through my cracked lips, "How did we ever sleep through this?"

"During the daytime, our bodies shut down," he rasped. "Since we're not active, our bodies need less of the energy taken from the blood, and use the rest to protect us from the daylight, 'till we can feed again."

"We should take shifts," I suggested. "Two of us sleep, two of us keep a lookout. Rotate once an hour."

"No," he coughed back. "If the cops try something, we need all four of us ready to fight right away."

"Look around, Chuck. None of us is any condition to fight anything. If at least two of us are able to get some rest-"

"No. If we need to fight, we'll fight. It'll be fine. You'll see."

I wasn't ready to concede, but I also didn't have the energy to keep arguing. My bloated, dehydrated tongue was taking up most of the space in my throat, so I simply nodded and let my head fall back against the wall. Another drop of sweat fell into my eyes, and they squinted shut involuntarily. I tried to open them, but they didn't budge. My eyelids were stuck fast like anchors on the ocean floor. I felt myself drifting away, falling into unconsciousness. "Chuck…Chuck, I'm falling…I'm…"

"CHUCK! ANSWER ME DAMNIT!"

The spell was broken by the man outside on the megaphone. My eyes shot open, and I leapt to my feet. "Chuck! He's back! He's back!" I nudged him with my foot, but he was sound asleep. As was Thomas. As was Barry. I was the only one awake in the boxcar.

"Chuck, are you in there?! Answer me, or we're coming in!"

"He's here, he's here!" I shouted back, taken aback by the volume and power in my voice. My tongue had given me a brief respite, and it couldn't have picked a better time.

"Who're you?!"

"I'm…I'm his friend! He doesn't feel like talking right now, so I am!"

There was silence outside the car. Then, "How old are you, kid?"

"None of your damn business!" I shot back.

"Do you really think this is gonna end well for you, son? Do you really think you chose the right side to be on?"

I felt anger welling up inside me. "What makes you think I chose this, huh?! How do you know whether or not I even had a choice?! You think I wanted to end up on some shitbox train, having a shouting match with a cop halfway across what's left of this shithole country?!

More silence on the other end, followed by "You know what, son? You sound like a pretty good kid to me, a pretty good kid who ended up in a bad situation he never planned for."

'You don't know the half of it,' I thought.

"But I tell you what, son. I'm giving you a choice right now. You've got the choice to throw open that door, come out here, and end this whole thing once and for all. We've got over two dozen guns pointed at that train right now, and if Chuck tries to stop you it'll be the last thing he does. What do you say, boy?"

I didn't answer right away. I knew the second I opened that door I'd burn up like a newspaper, with nothing but a pile of ashes to remind the world I'd ever been a part of it. As illogical as it was, a very big part of me wanted to say yes and walk out the door. To leave this whole impossible nightmare behind me. To tell myself not only was this not happening, that it had never even happened to begin with. To make things they way they were, so very long ago. I didn't even know I was doing it, but I had the door handle in my right hand. All I was thinking about was the fact that this man was giving me something I hadn't been offered for what seemed a very long time: a choice. Sometimes if you go long enough without something, and then you finally get it, you're so happy you don't even bother worrying about whether or not it's actually good for you. Denial breeds desperation. And after having gone so long only being able to make do or hang on for the ride or see where this or that takes me, I had just been given a real, honest to God choice as to how my new life was going to turn out. For better or worse, I was going to take it.

What finally brought me back to reality was the searing pain of direct sunlight on my left hand. Without consciously thinking, I had opened the door the tiniest of cracks and brought the poison directly inside. I immediately closed it. The action had been so small, I doubted if anyone outside had even noticed.

"So what's it gonna be son?" called the man on the megaphone at last. "You ready to come out and start fixing your life?"

I squeezed my wounded hand against my body, trying to completely cut it off from the light, hiding it behind my other hand. "Go fuck yourself," I spat, furious at having been tempted with the illusion of freedom. At a certain point, life just isn't fixable.

The man outside on the megaphone sounded disappointed. "Don't say I didn't give you the chance, kid. Tell Chuck his goodies are here."

"Send em' in!" Chuck barked. He was awake, and standing behind me. "In through the roof, like we agreed. And remember-*one man.*" He gave me a strange, probing look, offering appraisal without verdict. How much of our exchange had he heard?

He called Barry away from his corner, keeping his hawk's eyes on the roof overhead (how Chuck knew there was a door I wasn't sure. He must've noticed it when we first boarded). Moments later there was a scraping sound overhead, and the sound of footsteps. Finally, two knocks.

"I've got the stuff," an unfamiliar voice called out.

"I'm opening the door. Hand it down to me, fast. No tricks."

"No tricks," the man echoed.

Chuck grabbed hold of a handle overhead and threw the door open. Brilliant, excruciating light came down in a blinding column. He brazenly reached out into the light, shouting "Drop it! Now!" A large cardboard box feel into Chuck's waiting arms. He clutched it tightly and stepped back, yelling "Close it! Close it!" The unseen man reached down, caught the door, and slammed it shut. "Now scram!" Chuck hollered, and we heard the man's footsteps moving away from the roof. With the daylight vanquished, Chuck sat down and tore the roof off the box, inspecting its contents, ignoring the burns on his hands.. The scotch came in an unlabeled, bubble-wrapped brown bottle. He took off the top, sniffed it, and smiled, apparently pleased. Next came the pizzas, still hot to the touch, their fragrant smell filling the room. Underneath the pizzas was a cache of candy bars, and finally, at the bottom of the box, a large jug of water and a bar of Dove soap.

"Everything OK?" shouted the man with the megaphone.

"Out-*standing,"* Chuck replied. "Now just give us a little space, and we'll see you tonight."

"Count on it," called the man with the megaphone, and then there was silence from the outside. For the time being, things were looking up, and we sat down to dinner.

The pizzas were the first food to go. Although the four of us now subsisted on a very different food source, there was something emotionally satisfying about partaking in an old favorite. Chuck produced the final blood pouch from the blood bank and poured it into the scotch, shaking it thoroughly before passing it around. The candy bars served as dessert, something to lazily snack on as we drained the last of the scotch. As soon as the bottle was empty, Barry opened his water and soap and began washing himself. It struck the three of us as somewhat odd: we all stank, and so what? Should we worry about offending the sensibilities of our victims before we killed them? Still, Barry scrubbed and scrubbed. He worked especially hard to get the blood stains out of his clothes, but had no luck. He seemed disappointed. When he was finished, he passed around what was left of the water (a little less than half) for all of us to drink. Having eaten and drank, the sunlight didn't seem nearly so oppressive.

When all the food was finished, the trash strewn about the floor, Chuck consulted his watch. It was three o'clock. A little more than three hours away from sundown. There was nothing left to eat, no more negotiations with the police, these things replaced by a sense of listless boredom. This was evident in Thomas, who's eyes darted wildly about, and whose limbs shook almost imperceptibly with anxiety. He knew the hour of his reimprisonment was close at hand. Time dragged by at a greatly reduced rate. Chuck was polishing his damned broken scissors again, Barry was still contemplating the stains of his clothing, pausing briefly to straighten his tie. There had to be a better way to pass the hours than this. I decided now was as good a time as any to get some questions answered.

"Hey Chuck," I asked, breaking the silence. He looked up in acknowledgement. "How come your voice is always different before you feed?"

"Different?" He replied, slightly perplexed. "How?"

"Well, normally you have a pretty thick accent, you talk like you're from the South. But always a few hours before you feed, your voice changes. You lose your accent, you use different words. You sound more…I don't know…dignified."

He was silent for a moment, staring into his lap. Finally, he looked up and said "Have you ever been around a person you know, after he's had too much alcohol to drink?"

"Well, yeah."

"Doesn't his voice sound different? He slurs his words, talks about different things, changes his personality?"

"Yeah."

"It's the same as that." He once more turned his attention to his prized scissor, as if declaring the matter closed. I wasn't satisfied.

"But our voices don't change, do they? And people get worse at talking when they're drunk, but you get better."

"When our bodies use up all of the blood we've drank, they begin to change," he snapped back, clearly annoyed. "Our senses grow sharper, our physical abilities are greater, and certain…personality traits we'd rather keep to ourselves begin to manifest themselves. I'm sure you know what I'm talking about, *don't you*?" He said rather pointedly, looking from me, to Thomas, and back to me. "We can't control it, we can't change it, it simply…is. And we must learn to live with it, as all vampires must."

"How did…" It was a difficult question to ask, one I was not sure I would want to have answered. "How did the three of us become vampires? I can't remember anything beyond waking up on the first train."

"Neither do I," said Barry.

"Same here," Thomas chimed in

"I bit you," Chuck said dismissively. Our interrogating gazes didn't lift. "All of you." Still not enough. "Well, what is it you all want from me?!" he shouted.

"Why, Chuck," I said firmly. "We want to know why. Why you did this to us. Why you made us this way."

"Why?" He shot back. "Why do you care? Knowing won't change anything! Did you ever think that maybe there's a good reason why you don't remember?"

The three of us looked at each other nervously. It was a fear we had all shared.

"Fine," he said, tucking his scissor back into his coat. "You want to know how it all happened, I'll tell you. I was in Oregon, looking for the doctor, the Nazi who knows how to reverse vampirism. He was hiding."

"From the government?"

"From me." He answered my next question before I had the chance to ask it. "We've met before. Several times. Anyway, he found out I was coming for him, and took a plane across the country to New York. The gasoline is all but gone, but planes still fly, if you've got enough money, which he does."

"How do you know that's where he went?"

"By the time I made it to his house, he had already left, and his personal assistant was getting ready to do the same. He didn't do it fast enough. He told me where he was going, before he died. That's the third assistant of his I've killed.

"After I'd finished the business with the assistant, I went out for a walk. I had come all the way across the country in vain, and would now have to go back another way."

"How did you get to Oregon in the first place?"

"A man who drove one of the few remaining supply trucks for FEMA. He owed me a favor. Anyway, I was out on my walk, trying to think of a way to get back across the country, and fast, when I stumbled upon a train yard. It hit me that although there was very little gasoline left, trains, which run off of coal, would still be able to get about. There was a man at the front gate, a drug shipper. The yard had been abandoned, and he used the trains to move his product. I asked if he sent any trains to New York. He didn't, only to Canada, via a series of underground tunnels under the boarder. But the station that he was sending a train full of speed to on that night sometimes sent old engines to the east coast to be junked. He had a copy of their itinerary, and knew a single train was scheduled to leave for New York that night. For a little money, he agreed to let me stow away on one of his trains heading to the Canadian depot."

"He let me inside the train yard, and told me where I could find my train. I had just over half an hour before it departed. On my trip from Georgia to Oregon, the driver and I had run into a number of unfortunate incidents that would not have been quite so unfortunate had there been more than two of us. It would be even more dangerous to make the return journey alone. I would need company.

"I wasn't alone in the train yard by any means. There were several men, customers of the drug shipper no doubt, as well as the vagrants and bums who grow like weeds alongside train tracks. Men so old and feeble would only slow me down. It seemed I would be traveling alone after all, like it or not. I set off to find my train. And that was when I saw Barry."

Barry fidgeted in his seat. His face turned pallid white, his memory apparently jogged. "Chuck, don,'t," he begged. "Please don't tell them."

"You all wanted to know how it happened, and now you're going to find out. When I first saw Barry, he was asleep, propped up against an old, rusty train, half on the tracks, half off. There were lots of men sleeping next to trains that night, but none so well dressed. You were the most respectable-looking man I had seen that night, so I decided to make you my traveling companion by default.

"I came upon you swiftly and silently, getting my fangs in your neck before you could open your eyes. It was then that I discovered you weren't really sleeping after all. You were dead."

Barry swallowed hard. Tiny beads of moisture began to form at the corner of his eyes. He blinked them back. "You monster."

"There was an interesting taste to your blood," Chuck continued, ignoring him. "Quite bitter. I recognized it right away as arsenic. I wondered which of the vagrants you had angered, and how, in order to make one of them want to poison you. And while you were in fact dead, you had not been dead for very long. Five minutes at the most. I could still bring you back, if I wanted to. And I did. It took nearly ten minutes to siphon the poison from your blood, but I did, such was my dedication to you. It wasn't until I checked your pockets and discovered the glass bottle with the traces of white powder at the bottom that I learned who your poisoner was...yourself."

Barry's eyes were burning a hole in the floor.

"Now that you were taken care of, I began dragging you along with me to our train. I didn't take but two steps when who but our dear friend Ethan came stumbling around the train and ran right into me."

Goddamnit.

"Ethan, although clearly under the influence of some substance or another, apparently wasn't satisfied just yet, and was willing to do some very...*interesting* things to me for a little bit of money. Rather ironic that *I* was the one to do the biting and sucking that night, not him."

He can talk now. He'll pay for it later.

"This night wasn't turning out to be such a disappointment after all. These men were perhaps not my first choices for fellow travelers, but anything was better than trying to make it back alone. I was running out of time, and now had two bodies to transport rather than one, so I began the hunt for my train in earnest. When at last I found it, I was just in time. I threw them into the first unlocked boxcar I saw, and hopped in just as the train started moving. I was feeling mighty proud of myself, having so quickly reversed my fortune, when Thomas very nearly threw me off the train."

No expression from Thomas. He looked almost bored, in fact.

"In my haste to get my new friends and I on the train, I hadn't bothered to check if the boxcar I'd chosen was truly empty. It turned out it wasn't. Our fight was nothing short of spectacular. Had I been merely human, I daresay Thomas would've killed me two or three times over."

"You *were* especially hard to kill," Thomas offered noncommittally.

"As were you," Chuck replied. "It's a shame we couldn't have had this conversation earlier, on the first train. Right now I would've called your attention to the remarkably detailed imprint of my face that Thomas put in the wall. Would've made a great visual aid.

"Anyway, we kept fighting. I was a vampire, and he wasn't, so I won. I bit you and threw you in a corner like I had the other two. I was very, very sore, but also glad that I had found at least one human that I knew would be a worthwhile vampire. Everybody woke up the next day as vampires, with varying degrees of short term memory loss as is the norm. We were in California, about to head into the underground tunnel system that lead us into Canada. We changed trains at the next yard, and so began our little adventure together."

Nobody in the boxcar would look at each other. Each individual pair of eyes staked a claim to its own plot of unoccupied real estate.

"What's the matter, guys?" Chuck called out, his voice taking on a new degree of belittling coldness. "You wanted to know what happened, and I told you, didn't I? So what's the big deal? Now we're getting to know each other! We can put on name tags and talk about our zodiac signs and our SAT scores and our favorite foods! Mine's spaghetti! What's yours, Barry? Arsenic burgers?"

"You bastard!" he screamed, coming unglued. "You bastard! You ruined us!"

"Ruined what?" Chuck shouted back with more than equal fury, rising to his feet to loom over Barry. "Ruined a suicide and a drug whore and an escaped convict? There's not a whole lot there to ruin in the first place! You're all failures, all of you! You were a bunch of chemically imbalanced, maladjusted, social outcast fuck ups when I found you, and you still are, only now you have to fuck up other people's lives to keep going! And what gives you the right, huh? What makes you so much more important than the people you kill to stay alive?!"

Chuck had worked himself into a frenzy, hurling profanities and imprecations at everyone, including, albeit indirectly, himself. At this point I was struck by an idea.

"Chuck," I said, calmly, rationally, with no sign of menace or malice.

"What?" he growled back, turning on his heels to face me.

"How did *you* become a vampire?"

My question hit him firmly in the gut. The anger clouding his head was instantly burned away. He was standing fully erect, yet looked very, very small. The question hung in the air between us, floating like concrete. Seconds later, he still hadn't answered. I considered broaching the question again, but decided against it. His response was very important; it dictated how I would proceed.

"Man, fuck you," he called weakly, turning around and retreating to his corner. "you're not worth the time."

"Were you so much better than us when you were turned, Chuck?"

"As a matter of fact I was," he replied sharply.

"Oh, sure you were, Chuck. You were a hobo, weren't you, always eating beans out of a can, right? That would explain the smell."

"*I was not a hobo,"* he snarled back.

"Definitely not, Chuckie. I'm guessing prostitute. You've definitely got the prostitute look nailed, Chuck. How much for an hour, Chuck? How much for the *whole damn night?"*

"You have no idea what you're talking about!"

"Then give us an idea, Chuck. You turned us so you'd have someone to watch your back on your trip to New York. That's fine. I'm committed. We're all committed. We all know each other's stories now, we're not just anonymous vampire badasses who bad-lucked into each other. For better or worse, we're some kind of fucked up family, and you're the Dad, and I'd say if nothing else, you owe the kids a little explanation."

Chuck sat briefly in ponderous silence. "Fine," he said. "I suppose you have a right to know.

Chapter 5: Chuck's Revolution

"There is no loneliness greater than the loneliness of a failure. The failure is a stranger in his own house."
-Eric Hoffer

"As we discussed earlier, I'm very old, much older than I appear. I was born in 1769 in Paris, to an aristocratic family. My given name was Arnauld de-Chambeaux. My family had great wealth, and great influence, and therefore so did I."

Well, this was certainly not what I was expecting to hear. It was not easy to imagine the scarred, drawling brute I had come to know as French nobility, but as I've said many times before, stranger things have proven true.

"Mine was an easy life, a life of luxury and decadence, which I took for granted, as it was the only life I knew. I was married young, to the daughter of another privileged family. It had been arranged by our families, of course, but we cared for each other greatly.

"A few years later, the Revolution began to take form. It was still in its infancy, and we paid it no mind. There was another problem, however, that troubled us greatly; the vampires.

"As far as we were concerned, vampires were simply the stuff of legend, an imaginary menace. Every so often there would be sightings, in outlying rural areas, but those who claimed to have seen them were dismissed as foolish or insane. It was very similar to the way people in your times treat those who claim to have been abducted by aliens.

"However, as time passed, more and more sightings were being reported. People began disappearing, closer and closer to the city. Authorities were sluggish to take any action, at least until vampires were seen inside the walls of Paris itself. Weeks went by, and the vampires grew more numerous, until the aristocracy decided we had no choice but to save Paris ourselves. A party of young noblemen was assembled to become vampire hunters. I was their leader.

"We armed ourselves with the traditional banes of the vampire; wooden stakes and mirrors and crosses and garlic. Our first night out was in early July. There were roughly 30 of us. Of course, having lead the sheltered life of the aristocracy, none of us had ever seen a vampire. We were terrified, paranoid, in search of quarry we wouldn't recognize until it attacked us. But I would not let us turn back. We stalked the empty streets for hours, hands trembling with nerves, until we were thoroughly exhausted. It was then that the vampires saw fit to attack us, dozens of them, pouring out of alleys and sewers and abandoned homes. I stood and fought as the others fled. Needless to say, I did not last long.

"I woke up the next night in a chair, sitting at an empty table. I was not bound, nor was I injured. When I opened my eyes, I saw that I was not alone. There was another man on the other side of the room, an older man, his body covered with a dense constellation of scars and old wounds. When he saw I was awake, he came and sat down at the other end of the table. He handed me a mug and told me to drink it. It was thick, with a bitter taste, and yet I loved it more than anything I had ever drunk before. It instantly made me feel stronger, more alive. I thanked him, and asked what it was. He told me it was scotch and blood. And that's when I knew what I had become.

"He introduced himself as Grisson, and told me that although I did not know it yet, I was special, very special. When I asked him what that meant, he told me I would find out soon enough. He told me there many lessons I had to learn first. For my first lesson, I had to learn who I was, by learning who I used to be, and would never be again. He would tell me nothing more, and then he released me into the night. I was in one of the poorer neighborhoods of Paris, a little more than a mile away from my home. I was still very confused at this point, no doubt as you were when you first woke up after being bitten. I began to doubt that I really was a vampire. Perhaps I had only been kidnapped by a madman who was making sport of me. Strangely, that was a comforting thought. I ran home as fast as I could, thrilled that I was still alive, that I would soon have my old life back. When

I reached home, my family was thrilled to see me, to have me in their arms, alive. Then they saw the bite marks in my neck, and panicked. I tried to explain that they were wrong, it wasn't what it looked like, but they wouldn't listen. My father and his guards tried to kill me. They were attacking me with crosses and stakes, and the whole time I fought them off I was trying to explain, begging them to just listen, but they wouldn't. And as much as I hated myself for it, I felt just as strong an urge to kill them as they did to kill me. To feed on them, to drink their blood. And that's when I knew for sure what I had become. I fled the house and ran back out into the night. I walked the streets, thinking about who I now was, who I used to be, who I could never be again. My life as I had lived it up to that point was over. I could not go home; where else could I go? And that's when I understood what Grisson had meant. And so I went to see him again.

"He was in the same house, sitting at the same table, when I came inside. He asked me if I understood; I told him I did. He said it was time for my second lesson.

"Grisson knew what he wanted; scientists. Coming from my background, I knew where to find them. I warned him that they would be heavily guarded, owing to their high social status, but he assured me it wouldn't be a problem. I knew of a chemist who lived a few neighborhoods over, so I led Grisson to his house. Standing outside in the street, we hatched our plan. Grisson would kick down the door and go after any bodyguards; I was to run upstairs and subdue the chemist. I braced myself as Grisson prepared to kick in the door, and the moment it hit the floor I charged inside. I was nearly halfway to the stairs when I realized I was alone. From the corner of my eye I saw Grisson turn around and walk back into the street. My confusion gave way to anger, and that's when the first of the guards jumped on my back.

"A second guard, then a third, then a fourth piled on until I went down onto the floor. I was on the verge of panic, but I managed to get in one weak, desperate kick. To my surprise, the four men flew off easily, crashing into the wall across the room. I was too startled to move when yet another guard came down the stairs. He swung hard and punched me squarely in the face, although I hardly felt it. I grabbed him by the throat and effortlessly pitched him across the room and through a table. By this time my original four attackers were back on their toes, but they were fumbling aimlessly, tripping over furniture, swinging blindly. I was utterly confused, until the thought hit me; *they can't see me.* I had utterly forgotten that the room was completely dark. And yet somehow I could see them, in perfect detail. With my visual advantage, I disposed of them all quite easily. Suddenly, I remembered why I'd come upstairs in the first place...the chemist. I bolted up the stairs, heart racing, and flung open the door to his bedroom. Standing inside, before an open window, curtains fluttering in the breeze, was Grisson, holding the chemist's limp body over his shoulders. His chin was slick with gore. He peered over my shoulder, down at the carnage I'd left on the first floor. He looked impressed.

'I...I didn't know I could do that,' I gasped.

He grinned at me through a film of wet blood. "You do now."

"We left the chemist's house right away, Grisson carrying our trophy. I turned right, to go back to his house, but he turned left.

"We're going someplace else," he said. So I followed him. I thought little of our change of direction until I recognized the enormous, lavishly appointed building on the horizon; it was where my family, along the rest of France's ruling class, lived in luxury, isolated and protected from the less-desirable elements of French society. At least, until tonight.

"Grisson, no, we can't," I pleaded. "Give them time, they'll come around."

"They will *never* come around," he replied coldly. "But your worries are unfounded. We're going someplace else."

"Swaddled in shadow, we stole past the magnificent building, and my heart implored me to go home, to my parents, to my wife. But my mind knew better than that. I was now a monster and a murderer, acutely less than human. The comfort and stability I had known in the past was just that; in the past. Grisson led me through yet more alleys and underpasses until we arrived at our destination. It was a warehouse, but not just any warehouse; the largest, oldest storage center in the city. Many years before I was born, two very rich men had been locked in a legal battle for decades over its ownership. They both died within the same week, without a winner ever having been declared. Other parties had expressed interest in acquiring the property after the men's death, but the lawyers involved in the case now viewed each other as personal enemies, and with considerable financial resources allocated to them from their former client's wills, they kept the case tied up in court indefinitely. During the legal proceedings, no one was allowed within 50 feet of the warehouse, therefore no one was able to maintain or repair the ancient, crumbling structure. As the feuding lawyers grew older and physically deteriorated, so did the building. By the time the lawyers themselves finally died (coincidentally, within 72 hours of each other), with no decision ever having been reached, the building was in such bad shape no one else wanted anything to do with it. And so, as a result of enduring hatred and long-held grudges, the vampires of France had their first real home.

"All the doors were sealed years ago, so we had to climb over concrete rubble and then under what looked like a collapsed rafter to get in. The warehouse looked even larger from the inside, if that was possible. More shocking even than the size of the interior was its condition. Although from the outside the warehouse appeared to be on its last legs, inside there was furniture, candles, beds with blankets and pillows, everything required to lead a reasonably comfortable existence. There were even a few purely aesthetic touches, like paintings on the walls, three of which I immediately recognized as having been stolen from a neighbor's home a year and a half ago. But even more surprising than the building's interior were its occupants. There were vampires everywhere, some lounging on the furniture, a small group playing cards, a few of them even reading. However, most of the vampires appeared to be very busy, bustling about, running up and down the stairs, engaged in mysterious conversations, carrying mysterious things. One of them, wearing clean white clothing, with short blond hair, noticed Grisson standing near the entrance and ran over to speak with him.

" Grisson, apparently, was in no mood to talk. He merely dumped the body from his shoulders onto the other vampire's with a perfunctory command. "Take him to level four, and make him comfortable." He nodded and scurried away towards the staircase. Free of the dead weight, Grisson beckoned and lead me through the crowd.

"The fourth floor is the scientist's wing. You have no official business there. I'd be happy to give you a tour if we both have free time available, but realistically, that's very unlikely. We're both going to be very busy in the near future." He threw open a door at the end of the lobby, and walked into another expansive room filled with bread and wine, jugs of water, books, sporting goods, the occasional fiddle or drum and other miscellaneous pastimes and comforts of a decidedly human vein. "This is the recreation supply room," he said. "Many people, when dealing with the physical and mental stresses of having been Turned, long for the comforts of their previous lives. We keep these pleasant distractions on hand to keep them occupied. I'd suggest you visit the library at some point; it rivals any in the country."

"But why the food?"

"Again, comfort. Traditional food is obsolete to a vampire, as we take our sustenance from blood alone. New vampires are often loathe to give up food, so we allow them their old pleasures while they acquire a taste for new ones."

"We passed through another room, similar to the one before, and then another, before stopping in front of a massive spiral staircase."

"This is the grand staircase, the only one that gives instant access to all four floors. Very convenient." He started up the stairs, and I followed him. "Now that you know who you are and what you're capable of, you won't be on street patrol for awhile. You have a more important job to do indoors. Don't worry about blood, there's more than enough to go around, even for those who don't hunt. The Feeding Room is on level one; if you can't find it, ask someone for help. Most of the first floor is Reception; they're all very friendly."

"I have a question right now actually."

"Yes?"

"What is it exactly that you want me to do?"

"It's very convenient you should ask that right now, Arnauld," he said, walking off the staircase and pausing in front of a door with a decorative "3" carved above the frame. "You'll be working on the third floor," he said, opening the door to reveal a gigantic room with beds lined from wall to wall, dozens of people lying in apparent slumber.

"You'll be working in the Hospital."

"But...why? I don't know anything about medicine. I'd probably end up doing more harm than good!"

"Relax, Arnauld," Grisson said soothingly. "We have people to do that. You needn't be concerned with their bodies; it's their hearts and minds you're after."

"I still don't understand."

"You know what it's like to close your eyes as a human and open them as a vampire, no? To go from a decent man who loves his family, to a monster who must forsake his old life and drink blood to survive? It's not the easiest thing in the world, is it?"

"No."

"That's exactly what all of these people will be going through when they open their eyes and understand that something important has gone horribly wrong. You need to help them through that."

"But why me?"

"Because you're a hero, Arnauld. Their protector. The man who took up arms and lead the charge against the vampiric scourge, and so nobly gave his life in doing so. On top of that, Arnauld, you're of royal birth. These people have been raised from childhood to do what you say, to give their lives for you, and go to the grave with a smile at your whim.

"As we stand here at this very moment, Arnauld, important things are taking place inside this building. *Very important things.* Things that will rock this country to its core, things that will change the state of the entire planet. This is not a dying warehouse so much as a gestating nation. *And you will be its King.* A kingdom is only as strong as the people it rules, and those people lying in their beds, those are the people you will rule. And you will rule them very soon. But you will not rule them out of fear and malice, as so many kings in the past have. You will rule them with respect, with compassion, with loyalty, with love. Just because we must drink blood does not mean we are blind to its value."

"Without another word, Grisson left me to my work.

"As it turns out, Grisson had been quite right about our not having time to tour the fourth floor. Every night, from sunset to sunrise, the men and women who had been brought in by the street vampires would groggily open their eyes and ask where they were. I made it a point to be the first thing they saw; to treat any lingering pain, to make them comfortable, to learn their names, both first and last. To answer their questions, as best I could, which was often not very well at all. To hold them when they cried, to hold them down when their anger at what we had done to them boiled over. As time went by, I found that the best weapons in my arsenal were listening and food. Often times it took little more than a piece of bread and a five minute conversation to settle their nerves. After about two weeks, when the doctors declared them vampires of good physical and mental health, two rather personable gentleman, one old, one young (I suspected they were father and son, the resemblance was so strong) would come into the hospital and take them to second floor, known only as "Training." A few months later some would come back into the hospital as nurses or attendants; others I would see on the first floor, dealing with whatever mysterious paperwork the Reception workers often handled. Still others seemed to simply disappear.

"Weeks went by and I settled into a busy but comfortable routine. While no two freshly minted vampires were exactly the same, most of them had similar needs; a friend to see them through a time of jarring transition, and reassurance that they had not become the monsters of fairytale and folklore they had been taught to fear as children. I had been working in the Hospital wing for nearly a month when that pleasant routine was broken.

"There was a vampire on the fourth floor who had become "Mentally ill to the point of attempted suicide," as his chart read. Considered a danger to himself and others, he was being kept in restraints in a glorified closet. I went to see him, intrigued at the notion of a suicidal vampire, but confidant that I could help him get back on the right path the way I'd helped so many others. When I entered his holding room to see him, my stomach nearly leapt into my throat. I recognized him right away as the chemist Grisson and I had brought in on my first night in the warehouse.

"My first thought was to turn and run immediately; I could simply tell the doctors that he was beyond help and leave his care in their hands. However, I could not bring myself to abandon him. In no small way, I was the man responsible for his current situation. The very least I owed him was to try and help.

"I pulled up a chair and sat down in front of him. He was tied to a chair of his own, arms behind his back, legs bound with leather straps. His only clothing was a pair of dirty shorts. He hung his head limply in front of his chest. If he hadn't managed to kill himself, it appeared as though he had come very close.

"Hello," I said, trying to make eye contact, but his gaze stayed locked to the floor. "My name is Arnauld, and-"

"I know who you are," he rasped weakly, with what sounded like a mouthful of sand. Oh God, what else did he know?

"How do you know who I am?" I asked, trying desperately to remain composed.

"You have quite a reputation in our little society," he croaked. "You're a phenomenal salesman of the vampire lifestyle."

"What's that supposed to mean?"

"It means you convince people that they're better off for having lost their humanity. They're better off living as monsters. Don't get me wrong, it is fun at first. The extra strength and speed and heightened sensory perception are all very useful. On top of that, you don't even have to kill to eat, provided you have some sort of useful skill. But one day," he paused for a dry coughing fit, "One day you ask yourself, where did the blood in this cup come from?"

"That's a rather harsh way of-"

"It's a very *honest* way!

"You didn't let me finish, I was going to say-"

"We're *sick!* And the longer we go on being sick the sicker we make the rest of the world!"

"His outburst had overtaxed his frail body, and his head flopped sidewise as he wheezed for air. I leafed through his chart in the meantime, and found "method of self injury; intentional staking." There was a large, crusted scab on chest, partially hidden by his limp head.

"So you staked yourself."

"Yes. Tried to, anyway. That stake was originally meant for the man who did this to me, but of course they'll never tell you who did it. In a building this huge I'd probably never even run into him again." I swallowed hard. He continued, "I went too high."

"Excuse me?"

"With the stake; I went to high. Didn't even nick the heart. All they had to do was slice in and pull it out."

"I really didn't know what to say.

"I'm sorry," I settled on. I meant it.

"Don't be. If you can live the way you are now, that's fine. But I can't. I'm a scientist, not a parasite. I wanted to understand nature, not destroy it. I'm just ashamed it took me so long to figure it out."

"What are you working on upstairs?"

"For the first time he looked up at me, and I saw the whites of his eyes were nearly pink with blood. Even stranger than that, almost all of the color had drained from his pupils, leaving only a hint of brown behind a rising tide of grey.

"Hell if I know," he rasped. "Hell if anyone knows. They don't let us talk to each other. Every evening there are four different bottles on my table, with instructions on how to mix their contents. Very detailed, complicated instructions. And every morning, before I go back to sleep, I write down what the final mixture looked like, smelled like, tasted like, and so on. When I wake up the next evening, my notes are gone, and I have four more bottles to tend to. It's like that every single day. It never changes. Or at least it hadn't, up until two weeks ago. Then I was only given three bottles to mix. As of three days ago, they've been giving me only two bottles, which means they're getting closer."

"Closer to what?"

"I already told you, we don't know. Something evil, no doubt. What else could it be?"

"How can you be sure it's something bad? They've always taken good care of us here."

"But at what cost? At the expense of the lives of women and children and whatever poor soul couldn't run fast enough or couldn't afford a decent lock on his door. It's one thing for a few people to die so that other people may live, but we've been here for months. Hundreds of people have been murdered, and hundreds more will die the longer we stay here, feasting on the living." He was racked with another coughing fit.

"What do you want me to do about it, then?"

"Kill me," he gasped.

"I can't kill you!"

"Then help me…to do it…myself. Under my…foot."

I got down on my knees and looked under his right foot. There was nothing there. He began weakly kicking his other foot, and I grabbed it carefully and examined it. There was a small pouch stuck to the bottom of his heel with some sort of glue.

"Sawdust," he croaked. "Feed it to me."

"What will that do?"

"It's not…the stake in the heart, that kills, but…the wood. All vampires…allergic. Heart pumps splinters through veins. Quiet… death."

I opened the pouch and lifted his head. He opened his mouth as best he could, and I poured the fragrant dust into his mouth. He swallowed, and began wheezing violently. I reached for the small flask of cold water I kept on my belt and poured it into his mouth. The color began to drain from his skin almost instantly. His tongue dangled out of his mouth, and his eyelids shut slowly. I poured a final drink of water down his throat.

"Thank you," he said, in a barely audible hiss.

"I'm so sorry," I told him, feeling my own skin go cold and pale.

"No…I am." His head fell back to his chest. And he stopped breathing.

"I called a nurse to come pick up the body. Then I let her know I was taking the rest of the week off and left for my private room, locking the door behind me.

"Three days later there was a knock at the door. I ignored it as I had all other attempts to communicate with me. After a few more knocks, I heard a key slide into the lock and then Grisson was standing in the open doorway."

"Hello, Arnauld." I gave him a cursory greeting.

"What happened to that man wasn't your fault. Everyone seems to have agreed upon that but yourself."

"It was the chemist, Grisson. The chemist we brought in together."

"I know. Do you then believe I'm responsible for his death as well?"

"Yes. We all are."

He walked in and sat down at my table across from me. "Your honesty is admirable. But you cannot let one delusional man rule your mind from beyond grave."

"He wasn't delusional at all. He was the only person I've met since I came here that honestly understood what he and all of us had become."

"And just for curiosity's sake, what have we become, according to this man?"

"Parasites. Monsters who kill dozens of people a day, so that we can live while innocent people die. He couldn't bear to keep working on some mysterious project he knew would serve to take even more lives."

Grisson suddenly looked very troubled. "And this is why he killed himself, you say?"

"That's what he told me."

Grisson was nearly speechless. "Well, this is very sad news. Very ironic."

"What do you mean?"

Grisson produced a flask of his own from his belt, and poured a small amount of a thin, clear liquid into an empty cup on the table. "Drink this."

"What is it?"

"The defining accomplishment of our recently departed friend. Surely we at least owe it to him to try it."

I raised the glass and downed it quickly. At first it merely tasted like warm water, but a few seconds later I felt that familiar rush of energy and vigor unique to live human blood. I dropped the glass on the table.

"What is this?" I demanded. "This cannot be blood!"

"Technically, you're right. It's synthetic blood. Water mixed with the specific blood proteins from which we draw our strength. One glass a week will provide all the nourishment a vampire needs."

"How is it made?"

"It's a very complicated process, but fortunately its inventor left behind extensive notes. The first successful mixture was created the evening before he attempted to kill himself."

Oh God...

"Unfortunately, its manufacture is not completely nonviolent. It still requires human blood, preferably from a young adult female. But the blood from one young woman is enough to produce nearly a hundred glasses. Rather than killing hundreds of humans per month, as we'd unfortunately been forced to do previously, we can now feed all the vampires in France on fewer than ten human deaths per year. Our days of hunting in the streets are over. Tonight, we're sending a draft of a vampire/human peace treaty to the king. It's just a shame that the man responsible for this new era of peace couldn't be here to welcome it."

"Why didn't he know? Why couldn't you have told him what he was making?!"

"In hindsight, it's seems obvious that's what we should have done. But needless to say, this was a controversial project. We couldn't have news of it leaking out to the public. There are those among us who enjoy killing, who have nothing but hate for humankind, and regrettably it is these who we have depended on for sustenance as our ranks grew. Overnight they will go from being revered as providers to being essentially unemployed. We suspect some of them will even attempt to break away and form their own violent societies dedicated to war and terror. We are confident that in time most of them will come around; those who do not will have to be eliminated. But we could not afford to have this happen while we are trying to come to a peace agreement with the humans. I understand why you are upset, I am greatly saddened as well, but there's really not much we could have done in this case. Besides, you cannot accept responsibility for his suicide; it's not as though you yourself took his life."

"I was lost inside my own grieving mind when I managed to voice agreement, and asked Grisson to leave so that I may get some sleep. He agreed, and left me to spend the night inside my own tortured mind.

"Late the next night, on the cusp of morning, I was woken by Grisson. He very nearly threw me from my bed as he ordered me to get dressed and meet him at the fourth floor. I had 10 minutes.

"Although I wanted nothing more than to lie in bed and stew in my own vituperous grief, I forced myself to quickly dress and set off for the fourth floor. Under different circumstances, I more than likely would have chosen to ignore orders and spend the night in isolation. However, even in my exhausted, distraught state I had detected a trace of something very unusual in Grisson's voice; panic.

"When I arrived at the fourth floor, a vampire I recognized from reception was waiting for me in front of the door. We silently acknowledged each other, and then he opened the door and led me inside. On the other side of the door was what looked like a dining room, mostly occupied by a large table. The plates and utensils had been pushed onto the floor, along with a stray Bunsen burner and several sheets of paper filled with screeds of scientific jargon. All but two of the seats at the table had been filled by Grisson and various vampires I recognized as leaders of each floor's respective operations, along with three or four other, particularly nasty looking vampires I didn't recognize. They probably led the hunting parties in the streets. In total, there were about 20 of us. The two of us sat down and Grisson began to speak."

"First, I must thank all of you for assembling so promptly at such a late hour, and in such Spartan accommodations. I'm aware that all of you know about our recent scientific breakthrough, and," he shot a stern glance at the leaders of the hunting parties, who were all too happy to return it, "regardless of your personal feelings about it, surely grasp its significance. I know that you're also aware of the peace treaty we sent to the leaders of the humans last night-"

"-against our better judgment," interjected one of the hunters.

"Yes," Grisson replied coldly, "Against *your* better judgment. At any rate, the leaders of the French government have received and reviewed our petition. And we have just received word, less than half an hour ago, in fact, that it has been completely and wholly rejected." The assemblage of vampires looked uneasy, with the exception of the hunters, who appeared rather pleased with themselves. "They have informed us that, in their estimation, peace can only come when we and any remaining traces of our existence have been wiped from this earth."

"Then we shall wipe them from it first," declared one of the hunters.

"Given their truculent, bullheaded response I would like nothing more than to do just that," he replied. "But there is a problem. Within the hour, the sun will have risen again, and we shall once more be confined to the warehouse for the duration of the day. The French have informed us that their Army is assembling as we speak, and will be on our doorstep come midday." Many of the vampires gasped aloud; one even managed to choke on some nonexistent food. The eyes of the hunting vampires grew wide with shock, although they were quick to paint over their true expressions with a thick layer of stoicism. "The reason I have called this improvised assembly," Grisson continued coolly, "Is to determine what course of action should be taken in the interest of those we lead."

"Can we be sure they are serious?" asked a Reception vampire. "It could be a bluff."

"It's not a risk we can afford to take. If we idle, and they hold to their word, the outcome will be disastrous. Also, although we obviously cannot be sure, the haste with which they rejected our proposal could indicate they've been planning this for some time. Our hunting parties have met a suspiciously low amount of formal opposition. Perhaps their military has been holding back until now, in order to attack at full strength.

"What about an evacuation?" the head doctor suggested. "If we begin right away, there's a good chance we could clear the building in twenty minutes."

"Yes, but where would we evacuate to? With the exception of a few houses we've maintained as external bases, there's simply nowhere else to go."

"They could commandeer civilian homes," he replied.

"It sounds good on paper, but that kind of thing is easier said than done. Holding a family hostage is a very complicated procedure, and much of our population is occupational, and not sufficiently trained in combat-"

"Another brilliant oversight," quipped one of the hunters, while his allies sniggered agreement.

"Shut up!" Grisson barked, pounding the table in a lapse of temperament. "For the sake of the Lord, shut UP!" His antagonist shoved a finger into his face and snarled,

"You will pay me the proper respect unless you-unh!"

"In a sliver of an instant Grisson grabbed his probing finger and smashed it down upon the table with a thunderous sound. Grisson's force was so strong that the vampire was thrown an inch out of his chair, and a sickening crack declared that his ribs had crashed into the edge of the table. He landed back in his chair, clutching his hand, and for a moment a vengeful fire lit up his eyes, but then he felt the wind forced from his body and collapsed meekly into his seat. A heavy silence fell over the table, perforated only by the gasps of the injured vampire. His supporters were wide-eyed and slack-jawed with a blend of fear and reverence. Grisson's face, however, was awash in remorse. "Jean-Claude, are you hurt?"

"No," he choked through trembling lips. "I am fine."

"I am sorry," Grisson said, addressing Jean-Claude specifically. Then, he generally declared, "Needless to say, it has been a very stressful night. If we want to see tomorrow night, we must not allow our bonds to be frayed by petty grievances. Now, does anybody else have any ideas?" Only silence. "Anyone? At all?"

"Don't you have any ideas yourself?" asked another Reception vampire.

Grisson looked out into the expectant faces of those he had gathered before him.

"No," he sighed. "No, I don't."

"A few minutes later, the meeting had been adjourned. Finally a plan of action had been decided upon, although in truth it wasn't much of a plan at all. One of the hunting vampires had advised a defensive approach, sewing shut the curtains and hiding in the shadows, attacking whoever was bold enough to enter, with most of the hunting vampires being placed on the first floor. Obviously, there were countless scenarios and contingencies that this plan held no answers for, but in the absence of anything better, it had been adopted. Those who had been in attendance at the meeting left to inform their floor's population of what was to come, and to help locate potential hiding places. I went with the doctors to see our patients. There wasn't a single one among them fit for combat, so we simply helped them from their beds into whatever closets and crawlspaces were available, leaving them to their fates with encouraging words and small rations of blood and drinking water. With the last patient tucked away in relative safety, and the sun due to peek over the horizon any minute, I went to go see Grisson in his private room on the second floor. I knocked at his door, gently at first, then louder when there was no response. He still did not come, so I silently opened the door and peered inside. Grisson was kneeling in front of the opposite wall, in total silence and stillness. Not wanting to disturb him, I quietly slid away from the door, and began to close it when he suddenly addressed me by name and invited me inside. I entered cautiously. Grisson did not stir. "Why did you come?

"I, just, uh, wanted to talk to you about..." My voice trailed off as I noticed what Grisson was kneeling in front of. A nail had been set into the wall a few inches above his head, and hanging from the nail by a very simple rope was a small cross, roughly hewn from stone. "Grisson, are you...*praying?*"

"Yes," he said serenely, rising from his knees and turning to face me. "What of it?"

"Oh, nothing, nothing at all." We looked at each other in silence. "Do you pray, um, often?"

"Not as often as I used to," he replied. "I was a monk, a lifetime ago."

"Really?" I asked, utterly stunned. I had often speculated privately as to who Grisson had been before becoming a vampire. A religious figure never crossed my mind. "What happened?"

"The same thing that happened to you," he said dismissively. I took the hint and changed the subject.

"So, the cross isn't harmful to vampires?"

"No, that is a myth. See for yourself." He grabbed the necklace off the nail and placed it in my hand. The cross landed squarely in the middle of my palm. Sure enough, there was no pain or discomfort.

"Wow. Amazing." I handed it back to him. He smiled, and pulled the necklace over his head, dropping the cross between his chest and his shirt.

"A common misconception," he told me, "Although vampires traditionally aren't known for their religious devotion. So why have you come to see me?"

"I was just thinking about tomorrow. Do you really think the army will come?"

"Like I said at the meeting, we have no way of knowing, so we must assume they will."

"And what will happen if they do come? Is that the end? Of all that we've built, of everything?"

"Once again, we have no way of knowing. We will simply do all that we can to make sure that that doesn't happen."

"Grisson…I'm scared." He looked into my eyes, then into the floor, then into my eyes once again.

"I know. I am as well. We all are, and we have every reason to be. In a situation like this, all we can do is have faith that everything will work out. It isn't easy, I know. But he who has faith will never go into battle unarmed." At that moment, a thin beam of light shone through a crack in the wall and stretched itself across the floor. We felt our muscles tighten, our circulation slow, and our minds fill with the fog of exhaustion. Without a word, we both knew what this meant; the sun had risen on France, and perhaps set upon our budding revolution.

"Grisson and I went down together to the ground floor. It had been suggested at the meeting that the two of us remain cloistered away on the fourth floor, with a private guard, an offer we had respectfully declined. We had not taken a hands-off approach to the creation of our miniature country; we would not take a hands-off approach to its possible demise. We were pleased to see that the first floor had been suitably prepared for combat. Windows had been thoroughly boarded up; bookshelves were toppled over and turned sideways to impede the progress of invaders. From one side of the warehouse to the other, primitive yet deadly traps had been set and expertly concealed. Members of the nightly hunting parties were tucked away in every possible nook and crevice. The majority of our small army had been deployed to the first floor. The second floor concealed fewer fighters, and the third floor fewer still. By contrast, the fourth floor was entirely empty, the scientists having fled to several of the homes maintained as external bases by the hunting parties, taking their priceless research with them in the final fleeting moments before sunrise. There were a few hunters anxiously roaming the darkened first floor, among them the four captains who had joined us at the meeting. We spoke briefly with Jean-Claude, who assured us that all the scientists and their escorts had made it to safety, and that all preparations for battle had gone well. We thanked him and let him return to his men. Grisson and I pulled two chairs up from the floor and sat in the middle of the giant room, and so, with an intensely ironic lack of bloodshed and fanfare, the Lost Revolution of France began.

"Just like the four of us are doing right now, we waited, bored, silent, listless, anxious. Holed up in squalor. Minutes crawled into hours. Hours dragged into days. Days stretched into years, and still nothing. There was abject silence both inside and outside the warehouse. In truth, it had probably been four or five hours, sometime in the early afternoon, when our frazzled nerves and twitchy anticipation was beginning to give way to boredom, when the first deafening cannon blast rattled us from our complacency. Instinctually, every last one of us yearned to rush for the door and be done with this cowardly hiding, but we remembered ourselves, remembered the plan, and held fast. We would fight them inside, on our own terms. At the sound of the cannon we came back to life, knowing at last that the battle would soon be upon us. Moments later, the next blast rang out, followed by another sound, one that we all recognized right away despite our shock. One of the commanders ran to a wall, squinting through a peephole drilled at eye level. He turned around and addressed us a moment later.

"That wasn't cannon fire," he told us. "It was thunder. It's pouring rain outside."

"Grisson, myself, and the four commanding officers huddled in a small adjacent room. "We may as well call everything off at this point. The French army won't want to contend with a storm like this. They'll postpone and come for us later. At least this buys us more time to make a new plan."

"No," Grisson said. "If they're ever going to come, they're going to come today. They've been planning this too long to let poor weather stop them."

"We don't know for sure that they've been planning this a long time."

"We don't know *anything* for sure! Trust me, if they're going to come, they're going to come today. We have to keep our defenses up."

"You're certain about this?"

"We have everything to lose if we break formation, and nothing to lose if we don't. It won't be easy on the men, but they're strong, they can handle it. Are we agreed?"

"Fine. We'll defer to your judgment. Today."

"An excellent decision. Shall we rejoin the troops?"

"The six of us returned to the main room. Grisson grabbed my shirt sleeve and pulled me gently aside. "Keep your eyes on the outside. There're peepholes all over the walls. If you see anything, I want to know about it first." I nodded, and quickly found my own personal window to the outside.

"The day resumed crawling by, and although I did my best to keep a close eye on the damp, gray expanse beyond our walls, the pounding of the rain lulled me to sleep several times before I was awoken by thunder.

"It was many hours later, in the early evening, when I saw the first man outside. At that point I had all but given up on seeing any combat that day, and so apparently had the rest of the men. The majority of them had fallen asleep, with the few holdouts ambling about the room, trying to stay awake by staying on their feet. I was only bothering to look outside once or twice an hour, sleeping under a table the rest of the time. I came out of an especially long nap, woken by one of the literally walking dead bumping into my table. I slid out from under it, rose to my feet, and shambled over to my peephole for a perfunctory glance before searching out a better bed, and that was when I saw him. He was coming up the road, in the pouring rain, wearing red. As he came closer, the red smudge of his clothing sharpened into what was unmistakably a military uniform, albeit a very damp one. By the time he was close enough to see that, I could also see a massive red stain following in his footsteps.

"Once my brain caught up with my eyes, and I realized what I was seeing, my stomach leapt into my throat. 'Finally,' I thought, turning around to announce what I'd seen and call the room to attention. However, I managed to catch myself just in time, and rather hurried over to Grisson, who himself was on the verge of sleep at the back of the room. "Grisson, they're here!" I whispered, shaking him from his sleep. He woke with a start, asking "Really?"

"Yes! Come on!" I grabbed him by the arm and dragged him to the wall. He peered through the hole, got up, and made for the center of the room. I snuck a quick glance through the hole after he'd left; the large red cloud appeared to be fanning out around the warehouse.

"Attention! Everyone!" Grisson shouted from the center of the room. There was a hollow *Clonk!* as several men who'd been sleeping under furniture jumped to attention before remembering where they were. "The French army is indeed outside right now! There's no time to look, just trust me. Everyone resume your positions; we're sticking to the plan. Do not, under *any* circumstances go outside. We're going to make them come to us. Hold your positions, and get ready!"

"Grisson waived me back to my post. "Go and tell us what they're doing outside," he instructed. Hands shaking with anticipation, I once more dropped to my knees and pressed my face to the hole. "They've fanned out around the building, a few meters away," I called out to the room, apparently empty but with violent death tucked away in every crevice. "It looks like…they're wheeling in cannons. Eight of them."

"Hold tight, everyone," Grisson's disembodied voice commanded.

"They're getting ready to fire them, but…"

"But what?" someone called out.

"It's…It's not working, there's a problem. None of the cannons are working. I can't see what it is…it's too wet. They can't fire the cannons because of the rain!"

"Thank God," Grisson whispered.

"Minutes passed, without change. "What are they doing out there?" somebody asked.

"Trying to light the cannons."

"Still?"

"Yeah. I guess they want to stay as far back as possible. They're still not having any luck."

"How much longer are they gonna sit out there trying? You'd think they'd want to get the hell out of here before the sun…"

"His voice trailed off into silence. Throughout the room, throughout the entire building, even, everyone felt the change within their bodies. Wordlessly, simultaneously, a soft warmth rose up into our guts, tendrils of power snaking into our chests, our throats, our brains. Our blood pressure fell, our heart rates rose, and the hebetudinous mist of daylight burned away in the face of our nocturnally elevated consciousness. This wasn't completely unusual; it happened to all of us every 24 hours. What was strange, however, was the fact that it always happened at a very specific moment. The moment the sun

"…Sets."

"Everyone stood up, climbing up out of their hiding places, looking into each others eyes as if to ask "You felt it too?" Everyone had. Their eyes then turned to Grisson, sitting alone in the back of the room, smiling wickedly and absently fingering the cross that hung from his neck.

"Grisson, uh, why are you so happy?"

"Because," he said, climbing out of his chair and walking toward us. "Because our faith has been rewarded. Because if I know the French army, and I do (to this day I have no idea what he meant by that), they planned to bomb us, do as much damage as they could, and get as far away from us as possible before sundown, when the rules of engagement shift heavily in our favor. As a matter of fact, I'm sure that that's still their plan. The weather has turned circumstance in our favor. Although we instinctively know it the moment the sun sets, they must rely on their eyes to inform them. And with the heavy rain and cloud cover, there's no way they can see the sun itself, or accurately gauge its position." There was a moment of pregnant silence as the assembled crowd realized what this meant. "They," Grisson said heavily, pointing beyond the wall at the army on the other side, "Have no idea that we're ready for business. Who wants to go outside and tell them?" The mischievous smiles on the men's faces mirrored Grisson's own. "We've been hiding inside like cowards all day, waiting for our guests." He tucked his cross underneath his shirt. "Let us go forth and greet them."

"Whether or not there was an actual command, a battle cry, or a direct order, I cannot remember. All I do know is that moments later we were outside, having crawled over the debris, running uphill in the rain as the lightning flashed and thunder roared, towards a throng of soggy, terrified men who couldn't believe their eyes. Within minutes we had literally and figuratively bitten a huge chunk from their ranks. The next wave of men behind them at least had time to draw their guns, which of course were too wet to be used as anything but damp clubs. We were nearly halfway through the ranks when what was left of their army did the first wise thing they'd done all day and ran. At that point, it ceased to become a battle and became little more than a game. We ran them down like dogs, splashing through the flooded streets with their sodden uniforms bearing down upon them like their own mortality, and killed them for fun or sport or vengeance or whatever grievance we could think of at that moment. It didn't last very long, and we left their bodies in the streets, leaving them to open their eyes the next night underwater, briefly thrilled that somehow they'd survived the nightmare, before learning the awful truth and realizing that they weren't lucky enough for the simple luxury of a permanent death.

"When the first rays of tomorrow's sunrise breached the horizon, we were all safely inside the warehouse. The cumulative effects of stress and exhaustion had sent most of us into deep sleep, but Grisson and I sat awake in my room, passing a bottle of blood and scotch back and forth. His cross hung in front of his shirt once again.

"What will become of the soldiers who were bitten? Will they burn up once the sun rises?"

"No," he answered, following a long drink from the bottle. "Sunlight has no effect until 24 hours after conversion. They will sleep through today, and wake up tonight. After that, they will be bound by the same rules and desires that bind us."

"And then what? Do they come and live with us?"

"I would imagine that they will resent us, initially. Some of them will almost certainly try to attack us again. We don't need to win their hearts individually, just those of their commanding officers, who I made sure were safely brought inside. This was only a fraction of France's army, a little less than a third by my estimation. Should they try to rejoin what's left of the military, they will be killed immediately. Once they understand that this is their home now, our new nation will have its first official army."

"And so we went to speak with the leaders of our new military. One of our doctors injected them with a pale blue liquid, and they slowly woke up. When they sat up and yawned, we saw the fangs in their mouths were only half formed. They appeared to be having lots of pain in their mouths, so we very quickly explained what had happened to them and their troops, and how they should behave if they wanted to stay alive. Then the doctors injected them with something else, and they immediately went back to sleep. I went back to my bedroom alone and slept as well.

"Many hours later I woke up, startled by the noise downstairs. My heart skipped a beat as I realized I had slept way past sundown, when hundreds of potentially hostile vampires opened their eyes for the first time. I threw on a shirt and sprinted down to the ground floor, where much to my surprise, hundreds of soldiers were lined up, giving their names and ranks to some very overworked Reception officials, in exchange for clean clothes, a housing assignment, and a glass of synthetic blood. The whole affair was proceeding like clockwork under the watchful eyes of Grisson, the heads of Reception I'd met at the emergency meeting, and several strangers wearing heavily decorated military uniforms. Grisson spotted me on the stairs, looking bewildered, and called me over to meet his new friends. He introduced me to all the commanding officers as "Our Prime Minister," which needless to say caught me off guard, but I stifled my surprise and did my best to make a dignified first impression in my pajamas. When all the diplomatic pleasantries had been dealt with, he quietly excused us and led me to a smaller, private room.

"What the hell is going on out there?" I asked, letting my bewilderment surface.

"You miss a lot when you sleep in, don't you?" Grisson jibed cheerfully.

"Ha-ha, very funny. Now seriously, what's happening? And what's with the whole Prime Minister act?"

"Well, earlier tonight, when our new friends in the Army woke up on their own, I answered all their questions and we discussed their options quite thoroughly. And, given the circumstances, they made the wise decision and elected to throw in their lot with us. Then we went outside, where all of the soldiers were beginning to come to, and brought them up to speed. Soldiers are good at nothing if not following orders, so we brought them all inside to get their information, feed them and clothe them, and give them a place to live. Obviously, there isn't enough room in the warehouse for all of them, so half of them will live here with us, and we've commandeered a few nearby houses for them Each will house five people; four new soldiers and one senior vampire from the street patrols. And now that we have an army, along with our capital building, which contains a bureaucracy, a university, a hospital, and a research institute, it's only natural that we devise our government next. I took the liberty of giving you a title. You can make up mine, if you'd like."

"This is ridiculous. Our population nearly doubled overnight. Shouldn't we be worrying about that first?"

"That's exactly my point. With everything growing as quickly as it has, it's going to *take* a government to keep everything under control. When I told you we were building a nation, Arnauld, I wasn't joking. With the discovery of synthetic blood, we no longer need to be feared as killers, as drains on society. We can *become* society. It's not a whole lot right now, but what we do have is a strong foundation to build upon."

"That may be true, but we're missing one very important ingredient; land. Frankly, we don't have any. We only have control over one city block in a real country that wants us all dead."

"Yes, I suppose that is true. For tonight. We've just received a letter from the French government. They're ready to negotiate peace."

"Silence fell softly over the both of us. Grisson's silence was born of satisfaction; mine was born of shock.

"You're kidding."

"Nope.

"You have to be kidding."

"I don't, and I'm not."

I struggled to find my words. "What could have changed their minds?"

He shrugged happily. "No idea. They didn't say. My guess is that it might have something to do with the fact that they just lost a third of their army, not to death but to our side. Or it could be the rumor that they were attacked by vampires *before* the sun went down that has them a little nervous. At any rate, they want to meet with our leader, tomorrow at midnight, so make sure you get some rest."

"Wait, *I'm* meeting with them?"

"That's what I said, isn't it?"

"Grisson, I don't get it. You're the one who runs this place, not me. You came up with the idea and took over this building and turned it into a country. You oversee everything and run the meetings and lead us in battle. All I do is work in the hospital and follow you around, so why do you always act like I'm the one in charge?"

"Because you will be. I'm going to stay around a little longer, help you out from behind the scenes, until things get settled in. I did not become a monk because I wanted to establish and rule a new country. I wanted to be close to God and far away from human contrivances like governments and militaries that magnify and perpetuate the evils in our hearts. But when I became a vampire, I had no choice. I had to leave my old life behind for a new one of murder and vagrancy. But it doesn't have to be that way anymore. Under your rule, the unfortunates stricken with vampirism will have a place to go where they can lead a reasonable facsimile of their old lives. But first, you need to smooth things over with the French, so that we can finally stop killing and start building. You'll be meeting one on one with an ambassador in a house that splits the distance between their palace and our building. I wouldn't ask you to do this if you hadn't shown me that you are ready. This will be your first official act as leader."

"…"

"…"

"I won't let you down."

He smiled, and grabbed my shoulder paternally. "I know you won't."

I smiled back.

"Now go get some rest."

"I retired to my bedroom, and slept for the last time without the weight of a nascent country on my shoulders.

"I slept all day, and through half the night, before Grisson woke me at 11. We briefly discussed the demands I should make, and the concessions I could afford to give, before walking to the first floor. He told me the house I was looking for would have three candles burning in the window. He hugged me, told me to be careful, and turned me loose into the night.

"As you might imagine, I was dreadfully nervous, and as I walked I softly recited to myself the guidelines Grisson and I had agreed upon.

In an effort to relax myself I began taking deep, slow breaths. *In, out. In, out. In, out.* It was a soothing rhythm. I altered my walking speed to match it. *In, left foot, out, right foot. In, left foot, out, right foot.* It had the desired effect, and I felt my confidence returning. Preoccupied as I was with my nerves, I couldn't help but pick up on something else. Although it may have appeared that way at first glance, I knew very well that I was not alone that night. I may have been the only one bold enough to be walking in the middle of the street, but from the shadows I could sense many pairs of eyes monitoring my progress, not all of them human. The invitation had clearly stated that myself and the French representative would be coming alone, but neither side was taking the chance that the other side hadn't. One side of the road smelled like garlic and fear; the other, of blood and triumph. I did not envy the poor men who had been dispatched into the dead of night to ensure that an unstoppable foe played fair, armed only with trinkets and superstition.

"At last I came upon a home, humbly sized and decorated, with three long candles burning in its only window. I wrapped my hand around the doorknob and stopped to look about one last time, seeing no one yet feeling their gaze, before opening the door and stepping inside.

"I was pleased to be greeted by only one man, although it was not the man I would have preferred. His name was Gregoire, a man my own age with whom I had attended many years of school. We both came from powerful families, and our parents clearly wanted us to become best friends. Despite their pushing, we never got along well, barely tolerating each other for their sake. He was a sycophant, and weasely by nature, constantly sniffling and running to authority figures when he couldn't have his way. We were both sufficiently shocked at the sight of each other to briefly forget our nerves.

"Arnauld? Is it really you?" he asked, squinting at my face in the candlelight. I could see him plainly without effort. He was exactly as I'd remembered, albeit taller and thinner, with a whiskery mustache that emphasized his rodential features.

"Yes Gregoire, it's me." I lied out of politeness. "It is good to see you again."

"Yes, certainly, the same to you. If only it were under better circumstances. We were all most upset when we, uh…lost you. Such a shame, it is. You deserved a kinder fate."

"Thank you, but your pity is not warranted. I've adjusted to my new life very well."

"That is good to hear. Still, such a shame, if not for you, then for your family. Your wife was most distraught, but you needn't worry. I've been keeping a very close eye on her for you." His eyes narrowed snidely, and a sneer worthy of death crossed his mouth, but in a moment it was gone, replaced with a mournful gaze dripping with false sincerity. "Such a sad, sad misfortune." This was indeed the same scheming, passive-aggressive boy I had pummeled many, many times as a child, whose head I longed to smash into the wall once more, if only for old times sake.

"Yes, well, I'm sure she appreciates your supervision as much as I do. How funny that some of my new friends and I have been returning the favor without knowing it. Your own wife need never worry about going out alone; she hasn't been." It took him a moment to realize what I had just said, but when he did, the look on his face was even better than if I'd smashed him into the wall. He regained his composure almost immediately, and gestured amicably at the table in the middle of the room. "Shall we sit down and begin?"

"Nothing would make me happier."

"We took our seats opposite one another. Just as I'd gotten comfortable in my chair, Gregoire produced a quill, inkwell, and a thick stack of parchment. When he began stirring the inkwell with the quill his elbow bumped into the stack of parchment, scattering it beneath the table. He apologized and bent over to retrieve it, and I too ducked under the table to help. We had finally restored the stack of parchment and lain it on the table when, in the midst of taking my seat once more, I saw the shadow of a man, from the shoulders up, briskly walking past the candles in the window, projecting a silhouette onto the floor that vanished as quickly as it had appeared. I looked at Gregoire in suspicion; he had clearly seen it too.

"Did you come alone?!" he demanded, halfway between terror and betrayal.

"Y-yes," I stammered, taken aback that he'd had the gall to accuse me. "Yes, of course I came alone! Did you?"

"Yes!"

We sat in stalemate, trying to look unblinkingly in each others eyes while also keeping an eye on the window.

"Shall we go outside and have a look?" I offered.

"Oh, you'd like that, wouldn't you? We go outside and there just so happens to be ten of your friends out there waiting! How convenient!"

"Shall *I* go outside and have a look about then?"

"*Yes*, if you feel so inclined, go right ahead."

"Then I will!"

I nearly knocked over my chair, jumping up from the table and stomping over to the door. My hand was on the knob when I caught myself. I wasn't the one who'd set any sort of trap outside, and yet here I was, about to storm out into the waiting arms of whoever was skulking about the house, proving my innocence by stepping right into Gregoire's trap. My face burned bright red in the dark as I realized how easily I'd almost been manipulated. Instead, I took my hand off the doorknob and threw the deadbolt, locking us in, and whoever was outside out. I craned my neck in front of the window, but couldn't see anything with the glare from the candles reflecting off the glass. I walked back to the table and took my seat.

"Very clever, Gregoire, but not clever enough. The door's locked, so whoever or whatever is out there isn't coming in."

"Just as well, I'd prefer your friends stay out on the streets where they belong!"

We stared distrustfully at each other; Gregoire looked away first, sighing and slamming his fists on the table with great exaggeration. "Arnauld, friend, what are we doing to ourselves? We've been charged with drafting an historic document; it should be conceived in celebration, not suspicion. Who are we to let silhouettes and rampant imaginations spoil it?"

Feigning shame, I stared guiltily into my own lap. "Gregoire, you're right. We're behaving like the children we were so long ago. Let us start over, in better spirits."

"Excellent," he said, laying out a sheet of paper and pulling his quill from the inkwell. "Now, first and foremost, this is a treaty of peace, so let us address that issue right away. An unconditional cessation of all human/vampire hostilities, effective immediately. Do you agree?"

"Yes."

"Very good." He set his quill scribbling with short, scratchy strokes. "So, this 'Bloodless Feed' you claim to have developed for yourselves, it really works?"

"Yes, although we've told you, it's not entirely bloodless, it just requires very little blood. Our population's grown quite a bit recently, as you know, but we have enough blood stored to feed ourselves for the rest of the year. After that, we'd be more than willing to use any of your murderers or other prisoners condemned to death as, uh, raw materials. Trust me, their deaths will be very humane, and we only require six or seven per year…"

"Uh-huh, uh-huh," Gregoire mumbled, writing feverishly, working through page after page in seconds time.

"Gregoire?"

"Uhm-hmmm, yes, I see…" he muttered, scribbling ever faster, the occasional finished page jumping out from under his quill and flying into the air.

"Gregoire, much like your father and his father before him, ad infinitum, you engage in unconsensual romantic intercourse with sheep, cows, pigs, and other assorted livestock on a nightly basis."

"Yes, yes, uhm-hmmm…" he continued to write.

"And you like it."

"Yes, yes of course…" he was gathering momentum, his hands ablur as he continued writing.

"GREGOIRE!"

"What?!" he shouted back, spittle flying, pounding the table with both hands, snapping his quill in half. "See what you've made me do?!" he grunted, reaching into his shirt pocket for a replacement.

"Gregoire, I've spoken three sentences, and you've written eleven and a half pages. What in God's name are you writing?"

"Well," he said, stirring his new quill in the inkwell and calming down, "There're a number of legal and clerical issues that must be addressed when creating a new contract. In regards to the type of contract, the time and location, the number of witnesses present, the applicable document taxing information and the amount of stamps required and-"

"Ok, ok, ok, I get it. So, technically speaking, we haven't even really started yet?"

"Well...no."

"Jesus, Gregoire! You couldn't have taken care of all that beforehand? We're on a deadline here, and sunrise is only a few hours away, and if you think you're gonna stall until the last minute and force me to sign some bullshit that hands over all the power to you, know that I have no problem taking you home with me to finish this up at *my* house, on *my* terms, do you understand me?"

"Oh, don't be so dramatic. For your information, I *did* do most of it before you came, and you'll have every opportunity to look everything over. And don't honestly tell me you expected us to hash out, write down, revise, rewrite, and sign off on an entire agreement in one night? This is going to take weeks, if not months. The only thing we've done that's effective immediately is the cease-fire, which, as soon as you sign it, becomes official at sunrise. When we don't have to worry about killing each other, it should enable us to finish this more quickly. If that's alright with you, of course," he added spitefully.

"Uh, yeah, yeah that's fine. Sorry, didn't know."

Gregoire dropped his quill on the table and looked up at me mournfully. "Oh, think nothing of it. It's every bit as much my fault, I should have told you beforehand. We're letting the pressure and stress of this whole affair make us needlessly cross. We should break for some tea," he said, hopping up from the table and heading for the stove in the room's corner, already lit for heat.

"Oh, actually I'm not thirsty, but I appreciate the offer."

"Come now Arnauld, you speak too hastily. This is an incredibly rare Chinese tea we've only just acquired a few weeks ago. It tastes a little strange at first, I admit, but trust me, it grows on you very quickly. Just takes a moment to make, too," he said, loudly placing a pot on the stove that almost immediately began sizzling.

"Really, it's very kind of you to offer, but I think I'll pass."

"Arnauld," he began whining, as he always did in the face of noncompliance "We only have a very small amount of this tea, an appreciable fraction of which I've brought for you as a goodwill gesture, and we very likely won't be getting any more for some time. If you refuse now, it may be decades before you have another opportunity. And trust me, I know teas very well, and this stuff is good, ob-*scenely* good, and-"

"Actually, I think I could go for some of that tea right now," I conceded. It was the quickest way to shut him up.

"*Good man,*" he exclaimed a little too loudly, vigorously stirring the pot that was now boiling loudly. "You'll be so glad you did, this is top-notch, really exquisite stuff." He came walking back to the table, with a delicately inlaid cup in each hand, one of which he carefully placed in front of me before taking his own seat. "Give it a moment to cool, but not too long," he advised, still intently stirring his own cup. "Just cool enough that you don't get burned."

"Duly noted," I said cheerfully enough. Honestly, the stuff smelled absolutely horrid, but a bitter mouthful or two was a small price to pay to stop his nattering and sulking.

"In the meantime, let us talk," he began. "What would you include in this contract we'll be drawing up?"

"Well, first of all, on a personal note, I'd have my wife join me."

"What?" he gasped, nearly spilling his precious tea. "Here? While we're writing?"

"No, I think the two of us alone are perfectly capable of doing that ourselves. I mean afterwards, when everything's drawn up and the peace is established. I would like her to come and live with me, with the rest of us. Provided she wants to, of course. I don't intend to force her. But she should certainly be given the option."

He was very clearly taken aback, and also apparently somewhat offended. "But, but she isn't...she's human!"

"Yes, she is. As am I, and those I represent as well. At our cores, we are human, albeit a bit modified, with an unfortunate physical burden we have effectively eliminated. That is what this, *all* of this, is about. Of course, she would not be expected to assume this burden, unless of course it is her will to."

"And why, in the name of God," he spat, rising out of his chair with deliberate aggression, "Would she?!"

"Because," I said calmly, rising out of my chair as well, extending the pinky of my left hand, and bringing it down upon the top of his head, pushing him back into his chair. He tried to leap back up at once, but I held him in his seat, with one finger, and no apparent effort, "It has its advantages."

"Gregoire looked up at me, alight with cold fury at having been so easily humbled. Like a defeated, peevish child he powerlessly scolded me. "Your tea grows cold."

"So it does," I remarked flippantly, removing my finger from his head. I returned to my seat and downed a great gulp of tea like it was water. "Your tea sucks," I told him.

"Almost as soon as I'd told off him and his tea, I felt a great wave of nausea break over my head. As expected, the taste was atrocious, but that was the least of my concerns right now. All at once I felt my stomach and my brain churning in unison, and I gripped the edge of the table fiercely to steady myself. It accomplished nothing, as the muscles in my hands grew rigid, then swiftly relaxed themselves beyond the point of my control.

"You don't look well, Arnauld," Gregoire remarked, his voice echoing bluntly inside my head. "You don't look very well at all."

"I would have responded, but right now I was exhausting all of my energy trying to stay upright in my chair. Before I even knew I'd fallen, I hit the ground hard, but felt no pain whatsoever. The situation clearly called for panic, for crying out, for a last minute lunge at the door, regardless of who or what was on the other side. There was no point, however, as I felt my consciousness ebbing away, and as badly as I tried to hang on, my eyelids came down, and there were hands around my ankles, and, and…

"When I opened my eyes again, it was morning. My consciousness came back at once, in one quick burst, and I felt sick, seriously sick, as sick as I've ever felt in my life. There was a wide gap in my vision, and it was difficult to breathe, like there was a heavy weight on my gut. I wiggled my fingers, then my toes, and gave a quick prayer of thanks to whoever was listening that I wasn't paralyzed. Next I tried moving my arms, which were weak, and very sore, but fortunately compliant. I reached up to loosen my collar, to try and make it a little easier to breathe, but my arms hit something, and I realized why it was hard to breathe; there really *was* something heavy on top of me. It was fairly thin, so I wrapped my hands around it and threw it off of me to the left. Once it was off me, my vision returned to normal (it had really just been laying partially on my face, obscuring my view), and I could breathe much easier, though not as easily as I should have been able to. Fighting through the nausea, which was no longer a wave but rather a lake that had settled upon me, wide and deep, I sat up and looked at whatever the hell it was that had been on top of me. It was a giant wooden cross, as long as I was tall, as wide as I was wide.

'This isn't really happening,' I thought to myself.

"I now had a new symptom, in addition to everything else that plagued me. My left hand felt like it was on fire. I cradled it in front of my face, saw it was pink, like semi-cooked meat. My right hand was sore in the joints, but wasn't at all burned like the other. I looked to the left, where the cross had landed after I'd thrown it off of me. It had landed on a square in the floor, about three feet long and wide, where the sun was shining in painfully bright, its glare magnified through the glass window that gave it its shape. Conservatively guessing, this sunspot was perhaps six inches away from where my head had been while pinned down under the cross. Had I been laying a hand's length closer to the window, my upper body would've been turned to hot ash when the sun rose.

He tried to kill me.

"Taking the utmost care to stay far away from that lethal box on the floor, I rolled over to the other side of the room and pulled myself to my feet. When I'd risen to one knee, and reached down to pull the other leg up as well, I felt a piercing, acidic burning in my gut. I wasn't about to go back down to the floor, so I gritted my teeth and pulled myself upright, leaning against an unwindowed wall for support. Standing still, on two feet, the burn in my gut wasn't as bad, but it was still ferociously painful. It got better gradually with time, sleeping on my side helped it somewhat, but it was 48 years before that pain left me for good. I tried everything; opium, whiskey, every brand of snake oil, dozens of quaint home remedies, but nothing, *nothing,* ever made that pain go away except time. Took my mind off it, maybe, pleasantly distracted me for a bit, but that plague may as well have been from God's own hand. When my mind came back to me a little bit, I remembered who was really responsible.

It was poison. Poison in that damned tea.

"The fact that it had knocked me out until morning surprised and impressed me the most. Gregoire had used the good stuff, whatever it was, and quite a bit of it. I should've known, based on how bad that damned tea had smelled, had tasted. I'd bet there probably wasn't even any tea in my cup at all, just acid and pestilence and hot water. It would've killed a regular man hundreds of times over. I looked down at my chest for the first time since waking up. It was caked with dried, bloody foam. There was absolutely no sensation in my tongue while my stomach burned me alive on the inside for what I had allowed to happen to it.

Yep. That's poison.

"Now that I was back on my feet, and my mind was coming back to me, I began trying to reconstruct how I'd gotten from last night to here. Gregoire and I had been working on the peace treaty and fighting, mostly fighting, when he'd forced the tea on me

No. My mind, my sense of responsibility, wouldn't let me off the hook for what I'd allowed to happen. *No, he didn't force it on you. He offered it to you. He pushed it on you. But he never* ***forced*** *it on you.*

It still hasn't.

"Anyway, I'd taken the tea, let myself get all worked up about my wife, and drank the damn stuff. I fell on the floor and passed out. Several hours later, I wake up with the cross on top of me

What was up with the cross, anyway? Why not the stake through the heart, the old standby? It would've been just as easy (Hell, a lot easier, actually, less heavy lifting and assembly), but he decided to get creative. Also, why not drag me the extra few inches into the path of the window, just for insurance' sake?

"I've been asking myself those questions for years, hundreds of years, and I've never been able to come up with an explanation. But, for whatever it's worth, Gregoire got creative, and then he got lazy, and that's why I'm alive today. I don't know why, and I never will. I'm just thankful that I am, I guess. Most of the time.

"By this point, I was mostly awake and alert, which was a mixed blessing. On the one hand, I could start formulating a plan, a plan to get out of here, to find Gregoire, to make him wish he'd done the job right the first time in some of the worst ways imaginable. On the other hand, I could now fully appreciate just how much it hurt to stand, to walk, to breathe, to just be alive. And trust me, it hurt a *hell* of a lot."

For the first time since he'd started telling his story, a story I never would've imagined he possessed when I'd first goaded him into sharing it, Chuck, or Arnauld, or more accurately someone somewhere between the two, stopped talking. Up to this point he'd been going nonstop, picking up momentum like a rock rolling down a mountain, but now he'd hit a wall. I looked away from his face, down at his hands folded in his lap. They were shaking violently.

"And that's when I saw her," he continued, his voice no longer booming with tales of ancient adventures, now quivering just like his hands. "She was sitting in the corner on the other side of the room, propped up against the wall. It was…it was my wife."

Just like that, at that moment, the man telling the story stopped being Chuck, stopped being Arnauld, stopped being a vampire, stopped being our fearless, tactless leader, and became a man who'd been nursing a broken heart and a shattered spirit longer than the rest of us put together had been alive.

"Jeannette. Her name was Jeannette.

"I ran to her, ran through the sunspot, burning my hand all over again, but she…she was gone. We can bring them back sometimes, we can change them, and bring them back if they haven't been dead too long. But," he swallowed hard, breathed deeply, and stared at his feet. "He cut her head off. I thought I could bring her back, but I touched her and it…slid off."

"Oh God," Thomas whispered under his breath.

"There was nothing I could do. She was gone, and there was nothing…I could do. I laid her down, and took a handkerchief out of my pocket and I…said goodbye, and put it over her face. And that's when I first noticed the screaming.

"It was coming from outside, way, far away outside, but now that I'd heard it it just got louder, and louder, and louder, and louder, like it was filling up the air.

"So I moved around the room, where I could look out the window without getting burned. It was blindingly bright outside, not a single cloud in the sky. Once my eyes adjusted, I could see what was happening.

"It was the warehouse, and it was on fire. I was stunned at just how close it was to the house I was in. Last night, walking here felt like it had taken forever, but things…had been different then.

"Standing there, looking out the window onto the street, I had a perfect (if you could call it that) view. The first three floors were already on fire, and the flames were quickly moving up to the fourth. People I knew, good people, doctors and teachers and mothers with children were jumping out of windows, turning to ash in the air, landing as piles of bones. The first floor was completely engulfed, but people were still scrambling out, crawling away from the fire only to burn up in the sun. There was nowhere to go; burn inside or burn outside. And standing there, watching it all, celebrating, *laughing*, were the French soldiers, what little was left of them, the few we'd spared. They'd sat down to watch the show, the bastards. At least we'd fought em' fair, at least we'd given em' a chance!" Chuck was screaming at the air, reliving the worst day of his life all over again. His hands shook into a nervous blur. The blood from his palms started seeping past his nails and through his knuckles. His voice was an indescribable blend of diction and drawl.

"Do you know what I did?" he asked us. "Do you know what I did then?" A fat teardrop of blood leapt out of his hands, landed on the side of his boot, and slid down to the floor. "I ran away. My people, my family, were being burned alive down the street. Jeannette was dead in the corner. And I wobbled over to the window and found a pair of scissors behind the candles. I cut the curtains from the wall, threw them over top of me, went out the door, and took off away from the warehouse as fast as I could go. I kept my head down, stayed in the shadows of the houses as best as I could. For about two minutes, anyway. The sun was too bright, the curtains were too thin, my body was too weak, and I knew I was dying. Not quickly, like the ones back at the warehouse, the ones who stepped outside or walked into the fire and that was that. I was the coward, the one who tried to run, and this slow, prolonged agony was my reward. So I kept running, and I felt the skin on my back going chalky, starting to burn up under the curtains, and just when I thought to myself

Finally, this is the end, no more poisons and crosses and curtains and sunlight and fire, for the old things have passed away, and praise the Lord at long last so have I

"I fell. I was all covered in curtains and couldn't see where I was going, but I tripped, and I hit the ground hard, so hard I rolled out of my makeshift armor entirely, rolling until I finally crashed into something and stopped. I waited for the sun to finally finish me off, to just get it over with for the love of God, but it didn't happen. When I opened my eyes, I saw I'd stopped in a tiny strip of land between two houses, in a tiny island of shade only a few feet wide.

"I couldn't believe it. Despite the best efforts of Gregoire, the sun, and the army of France, I simply refused to die. Resuming my mad dash out of the city was out of the question. I wouldn't have even been able to make it back into the street to put the curtains back on, much less escape to safety. If I wanted to survive, and I wasn't even sure if I did, I would need to find somewhere to hide until sundown, when I would hopefully be well enough to finally flee Paris. But where to hide? I scanned the street intently, but there was nothing. The entire world was exposed and bathed in sunlight. I decided that I would have to make that dash for the curtains after all, and just hope that I was able to squirm underneath them in time. It was a bad plan, and I was almost positive it wouldn't work, but I had made up my mind that I wouldn't blithely give in to death. It just seemed too disrespectful, to Jeannette and Grisson and all the others who'd gone down trying. It wasn't until I was standing with my ankles pressed together in my tiny oasis of shade, bracing myself for my final attempt at escape, when I noticed something I should've seen right away; the front door of the house behind me was wide open.

*How could you **possibly** have missed that?! Dumbass!!!*

'Thank God,' I sighed aloud, quickly abandoning my former plan. I realized that that was the first time I'd ever positively acknowledged God out loud. I immediately thought of Grisson, a man who could be so violent, but in the name of a much greater peace. A man who sanctioned great harm against hundreds of people, but who also provided for their recovery, and treated them with love and respect. A man who was a vampire, but a man who wore a cross around his neck at all times. It was a little after nine o'clock in the morning, and his bones had surely begun to bleach by now, his ashes long ago scattered by the wind.

"I walked inside the house and found it empty. Whoever lived there had probably gone out to see the show, gone to see the monsters finally get theirs, and forgotten to lock the door on the way out. They must've left early, trying to get the best seats. Probably even packed a lunch, the tacky motherfuckers. The thought of it made me sick, not just mentally, but physically. I was very dizzy, and my stomach began its fiery churning again, worse than before. Doubled over I wretched dryly, holding back the vomit with sheer will. I didn't want to give these ambulance-chasing fucks a reason to search their house while I was laid out under their bed or in a closet for the day. The need to vomit suddenly passed, and I was greatly relieved. Then it returned, stronger than before, with a headache that made nebulous green blobs appear when I closed my eyes. Just as quickly, it was gone, then back, then gone, then back, then gone, then back.

Fuck this.

"I shoved my middle finger down my throat, aiming diagonally out of a window that had also been carelessly left open. The less said about what came out of my mouth and went through the window, the better. Normally throwing up, though never fun while you're doing it, almost always makes you feel better as soon as you get it over with, but not this time. I felt enormously weak, as though I'd just vomited up my strength rather than bile. I knew I had to find a hiding place, and fall asleep fast. I started up the stairs to the second floor, but made it less than a third of the way up before falling to my hands and knees. I crawled up a little ways further, but I was completely exhausted before I'd even made it halfway. I had to throw up again, and my joints were locking up, and I'm sure by now it's lost a lot of its effect and you're as tired of hearing it as I am of saying it, but I knew this was the end. All the pain and exhaustion and frustration and grief had reached a boiling point, and that's when I decided that enough was enough. It was a little embarrassing, to survive betrayal, poison, and life-size religious iconography on top of the murder of your wife and best friend and the genocide of your people, only to finally be defeated by stairs, but I wasn't all that worried about my reputation at this point. I decided that in light of all that had happened, it was pretty obvious that something or someone beyond my comprehension wanted me to survive this whole mess, so I closed my eyes and let myself take a little nap right there on the stairs. If I woke up in time with enough strength to make it up the stairs into a decent hiding place before the mister and the missus came home, I'd do just that and be thankful for the blessing. If I never woke up, on the other hand, I wouldn't consider it that big of a loss.

"And, just as surely as I sit before you now telling this story, I was right. I woke up about an hour or two later, still by myself, feeling marginally better, with enough strength to make it up the stairs and literally lay low under a bed for the rest of the day."

"That was an incredible story," Barry said, after a short pause. "But, if you don't mind my saying so, that has to be one of the most anti-climactic endings I've ever heard in my entire life."

Chuck looked at him sharply, slightly annoyed at the interruption and said "I can see how you'd feel that way, seeing as how I'm just *now* getting to the ending."

"Oh," Barry said, looking embarrassed, then "Whoops." Not 'Sorry, go on,' or 'Please continue,' just 'Whoops.'

Chuck looked a little bit more annoyed, then muttered "Dumbass," under his breath, not because he was afraid of Barry hearing his insult, but because Barry just wasn't worth the extra volume. I mean, here's Chuck, telling this huge, fantastic story where his wife and his best friend and everyone he knows gets murdered and he spends a whole day cheating death, and Barry interrupts him, and all he can say is "Whoops." It wasn't intentional, and it wasn't the kind of particularly telling little episode that really solidifies your opinion about someone, but I kinda had to agree; Barry was a dumbass.

Barry just took it like he always did, looking cowed for a moment, then shrugging it off, looking anxiously at Chuck, waiting for him to continue. I couldn't fault him here, because I felt the exact same way, and so apparently did Thomas, looking engaged but noticeably more relaxed. Chuck wiped his hands on his pants and resumed his story.

"As I said earlier, I woke up on the stairs a short time later, still by myself, and although I felt far from great there was at least some improvement. I made it up the stairs and found my way into the master bedroom. The bed was easily big enough to hide under and high enough off the ground that I could comfortably lie underneath. My plan was to hide out and rest under the bed for a day, maybe two, then sneak out at night and get as far away from here as possible. It goes without saying that it had been a very bad day, but I had survived, unlike so many others, and I was content that the worst of things were behind me. I fell asleep almost immediately, thinking about how good it would feel to walk out of Paris and never look back.

"If you've been paying attention up to this point, you should know by now that nothing ever turns out the way I plan it, so you shouldn't be all that surprised when I tell you I woke up a little earlier than I'd expected, with five men holding me down and a sixth standing over me. Once again, this is one of those situations where, without the proper perspective, we'll never know exactly what happened. Maybe the owners of the house came home, saw the present I'd left by the window, and decided to search the place just to be safe. Or maybe after they'd finished burning down the warehouse the army sent people door to door checking houses to make sure the extermination was complete. Or maybe my luck just finally ran out and I ended up selecting the home of Mr. and Mrs. Paranoid who look under the bed for monsters every night and finally found one. But, however it came about, the result was still the same; the bed was flipped over, and I was on the floor, caught unawares and outnumbered.

"The five men holding me down were playing it smart. Rather than dog piling on me like amateurs, each of them took a limb, and I guess the guy who got the short straw had me by the ears, shoving my chin into my chest. It was a pretty rude way to be woken up, and I was majorly pissed at myself for giving them the chance to hold me down; I should've been up and running for the door the moment the mattress flipped. But, I hadn't, so in keeping with the theme of the day, I would just have to make do with what I had and hope I got lucky. I immediately went into scary-vampire mode; thrashing, hissing, spit flying everywhere, and of course, fangs way out."

It was pretty obvious right away that the Chuck finishing his story was very different from the one who'd started it. Whereas before he'd been very emotionally involved, very clearly struggling to get through the tougher spots, this Chuck was much more amiable and detached, more like he was telling the funny story about a friend who got caught in his zipper at a wedding than describing an attempt on his life. Accordingly, I was expecting a resolution that was much less dark or violent, but that turned out not to be the case at all.

"For those of you taking notes, I feel compelled to use this incident to illustrate an important point, one that has served me very well in life and that you'd be wise to remember. 'As long as you can intimidate, you're never truly unarmed.' These guys probably felt pretty tough going in six-to-one against a man passed out under a bed, but once I showed some spirit, that leveled the playing field a little. Not a lot, mind you, but it was better than it had been before.

"Awww, Jesus William it's wakin' up! It's wakin' up!" The guy holding my head suddenly didn't sound so tough after all.

"Mind the Lord's name, Andrew," replied the man standing over me, calmly reaching into a large bag slung over his shoulder dangling against his hip, but keeping his eyes fixed on me. "As well as its fangs."

"I keep up the angry-demon act, shrieking and spitting and almost getting my head free several times.

"Awww it's gettin' mad, it's gettin' real mad William, can't ya hurry it along a little bit-"

"Hey! Watch its head!" One of the men minding my arms shouted. "You almost lost-"

"Oh, yeah, that's real easy for you to say," the man behind my head snarled back. "Why don't you come watch the head, Mr. I'm Too Scared to Watch the Head!"

"The fact that you're calling him Mr. I'm Too Scared to Watch the Head implies that he's already too scared to do so, so there's really no point in offering him the position," helpfully offered one of the men holding my leg.

"Easy for you to stand back there and comment, you only have to hold a leg!" shouted the man holding my other arm.

"Oh, so you think its easy holding a leg?" the other leg-holder barked back. "Legs are the strongest limbs of the body, you hear me? The strongest limbs!"

"EVERYBODY SHUT UP!" William commanded. He'd found what he was looking for in his bag; a long, wooden stake, sharpened to a very fine point, black tape wrapped around the blunt end for an extra solid, no-slip grip. "Fight about it later, I'm about to stake him!"

"At the mention of the 'S' word, everyone grew silent, and straightened their act up immediately. They fell upon me once more, casting their entire body weight upon each limb. The skittish man charged with holding my head pulled it back from my chest, turned it sideways, and pressed it into the floor. I kept fighting, trying to get my head free, but he was a fat man, leaning on it with his entire considerable weight. He'd been chosen for his job not for his courage or strength, but for his gut. William was bent over me now, looking intently into my chest, the stake raised ominously over his head.

"I'm sure I don't need to tell you this, but I was mortified. This time, there really was no way out. Then, with all the weight of the five men bearing down on me, I felt the bulge in my back pocket being pressed uncomfortably into my ass. In that moment, that brief second after I remembered what was in my pocket and before the stake came down, I had my plan. A good plan? Absolutely not. But a plan nonetheless. I looked up sideways, through the fat man's fingers at William's stake, waiting for it to come down.

"And come down it did.

"It came lightning quick, with astonishing force, a little bit faster than I'd anticipated, but not too fast for me to adjust to. While this William and his goons could hold down my head and my limbs easily enough, there was one joint they couldn't suppress so easily; my hips. At the last possible instant, before the stake hit, I threw my hips as quickly and violently to the right as I could. It wasn't enough to move my chest out of the way entirely, but it was enough to move it a little bit, and, more importantly, change its angle. The stake hit with remarkable, punishing force, but it hit a little bit less than an inch from my heart, and at enough of an angle that it hadn't been able to go all the way through me and into the floor.

"Just as planned, I'd feigned death the moment the stake hit, although at first I wasn't even sure if I was faking or not. But once I realized how much pain I was in, and then realized that I *could* realize anything at all, I knew I was still there. I immediately stopped fighting my attackers, and went limp on the floor under their hands. They looked at me, dumbly, for a moment (a very, *very* long moment), and then one of them asked,

"Is that what it's supposed to look like?" and nobody answered right away. William, showing his first sign of uncertainty, stuttered "I…I think it is. Yes, I do believe it is. We've killed it." And then, giving the stake a final, halfhearted push for good measure, which quite possibly hurt more than everything I'd endured that day combined, he stood up and took a step back from what he assumed was my lifeless body, perhaps to admire his handiwork. When the others saw him do this, they followed suit, and my window of opportunity opened. As quickly as a man who's been poisoned and impaled in a 24 hour period could, I reached into my back pocket and pulled out what I hadn't even consciously remembered putting there in the first place; the scissors with which I'd cut down the drapes that morning. With one swift, slicing motion, I cut open the leg of the man who'd been holding my right arm, and his calf muscle fell out onto the floor, wetly. He went to one knee screaming, and I reached up and cut his throat. The fat man who'd held my face bent over to help him, and took the scissors in the neck as well. The other three men ran screaming out the door and down the stairs, and William, brave William, the fearless leader, was quite visibly torn between joining the half of his team who'd fled and the other half who'd been killed by what he probably now assumed was some sort of unkillable vampire god, decided not to finish the job and ran out the door himself.

"At this point, I'd rid myself of the four living members of the team that'd tried to kill me, which was good, but now I was left lying on the floor of someone's bedroom with two dead bodies and a stake in my chest, which, needless to say, was not so good. I was hesitant to move too much, afraid I might jiggle the stake into a major artery, so I decided to try and extract it while I was on my back. At this point I was so weak from the day's combined abuse and my last desperate flourish that'd saved my life that it was hard enough just getting my arms up from my sides and around the stake. I tried to pull it out, but had only the energy to wiggle it a bit, and if that wiggle was any indication, this thing was going to hurt just as much going out as it did coming in. I simply wasn't strong enough, and the allergic reaction from the wood was starting to take effect, blurring my vision and causing a great headache. Also, I had lost a lot of blood, and naturally that wasn't helping matters at all. I had to get some blood back into me, and fast. Fortunately, the calf muscle that had fallen out of the first man's leg had landed within arms reach. I abandoned my first attempt to pull the stake out, instead grabbing the dislodged muscle, putting it in my mouth and chewing it like a wad of beefy gum. The taste was disagreeable at best, but there was plenty of blood inside, and that's what mattered. I could feel my strength beginning to return immediately, but I knew it wasn't yet enough. Thankfully, the fat man who'd held my head had also fallen within reach, and appropriately enough, he was bleeding like a cut pig. I had to reach behind my head, grab onto his shirt, and pull myself backwards a few inches to get close enough to his neck, but somehow I made it happen. Having sufficiently drained him, and feeling significantly better because of it, I once more turned my mind to the matter of stake removal.

"The allergic reaction to the wood had slowed my breathing considerably, and reduced my vision to an ill-defined portrait of dark colors and nebulous shapes, but all of the blood I'd consumed had returned much of my strength, and restored my ability to think clearly. Above all else, I knew I was on a very slim timetable, and it wouldn't be much longer before angry citizens would descend upon the home with torches and Bibles and slices of garlic bread blessed by the Pope. I had to get the stake out, but even more than that, I had to get it out fast.

"Summoning all of my newfound strength, I tucked a roll of my shirt in my mouth, grabbed the stake with both hands, closed my eyes and pulled. Once again, I was only able to wiggle it, but that tiny wiggle unleashed a tidal wave of pain. I bit down harder, dug my nails into the side of the stake, wholly committed, and pulled, and pulled, and pulled, and *God did it hurt*, but even worse, it still wouldn't budge. Right away, I knew something was seriously wrong, because as hard I was pulling, it made no sense that the damned thing wouldn't even move an inch. I had been hoping to avoid this, but I knew there was no other way. I was going to have to focus my gaze and actually look at the damned thing to try and figure out what the matter was.

"The matter was, as it turned out, that when the stake had gone in at an angle, missing my heart, it had ended up going several inches through the skin and partially under a rib. That was why trying to pull it out had hurt so badly and been so difficult; if I was going to pull this thing out, I would also end up leveraging one of my ribs out of my chest."

Barry looked like he was about to puke. I wasn't quite there yet, but I was getting close.

"So, naturally, due to the unfortunate angle at which the stake had entered my chest, simply yanking it out was out of the question. I would need to take a more refined approach. I was going to have to cut away enough of my chest that I could pull the stake out from under the rib, then finally out of my body. I had no idea how I was going to make that happen. I wasn't a doctor; I had no anesthesia, not even a scalpel to actually do the job with. I looked over at the fat man's body again, who knows why (I doubted he'd have any suggestions on the matter), which was when I saw the handle of the scissors sticking out from under his arm."

Oh God. No way. No fucking way.

"I really didn't have much of a choice in the matter. I could cause myself a lot of pain, and possibly save my life, or I could choose to simply lie here in a lot of pain, until the townsfolk finally worked up the courage to come inside, or light the house on fire, which would also be a lot of pain, only with a zero percent chance of survival. I knew what time it was; it was time for amateur surgery.

"I was holding the scissors, asking myself if I could really go through with this, all the while the heart my hands would soon be so near pumped fragments of the poison wood through my body. My brain was gradually turning off, dimming itself like a light. I was losing the capability to think, to reason; worst of all, I was losing my ability to fear. A fractured state of peaceful abandon was clouding my mind, assuring me that everything would be alright, although it wasn't too clear on the particulars. I let the back of my head sink back onto the floor, and I began to close my eyes, beset by a great drowsiness.

You're only going to sleep, my mind told me. *There'll be time to address all this nonsense in the morning, but right now, you need your rest.*

"I closed my eyes, and I relaxed my muscles, and before I knew what I was doing, I dropped the scissors.

"They fell to the hard wooden floor, landing on their brass handles, with a loud, piercing, surprisingly musical *chiNG-*

"And then my eyes flew open, and I knew where I was, knew I wasn't sleepy, but dying, and knew that all of this nonsense couldn't wait till morning, that this nonsense was going to be death of me if I didn't sort it out right there and then.

"I picked up the scissors, lined up where they needed to go, and put them on my chest, one hand doing the aiming, the other supplying the muscle. I was ready, I was set, but I couldn't bring myself to watch me do it. I let my eyes wander about the room, finally setting on the fast-blurring form of the fat man's bloodless body. I counted it down, on 3, 1…2…

"Then I realized I was breathing wrong. If I pushed in on 3, I would be exhaling right when I cut, and that might throw off my aim, so I slowed down, reset my breathing, and counted off for real this time, 1…2…

"*Then* I realized how much my hands were sweating, and you don't go about cutting into yourself with sweaty hands, I mean, you could lose your grip, to say nothing of the sanitary concerns, so I held the scissors in one hand, wiped the other, vice versa, and steadied my freshly dried hands, inhaled at the appropriate time, and 1…2…

I CAN'T DO THIS

"It was my brain, my god-damned chatter-boxed brain, the betrayer, the Brutus between my ears that found a different detail to nitpick every time I got ready to do this, and I just couldn't shut it up, couldn't do it to save my life, literally, when a different voice altogether spoke up

YOU WILL IF YOU WANT TO LIVE.

"It sounded very similar to my brain, this new, commanding voice, but there was something very different about it. Whereas my brain tittered about, panicked, squawking about minutia in a self-defeating attempt to save its own skin, this voice *proclaimed,* with maturity, and confidence, and poise, and an elegant simplicity grounded in truth. And even still, for all of its firmness and its strength, there was the sense that no matter what I decided on the subject of life or death, this voice would be ok with that, would understand that everything we know and worry about and experience isn't nearly as important as it seems, that there's *more*, a deeper depth and a higher plane all at once, and it's been there before, and it'll go there again, when the timing is right. I'm not saying it was my soul, or anything like that, it just was what it was. I didn't know what to call it then, and I still don't know what to call it now, but whatever it was, it had spoken.

"The two competing voices inside were both demanding my attention, demanding to be heeded, so much that it grew to the point I couldn't hear either one clearly. I needed another opinion, so I looked harder at the fat man's body, making him the tie-breaker. I looked at him expectantly, the cold sweat no longer falling from his forehead, eyes lazily half-shut, waiting for an answer from my gory muse. Last time, he'd given me the scissors, and I needed him to come through with a big idea one last time. And that's when he woke up, and he came through for me. Came through in a big way.

"He lifted his head up off the floor, opened his eyes all the way (for no real reason, as they'd already rolled back into his head), and gave his last words a second shot.

"William could do it," he whistled through the holes I'd torn in his throat, and went back to death.

William? I thought. *This guy resurrects himself to give me advice, and all he can talk about is his asshole friend? Fuck William. Fuck him.*

"And that's when I did it, sweaty-palmed and exhaling all the while. I manned up, grew a pair, and did it. Did it hurt? Yes. Did it need to be done? Absolutely. And once I stopped contemplating the metaphysical and got good and pissed, I could do it. That's another lesson you all could take away from this. 'Don't over-think it.'"

I looked at Thomas. Thomas looked at Barry. And Barry was looking at me. Was he serious? The story, up to this point, had been fantastic, certainly, but with a cogent grounding in plausibility. It's wild, yes, but is it possible? Were it someone else, perhaps, I probably would've said no, but Chuck is not a 'Someone else,' and you only need hear him tell it to know that there may be an occasional stretching of the truth, but Chuck *believes* this, 100%. And as I said above, it could happen. Hell, even my story, or Barry's story, mundane as it might be in comparison, would seem impossible to most folks. But it's the honest truth.

But now we're expected to believe Chuck's anonymous would-be co-murderer came back from the grave to taunt him into cutting himself up to save his life? What made it hardest to deal with is the fact that yes, Chuck definitely believes what he's telling us, but very clearly he believes this part the most. An unsettling, unspoken wave of concern rippled through Thomas, Barry, and myself. Is this guy insane? Did *any* of this actually happen?

These were questions to be answered at a later date, because Chuck, dishonest, insane, or capable of raising the dead with a look, was a hell of a storyteller, and he was still going strong.

"Anyways, getting back on track," he said, assuming we'd been given sufficient time to make the proper mental notes. "After much ado, I'd finally made the cut, and I was inside. It was painful, I won't lie to you, but it wasn't *as* painful as it should've been. After awhile you develop a tolerance, which brings me to this point, fishing around inside my chest with a pair of scissors and not minding all that much. The scissors had gone more or less where I needed them to, though actually a little bit closer to less; I guess I shouldn't have exhaled after all. The blade had gone in deep enough, but once again, the angle wasn't right, and instead of slicing in underneath the stake, it cut through my chest and into the stake itself, about a half-inch above the point. A minor miscalculation, no big deal, until I tried to pull the scissors out for a second attempt and discovered they'd gone too deeply into the stake to pull out, which meant there was now something *else* stuck in my chest.

"At first, I was livid. Why the hell were all these sharp things getting stuck inside me? I tried wrestling with the handles a little more, but all that did was hurt me even worse. I made myself stop and take a break. It was time to rethink my strategy.

"Fortunately, and, well, gruesomely, I had managed to make a big enough hole in myself that I could get a decent view of the situation. The scissor blade had embedded itself pretty deeply inside the stake, but close enough to the point, where the wood was thinnest, that I figured I could twist the scissors hard enough to snap off the tip and remove the two separate pieces easily. I tucked a fresh roll of shirt in my mouth (I'd bitten through the first roll somewhere between now and the beginning), locked my hands around the finger holes and pushed.

"Jesus Christ, you would not believe how much that hurt.

"I was twisting and twisting and twisting, trying to break the stake but it felt like my rib was going to give first. Either way, it didn't matter. After all the hemming and hawing of before, for the first time since starting I was really, truly committed. The stake was coming out, and it was coming out *now.* If it took a rib with it, well, that's life.

"I kept going, pushing, pushing harder, feeling the rib quaking in place, shaking my chest, my arms, my hands. Finally, I felt the wood fibers starting to stretch, screaming to hold on, to stay inside, stay whole. I knew it was gonna break, but I also knew the rib was gonna break first. I thought that if I could shift my grip, make the angle a little sharper, I could split the wood without losing the rib. I bent at the waist, slid my right hand above my left wrist, wrenching down and away, gave one last twist, heard the white-hot scream of steel grinding steel, and that's when the stake, the scissors, and my body all broke at once.

"The stake was the first to give out, and also the least dramatic. With a dull *crack* the wide, club-like end snapped from the tip, falling off of my chest like a tiny cut tree and rolling onto the floor. Next to go were the scissors, which finally stopped shrieking when the two halves had been bent so extremely they split apart inside of me. Last one to go, of course, was me; I didn't lose the rib, which was nice, but half of the broken scissors got launched out of my chest and across the room, blade up. I looked down at my chest; there was the initial cut, where the bleeding had already climaxed and was now slowing to a steady, subtle flow. Connected to that point, making 2/3 of that triangle, what's it called…isosceles, that's the one, was the exit wound. It was a much cleaner cut, as it hadn't had to partake in the messy digging that followed the first wound, but it must've hit something important, because you wouldn't believe how much blood came out of that long, thin line. Not an arterial spray or anything dramatic like that, it just all bubbled out suddenly and ran all over me and the floor. Normally, I would be pretty upset if something like that happened, but not this time, cause now all I had to do was pluck out the tip of the stake. It was sitting in some really gooey, important looking red stuff that stung like electricity when I touched it. It looked so small and non-threatening, more like an errant splinter than a mortal threat. Easily, cleanly, it came out; no shrapnel left behind. It was half the size of my thumb and pitiable to look it, but it was my trophy, and now that I had it I could lay my head down in peace.

Arnauld de Chambeaux, you've just survived amateur surgery; what are you going to do next?

Run.

"What if they came in just now? All torches and strength in numbers and righteous indignation at your survival and tore you to pieces, having just done that to yourself and lived? It was a terrifying thought, but it made me haul ass.

"I leapt up from the floor, landing feet first, upright and ready to run. It was a foolish, victory-dance sort of thing to do, especially for someone who'd lost as much blood as I had. The room blurred and spun out, but when it refocused and stopped it landed in the same place, so that was good. I wanted out of there, the faster the better, but first I had some clean up to do.

"For starters, I was bleeding all over the floor. The first cut had more or less run dry, but that last one was a trooper, rewetting itself with every heartbeat. Before I could go anywhere, I had to stop the bleeding, and it is here that the fat man, Andrew, did me his final favor. Using the half-scissor still in my hand, I cut off his coat, leaving both sleeves intact. I took off what was left of my own shirt and wadded it over the wound, and tied his sleeves over top of it around my torso like a tourniquet. I walked over to the window and threw out the tiny point of the stake, wishing never to see it again. I slid the arm of the scissor I'd done the cutting with into my pants pocket, thinking, in the biggest underestimate of my two-odd centuries on earth, it might come in handy in the future. I left the blade that had rocketed out of my chest where it had fallen; it sounds ridiculous, but I felt a bit betrayed by it. Its brother, the good twin, had cut with a purpose. The other half, excuse the pun, had cut and run as soon as its job was finished, at the expense of keeping my chest in one piece. I abandoned it, ephemera for whatever brave soul dared enter first, to mull over on his own time. I thanked Andrew a final time for his wisdom, creativity, and generosity, not sure if he could still hear me, but wanting to express my gratitude just in case. I looked down, next to where his body had fallen, at my improvised operating room, and for the first time fully realized just how dearly I'd paid for my life.

The blood sat thickly on the hardwood floor, forming the silhouette of my body as I'd operated. From my waist to the top of my head, the outline could be clearly traced, the curve of my shoulders drawn with astonishing clarity. It looked like the top half of an armless snow angel, sketched in blood. It was a hideous thing. I hated it instantly. Even so, I thought about leaving it alone, for posterity's sake, to stain and settle into the floorboards and local folklore at the same time. The Hideous Vampire Stain, they'd call it generations from now. At midnight, when the moon is most full, the Stain will return, no matter how many times the floorboards are replaced. Parents would use it to frighten their children, children would use it to frighten weaker children. Right then was when I recognized how much had been lost today.

"Two sunrises ago, we were a few discussions, handshakes, and signatures away from an unheralded historical event, the establishment of a peaceful vampire nation officially recognized by France herself. Not only that, but we had already subverted the vampire's intrinsic need to kill his neighbors in order to live. With the synthetic blood formula and a treaty with France, the world would change in an instant. Those unfortunate enough to be bitten by a vampire would no longer be forced into a life of vagrancy and murder. Rather, they would come and live with us, and do respectable work, and live an honest life similar to the one they'd known before. We were on the precipice of legitimacy, of crossing the realm from ghoul to citizen with a controllable chronic illness, and in one day's time we'd fallen from that to a ghost story. Children would sneak out of the house at sleepover parties to come in here and touch the floor where one of *them* had bled. In one day, we once again became things that went bump in the night. We'd lost our humanity. I cried, silently, and a tear fell on the floor next to the blood.

They'd never talk about that. Never even notice. It's just our blood they want. Nothing else.

"I kicked it, splattering the blood indiscriminately all over the wall. And I ran down the stairs, out the door, into the street, and out of Paris forever.

"Twenty minutes later, and I was long gone. I climbed to the top of a hill to rest for a bit, catch my breath. At the top, I could see the whole city. The moon was full, shining behind the burned out husk of the warehouse. Looking down, I could see the house I'd just fled, sitting silently in the dark. A few minutes later, the first torch approached it, bobbing cautiously up and down in the darkness. I could see the outline of a dark blob following behind it, bobbing up and down with it, stretching down the street. They'd finally worked up the balls to go inside. I told them to fuck off. I knew they couldn't hear me, but that was ok. I said it because despite their best laid plans and most earnest efforts, I was still alive to say it, that was victory enough

"By the end of the night, I'd put enough distance between myself and the city to feel comfortable. I found a small, secluded, wooded area, with a small stream and a cave big enough for me, a few bugs, and little else. I stayed there a few weeks, resting, healing, feeding on whatever small animals I could catch. Once I was more or less myself again, I moved onto someplace else, sleeping by day, traveling by night. It was certainly an alright place, but it just didn't feel like home, so after a little while I left again. I've pretty much been doing that ever since, I guess. It's not a bad life, really, as long as you keep moving. Always moving."

Chapter 6: Capture

"Acceptance of one's life has nothing to do with resignation; it does not mean running away from the struggle. On the contrary, it means accepting it as it comes, with all the handicaps of heredity, of suffering, of psychological complexes and injustices."

-Paul Tournier

Chuck stopped talking, and didn't start again. It took a few seconds to register; he was done. He had finished his story. We all looked at him, expectantly, more out of habit than anything else. For the first and only time I would ever see it, Chuck was actually shy. He looked at us emptily, in effect saying "What else do you want?" He looked down at his boots, bounced his ankles idly up and down, distracting himself and giving us something else to focus on besides his face. The four of us were completely silent, the only sound that of the soles of Chuck's boots squeaking on the floor. I recognized that squeak. One day in high school, sophomore year, January, the first day back from winter break, there was a new student in history class. We were all sizing him up, the way new kids have always been sized up on their first day and probably always will be. We had had a few new students that year, most of them were weirdo private school kids whose parents' checks had bounced or something, but this guy seemed alright. He looked like us and dressed like us and walked and talked like us, within an acceptable margin, so we figured he'd be ok. There was only one desk left open in the room, in the back corner behind Ike Herzog. Ike Herzog was a cool guy who'd gotten an extended winter break, but had paid a steep price for it; four days before break started, Ike's mom got killed in a car wreck. Needless to say, we hadn't seen him that week, and although a few of us went over to his house the day after Christmas to try and take his mind off everything, nobody answered the door. Nobody had heard from him since that last Monday when he came to school with a turkey sandwich and two parents. Some kids said he'd transferred, a few said he and his dad had moved out of state overnight, but it was all idle speculation. The first day back at school arrived, and, to everybody's surprise, there was Ike Herzog himself, back at his old desk, five minutes early to class.

We were all thrilled; as I said above, Ike was a cool person, a good person, not popular because he picked on people weaker than he was, but because he treated everyone like a friend. Everybody was hanging around Ike, shooting the breeze, being real nice to him, but nobody dared ask him what he had done on his break, or even say something like "I'm sorry." We wanted to, desperately, to tell him we were sorry, to ask him what we could do, to acknowledge this horrible thing and let him know we were there for him, no matter what, cause he was Big Ike and he deserved to hear those kinds of things the way anyone good who has something terrible happen to them should, but one glance was all it took to see that Ike wasn't so big anymore. He'd lost weight, his hair was a mess, he looked shorter and sicker and more fragile. His eyelids hung lower than they used to. He was on the verge of collapse, and he was silently begging us not to break him, begging us to carry on like everything was normal in the hopes that maybe someday it would be again. It was the very least we could do for Big Ike. Then the bell rang, and the teacher, Mr. Swanson, walked in with the new kid.

Mr. Swanson was an old dude, real old, who'd transferred here at the start of this year. He just needed one more year in the public education system to get full retirement benefits, and as long as we turned in homework that at least looked like it could be legitimate, didn't start fistfights, and only smoked near the vent, he wouldn't get on our case and everyone was guaranteed a passing grade. That was the first thing he said to us, after he finished taking role on the first day. We admired straight-talkers almost as much as people who expected little to nothing of us, so we said ok. We had free run of the classroom while Mr. Swanson sat behind his desk with a book and tuned us out. The student-teacher relationship was as symbiotic as could be. We'd made it through half the year without a single incident, and then Mr. Swanson introduced us to the new kid, Henry Weams. Henry said hey; we said hey back, and Swanson told him to take the last empty desk in the back and "Just follow the other kids' example."

And that's exactly what he did. He took his seat and produced a notebook and a previously sharpened pencil, and for the first time that year, a history book was not only placed on top of a desk, but opened. Mr. Swanson finished role call, sat down behind his desk, and opened up his newspaper (he always read the paper on Mondays). Instantaneously, the class came to life, and Henry heard the rustling of comic books in the front seats, smelled the tobacco smoke being drawn over his head into the ceiling vent, and saw the entire left side of the classroom pushing their desks together into a fearsome paper-football arena. An instantly likeable smile, not unlike the one previously worn by Ike, danced across his face as he realized the extent of the free ride he'd been given.

"Holy shit!" he cried gleefully, closing the textbook and dropping his pad and pencil to the floor. "Is it always like this? Hey...Hey, you!"

"W-What?" Ike stuttered, turning to see who'd poked him in the arm.

"The teacher, he's not even gonna try to stop this?"

"Umm, no, he...he never has before," Ike said, awakening from his own grey thoughts to the outside world. "As long as it doesn't get too loud and nobody fights, we can do pretty much whatever we want."

"Seriously?"

"Yeah."

Henry's face lit up again with that same irrepressible smile. Ike just looked at him blankly. He'd forgotten how to do that.

Swiftly, Henry's hand shot down into the front left pocket of his jeans. It rooted around for a moment, and when it reemerged it was wrapped around a smartly polished Fireball yoyo, glossy black with candy apple flames racing down the sides. Henry slid his middle finger through the end loop and started winding it. "Do you like yoyos?" he asked, with one eye on Ike and another on Mr. Swanson, as though he still couldn't believe he could take out and wind a yoyo right in front of a teacher and get away with it. Amazingly, a hint of a smile tugged at the ends of Ike's lips. It wasn't a real smile, but it was close. Given the circumstances, that alone was remarkable.

"Yeah."

Having finished winding the Fireball, Henry's left hand was twitching with potential energy. "C'mon, get yours out."

"Oh, I don't really carry one with me anymore. I used to, when I was younger."

"That's cool, I've got a spare in my backpack. The string sticks a little, but all in all it's not too bad. You can use it if you want to, uh…"

"Ike."

"Ike, gotcha. So, whaddaya say Ike?"

Ike smiled a little more. Still not quite a full one, but definitely getting closer.

"Sounds good to me."

Henry began digging through his backpack, tossing aside the pens and spiral notebooks he knew he'd never have to bring to history class again.

"Argh, dammit I know it's in here somewhere…A-ha!"

He resurfaced holding a silver yoyo that had clearly been lovingly abused, the flecks of glitter in the paint shining subtly under the hand oil finish hours of practice had unwittingly applied. He admired it for a moment, inspecting it for signs of change the way one looks at an old friend they haven't seen in a long time. The string was fraying in a few places, but this actually made it look tougher, offered tangible proof that it could handle a little action. Henry finished appraising it and passed it to Ike.

"I know it looks a little rough, but trust me, that's a great yoyo. I can't remember how long I've had it."

"It looks just like my old one," Ike remarked to no one in particular, throwing it down and letting it spin a few inches above the floor before pulling it up with a flick of his wrist. He did it again, holding the spin longer, seven or eight seconds before calling it back into his hand. "Man, this really takes me back." And there it was, unmistakable; Big Ike Herzog's smile.

"Not bad, buddy, not bad at all. But check this out." Henry got up out of his chair and dropped to one knee. Swinging his shoulder violently, he launched the yoyo hard out of his hand, like he was pitching a softball. As soon as it had left his hand he gently dipped his right shoulder towards the ground, lowering the yoyo to the point that it was actually rolling along the tiled floor. It rolled between the feet of three unsuspecting students, spinning furiously at the end of its leash. Henry held it there, eyes squinting, lips pursed, deep in concentration. A few seconds later, he subtly jerked his wrist, and the yoyo came speeding back at him, bouncing along the floor like a stone skipping on water. It landed back in his palm with a meaty, satisfying *thwack.* I was rather impressed. So was Ike.

"That one's called The Creeper," said Henry, his hands automatically rewinding the Fireball in seconds. "It's not nearly as hard as it looks," he said sheepishly when he saw Ike staring at him slack-jawed. "I betcha you could learn it, no problem. Throwing it's easy, it's just getting it to come back that takes a little work. Go on, give it a shot."

Ike hopped out from behind his desk and kneeled down on the floor next to Henry. He pitched his yoyo even harder than Henry had; it hit the floor spinning like a hurricane. He threw his arm hard to the left, somehow keeping it balanced and rolling upright. Ike left it rolling at the end of the string, yearning to fly off its tether for several seconds before remembering there was a part two to this trick, but by that point it was too late. It simply didn't have enough power to get back to its destination, and it fizzled out and tipped over a foot and a half away from Ike's hand.

"Not a bad first attempt," said Henry sincerely, "But you left it out there a little too long. As soon as you feel the line start to lose tension, that's when you gotta pull it back in. Try it again."

I would imagine Ike did make another attempt, but I wasn't able to watch any further. My undisputed paper football crown was in jeopardy, a matter which required my undivided attention. Even so, it felt really good to see Ike smiling again. I knew that a new friend and a rediscovered hobby doesn't make the death of your mother even-steven, but at least Ike would have something to distract himself with through the worst of it, during that awful period where time starts piling new thoughts, feelings, and events over an open wound to fill in some of that painful emptiness. Ike and I ate lunch together at 12:30, and I vowed to check in on him then just to see if there was anything

I could do for him. Until then, I was content to leave him and Henry to do their thing while I did mine.

Anyone who's ever spent time behind a school desk, a cubicle wall, or prison bars knows that time is not a rigid construct. The big hand of a clock might hold a steady pace when you look up at it, but as soon as you look away it knows the coast is clear, that it can run as fast or as slow as it goddamn pleases, and usually it does just the opposite of what you want. I was busy with my paper football, Mr. Swanson was busy with the financial section, Ike and Henry were busy with their yoyos, and everybody else had their own hobbies or pastimes to occupy themselves. No one was paying much attention to the clock at all; a bell rang at 12:30, and then we'd go to lunch. There was a constant low level murmur of conversation and activity, the white noise soundtrack to a dozen or so islands of interaction peacefully coexisting next to each other.

I read Scientific American magazine, and because of that I know one of the things that baffles scientists who study herd behavior is that they can't figure out how flocking actions are initiated. A bunch of birds sit on a telephone wire, then all of a sudden they all take off at the same time. A bunch of lemmings are sitting in the forest, then all of a sudden they're all barreling head-first off a cliff. These groups don't have leaders, so how do all the animals know to do the same thing, at the same time?

To put it in human terms, everyone's been out to a party where there're lots of people, lots of different conversations going on at the same time. Ever notice how all these groups go on chatting happily all night, until 10:41 pm when every conversation stops at the same time, just as some poor shmuck who didn't get the memo is dropping the punch line to a joke about how fat the host is? Nobody knows how or why it happens, and yet it always does, and always at the worst possible time.

I had just vanquished my second paper football opponent of the day, final score 28-14. Two other guys down the table were arguing over who had the next shot at me; one of them demanded to see the official tournament bracket we'd drawn up last month. Action stopped at the table while someone dug it out of a desk. Three kids in the front of the room each turned over the last page of their respective comic books at the same time, and sank contentedly into their chairs. All of the smokers, each smoking cigarettes at different stages of decomposition, inhaled simultaneously. Swanson turned the page of his newspaper; the other 12 or so kids in the room I never paid much attention to similarly stopped doing whatever they'd been doing before and were silent. All the birds had hopped off the wire at the same time, except for two; Ike and Henry.

Ike was rewinding after what looked like another fruitless attempt at The Creeper. Henry was ready to take his turn. Ike remarked, to no one in particular, "I think I must be fingering it wrong."

Henry replied "Thanks to me, at least your mom never has to worry about that."

Everyone had heard. Shocked outrage dawned over all of our faces, except those of the smokers, who had all gasped and swallowed their smoke and were now fighting to breathe.

Henry looked around the room and saw that 25 people who'd been previously ignoring him were now looking at him like he'd slaughtered an infant with the partially eaten corpse of a puppy. Henry knew he'd crossed some kind of line, but he had no idea how badly. He shrugged and smiled weakly in a submissive gesture. "I was…I was just kidding around guys. What's…what's the big deal?"

Henry turned around and looked up meekly at Ike. They looked at each other, each wearing identical masks of bewilderment. Ike couldn't believe what had happened; Henry still didn't know what he had done. And as the walls began to close in with the force of sheer awkward silence, for the first time in my life I heard that same sound Chuck was making; the sound of a rubber soled shoe bouncing frantically on the floor, the sound of a nervous tic personified, begging for a peaceful resolution, but more importantly for the blinding spotlight to go somewhere else. I don't know whose foot was responsible for it, but I've never forgotten that sound. It sounded exactly the same when Chuck did it too. It's one of the most universal gestures in the human vocabulary.

Ike punched Henry. Hard. I could see his face while he did it. It was the first time I'd ever seen anger on Ike's face, and it swallowed him completely. Henry was bleeding before he even hit the ground; he'd taken the punch directly on the nose. He hit the floor and crumpled under a desk, not even twitching. Mr. Swanson was the first to react, throwing down his paper and leaping out of his chair as fast as a guy his age could.

"Hey! Just calm down!" he yelled, racing to put himself between Ike and what was left of Henry, but Ike was already calm, if you could call it that. Catatonic is probably a better way to describe it. He made no further attempt to go after Henry, rather watching impassively as Mr. Swanson pulled Henry out from under the desk and looked at his face. "It's broken. Badly. He's gonna need an ambulance. Jesus." He sounded annoyed, rather than awed. He was going to have some explaining to do.

The ambulance came to get Henry, and Mr. Swanson and Ike went to the principal's office. In light of extenuating circumstances, Ike got a three day suspension. Mr. Swanson got five. Henry got two weeks in the hospital and a new nose. His family moved away as soon as he was released.

Neither Ike nor Mr. Swanson came back to school the next year. Swanson got his full pension, but was asked to retire at the end of the year; I don't think he was all that broken up about it. Ike dropped out at the end of the year and went to trade school, where he learned to be a train mechanic. A few years later he was in the local paper, one of a few kids going up to the Yukon right after the second Gold Rush started, the one that eventually brought back the Miner's Flu. He went up on one of the first two trains to go, so I guess that means there's a 50/50 chance he was on this train, back when it was the great economic hope of a new generation and not $400 worth of scrap metal. I totally didn't remember that when I started telling this story. That's a pretty wild coincidence.

Things were still quiet in the train. Chuck's foot had stopped squeaking; we'd all had the good sense to give him his space when he wanted it. The tension in the train was beginning to subside; we were all silently mulling over what we'd learned about Chuck's past. Some less silently than others.

"Hey, I think I know how that dead guy was able to talk to you," said Barry.

"And how's that?" Chuck muttered, still staring at the floor and sounding less than enthused to have the subject brought up again.

"Well, you said you bit him and drank his blood, right? I bet you just turned him into a vampire, and he woke up quicker than normal. Maybe that's how it works with fat people, or something."

"No," Chuck replied. "Juvenile vampires can feed, but they can't pass on vampirism until about a year after they're turned."

"How's that work?"

Chuck looked very bored. "Our fangs work two ways; they suck blood in, but they can also spray blood out. A juvenile vampire, one whose been recently turned, only uses them to suck in blood. After about six months, a small muscle above the roof of your mouth will begin to develop. It's another six months before that muscle is strong enough to do anything. At that point, the muscle increases the suction power of your fangs, enabling you to feed more efficiently. While it's doing that, the muscle also sprays a small amount of your own blood through your fangs into the person you're biting. That's what actually turns them into a vampire; not having their blood drained, but the transfusion of infected blood."

"Woah. That's fascinating."

"Yes. Yes it is. Glad to be of service." There was a momentary pause.

"Do you feel it?"

"Feel what?!"

"The muscle…thing!"

"Yes, you feel it." Chuck's exasperation level had dipped down to 'slightly annoyed.' "Roughly six months from now, your mouths will swell up a little and be sore for a few days. Hopefully you'll have fed before this happens; if not, tough. You'll still be able to feed, if you're that desperate, it'll just hurt. It's like teething, and it passes in a few days. Six months later it'll happen again, and then you'll know you're a live grenade. The muscle itself feels like a little piece of gum on the roof of your mouth you can't get rid of; eventually you forget it's there. You should start decapitating your meals when you're finished with them at this point, otherwise they'll literally come back to haunt you. If you should forget this, or have any further questions, don't worry, it's all in the handbook."

Barry's eyes lit up. "There's a handbook?"

Chuck slapped his palm into his forehead. "No numbnuts, there isn't a vampire handbook. Maybe you could write one and sell it to weird kids at high schools.

"In all seriousness, there's a lot to know about being a vampire, a lot of things most people don't know, but I do. And before we all go our separate ways I'm going to make sure you know it all. That's the least I owe you. But right now, I'm tired of telling stories, and we have a big night ahead of us, and I'd really like to get some rest. I'd suggest all of you do the same. We've got a lot of travel ahead of us, and lots of time to talk, but now isn't one of those times. Ok?"

"Ok."

"Good."

Chuck stuffed his scissor in his pocket and lay down on the floor. He yawned, stretched, closed his eyes, and lay still. Barry, by contrast, stayed propped up in his corner, both eyes open, wringing his hands. It was kind of a weird thing to do, but Barry's kind of a weird guy. I was more inclined to follow Chuck's example. I too lay down, but sleep didn't come so easily for me. Still, it was nice to finally have a moment's peace inside the train. As it turned out, a "Moment" was being a little generous.

"Chuck, I know we agreed to stop talking for now, it's just that-"

"Goddamn it Barry, WHAT?! What is it now?"

"Well, you don't need to get all pissed about-"

"That's where you're wrong Barry, I DO need to get pissed because you won't stop talking trivial bullshit when we've got some seriously non-trivial stuff coming our way, and I need some goddamn sleep. Now say what you've gotta say Barry, and then that's it!"

Barry swallowed hard and steeled himself. I could visibly see him second-guessing his decision to speak up, but it was too late to go back, and he knew it.

"I don't believe you."

"You don't believe I want to go sleep and take a break from your bullshit? I don't mind coming over there to convince you."

"No Chuck, it's bigger than that. I don't believe your story. I don't believe you are who you say you are. What you told us was a hell of a story, and you told it well, but I think a story is all it was. You really think a dead guy you killed came back to life and basically tricked you into saving yourself? My concept of what is and is not possible has been blown wide open in the past few days, but I've still got to draw the line somewhere, and your story is that somewhere. I'm not saying I deserve your autobiography, but I don't deserve to be lied to. How can I trust you about little things like anatomy if I can't even trust you about who you are?"

Oh man. I wasn't sure exactly how bad Barry was gonna get it, but I'd guess a lot worse than Ike gave it to Henry.

Chuck opened his eyes, sat up, and looked at Barry. To Barry's credit, he met his gaze unblinkingly. When Chuck spoke, he was almost too quiet to hear, but I could hear him.

"You want proof."

"What?" Barry asked.

Chuck responded, louder. "You want proof. That's what you want, huh?" He got up, and slowly walked to the middle of the car, facing Barry, towering over him. "You…want…proof." He reached into his pocket and pulled out his scissor. "An old half scissor. Doesn't prove anything, right? Not by itself it doesn't. Hold this. Go on, take it."

Barry sheepishly reached out and very carefully took the scissor from Chuck's hand. He looked like he was about to pee his pants. Thomas was in his default position, eagerly watching what was going on with his fists folded in front of his face to hide his expression. I noticed I was doing the same thing without realizing it.

"However," Chuck continued, the entire room captivated. There was no way I could even guess what was going on in his mind. "Given the proper context…"

Chuck whipped off his leather jacket in an instant and let it fall to the floor. It was the first time the three of us had ever seen him without it. For the first time it was possible to distinguish where the jacket ended and where Chuck began, and it was startling. With the jacket on, he was a proper menace, a thug of sizeable build with wide arms and the broadest shoulders I'd ever seen. Without the jacket, he was thinner than a fencepost, a skeleton with dirty pale skin pulled tightly over its frame. He wore a wet brown t shirt that I suspect was initially white, and it contrasted starkly with the pallid flesh of his arms. He somehow managed to look severely wounded and infinitely durable at the same time.

He reached back and pulled the moldy shirt up over his head and dropped it on top of his jacket. The skin of his etiolated torso was even whiter than that of his arms, except where purple scar tissue was inlaid into it like constellations. There were scars from gunshots and stabbings and countless other wounds of no discernable origin, raised up in gnarled violet welts. It was a novel of suffering written in his flesh. There were wounds on his lower back and right side that looked different from all the others. These were precise, surgical, and all the more ghastly for their calculated cleanliness. A few inches above his navel, there was a round wound where some spear-like object had entered his abdomen, with a matching exit wound on his back. Branded into his left shoulder was a six inch cross with a halo hung round its top. These wounds, morbidly fascinating as they were, weren't the real story. That was carved into his chest.

Right where'd he'd described, exactly as he said they'd be, were the scarred outlines of the wounds he'd endured in carving the stake out of his chest. The skin over his heart was a bulbous purple lump, with two clean lines bisecting out of the main injury.

"Get up," he commanded Barry. Barry didn't get up. He was too horrified and nauseated to move. Dumbly, he sat on the floor, transfixed. "Get up," Chuck tried again, and got the same reaction. This time he grabbed Barry by the shoulders and yanked him to his feet. He grabbed the back of Barry's right hand, the hand holding his half scissor, and pressed it to his chest. The blade of the scissor was the exact length and width of the cuts extending away from his heart. Chuck turned slowly to the left, then to the right, showing myself and Thomas what Barry was seeing up close. No sound was coming out, but I could see Barry's lips moving. I'll never know for sure, but to me it looked like he was saying "Wake up. Wake up."

"Do you see it?" Chuck barked at him. "Do you see it? Do you understand what it means?" Barry's mouth was twitching too strongly to form a response. He choked on a single syllable, "I…I…" The moment dragged on uncomfortably. As Barry became more and more terrified, he became less and less articulate. Chuck was losing patience. His sinewy muscles flexed, and his face contorted into something that was essentially a scar in and of itself. Thomas and I shot each other a nervous glance. It was too soon to predict specifics, but we both knew this was going to end very badly.

Chuck reached out for the scissor with his other hand. He had slid his index finger into the loop at the base when a piercing metallic blow was struck on the wall of the boxcar from the outside. All of us jumped and shuddered at once. The same sound rang out again, the sound of a truncheon on corrugated steel. We heard it another three times, followed by the voice we'd heard over the megaphone earlier. This time he was close enough not to need it.

"Keep it down in there!" he shouted. Seconds later, he followed with "Sun's coming down, Chuck. You and your friends won't have to wait much longer."

Chuck let go of Barry, pulled the scissor from his hand and put it in his own pocket. In the ensuing silence, we could hear the footsteps of the man outside walking away from the boxcar. Chuck dressed swiftly and silently, and each of us sat in our corners, lost in our own heads.

A little less than an hour later, the sun went down. We didn't have to look outside to know; as always, each of us felt the instinctive tingle privately. Normally, this was a good thing. It meant that it was our time, that control of the world had been handed off to us for the next twelve hours or so. Tonight, it meant we were giving up control entirely. Thomas was the only one who spoke when it happened.

"Shit," he said. I had to agree with him.

We were undisturbed for the next ten minutes. The room was too tense for conversation. All sounds were magnified, and something was always moving at the edges of peripheral vision until further examined. Thomas spoke for the group once again.

"Why haven't they come for us yet?" he blurted to no one in particular. "I just want to get this the hell over with."

"Maybe they don't know the sun's down yet," Chuck offered. "There could be clouds."

"Maybe they want us to come out on our own," volunteered Barry. "You know, show some initiative." I couldn't tell whether he was kidding or not.

"More likely they're just letting us squirm," I said. "It might not have felt like it, but we've been in control all day. Now it's their turn, and they're enjoying it. Probably imagining us having this exact conversation right now."

"We're gonna get our asses kicked, aren't we?" asked Barry. He spoke not like a small child dreading a flu shot, but a man stoically resigned to performing an unpleasant task. It was the first time I'd ever heard a hint of courage from him. For some reason, that made me feel really good. *Wow, even Barry's growing a backbone*, I thought. *Maybe we can actually pull this off, somehow.*

"Not as badly as we're gonna kick theirs when we get out," I replied. He smiled at me, and I smiled back. I realized something; *Barry's my friend. Ho-ly shit, I am actually friends with Barry.* Barry was cracking his knuckles, then twisting his head with his hands to loosen up his neck. *He's getting ready to fight. I'll bet he hasn't done that since he killed that girl. Remember her, the one with the eyes missing?* Goddammit. We were actually having a moment, Barry and me, and my mind has to go and bring that up. You know, come to think of it, he's never actually told us what happened there. Maybe it wasn't what it looked like. *Oh, really? What else could it have been?* Look, it's not like the rest of us were volunteering at a soup kitchen that night. Maybe there's something else out there, something like us, but worse, and Barry was just the unlikely guy who found his leftovers?

That was a profoundly unpleasant thought. Arguing with yourself never does any good. Rather than settling on A or B, instead you land on C, and it's worse than the other two choices combined.

Official ruling: Barry gets the benefit of a doubt. There's not enough time, and besides, I don't want to break his balls the moment he grows them. He's clear until proven otherwise.

"That's a good idea, loosening up," I told him. "Everybody, c'mon, stretch out a little. It's better than sitting here quaking. C'mon, stretch it out." I got up and started stretching my calves behind my back. Chuck did the same. Thomas sat in his corner looking ashen.

"Thomas, you look like you're trying to quit smoking, buddy," I teased.

"No," he replied. "I'm trying to quit prison. It's proving more difficult than I thought." He was dripping nerves and sarcasm.

"Well then, we'll have you 12-stepped out of there by tonight, promise. Just get up and stretch. It'll make you feel better." He grudgingly complied.

"Chuck?" I said.

"Yeah?"

"You strike me as a man who's been apprehended by the police more than once in his lifetime." Chuck actually smiled.

"You would be correct."

"Got any tips for us?"

"Keep your head down. Cover your groin. Don't get killed." Everybody laughed, even Thomas, a little bit.

"Have you ever considered motivational speaking?" I asked. The laughter settled down.

"Seriously though," he said, "That's the basic idea. Don't make it any harder on yourself-"

The door to the box car slid open so violently it nearly bounced off its rails. On the other side were about twenty men. Everybody was wearing either blue or green hooded sweatshirts with bulletproof vests on top. Half the blue suits had riot shields, and all of them had at least one handgun. The green suits had considerably larger weapons, mostly assault rifles with the occasional shotgun, and waist belts loaded with hand grenades and large knives and other holstered tools of the trade. At the back of the crowd, behind two more shielded blue suits, were three men dressed head to toe in black fatigues. Two of them were wearing riot helmets. The man on the left was holding a long, Japanese sword. On the right, what looked like a grenade launcher. The man in the middle had no helmet or weapons of any kind, just a megaphone, expensive sunglasses, a bad mustache, and a two-way radio on his belt. He was grinning proudly.

Chuck concluded, "Than it's going to be."

"Good evening boys!" called the man on the megaphone. "Nice to finally see ya!"

"Likewise!" hollered Chuck, raising his hand above his head in an exaggerated wave. When he did so, over 20 guns clicked to life at once and drew a bead on his head. "Aren't you a friendly bunch," he said

"The friendliest," deadpanned the man on the megaphone. "Now, getting down to business, my name is Mr. Scott, and effective immediately, I own you. All of you. I decide whether you live or die, and how quickly or slowly it happens. If any of you want to get out of this train alive, you'll do exactly as I say. The more you cooperate, the less I hurt you. To a point, at least. Now, all of you: hands behind your head. Slowly. But not too slowly. Do it wrong, and I'll make sure you know it." All four of us, even Chuck, slowly lifted our hands from our sides and placed them behind our heads. The gunmen took their focus off of Chuck and spread their line of fire the length of the boxcar.

"Well done boys. Now, about the girl." Mr. Scott took off his aviator sunglasses and squinted into the boxcar. "Where's the girl?"

Chuck looked at him blankly. "Who?"

"Don't fuck with me," he commanded. "The girl. The one you were holding hostage. Where is she?"

"Ohhh... *That* girl," Chuck replied. "Kind of a funny story there. You see, we never *really* had a girl in here, in the strictest sense. One of us just does a really good impression. The pizza was terrific, by the way. The scotch, eh, well...you did the best you could. I know things are difficult, what with the country having fallen apart and all. But hey, you did your best, and that's what matters. Luckily, I'm an understanding kind of guy."

"I'm not," Scott replied. "Bean bags, one round each, abdomen."

There was a whooshing noise, and I went down on my back. It felt like I'd been hit in the ribs with a sledgehammer. I curled up in a ball, gasping for breath. There was a black, fist-sized bag on the floor next to me. Poor Barry had been blown back into the rear wall and had fallen like a lump. He wasn't moving. Thomas was in a position similar to my own. Chuck was wheezing, standing on one knee. He was the only one of us who hadn't gone down.

"That," continued Mr. Scott over the megaphone, "Is what's referred to as a 'Bean bag bullet.' Hurts, doesn't it? At first, I was skeptical about non-lethal weapons, but I've acquired the taste. You've got ten seconds, then I want you back on your feet, or you'll get it again."

Chuck was still struggling for breath, but he was back up on two feet, doubled over. Thomas was on one knee, struggling to get the second one up. Barry had just opened his eyes. He was bleeding out of his mouth. I pushed myself up with my arms, tottering on both knees. With a final push I rocked up to my feet. Barry still hadn't moved.

"Well done boys, with two seconds to spare. You have five more to get your friend up or he gets another one in the face."

"C'mon Barry, just lean up against the wall. You can do it." I had his left arm, Chuck had his right. Barry spat out a mouthful of blood and took hard, lunging breaths.

"Workin'…on it," he stammered.

"We don't have much time. Just get on your feet and lean up against the wall. Let the wall hold you up." Chuck and I were pulling, but the two of us could barely keep ourselves upright. We tugged as hard as we could, but Barry was all dead weight, and barely conscious.

"Time's up. Gangway," called Mr. Scott.

"He's hurt," Thomas yelled back. "Give him time."

"I don't know who you are, but unless you want to get hit again, you'll get out of the way."

There was no response. Finally, Scott gave the order. "One bean bag, wherever you want it."

I braced for another hit. There was another whoosh, but I didn't feel anything. I looked behind me and saw Thomas face down of the floor. He had been standing in front of us, covering Chuck and I while we tried to get Barry on his feet. Thomas grunted, spat a little blood of his own, and started pushing himself back to his knees.

Barry was finally showing signs of life again. He pushed with his legs, Chuck and I pulled his arms, and we got him up. We pulled Thomas up next. He was leaning against the side wall with his arms wrapped around his stomach.

"Well, wasn't that touching," Scott said flatly. "Let's proceed. If you're holding a weapon, slowly take it out and lay it on the floor."

Chuck very calmly reached into his back pocket and pulled out the pistol he'd taken from me so long ago. He softly placed it in front of his feet and stood up.

"Only one handgun?" Mr. Scott asked. He turned and whispered something to the man next to him holding the grenade launcher. The man nodded. Scott got back on the megaphone. "Everybody empty your pockets, placing the contents on the floor in front of you, then turn them inside out."

Barry took out a leather wallet and dropped it on the floor. All of my pockets were empty (I'd left the sketchbook in the corner), so I just turned them inside out. Thomas didn't even have pockets, so he just stood there looking like he was trying not to throw up. Chuck hadn't moved.

"You too Chuck," said Mr. Scott. "You don't want to waste any more of my time."

"I've got nothing important," he replied. "Just some scissors."

"I decide what's important," Scott declared. "Take them out and empty your pockets. Now."

Chuck reached into his front pockets. He stood silently, hands hidden, staring over the riot shields and rifles directly into Scott's eyes. Finally, he removed the half-scissor from his pocket and laid it on the floor, never breaking Scott's gaze as he did so. He reached back in and swiftly inverted his pockets. It was an inherently submissive gesture, but Chuck turned his pockets with such defiant flair it was as if he'd just flipped everyone off instead.

"Nice," Scott commented dryly. "Now, everybody turn around and get on your knees."

"No can do, Mr. Steve," replied Chuck.

"It's *Scott*," he shot back.

"Steve, got it. Anyway, we can't turn around. What's to stop you from shooting us in the back if we do?"

"What's to stop me from having you shot right now?"

"Your cheerful disposition?"

"Right. If I wanted to shoot you, I'd have done it a long time ago. If you won't cooperate, we can come in there and bring you out, but I guarantee you won't like it as much."

Chuck looked over the raised weapons at Mr. Scott, then down at the floor, and blankly to his left and right. He didn't want to admit, it, but he was out of ammo. "Ok guys, let's do it," he said, loud enough for us to hear but not Mr. Scott. "It'll be over soon." He sighed, turned around, and slumped to his knees, as did the rest of us.

"See, that wasn't so bad, was it?" Mr. Scott taunted. "Move in and cuff em'," he commanded. Behind me, I could hear hard rubber boots clanging against the floor. Gloved hands grabbed my arms and wrenched them behind my back before clamping on handcuffs tightly enough to block the blood flow to my hands.

"Secured!" shouted a faceless voice behind me.

"Bring em' out!" responded Scott. Two more hands grabbed me by the elbows, dragged me back a few feet, and literally pitched me out of the car. I fell about three feet to the ground and landed back-first on my elbows. The momentum rolled me over backwards and I ended up rolling into a standing position, and that's when I took the first nightstick blow to the back of my knees. I went back down, and from there it was just a hailstorm of fists and clubs. Behind me, I could hear Thomas yelling, and then a gunshot went off, and someone shouted "Get the taser!" and I felt a burst of white-hot lightning between my shoulder blades. I fell over on my side, all of my muscles twitching and contracting to the point of implosion, and I could smell something burning. There was a second burst of electric agony under my chin, and a boot hit me in the face but I couldn't feel it. Seconds later I blacked out.

Chapter 7: Marty Hendrix

"Every form of addiction is bad, no matter whether the narcotic be alcohol or morphine or idealism."
- Carl Jung

When I opened my eyes again, I was lying on my back, but my hands were no longer bound. The floor was especially hard and cool. It felt good between my shoulder blades. Underneath my jaw, my skin felt like it had been brutally sunburned. My left thigh was twitching uncontrollably. As I gradually regained consciousness, I realized my leg was burned like my chin, though at least my jeans had offered a thin layer of protection. All of my muscles were throbbing out of time. With great exertion, I rolled over onto my stomach and lowered my jaw onto the cool concrete. The floor was abrasive, but cool enough that I didn't care. I exhaled deeply with gratitude. I lay there for a few moments longer, trying to draw as much of the blessed cold into my raw chin as I could. Eventually my body heat prevailed, and rather than slithering away to find a new spot, I got up and began about the business of figuring out exactly where I was.

Surely enough, we were in jail. The cell was surprisingly large, with a slab concrete floor, three windowless cinderblock walls, a sliding barred door, a small toilet in one corner, and two cots mounted on opposite walls. Thomas and Barry were sitting morosely on one of the cots, each favoring different parts of their bodies, their glum faces pockmarked with bruises and dried blood. I cast a quick glance through the bars at what was outside; just a long empty hallway and a desk. Satisfied that we were alone for the moment, I sluggishly limped over to see Barry and Thomas.

"Hey guys," I said, leaning into the cot for support.

"Hey," they both wheezed back simultaneously, neither bothering to look up from their own wounds. There were several seconds of silence

"God that sucked," Barry exhaled, and spat out a little more blood on the floor.

"I concur," said Thomas.

"What happened?" I asked.

"They cuffed us and threw us out of the train," Thomas replied, pausing to wipe blood from his nose with his wrist. "Then they beat on us for awhile, then we woke up here. I came to first, then Barry, then you."

"How long were we out?"

"No idea."

I looked down at the floor and sighed. My muscles were still quivering involuntarily, but I was gradually regaining control. The bottom of my jaw still felt like it had been run over a hot cheese grater. "Is there room up there for one more?"

"Sure," Barry replied absently, staring into his lap while massaging his temples.

With a great deal of effort I climbed onto the cot, using my arms more than my legs. It was only slightly softer than the concrete floor I'd come from, but comfort was in short supply and I was in no position to be picky. With the three of us sitting together on the cot, there was hardly any elbow room, but nobody complained. At the moment, our central nervous systems had more to worry about than personal space.

"I'm surprised this ratty thing can hold all of us," said Barry, still grinding his fingers against the side of his head.

...All of us?

"Holy shit, where's Chuck?!" Thomas whipped his head around and pointedly shushed me.

"Other cot," he whispered, pointing across the room. There was an ill-defined lump lying prone on the second cot, with a white sheet thrown over top of it. "They think he's dead."

"Wait, what?"

"Don't worry, he's ok...ok enough. You heard the gunshot go off, right? After they threw us all out of the train?" I thought back to those fleeting, panicked moments between falling out of the boxcar and waking up here.

"Yeah, I heard a shot. Only one though."

"Exactly," Thomas replied. "I think somebody's gun went off by mistake. If they'd wanted us shot, we'd all have been shot, no doubt about it. But the fact that there was only one shot makes me think it was an accident. Anyway, Chuck was on his feet when the gun went off, and as soon as he heard it fire he went down. They kept working him over, but he just laid there, still as could be. I'd imagine by the time they looked him over for a bullet hole he was already so bloody and torn up that they couldn't see much of anything. They dumped him on the other cot and put a sheet over him, probably to scare us into being compliant."

"He's…he's still alive though, right?"

"Oh yeah, definitely. A bit worse for the wear, just like you and me, but still totally alive. If that's what we're considered, at least."

"So where was he really shot?"

"Nowhere. He didn't take the bullet. That honor belonged to me." Thomas groaned and twisted at the waist, showing me his left thigh. Halfway between his knee and his waist was a four-inch chunk of bloody, ragged flesh. Strands of frayed fabric from his pants clumped around the wound, mottled and stuck fast in all the dried blood.

It took me a moment to speak. "A…a bullet did that?"

"No, my fingernails did," he replied. "Thankfully it just hit the outside of my thigh. I didn't have to dig in too deeply to get it out. All the same, it's not something I'd like to do again."

"You need to tourniquet that."

"That's what I said," Barry said.

"Nah, it's no big deal. It's already stopped bleeding."

"It won't take much to start it again."

"I told you, I'm *fine.*"

He wasn't budging, so I tried a new approach.

"You've lost a lot of blood."

"Captain Obvious strikes again."

"Just shut up already. You need blood."

"We'll get some. Soon."

"No, I mean *right now*. You think it's gonna be easy breaking out of here? We need you in peak shape, and you're anything but with your leg torn up and all that blood loss. I only lost a little through my nose. Take some of mine."

I raised the veiny inside of my wrist to my right fang. I could just taste the dirt and sweat on my skin when Thomas's hand shot out and grabbed my arm with unexpected force.

"*No,*" he whispered intensely, nose to nose with me. "Nobody exchanges blood. Under any circumstances."

"Says who?" I barked, yanking my arm out of his grip.

"Chuck," replied Barry.

"What?"

"The last thing Chuck said before they pulled us out of the car was that none of us should share our blood, for any reason. He didn't have time to explain, but it seemed pretty important to him. Also, he wants you to go talk to him. Tap him on the shoulder three times so he knows it's you."

I wondered why Chuck was always so cautious about contact with vampire blood. He almost certainly knew something we didn't. I wanted to ask him about it, but decided it could wait until after we were out of here. I climbed off the cot and apprehensively made my way across the cell. I paused to look out through the bars one more time. The hall was still totally empty. I briefly wondered why they'd go through so much trouble to capture us alive, only to leave us unguarded. Sometimes you should just be thankful and not ask questions.

Standing over the cot, looking down at the huddled mass under the sheet, I could clearly see whatever was under there was human, or at least human-shaped. It was lying on its right side, facing the wall, left shoulder pointing up. With great trepidation, I reached out and quickly poked its shoulder three times. Nothing. I looked back at Thomas and Barry. They both shrugged together. I tapped him again. Still no response. I pulled back my arm and slapped him on the shoulder as hard as I could. "Hey!" I whispered. "Are you dead or not?"

There was a grunting sound, and the body underneath the sheet rolled over. "What the hell was that for?" it wheezed.

"You were ignoring your little three-poke signal."

"Fell asleep. Sue me."

"You don't sound so good, man. Let's have a look at…oh."

I pulled back the sheet enough to reveal the upper half of Chuck's body. He was recognizable, but barely. His whole face was an ugly purple and red, and the left cheek looked like it had been crushed inward. His right eye was entirely swollen shut, and in the process of turning from green to yellow. There was almost nothing left of the white shirt he wore under his jacket, and the exposed skin was littered with bruises and taser burns. He had two stab wounds in his gut. One was shallow; the other was not. Both had already stopped bleeding, but there was blood in various states of coagulation all over his skin and clothes.

"Oh, Chuck. They fucked you up bad, man."

"Eh, I've had worse."

"Can you walk?"

"Probably. They dislocated my knee, but I popped it back in when no one was looking. It hurts, but it still moves ok."

"You've lost a lot of blood."

"Easy come, easy go. Most of it's borrowed anyway."

"I'll give you some of mine. I hardly got beat up at all, compared to you."

"Thanks, but that's not necessary. I'll get some myself, before too long."

"Then tell Thomas to take some of mine. He's got a bad leg wound, and an attitude to match."

"Go to hell," Thomas called flatly across the room.

"Exhibit A."

Chuck smiled, although the left half of his face was too busted to move. "Trouble in paradise?" He winked with his one functional eye.

"What'd he say?" Thomas yelled.

I leaned in close and grabbed him by the collar of his jacket. "Swear to God, I'll finish you off myself," I whispered in his ear. "This is neither the time nor the place."

Chuck was obviously stifling laughter. "You're right about the time, I'll grant you that. But after all, we *are* in prison. Stranger things have happened. C'mon, explore those feelings."

"What the hell are you two talking about over there?" Thomas shouted again.

I put my thumb on what remained of Chuck's left cheek and pushed. Not too hard, mind you, just hard enough to shut him up. The right side of his face twisted in pain. It was cruel, I know, and I didn't enjoy it, but I wasn't about to let Chuck's mouth make a bad situation worse for the second time in one day. Anyway, there was something about Chuck's behavior that seemed a little off to me. If I had to hazard a guess, I'd say he was probably concussed. Yet another liability to be taken into account.

I pulled my thumb off his face and Chuck's entire body visibly relaxed.

"That was not a nice thing to do," he said, sounding more wounded emotionally than physically. It was kind of creepy to hear.

"I'm sorry, but I had to get you focused again," I explained. "Why did you want me to come and talk to you?"

"Because," he replied, "It's time we got out of here."

"I couldn't agree more. So, what's the plan?"

"We need to get the guard inside the cell. He's gotta be kept alive too."

"Uh, Chuck…there's no guard here. The only thing outside the cell is a desk and an empty hallway."

"Actually, there is a guard," Barry chimed in. "He just hasn't been by in awhile. Based on the conversation he was having on his walkie-talkie, he's more interested in buying weed than guarding us."

"Just one guard?"

"Yeah."

"Armed?"

"Of course?"

"Big guy?"

"Hardly. Young, too. Couldn't have been much more than 22, 23 tops."

"Good, good. So, how do we get him inside the cell?"

"Well, as far as these guys are concerned, I'm dead of a gunshot wound, right? I'll start coughing and twitching and freaking out. At that point, you get panicked and run to the bars, screaming for help. The guard runs in, and you tell him I'm alive, but hurt badly, and he needs to get in here and help you save me. Unless he's already bought his weed and smoked it all, he is *not* going to want to come in here alone with the four of us. This is where the plan hinges on you, Ethan. Do or say anything you have to in order to get that man inside here."

"I can do that," I said. I had no idea how I was actually going to do that.

"Once he's inside, we take him hostage, and he leads us out of here. Sound good? Thomas, Barry, you guys are the back-up muscle on this one. If things get out of control, by all means help us out, but if this goes smoothly all you'll need to do is sit on the cot looking surprised. Now, there is a very real chance this guy will come in here, see what's going on, and turn right around and go get a superior, or a medic, or back-up. If that happens, well, we'll wing it and do the best we can. If he goes and gets a medic, then he'll have to open the door to get in and see me. If that door opens, *do not let it shut*. You got that?"

"Yeah, I got it," I answered. "It's just that, well, this whole thing sounds like a glorified version of faking a seizure to get out of a math test."

"You know, I actually tried that one time," Barry helpfully chimed in from the cot.

"*Really*?" said Thomas, suddenly interested. "How'd that work out?"

Barry shook his head. "Didn't take."

"Hmmmm," Thomas grunted sympathetically.

"Hey, can we at least *try* to stay on task here?" Chuck snarled.

"Sorry, continue," said Barry.

"Look, I know it's not much, but at the moment it's all we got. I wouldn't try it if I didn't think it could work. You ready to do this?" Chuck asked me, looking up from his cot.

"Sure. Why the hell not?"

"Good man," he said, crawling under the sheet and resuming his original position. "Remember, we need him alive."

"No problem."

I stood by the cot, ready for action. Our plan sucked, and half our team was seriously wounded. Still, it would be more fun to do it this way than to let them kill us on their own terms.

From beneath the sheet Chuck started gagging and wheezing, tastefully garnished with a hacking cough. I took up my position in front of the barred door.

"Hey! Hey! We need somebody in here! It's an emergency!"

I waited a few seconds; nobody came. I tried again; still nothing. Chuck was still dutifully hacking and twitching away under the sheet.

"Shit! Nobody's coming!"

"Shake the bars! Thomas yelled over Chuck's surprisingly convincing performance. "Keep yelling and shake the bars!"

I grabbed two of the bars in my hands and shook as hard as I could. The sound was enormous; it reverberated through the empty hall. I kept shouting, but I couldn't even hear myself over the clatter of steel and cement. Seconds later, a man came running down the hallway into view. He was wearing the green uniform, and carrying an assault rifle. Just as Barry had said, he looked barely old enough to hold it. He pointed his gun at me, and I stopped rattling the wall.

"What the fuck is all this noise about?" he spat, keeping the gun pointed at me but scanning the rest of the cell with his eyes.

"We've got a situation here," I explained, trying to strike a balance between competent confidence and desperation. "It's Chuck. He's alive, but he needs help. *Now.*"

"Chuck?" the guard asked, his face betraying a hint of confusion. "He's the one that was shot and pronounced dead, right?"

"Does he look dead to you?!" I yelled, gesturing pointedly at the cot. Chuck's performance was still going strong.

"Holy shit…" whispered the guard, finally lowering his gun.

"Holy shit is right," I shot back. "He's not dead now, but he will be soon unless you get in here and help me save him."

"Wha-what do you need me for?"

"Well, for starters, you can hold him down while I figure out what the hell is wrong with him, and we'll take it from there, ok?"

"I, uh, I dunno, I should probably go get someone-"

"Dammit man, there's no TIME! I know your bosses wanted Chuck alive, but some asshole's gun went off and killed him. Or almost killed him. If you get in here now and help me save him, you can walk out of here like Jesus Christ and go tell your bosses that you just resurrected public enemy number one. I'd imagine they'll be pretty pleased, don't you?"

The guard had one hand on the handle of the door. The other was on the ring of keys hanging from his belt. He was looking inside the cell, but he wasn't moving.

"Please man," I pleaded. "No tricks, swear to God. I just don't wanna watch my friend die."

He closed his eyes and lowered his head. A moment later, he inhaled and sighed deeply. "Ok," he said, sticking a key in the lock and twisting it hard. He grabbed the handle and threw the sliding door all the way open. "Let's get your friend patched up."

The moment he opened the door, guilt ran through me like a sword. This kid (and that's what he was, a kid) couldn't be browbeaten or tempted with personal gain, but a favor for a desperate stranger trying to save a friend had broken the dam. Even worse, I was delivering him into the hands of a badly beaten Chuck, who was no doubt looking for vengeance on somebody wearing the same uniform as those who had done the beating. I lowered my eyes as he stepped into the room and made his way to the cot.

"Thank you," I muttered. "And I'm sorry."

He was less than a foot away from the cot when Chuck pounced. Tossing aside the sheet and leaping into the air, he overshot, nearly landing on top of the guard, who was knocked backwards into the wall. Chuck went down on one knee, grimacing, and the guard swung his rifle up at Chuck, who swatted it away. It flew through the air, hitting the floor and sliding underneath Thomas and Barry's cot. The guard was dumbstruck as Chuck got up, wrapped a hand around his throat, lifted him off the ground and pressed him up against the wall. He kicked his legs and tried to pry Chuck's hand from around his neck, but it was futile. He wasn't coming down until Chuck said so.

"Thought you could kill me, huh?" Chuck growled. "I don't die easily. Do you?" He was still kicking, but weakly.

"Put him down, Chuck," I said. "He gets the point."

"You already did your part. This is no concern of yours," Chuck replied without looking at me. The guard's eyes were beginning to droop.

"Actually, it is my concern, because I'm the one who was responsible for getting him in here, and I'm *telling* you to *put him down*." His lips were beginning to turn blue. A sadistic half-moon grin lit up the side of Chuck's face that still worked.

"What's the matter, fag, got a crush on this one too?"

I walked up perpendicular to Chuck's left shoulder, wrapped both hands around his waxy, muscular neck, and squeezed until the bones in my fingers popped. Sweet Jesus Lord Almighty, it felt fan-motherfucking-tastic. I squeezed and squeezed and squeezed and squeezed , and the more pressure I applied the better I felt. The look of shock on Chuck's face when he couldn't breathe and figured out why was priceless. He wouldn't even look at me when he was insulting me, and now I was in charge of his oxygen supply. The next time he called me a fag, he would make sure to look me in the eyes while he did it.

I was so engrossed in the newfound joy of throttling that I completely forgot a very important factor in the current equation; Chuck's free hand. He reached out and easily wrapped it around my neck, squeezing with a might that shouldn't have been possible. My head spun from the sudden lack of air. I dropped to my knees, tried to get up, but I was too dizzy to even get one foot back on the ground. My eyelids started to flutter as well, but suddenly Chuck's grip loosened considerably. I now had enough wiggle room to lift my head, and I saw that the guard, still hanging three feet in the air, had gotten both of *his* hands around Chuck's neck. This kid was a fighter. I was flushed with pride, or lack of oxygen. Probably both. Chuck's face looked enraged and sleepy at the same time. Four hands beat two, and he knew it.

"That's enough!" yelled Thomas, cocking the guard's assault rifle and pointing it at the three of us. "On three, I want everybody to stop choking each other. One…two…three!"

I let go of Chuck; Chuck let go of me. The guard let go of Chuck, and Chuck did the same, letting him fall to the floor in a heap. All three of us had finger-shaped bruises on our necks, and were greedily sucking in air. Chuck was doubled over with his hands on his knees, wheezing. He looked up to meet my gaze, but I couldn't read his expression. It didn't look pleasant though. Thomas, the voice of reason with the M16, was directing traffic.

"Chuck, Ethan, opposite sides of the cell. Have a seat, catch your breath, and don't cause anymore trouble." Chuck and I retreated to our respective corners, like boxers pulled out of a furious exchange by the bell. Thomas lowered his gun and went to check on the guard. He put down the gun and kneeled on the floor in front of him.

"Hey...hey buddy, are you ok?" he asked with a surprising gentle sincerity.

"Yeah," the guard croaked, still lying on the floor. "Juz' catchin' my breath."

"Good, glad to hear it. What's your name?"

"Marty."

"Well Marty, first of all I want to apologize to you on all of our behalves. We did trick you to get you inside the cell, but it was never our intent to hurt you. Chuck just gets a little wound up sometimes. He's sorry for that too."

"Like hell," Chuck mumbled under his breath. Thomas not so subtly pointed at the rifle lying next to him, and fixed him with a withering stare.

"Thanks," Marty gasped, now sitting upright against the wall, the color slowly returning to his face. "What do you want with me then?" he asked.

"We need you to help us get out of...wherever we are, and back onto our train. Get us on that train, and we swear you'll never see us again. We'll cover our tracks, too, make it look like it was someone else's fault we escaped. All you have to do is help us get out of here, and you won't get hurt, and in a few days this whole thing will blow over and your life will be back to normal."

"And if I say no?" Marty wheezed, trying to sound big but lacking the air to pull it off.

"You don't want to say no." Thomas said flatly.

"No," said Marty, managing to sound a little bigger this time, but not much. Thomas grabbed the rifle off the floor with one hand and stuck it in Marty's face.

"Seriously, Marty?" His tone was paternal, but impatient. "We don't have time for games. If 'No's" your final answer, I'll respect that. Unfortunately, by 'Respect that,' I mean, 'Shoot you.'"

"Fine. Keep that guy away from me," he said, pointing at Chuck, "And I'll get you guys out of here."

"Good man," replied Thomas, lowering the gun and extending a hand to pull Marty up.

"Ok guys, follow me. The train's not too far from here."

"What about the other guards?" asked Barry.

"There are no other guards on this floor tonight. Third Wednesday of the month; everybody's on night maneuvers."

"That's rather convenient."

"Not for me," replied Marty, with a trace of bitterness. "If we take this corridor south long enough, we'll pass right by the rear of the train. Once I get you there, the rest is up to you guys."

"Actually, we've got a pit stop to make first," said Chuck.

"And just what is that?" Thomas asked.

"We need to get our things. What you confiscated when you pulled us off the train. We need those things back."

"Do we really have time?" Thomas was clearly losing patience with all the delays.

"We'll *make* time," Chuck declared.

Thomas sighed. "Marty, where are our things?"

"In temporary storage. That's located north, but it's less than a two minute walk. I have the key, too."

"Fine, fine," Thomas conceded. "Take us there first."

We filed out of the cell, Marty on point, followed by Thomas, Barry, and myself, with Chuck bringing up the rear. We turned left and headed down the hallway.

"I could kill you, you know," Chuck whispered in my ear.

"Sure, sure," I answered, never breaking gait or turning to look at him. "Very scary."

"Cut the chatter back there," called Thomas. I could almost feel the heat of Chuck seething behind me. It felt good. Not "Choking him" good; but still, rather enjoyable.

We arrived at a thick steel door with a small barred window. Marty pulled his key ring from his shirt pocket, identified the one he needed, and opened the door. We stepped inside to a large room with a tiled floor and dozens of lockers built into the walls. There were many different shapes and sizes, some tall and thin, some short and stout, one that took up nearly an entire wall and several others barely larger than my hand. All together, they covered all four walls from floor to ceiling. The only surface not covered by a locker was the back of the door.

"Let's see…If I remember correctly, your belongings are in E1." Marty quickly scanned the right wall. "Found it." E1 was a disappointingly conventional locker, three feet high and one foot wide. Marty once again flipped though his key ring, produced a small black key, and opened the locker.

As soon as the door was open, Chuck eagerly pushed his way to the front of the line and began furiously scanning the shelves. On the bottom shelf, he found what we all knew he was looking for; the one-armed scissor. He turned it over in his hand, inspecting it admiringly. Satisfied, he pocketed the scissor and stepped to the side. Barry was up next. He grabbed his wallet from the top shelf and flipped through it half-heartedly. "I don't think $35 and a driver's license will be all that useful," he said before dropping it back on the shelf.

Now it was my turn to go through the locker. Surprisingly, I found my pistol, still loaded, on one of the middle shelves. I thought one of the soldiers might've helped himself to it, but in all honesty it wasn't that great of a pistol, and if our encounter on the train was any indication, these people certainly weren't short on weaponry. I tucked the pistol into my waistband and made a final sweep of the locker. In the back left corner of the bottom shelf I was surprised to find not only my oft-neglected sketchbook but also the pencils I'd taken with it. I'd meant to hide the sketchbook atop one of the overhead support shafts that connected the walls of the boxcar to the roof, but in the chaos of our apprehension I'd totally forgotten about it. I was surprised they'd even bothered to throw it in the locker with our other belongings. The pencils had all been snapped, but were still long enough to sketch with, and the erasers were still attached to their respective ends. Somehow, I'd gotten lucky again. I rolled up the sketchbook and crammed it into my back pocket. The pencils went with it, and I backed away from the locker to give Thomas his turn.

Thomas, still holding Marty's gun, stepped up to the locker and immediately shut the door.

"Nothing for you?" Marty asked.

Thomas shrugged. "Nah, I travel light. Ok, let's head for the train."

"Actually, there's one more stop we need to make. Last one, I swear."

Thomas was exasperated. "Goddamnit Chuck, what now? We've gotta get the hell out of here!"

"I know, I know, and we will, don't worry," Chuck replied solicitously. "I'm just as eager to get out of here as the rest of you are, believe me, but these assholes have something that we need, something that's going to make things a hell of a lot easier once we get to New York."

"Oh yeah, and what's that?"

"Information. Marty, which way is it to the archives? They're still in the basement, right?"

"Um, yeah," he answered, taken aback. "How do you know about the archives?"

"I've been here before," Chuck replied. "On one of my first cross-country trips. I found the archives, but I had another job to do, and didn't have time to get what I needed."

"This wouldn't happen to have been four years ago, would it? When all those bombs went off?"

"Well, there weren't *that* many bombs," he said, smiling demurely.

"Jesus Christ, no wonder they were so pissed when they thought you died outside the train. Now I know why they wanted you alive so badly."

"And here I am, happy to oblige. Anyway, the archives. Let's move."

"Ok, but I've only got first floor keys. The locks for each floor are different."

Chuck was growing impatient. "Well, where *are* the basement keys, then?"

"There'll be two guards in the basement. One will have the keys to all the basement rooms. The other will have keys to the archives."

"Alright then, let's get those keys."

"Chuck," I said.

"Yes?"

"Are you absolutely sure this is a good idea? I mean, who knows when the other soldiers are coming back, or what kind of security measures this "Archives" place has, or what time the train is leaving, if it hasn't left already, and-"

"For shit's sake Ethan, will you just shut up and trust me? I've gotten you halfway across what's left of this country, haven't I? Haven't I? That's not a rhetorical question."

"Yes, but-"

"Yes but nothing, asshole! I've gotten us this far, and if I'm gonna get us the rest of the way then I need what's in those archives, and the more time we spend arguing about it the better the chances are of the things you just described happening. So will you do me a favor and just shut up and trust me? Everybody? Trust me for just a little bit longer, and I promise you I won't let you down. Is everybody ok with that?"

The four of us all nodded silently.

"Thank you," Chuck said. "I wouldn't ask this of you if it wasn't absolutely necessary. I've been something of an asshole lately, and I know that. Getting beaten up and going to jail are two of my least favorite ways to spend an evening, and I've been taking it out on all of you, and I'm sorry. I really am. But right now, we've gotta remember why we're doing this, why we're going to New York. I'm sure you've all got private reasons of your own, and that's fine, but there's also the Big Reason, and everything we need to know about the Big Reason is downstairs in those archives. Once we get there, this whole trip is gonna make a whole lot more sense to all of you, I promise. But first, we have to get down there. Marty, lead the way."

Marty led the way. We left the locker room, turned around, and went south through the long hallway for about ten minutes. Marty unlocked another heavy door, and on the other side were two long staircases leading into darkness.

"Which one?" asked Chuck.

"They'll both take us to the basement. The one on the right takes us closest to the archives, but we'll have to go right past the guards. We can sneak up on them if we take the left staircase, but it'll take us longer to get there."

"We're on a tight budget time-wise. We'll take the right staircase. I'll take point. Thomas, I want you on my right, Ethan, on the left. Have your guns ready to go. Marty, you stay behind me and navigate. Barry, keep an eye behind us. If you see something, say something. Everybody cool?"

We all nodded. Thomas and I cocked our weapons and moved into position. The five of us took formation and began our silent descent.

Once we passed the overhead light illuminating the last few steps of the staircase, the basement was totally unlit. None of us thought twice about this, until Marty spoke up.

"Dammit, I should've grabbed my goggles before we came. I can't see a damn thing."

"Don't worry, it's not a problem for us," Chuck answered without thinking.

"It's not? How?"

"We, uh, we eat lots of, carrots. Good night vision. Just keep a hand on my shoulder and try not to trip over me. If I describe what I see, can you still direct us?"

"Sure. The basement's easy. Keep going straight and you'll hit a fork in the hall. Go right. Follow it to the end, then go through the double doors. There'll be one more staircase, a lot smaller than the last one. At the bottom, there's a hallway. That's where the guards will probably be. The door to the archives is also in that hall. It's pretty unassuming, except for the five or six locks, but one of the guards will have the keys."

"Wow Marty, you really know your shit."

"Thank you," he said with mock exasperation. "About time somebody else picked up on that."

"They keep you on guard duty all the time?" Chuck asked, genuinely interested.

"Pretty much. It's all politics and bullshit around here. I kiss just enough ass for a gun, a bed, and three meals a day. But I get to meet interesting people, and be choked and kidnapped by them."

"Sorry Marty," Chuck said. "It was just business."

"Don't sweat it. This is more excitement than I've seen in a long while. Before you guys leave, we need to get a picture for my scrapbook."

Chuck laughed. "You're one funny son of a bitch, Marty."

"I'm just glad to have an audience."

"Right then, let's keep moving."

Marty's directions were spot on. We were approaching the second staircase when I heard a sound.

"Everybody stop. Be quiet."

I strained my ears for more detail. Below and to the right there was shuffling, the subtle click of glossed paper being flipped on wood, with a percussive thump every fifteen seconds or so. One man, no, two men, having a clipped, monosyllabic conversation.

hit

stick

bust

"They're playing blackjack," I said.

"How can you possibly hear that?" Marty asked incredulously

"Uh, carrots. Baby carrots," I amended. "Good source of Vitamin D, and, uh…Riboflavin?"

Marty shook his head. "You guys are weird."

"Blackjack eh," Chuck thought out loud, approaching the staircase. "This should be easy."

"Wait, are you guys gonna…kill them?" Marty asked.

All of us went silent. This wouldn't be fun news to break, but the moment he came down those stairs he'd see through any lie we thought up.

Surprisingly, Barry decided to field this one. "Well, Marty, it's just, the thing is-"

"-Cause that's totally fine by me," he interrupted. "I know those guys, and they're assholes. Especially Tony, the tall skinny one. He cheats at cards."

The four of us stared at him, aghast. Barry's eyes darted back and forth shiftily.

"What? He listens to crappy music, too. The Bee Gees and shit."

Chuck shrugged. "Eh, I've killed people for less. Put the guns away, guys. We'll do this one manually."

"They'll have guns," Marty warned us.

"I figured as much. You wait here; we'll call up when we're done." Chuck signaled us with his hand and started clomping down the stairs.

By the time the rest of us hit the bottom step he was already off and running at the guards. They were seated around a tiny wooden table, situated underneath the one overhead light in the hall. Chuck had already violently overturned the table before they had the chance to stand up. Both of their rifles were leaning against the wall, just over an arm's length away, three inches from giving them a fighting chance. The taller of the two, Tony, He Who Cheats at Cards and Likes The Bee Gees and Shit, managed to get to his feet and reach for a sidearm. Before he could draw Chuck had a hand on either side of his head, and he twisted violently, cleanly breaking the neck. He swung his arms so wildly that his elbow struck Tony's companion in the face. He tottered backwards into Thomas's waiting arms, and in a perfect imitation of Chuck's technique, he snapped this one's neck too. It was almost like rewinding a movie. I was much more disturbed by the skill of his mimicry than the fact that we had violently killed two men in the middle of a card game, before they could even scream, and now we were just standing around like it was another day at the office.

Chuck reached down and grabbed Tony's lifeless body by the hair. "Well, who's hungry?" He bit into Tony's neck and started feeding. A few seconds later, his eyebrows raised in shock, then furrowed in disgust. He withdrew his fangs and dropped Tony on the floor. "Ugh, he's anemic. I hate it when they're anemic. It's like opening a bag of chips and finding it half full." He stepped over the body and knelt beside Thomas, who was cradling the head of the other man in his arms. The untrained eye might have interpreted this as a sign of remorse or regret, but I'd seen Thomas do this before and knew what it really meant. He was searching for the biggest vein. Thomas was efficient like that.

"How about this guy?" he asked Thomas, we took a quick bite and replied "Seems normal to me."

"Good deal," Chuck said. "We did the killing, so Thomas and I will split this one. You two can help yourselves to Mr. Half-Empty over there." The two of them began feeding in earnest. Barry and I shrugged at each other. It wasn't worth the fight, and they had a point. Besides, Chuck and Thomas had taken much more damage and lost more blood in being captured than Barry or myself had. They needed it more than we did. The two of us kicked aside the overturned table and started on Tony. His blood was a little thin, and I wouldn't have minded getting a little more before he dried out, but as a light meal, he was serviceable. Chuck finished up, and wiping the blood off his lips, called down for Marty to join us.

"Well, that was fast," he called back from the stairwell. "Quiet too. Didn't even hear a shot go off...Uh, why is your friend sucking on that guy's neck?" He'd reached the bottom of the stairs and was surveying the aftermath. The three of us were finished, but Thomas was still going after the last few ounces. Caught in what could generously be called a compromising position, with a mouth full of neck precluding him from explaining himself, Thomas froze in silence.

"It doesn't make him a bad person," Barry meekly interceded.

Marty shook his head in confusion and disgust. "Look, I'm glad for the company and all, but I can honestly say you are four of the weirdest people I've ever met."

"It's not what it looks like," he tried again.

"Dude, I don't even *know* what this looks like. And I don't *want* to know. That way it's just one less inexplicable thing I'll have to explain when tonight is over."

"That's the spirit," said Chuck. "You don't ask and we don't tell. I believe you're familiar with the policy. Now, where are the archives?"

"You tell me, carrot-eyes," Marty answered. "It's one of these rooms in the dark, with a bunch of locks on the door. You find it while I grab the keys off of Tony." Chuck made his way down the hall, inspecting the doors one by one. Meanwhile, Marty was rifling through Tony's pockets, searching for the keys. I hoped he wouldn't ask about the bite marks. He didn't. After some searching, he found the ring of keys and turned around to follow Chuck. The second his back was turned Thomas removed his fangs from the body, laid it down silently, and hopped to his feet, looking "Relaxed" the way guilty people do when they're trying to look innocent. It was very Charlie Chaplin. I had to stifle a laugh.

"Found it! I found it!" Chuck shouted from down the hall, his voice almost cracking with excitement.

"Follow us," I told Marty, and the three of us set off to join Chuck, with Marty following close behind. It was only seven or eight doors down from where the guards had sat, and very unassuming, save the iron bar welded above the doorknob with five keyholes cut into it.

"You see the keyholes?" Chuck asked anxiously.

"Yes Chuck, I see the keyholes," Marty responded with detectable sarcasm. Chuck was no fan of backtalk, and Marty probably would've been slapped, best-case scenario, for mouthing off, but it seemed like Chuck hadn't even heard him. He was clearly preoccupied with the prospect of getting at whatever was behind that door he'd dreamed about opening for so long.

"There's gonna be some trial and error involved, at least in the beginning, anyway," Marty told us, trying one key on the bottom lock, then another, then another, then another. Chuck looked like he was about to burst. The ninth key Marty tried was the correct one, and Chuck nearly jumped when he heard the click of the lock successfully turning.

"Bullseye," said Marty, counting off the next four keys on the ring and proceeding to unlock the next three keyholes. His hands froze in front of the last keyhole, and he turned his head to ask Chuck a question.

"I'm not gonna regret this, am I?"

"Just open it already."

Marty swallowed and opened the last lock. He pocketed the keys and pushed the door open. The room was just as dark on the inside as the rest of the hallway. Marty cautiously entered, and the moment his foot broke the plane of the doorway, the archives sprang to life. Overhead lights flashed on like explosions, running across the ceiling in parallel lines, blinding us in a violent wash of fluorescent light. I turned my back on the painful brightness and could hear all manner of machines clicking and whirring and rousing themselves from hibernation. There was the sound of something like an army of typewriters clicking away furiously, shuffling reams of paper at a time. Another sound, pinging like sonar, rose and fell in volume, wavelike, over the din of the other machines.

I could hear Chuck shouting behind me, but he was unintelligible over all the noise. I turned around and saw that he was quite visibly screaming at the top of his lungs, but any sounds he made were devoured by the machinery. He was gesturing frantically at Marty, waving his arms at the ground. Marty only shrugged and pointed at his ears. Chuck began waving his arms more emphatically, and in return Marty shrugged more emphatically. Having realized he was wasting his time, Chuck threw his hands up in the air in a final display of frustration and began scanning the nearest wall. Marty squinted at him in silent confusion. A few seconds later, Chuck raised his hand and pushed something on the wall. The lighting system was the first to react. It remained on, but cut its brightness roughly in half, leaving the room visible, but not painfully so. The sonar, if that's what it was, pinged, screeched, and went quiet. Next to go was the invisible typewriter brigade, whose clicking slowed abruptly, like it was powered by a fading battery. Over the next few seconds, the clicking petered out to silence, and the shuffling stopped. There was still a low-level humming and whirring, accompanied by a slow, steady tick that sounded a bit like a large metronome. The white noise of the machinery was audible and omnipresent, but low enough to be comfortably talked over.

"Good idea," said Marty, no longer shrugging or pointing at his ears. "How'd you do that?"

"Got lucky," answered Chuck. "The power control is over on that wall. It has three buttons, red, yellow, and green. The green button was glowing, so I pushed yellow. I guess that turns off everything that's nonessential, and noisy as hell. Good thing that worked; I was about to lose my damn mind."

"I know what you mean. But now that we're down here, and we can talk again, I'd like to know just what this place is," I said.

"This," Chuck answered me, "Is Fort Bulwark, the one and only staffed and operational military base remaining in the United States. After the Yukon Flu and the gas shortage collapsed the government, the smart people in the military realized things were about to get very violent. So they simply grabbed as many weapons and supplies as they could carry and took off. Everybody in the east headed west, and everybody in the west headed east, and they crossed paths in the middle of the country at Fort Bulwark. Hiking across a lawless, disease-riddled country is never fun, especially with a rocket launcher strapped to your back. When each side heard from the other that things were no better on their side of the country, they decided to stop moving and put down stakes here. Within a few weeks there were more soldiers and supplies in and around this fort than in the actual recognized armed forces, at which point the few men who hadn't deserted did so and either came to Bulwark or tried to get out of the country. By now the fort was grossly overpopulated, so they turned it into a compound, creating new buildings and fortifying the old ones. Things had gotten so desperate on the outside that law enforcement officials started shutting down police stations and taking what was left of their personnel to Bulwark. The police became something of an underclass, charged with most of the manual labor and other dangerous jobs, like raiding the surrounding areas for provisions when the original supplies ran low. It wasn't long before they'd cleaned out all of the food in the immediate area, and with the threat of starvation looming, the stage was set for an internal conflict that probably would've wiped out every remaining American soldier and policeman. However, just before it came to that, and I mean literally, just before, an old naval communications officer finished a pet project he'd been working on for some time; a satellite dish. At first he only intended to use it to pick up a few more TV channels, to keep the men occupied. When he finally got the thing wired up and running, he realized he'd built it a little too well; not only was he picking up television signals, which anybody with perseverance and a pair of rabbit ears can do, he was also getting other transmissions, most of them in English, but in a few other languages as well. It was another day before he figured out where the signals were coming from; spy satellites, secretly launched in the early 70's, when America was winning the space race.

"There wasn't a whole lot left of America anymore, but her satellites didn't know that. They just kept spinning around the globe, intercepting other countries' communications and sending them back to earth, just as they'd always done. The only difference was that now someone was listening again. When he decided to hook his satellite up to a printer, the archives were born. And this guy wasn't just a great scientist, he was an entrepreneur. He called a conference the night before everybody was going to start blowing everybody else up, and explained to the higher-ups what he'd built, how it was beneficial, and what would be needed before they could truly capitalize on it. Now that the men had something to do other than try to steal each others' food, they forgot for a moment how desperate things were and began assembling the materials their CO's had asked them to. One long and hungry week later, Fort Bulwark possessed four receiver dishes with internal printing technology and one two-way dish, capable of listening and talking at the same time. According to their intelligence, a small fleet of Thai battleships were heading for a major commercial dock in southern Japan. They sent Japan a signal, letting them know they had some useful military information, and would be willing to trade it for some food. The Japs were skeptical, as was to be expected, but in a gesture of goodwill, Bulwark sent them the ships' coordinates anyway. Two days later, Japan sent a signal back; they'd sunk all the battleships miles off-shore, in international waters. That night, a Japanese supply plane flew over Bulwark and dropped a month's worth of rations, along with a very lucrative contract aimed at procuring their services long term. Word got out to other countries that American satellites were "Talking" again, and they all sent gifts and contracts of their own. Three months later the fort was getting regular air-drops of food, water, medicine, weapons, ammo, construction materials, and of course, the equipment to build more satellite dishes. And that's the story of how a few thousand grunts, deserters, and thieves became the foremost information superpower in the world."

"That's...wow. But I still don't understand what this room is, and why it's so important to you."

"This room," he continued, "Is every bit as important to you as it is to me. To the rest of you, too. And to millions of others as well. As the fort became more established, it built more and more satellites, until it could pick up transmissions from every American satellite, 24 hours a day. Needless to say, this was a lot of raw data, and it was hard to tell what information would be useful to what country as it was streaming in. So the people in charge had this room, the archives, built. The receiver satellites pick up transmissions and send them to the machines here, which print out hard copies of the info they receive. Information officers read through the print-outs, figure out what's useful and what isn't, then separate the useful info according to which countries might be interested in it. That information then goes back out on the two-way satellites to the countries that've contracted out for it.

"That's their main job, but the archives serve a second purpose as well. Every single piece of data the fort receives is also printed out a second time, regardless of whether or not it was deemed useful by the info officers. These copies are alphabetized and filed away somewhere down here, just in case they should come in useful later. All manner of information comes through these satellites; weather reports, astronomical activity, current events, financial news, etc, etc. However, one of the main uses of these satellites, after they were first launched, at least, was to send information from country to country regarding the movements of fugitive war criminals following World War II. Once a war criminal showed up in the system, a file was created for him, and all information pertaining to his activities went into that file. That's why the four of us are here. We've come for the file of Alfred Deutchner."

"Deutchner? That sounds familiar," I said.

"It should. I told you about him earlier. One of Hitler's personal physicians, the one who escaped the bunker?"

"I didn't think anybody escaped Hitler's bunker," said Marty.

"Well, this guy did," Chuck shot back defensively. "And he has information about Hitler's medical history that could do the world a lot of good. But first, we need to find him."

"You guys aren't Nazis, are you?" asked Marty, eyeing Chuck with renewed suspicion.

"No," Chuck answered, with an affected calmness I knew masked an impending loss of temper. "Hitler had an unfortunate illness, which he kept secret, that many people still have today. It's not common, but more common than you might think. Deutchner cured it, made it out of Hitler's bunker, and went on the run. We know now that he's somewhere in America, but he keeps moving back and forth between the coasts. I suspect he's in New York, or will be arriving there shortly, but there's no way to know for sure. Unless, of course, your satellites are still tracking him. I doubt he's even bothering to use an alias anymore, but I'm sure he's withdrawn money from one of his foreign bank accounts recently. He always does before he makes a long trip. If we find out where and when he made the withdrawal, we get a rough idea of where he is based on how long ago it was made. Then, we go find him, make him talk, and start curing people."

"Wow," Marty said, obviously impressed. "That's a hell of a plan."

"I've been chasing him for a very long time. The low tech approach isn't getting it done. I'm ready to try something else."

"What disease did this guy cure?"

"Lung cancer."

"No shit?"

"None to speak of."

"And he's just keeping it all to himself? *Asshole.*"

"I agree. Now where's his folder?"

"No clue. This was Tony's beat, not mine. Besides, you seem to know a lot more about this room than I do."

"Fine. Everybody, start looking. I'm guessing it'll be in a file cabinet or locker of some sort, or maybe in one of the machines. Let me know as soon as you find it." Chuck swept the center of the room, looking over and under and inside every machine in his path. Thomas and Barry moved along the right wall, searching for drawers, storage facilities, doors to other rooms, or anything else of interest. Marty and I did the same, on the left. We talked to each other as we searched.

"Your friend is pretty bossy, huh? Mixed with a delightful pinch of sadism, of course."

I smiled. "Yeah, that's Chuck. He's a bit lacking in the interpersonal skills department. Don't take what he did to you personally. He's hard on everybody at first. You should've seen the way he used to kick Barry around."

"Which one is Barry?"

"Dirty white shirt, green tie."

"Ah. He's with the man in the prison uniform who has my gun and chews on dead people?"

"Yeah, that's Thomas."

"Is he really the guy we should be trusting with a fire arm?"

"He's the most stable of the four of us. I'm sure he'll give you your gun back if you just ask him. We'll just take the other two guns outside the door."

"That sounds reasonable enough. So how long have you four been friends?"

"Uh, not that long. Maybe a week or two."

"Seriously? How did you all meet then?"

"Chuck sort of…arranged our first get-together." It was technically true.

"It always comes back to Chuck, doesn't it?"

"Yeah, I suppose you're right. He's just that kind of guy. He's a violent, grouchy, bigoted asshole, but the truth is, and he'd never admit this, by the way, but once you're in with Chuck, he takes care of you. There's actually a decent person inside that mess. I never told him this, but he's really changed my life. Before I met Chuck, I was just sort of drifting. There wasn't a whole lot of purpose to my life. Then he shows up, and now I'm chasing a Nazi across America to cure a disease. For the first time in my life, I have a real goal. I'm going to change people's lives, for the better. That wouldn't be possible without Chuck. Being around him, it takes a lot out of you, but you get it back, and then some."

Marty and I walked along in silence, absently checking the wall for anything abnormal. It was a minute or so before Marty spoke again.

"So, lung cancer, huh?"

"Lung cancer," I confirmed, sticking to the cover story.

"My old man died of lung cancer a few years ago. Killed him real slow." We were using the excuse of searching the wall to avoid looking at each other.

"I'm sorry," I offered, unsure of what to say.

"Thanks. I am too. He was…he was a good man." More silent searching. "I'd sure like an hour alone with that asshole you guys are chasing. He maybe could've saved my dad, and who knows how many others."

I had an idea. "Come with us, Marty."

"What?"

"You heard me. Come with us. You yourself said you were unhappy here. Living with people you hate, stuck in a pointless job, doing just enough to get by. Life is too short for that, isn't it? Leave here. Come with us."

"Eh, it's not as bad as I made it out to be. The food is pretty good, and we get movies on Sunday, and-"

"And when all that's done, when you're dead Marty, what are they gonna say at your funeral? 'Here lies Marty. He ate pretty good food and watched movies on Sunday.' That is, if any of these people who leave you behind to pace empty hallways all night show up. You think they'll show up at your funeral?"

"I don't see what that has to do with anything."

"You keep living this life, when you die, you die. Sure, it's comfortable, but it's empty. When it's over, there's nothing left behind. Time is gonna wash your memory away like dust on a windshield, Marty. We can give you more then that. This will be a hard trip, I won't lie to you, and I wouldn't invite you along if I didn't think you could handle it. But if you make this trip with us, Marty, I promise you, you'll never have to fear death again. Do you know why that is? Because every time this cure saves a life, you come back a little bit. The person you save doesn't even have to know your name, or what it was you did, and it'll still work. You will be reincarnated as an endless stream of good deeds. You will live on in the lives of wives who didn't lose their husbands, of brothers who didn't lose their sisters, of fathers who didn't lose their sons. That's immortality, Marty, in the best way possible. It's not never dying, it's never staying dead. Do you want to be immortal, Marty?"

Marty was looking at me again, but he wasn't speaking.

"You're lucky," I continued. I was on a roll now. "You're lucky because this is entirely your choice. Not all of us got to have that luxury. By the time I realized I was doing something positive, I was already 1/3 of the way across the country and in too deep to go back. When we find this guy and start saving people, it'll still be great, but it could've been better. It can and *will* be better for you, if you choose to come with us, because you'll have chosen to help the world of your own free will. I just sort of stumbled into it. You'll be able to say it was your intention all along. The intent enhances the end result. Does that make any sense to you?" I wasn't even sure if it made any sense to me. I just started talking, and that's what came out. Marty, meanwhile, still hadn't answered. He looked at me, hard, then turned his appraising stare on Chuck and Barry and Thomas.

He finally replied. "It does." He smiled. "And I'll think about it."

We went back to quietly searching the archive wall. I think we both knew he wanted to come; I could tell he was on the verge of acceptance, he just needed some time to process. That was fine. It was a big decision to make. I wasn't planning to have him turned into a vampire, at least, not unless he decided that was what he wanted. There would be time to open that can of worms later. Truthfully, he would be more useful to our mission in his current state, able to move freely throughout the daylight. Still, if he wanted to join our team, so to speak, I wouldn't have a problem with it. I would just make sure that unlike the rest of us, he knew what he was in for. As I said above, I wanted everything to be his choice. If we were going to do this, we would do it with fairness, and honesty.

I felt a sudden pang of guilt at the realization that despite all my idealism, there was a fairly important piece of information I'd concealed from him.

"Hey Marty."

"Yeah?"

"Assuming you were to come with us, would it bother you much if it turned out that this guy hadn't cured lung cancer, but something else?"

"Well, that depends. Is the 'Something else' just an inconvenience, like athlete's foot, or would it still be something serious, something life-threatening, just not lung cancer?"

"Definitely the last one. We don't know everything about this guy, but we know he was messing with some very serious stuff. Way beyond athlete's foot."

"Then the answer is no, it wouldn't bother me. Helping people is helping people, right?"

"Yeah," I replied. "Helping people is helping people.

"Not that I've agreed to anything yet. I'm still thinking."

"Absolutely. Take all the time you need."

"Hey! We found something!"

It was Barry, calling unseen from several yards in front of us. We followed his voice behind a huge gray monolith of a machine that hummed softly, and had a series of flashing yellow lights running up and down its considerable height. Behind this machine, carved out of the wall, was a very long and narrow hallway, only wide enough to accommodate one person at a time, that stretched many yards into the distance before disappearing into darkness. No one had gone in yet, though Chuck was nearly salivating at the prospect of doing so.

"The walls are lined with filing cabinets," Barry observed. "Hundreds of them."

"I'd say that if whatever you're looking for is here, it'll be in one of those cabinets," said Marty.

"Oh it's here," Chuck replied. "It's definitely here. Now it's just a matter of finding the actual file."

Marty produced a small flashlight from his back pocket. "There're letters on the drawers. They must store their files alphabetically."

"Well, get in there and start checking the 'D's,' man!" Chuck looked like he was going to burst a vein from impatience.

"Right, check the 'D's.' We're searching an alphabetized storage system for a man whose last name begins with the letter 'D,' and you want me to go check the "D's.' I swear, we'd all be lost in this crazy mixed-up world if not for your leadership and problem-solving skills."

I liked this guy.

"Go check the 'D's.' *Now.*"

"Sir yes sir," he grunted with comedic obedience, and before Chuck could get in the last word he was already walking down the narrow hallway, casually sweeping his flashlight back and forth while jingling his keys. I really liked this guy.

The four of us watched Marty moving down the hallway, his body gradually melding with the darkness until all we could clearly see was the light of his flashlight rocking back and forth. We could hear his keys jingling faintly, but they sounded like they were coming from miles away. Minutes ticked by, until Marty could no longer be seen or heard.

"Do you think something happened to him?" Barry asked.

"Maybe he found an exit," Chuck theorized. "Maybe he made a run for it. He'll pay if he did."

"I really doubt he'd do something like that," I answered, not yet willing to let the others in on his recruitment until he gave confirmation.

"Based on what?" asked Chuck.

"Based on the fact that he already had the chance, when we were breaking up the guard's blackjack game, and he showed no interest in doing so."

Chuck was quiet for a moment, planning his next argument. "Maybe he didn't run then because he knew he'd have a better opportunity later. Maybe this was his plan all along, to leave us waiting here while he runs through this rat hole and comes out the other side."

"I think," Thomas declared with effortless authority, "That this is a very long tunnel, and we should give him some more time before we start jumping to conclusions of any sort."

"So we just sit here and wait and see if he comes back?"

"That," Thomas answered "Is exactly what we're going to do. You're stressing too much, Chuck; try and relax. You'll get what you came for."

Chuck sat down and sighed, resting his back against the concrete wall. "If any part of this goes wrong," he muttered, eyes closed, "It'll be on your heads"

A bright beam of light washed out of the tunnel and spilled off onto the side of the big gray machine. It wasn't sweeping back and forth, but holding a steady line. We all saw it at once, and scurried to look down the tunnel. Marty was making his way back to us, nonchalantly, with his flashlight in one hand and a thin manila folder by his side in the other.

"Looks like our heads are gonna be just fine," I quipped. Thomas looked at me out of the corner of his eye and smiled. Chuck gave us a look, but it was more playful than anything else. "For now."

Marty stepped out of the tunnel, squinting in the relative brightness. "Man, I need some space. Let's get back to the main room." One by one we slid between the grey machine and the wall, returning to the massive open space that had greeted us when we'd first opened the door.

"I had no idea that thing went so far back. I walked that whole time and only got to "D," and that's less than 1/6th of the alphabet. It must go on for miles, might even run under the whole base."

"Let's see the file," Chuck said, ignoring him. Marty handed it over to Chuck, who snatched it out of his hands and immediately flipped it open. He held it close enough to his face that only he could read it. His eyes darted almost comically back and forth as they scanned the first page. As he flipped to the second page, then the third, then the fourth, the expression on his face morphed from excitement, to surprise, to serious contemplation, then finally and most severely, to white-hot, barely contained rage.

"Where is the rest of the file," he said. Grammatically, it was a question, but there was no inquiring tone in his voice, no inflection of any sort. In fact, it was the only time I'd ever heard Chuck speak with no emotion whatsoever. In hindsight, that should've clued me in that something bad was coming, but my mind was solely focused on finding out what was inside that folder, and it entertained no other thoughts.

"That's…that's it," Marty stammered. For all our heightened senses, it was Marty who first felt the storm brewing.

"Where is the rest of the file," he repeatedly blankly.

"I swear, that's all there was. I even checked the files on either side of it. This was the only one with your man's name on it."

"This," he paused, closing the file and holding it up to his face, "Is incomplete and inaccurate. Where is the rest of the file."

"Look buddy, I don't know what to tell you, but-" And that was as far as he got. Chuck grabbed him by the shirt and threw him into one of the machines. It was similar to the large grey one we'd seen earlier, but smaller and with an anodized black shell. He smashed into it with a terrific hollow clang that reverberated long after he'd fallen motionless to the floor. The three of us were stunned, but it wasn't until Chuck had turned back around to face us with violence etched into his features that we all noticed the same key detail at once; both of his hands were empty. In throwing Marty, he'd lost his grip on the folder, which was now lying on the floor about ten feet away.

It was only a fraction of a second before Chuck noticed us noticing his hands, and realized what had happened. All four of us dove for the file at once. Through good fortune and proximity, I managed to land on top of it first. I drew myself into a ball atop it and braced my muscles for the impact. When the other three hit me, it was like being sideswiped by a car and then pinned under it. Fists and elbows swung wildly above me. Knees and feet clamored onto my back. I simply kept my head down and stayed in a defensive position until the dog-piling was over. Suddenly the weight rolled off of me like a wave, followed by the squeaking of shoes frantically trying to gain purchase on the tiled floor.

Thomas yelled "Freeze!" and I heard him cock Marty's gun.

"You wouldn't," Chuck snorted, full of bravado.

"I would," Thomas answered, his voice steeled. "Now back up. Slowly."

"I don't feel like it."

"Do what he says," chimed in Barry, sounding impressively resolute himself.

"Oh, look who thinks he's a tough guy now," Chuck taunted.

"Look who never was," Barry replied. Chuck didn't say anything, but I could imagine the look on his face.

"Ethan, it's safe to get up. Are you alright?"

"Yeah, I'm fine," I answered, rising slowly to my feet. "Somebody kneed me in the neck, but I'm fine."

"And you've got the file?"

"Yeah."

"Good. Barry, go check on Marty. Chuck, you stay where you are."

"Look who's full of orders when he's the only one armed."

"Would you just shut up for five minutes? I said DON'T MOVE!"

"Marty's alive, but unconscious," Barry called out, moving him into a seated position against the black machine and checking his pulse. "Heartbeat's fine, but he took a bad knock on the head."

"Thanks. Keep an eye on him, let us know if anything changes. Ethan, take a look at the file and tell us what it says." I didn't have to be told twice.

"You're wasting your time," Chuck said petulantly.

"I said shut up!" Thomas yelled again.

I opened the file to the first page and began to read. It was full of Deutchner's identifying info, things like height, weight, eye color, hair color, blood type, fingerprints, etc. There was a single black and white picture photocopied at the bottom that showed him standing with two other Nazi officers. Deutchner was circled in red. He was tall and blond, with sharp, Teutonic facial features. Basically your typical Nazi, except a little bit older, in his mid 40's perhaps. The second page was titled "Background and Postwar Activities."

Alfred Deutchner, born January 2nd, 1888, Hamburg Germany. Studied medicine at university, received degree in haematology 1913. Worked briefly in small hospital (unknown) prior to joining Nazi party at its inception. Headed a new Nazi medical research department (unknown, records destroyed). Spent 8 years at Dachau with research initiative before transferring to work as one of Hitler's personal physicians, apparently at Hitler's own insistence. Confirmed to have been in Hitler's Bunker at time of his death, but escaped (method/ tactic unknown), and fled Germany posing as a civilian baker.

Traveled itinerantly throughout southern Europe/northern Africa for 15 years under many aliases (unknown, records destroyed). Arrived in United States October 1962, stowed away on cargo vessel. Fearing war crimes persecution, he traveled extensively between the east and west coasts for 4 years. No record of activities, 1967 (nonexistent). Resurfaced in Chicago, early 1968. Died in his hotel room November 11th, 1968. Cause of death unconfirmed, heart disease suspected. Buried November 15th, 1968, in Dranesville cemetery, under the name Jonathan Winkler (pictures follow). No known estate.

The next page was a series of color photographs stapled to a sheet of blank paper, flipbook style. The first three were overhead shots, taken from an airplane or satellite of some sort. The last of the three, zoomed in the furthest and of the highest resolution, showed an open grave and a casket beside it. On one side of the grave was a man reading from a book. On the other side stood four men paying their respects. The next photos were taken from the ground, and were much sharper than the aerial shots. One showed the man standing by himself, a priest, reading from an old Bible. Another showed three of the four men who'd come to see Deutchner off (I assumed the mysterious fourth man who didn't appear in any of the ground pictures was the photographer). I recognized two of them as the men who'd been standing with Deutchner in his original identifying photo, older and grayer but clearly still the same men. One of them was staring into the open grave and appeared inconsolably sad, bearing the burden of his grief with the silent dignity often seen on elderly people who have watched too many friends go into the ground. The other man appeared anxious and paranoid, torn between honoring his old friend and keeping a low profile. I didn't recognize the third man, standing at the foot of the casket and wearing a long black coat. He was younger than the others. Individual shots of these men were also included, but they were all still doing more or less the same thing they were in the group picture. There were two more pictures included; one, a shot of Deutchner's headstone, small and unostentatious, inscribed with his assumed name and actual dates of birth and death. The final picture was the most provocative, it was a close-up of Alfred Deutchner's dead body in the casket, now opened. He looked older than he did in his identifying photo, but he definitely didn't look 80. He did, however, definitely appear dead.

I flipped to the fourth and final page. No way was Deutchner dead. No way he had been dead for over a decade. Surely the final page would be titled something like "After the Fake Funeral" or "What *Really* Happened" or something to that effect. Actually, it was a blank title page. Well, not totally blank. "Copyright Atlas Incorporated, 1977" was written in fine print on the bottom right hand corner. But other than that, yeah, totally blank.

Chuck had some serious explaining to do.

"He's dead."

"What?" Thomas turned his head, keeping one eye on me and one eye on Chuck. "Who's dead?"

"Tell him, Chuck. Tell him who's dead."

A hint of embarrassment twitched across his face. "I told you, the information in that file is-"

"Shut up! Just shut-up! For Christ's sake, will you just tell us the truth for once?!"

"I've *been* telling you the truth the entire time! It's that file that's wrong! They must be hiding him somewhere around here."

"And why the hell would they do that?"

"Because he's *not dead*!" Any hint of embarrassment had been swallowed by denial and indignation .

"Chuck," I seethed, trying to control my temper but not doing a very good job. "You pulled the three of us out of our lives, turned us into fucking vampires, and took us halfway across the country to chase a man who's been dead for a decade. You're going to have to do a hell of a lot better than that."

"I don't owe you anything," he snotted.

"You owe us our lives back, is what you owe us! Can you do that? Can you fix it like it was before you ruined everything?!"

"It looked to me like the rest of you had done a pretty good job of ruining your own lives by the time I found you. You all should *thank* me. You should thank me for what I gave you, what I made you."

"Murderers? We should thank you for making us murderers?"

"No. You should thank me for making you powerful. Making you strong. Heightening your senses. Giving your lives a purpose."

"But that's just it Chuck, there was no purpose! We thought we were doing something good, but we were just the cast in your crazy-ass game of make-believe! You said our lives had no purpose, well *your* life hasn't had a purpose since you fucked up and let your little vampire nation-state get slaughtered 200 years ago, and you can't handle that so you run around chasing ghosts and redemption when all you're really doing is just adding to the body count! How many more have to die, Chuck? How many more have to die before you can face reality and admit you blew it?"

"At least one more," he said, pulling the half scissor out of his pocket.

"Chuck, put that away," said Thomas. He knew he would be caught in mine and Chuck's crossfire, but he also knew that if there was any hope of maintaining order, he had to stay between us with the gun. From behind him, I could see the barrel of the rifle fixed on Chuck, begin to quiver slightly.

"This doesn't have to be your fight, Thomas. Just step aside, and I give you my word-"

I heard another gun cock and saw Chuck wince slightly. "I…am getting *seriously tired* of you beating me up." Marty was standing behind Chuck, grinding the barrel of a pistol into the base of his skull. The sweat from his forehead was running into the tears on his cheeks, and the look on his face suggested he was moments away from screaming and pulling the trigger and dropping to his knees and pummeling the corpse with his bare hands until his rage and emotional exhaustion had burned out and evaporated. I am fairly certain that the proverb *beware the wrath of a patient man* was coined under similar circumstances.

"The file says…what the file says. If our intelligence was bad, other countries wouldn't pay for it and everybody on this base would've starved to death years ago. Now *I myself* don't know what the file says, but Ethan seems pretty pissed about it and Thomas has a gun pointed at your head and it was Barry's idea for me to get up and do this, and I trust them a lot more than you so that tells me somewhere along the line you fucked up big time. You also fucked up big time when you threw me into that machine for no damn reason. That makes two strikes, and if you do anything from this point on without my sole and express permission, that will constitute your third strike, and I will personally make sure that you die"

"You do realize I could spin around and rip your head off before you had the chance to fire a single shot, don't you?"

"Maybe you could, maybe you couldn't. What I do know is that if you did that, then Thomas would plug you in the face before I hit the ground. You could kill me, but in the act of doing so you'd also kill yourself. You, my friend, are caught between a rock and a disagreeable alternative. Sucks, doesn't it?"

Chuck was silent.

"That's what I like to hear."

"Everybody shut up for a minute." Barry had his ear pressed against the door where we'd come in. "Oh man. I hear people coming. It sounds like they're in a hurry."

"What? How many?" asked Thomas, splitting his gaze between Chuck and the situation developing behind him.

"I don't know, I can't tell. They're running down the big staircase, I think. It all sounds like *stompstompstomp* to me."

Leaving Chuck's containment in the hands of Thomas and Marty, I ran to the door and pressed my ear next to where Barry was listening. "I hear it too. What now?"

"We could hide," Barry offered. "In the tunnel. We can see in there, they can't."

"No way out," countered Marty. "They'll see the bodies outside and search every inch of this place. All they'd have to do is toss a grenade inside and we'd be killed or trapped."

"Let's fight them," Chuck suggested to no one's surprise.

"I don't trust you," Marty and I answered simultaneously.

"They're through the double doors, headed for the small staircase," Barry told us. "Whatever we're gonna do, we need to choose fast."

"I can get us out of this," Marty said quickly. "Everybody kneel against the wall, hands behind your heads. Thomas, throw me my gun."

"Like hell I'm gonna-"

"Actually, you are," Marty growled, grabbing one of Chuck's arms at the wrist and wrenching it behind his back. Using the pistol wedged against Chuck's neck he pushed him face first into the wall, then kicked him in the back of one knee, then the other. Chuck dropped to his knees, and Marty twisted his arms behind his head. "Now stay still and be quiet." Amazingly, Chuck did exactly that.

"That was awesome!" Thomas said, grinning excitedly.

"Thank you. Now please give me my gun and do the same." Thomas ran and slid on his knees, coming to a stop inches in front of the wall. He threw the rifle back over his head, and Marty caught it one-handed.

Barry gave his last report. "They're in the hall outside. They just found the bodies."

"Enough with the play-by-play, get against the wall! You too Ethan!" Barry and I bolted for the wall. We tried the same trick Thomas did, sliding in knees-first, but Barry came in too slow and had to waddle in the last few inches, whereas I went in too fast and smacked my forehead on the wall. I had just gotten my hands behind my head when the door burst open and I heard unfamiliar voices address Marty.

"Hendrix! The blacks are back! And the-what the hell are *they* doing down here?! Who said to let 'em out?!"

I heard at least five distinct guns cock, and didn't have to guess where they were pointed. 'Start talking Marty,' I thought to myself.

"Commander said to bring them down here and run background checks. A little over an hour ago. Tony let us in. You can lower your weapons; it looks like you guys beat most of the fight out of them when you took 'em off the train."

"Tony is *dead* Hendrix!"

"Wait, what?! He was just outside the door!" Thankfully, Marty was a surprisingly competent actor.

"He still is, Hendrix. Him and the other guy, what's-his-name, both dead. Stabbed in the neck with something, but there's no blood. You didn't hear anything?"

"No, I didn't. The machines get kinda loud in here."

There was a moment of silence. "These four have been under your watch the entire time?"

"The entire time, sir. When they weren't in the cell they were up against the wall, just like they are now. Did you say the blacks were back earlier?"

"Hell yes they're back! The west guard tower is burning down right now!"

"But it's Wednesday, night maneuvers. They never come during night maneuvers."

The other man sighed. "It's just been that kinda night. Get these four back in the cell, then get outside immediately. Just follow the smoke."

"Yes sir. Right away."

"Good. We'll see you there. Ok guys, back outside!" The door slammed, and I could hear several pairs of boots stomping back up the stairs, the sound fading out until it ceased entirely.

"Ok, we're clear," Marty announced. "We need to get to the train right away."

"What do you mean, 'We?'" Chuck asked, rising to his feet with the rest of us.

"I'm coming with you."

"What?!" Chuck cried incredulously.

"I think it's a good idea," I told him.

"I do too," said Barry.

Chuck was dumbfounded. "What...why would you even want to? You don't believe me, remember? Your damn file says I'm full of crap."

Marty shrugged. "Maybe, maybe not. I certainly wouldn't mind being proven wrong on that account. And even if you are wrong, going with you gets me far away from here. I'm not about to run out there and die for a bunch of tools who could care less what happens to me. There's gotta be something out there better than this. If I stay here, I won't find it."

Chuck stared hard into Marty, without speaking. A moment later, he asked for the final vote. "Thomas?" There was a clearly plaintive tone to his voice.

Thomas regarded Marty, much as Chuck had just done. "So far," he began, with a smile tugging at the corner of his mouth, "I'm impressed. I say he comes with us."

Chuck sighed with mock exasperation. It was a gesture of submission, but surprisingly, a good-humored one. "Let's hope these three are right about you. Welcome aboard."

"Thank you," Marty replied with genuine sincerity. "I promise I won't slow you down."

"I know you won't. Lead the way, sport."

"Will do," he said earnestly. "Unfortunately, your train is on the western side of the compound, but I believe there's a hall that winds around the kitchen that can get us close without having to go outside."

"Sounds good."

"Alright gentleman, let's get out of here." Marty raised his rifle to his shoulder and headed for the door. We followed him single-file, first Chuck, then me, then Thomas, then Barry. Marty had his hand on the doorknob when Chuck interrupted him.

"Hey, Marty?"

"Yeah?" Marty answered, turning his head to look over his shoulder.

Chuck placed a hand on either side of Marty's face, and twisted so violently his head nearly made a full rotation before rebounding back, the life snatched from his irises. The snap was deafening. He crumpled to the floor. Chuck pushed his body to the side with his boot.

"That," he said, looking back to face us before opening the door and stepping into the hallway, "Is what I think about what you think." And then he left.

I looked down at Marty, and Marty looked up at me with the sightless eyes of the dead.

I could make Chuck bite him, I thought. *I could make Chuck bite him and bring him back.*

But I knew that even if I could force Chuck to do that, I realized it would be pointless. His neck had been so thoroughly snapped he might as well have been decapitated. That was the ultimate death. No coming back from that. I decided that Chuck would get the same.

I stepped into the hallway and silently pulled my pistol from my pocket. Chuck was walking nonchalantly toward the stairs, his back turned, like he was leaving the post office instead of a murder scene. The back of his head was perfectly exposed. I threw the hammer and aimed my shot, but before I could take it a hand gently wrapped around my wrist and pushed it down.

"That won't bring him back," Thomas whispered calmly, and in that moment I hated him entirely. His stoic temperament, his unflappable rationality, his unconscious mimicry of the man who needed a bullet in the head more than anyone I'd ever known. He held me by the wrist, and he paralyzed me.

"He shouldn't have done that to him," I choked out. It was the understatement of the year, but it was all I had. "He shouldn't have done that."

"I know, he whispered again. "It was wrong, very wrong, and he'll be held accountable for it. But now isn't the time. We need him to get out of here alive."

"Why?"

"He's been here before. He knows this place. He knew all about the archives. I'd bet he knows a way out of here. If you kill him, we could wander this place for days, until they find us and shoot us. As much as it hurts, we have to let him walk away from this. For the time being, at least." He had a point. Goddamn Thomas and his goddamn points.

"Ok," I said, consciously steeling my voice. Thomas let go of my hand. I looked down at the floor. "Where are the other guns?"

"The other men probably took them when they took the bodies away." He revealed his right hand to me. He was holding one of the assault rifles. "I've still got this one. It's fully loaded." He didn't have to say where he'd gotten it from. We both knew it was a parting gift from Marty.

"Thanks, but you keep it," I told him, putting the pistol back in my pocket. Thomas was smart to have grabbed it, but if I'd taken possession of it, it would have been like I was looting his body.

"Once we're safe, we'll figure out what to do about Chuck, but we need to get out of here first. Ok?"

"Ok."

"Good. Stay close to me." He started up the stairs after Chuck.

Barry, who had been watching from the doorway, walked up beside me. We both looked straight ahead.

"You know, I would've let you do it," he said.

"Thanks."

When Barry and I got to the top of the stairs, Thomas and Chuck were waiting for us. "You're gonna have to move a lot faster than that," Chuck said.

You're not about to make not shooting you any easier, are you? Of course you're not.

Chuck led us back the way we came, past our cell, into new hallways and new staircases, always higher and higher. I hadn't realized just how far underground we were. Whereas Thomas and I had the sense to keep our heads down and our weapons out, Chuck simply strolled through the compound like he owned it, busting through doors with little to no concern for what was on the other side. Thankfully, the entire building appeared to have been emptied. As we moved closer to the surface, we could hear gunshots, explosions, and indistinguishable yelling getting louder. The acrid stench of smoke grew more pungent as well.

"Something's going on outside," Chuck helpfully noted. I could literally feel my trigger finger itch. We kept moving. The noises outside escalated from noticeable to deafening. Finally, we reached a massive, windowless set of steel double doors. "Ok everyone, this is it. 1…2…3!" We pushed through the doors and charged outside.

Chapter 8: The Battle of Fort Bulwark

"I've had a perfectly wonderful evening. But this wasn't it."

-Groucho Marx

We came out on the train tracks, about a hundred yards east of the fire, and walked into absolute chaos. The guard tower, at least three or four stories tall, still stood for the time being, though it was completely engulfed in flames. Several men were attempting to put it out with a fire hose that ran back into the compound, but they kept dropping it as they tried to dodge bullets that seemed to come from the shadows themselves. Jeeps with machine guns loaded in the bed were tearing through the mud and ash, strafing the men that were vainly returning fire, then the other jeeps that roared out to confront them. A grenade went off, and men screamed. Two massive tanks were rolling towards each other in what promised to be a very interesting game of chicken. Watching from the outside, through the darkness and smoke, it was nearly impossible to tell what was going on in this brutal, confusing affair. We were able to catch fleeting glimpses of the silhouettes of men advancing upon the defenders of Fort Bulwark, killing them, and disappearing. Back into their ranks? Into the fort itself? It was impossible to say. The two tanks were now within each other's range, and commenced firing. It sounded like the end of the world.

"What the hell is going on?" Thomas asked.

"Uh, guys," Barry began, "Look behind you."

We turned around and saw there was smoke in the eastern sky as well. It wasn't produced by a fire or an explosion, but rather by the Yukon Glory itself, as it rolled away toward the horizon.

We all looked at each other. Nobody said anything. Each of us wore identical expressions of dumbfounded shock. Then, we ran. Faster than we'd ever ran in our lives. The train wasn't too far gone; we could still catch it. We ran, and we ran, and we ran some more. We were getting tired, but the train was picking up speed. Finally, it disappeared over the horizon, the black cloud of smoke left in its wake dissipated, and the Yukon Glory was lost.

The four of us were doubled over, hands on our knees, sucking desperately for air. We gasped rhythmically, in unison, like a chant. Our paralyzing lack of options hung over us even more thickly than the smoke in the air. Thomas was the first to speak.

"Ok…what…now?"

Barry shot him a look of exhausted anger and disgust. "What… *now?!* We're fucked! This…is a fuck!"

"Wait…*what's* a fuck?"

"This! *This!*" Barry exclaimed, spreading his arms wide. One hand pointed at where the train had been; the other, back towards the burning tower and the thundering tanks. "*This,* is a FUCK!"

"Oh…gotcha."

Thomas sat down, and we all did the same, forming a loose circle. It was pow-wow time. Barry faced the battle at the fort. I faced the Yukon Glory's last known whereabouts. Chuck sat at my left; Thomas at my right.

"Well, we have to do something," I said finally.

"And that something is…." Chuck smarmed. Nobody knew what that something was.

"Maybe we can wait for the battle at the Fort to blow over, then sneak back in."

"Then do what?" Barry asked.

"I don't KNOW, Barry," Thomas replied, clearly annoyed. "But we can't just sit on the train tracks feeling sorry for ourselves. Maybe there's something at the Fort that we missed, I don't know. At least I'm contributing, *God*."

Barry's eyes suddenly grew very wide. "Guys, look behind you. Slowly."

"Seriously dude, that's not funny," I told him.

"I know it's not. But you really need to get up and turn around. Slowly."

The four of us rose from the ground and turned to face the battle at the Fort, careful not to make any sudden moves. Two men had materialized on the train tracks, perhaps twenty yards away from us. They were dressed entirely in black, and had equally dark shoulder-length hair. The only flesh visible was that of their faces and hands; it was pallid and hairless, and appeared to be stretched a little too tightly over their bones. Their most distinguishing feature, however, was the hazy, deep-red aura that hung about their bodies, outlining their frames in an eerie, unnatural glow. They both stood stock still, the crimson fog swirling casually about them, regarding us dispassionately.

"They're glowing, right?" I asked no one in particular. "Other people see the glowing?"

"I see it."

"I see it." Thomas and Barry answered.

"You have got to be kidding me," Chuck said. I could see beads of sweat crawling down the side of his face. He was actually trembling.

Barry was maintaining his composure better than Chuck. "These guys are creeping me out. What should we do?"

"Shoot them," Chuck gasped. He was the only one of us still breathing heavily. "Thomas…shoot them."

"I'm definitely getting the creepy vibes too," Thomas answered, "But they haven't actually…you know, done anything yet."

"They will," he said, with a slight quiver in his voice. "It's just a matter of who does it first, and this time, it's going to be us. For everybody's sake, just trust me and shoot them."

Thomas and Chuck locked eyes for a moment, then Thomas relented and raised Marty's gun. "Hey! Hey you!" he called out. Chuck winced and muttered something under his breath. "Who are you? What do you want?" Neither man moved. "If you don't answer me, I'm going to shoot!" They didn't answer him. He swallowed hard and refocused his aim. "Last chance!"

Chuck turned to him and snapped "For God's sake, if you're not going to-" but he was cut off by the sound of the gun. Thomas squeezed off two shots, which landed squarely in the chest of each man. They both took a step back, but they reacted more like they had been shoved with one arm than shot with an assault rifle. The red mist surrounding them darkened and swirled more animatedly.

"How did they-"

"Shoot them again," Chuck ordered through clenched teeth. "Shoot them like you mean it."

"They still haven't done any-"

"DO IT!" he screamed, and Thomas gritted his teeth and held down the trigger. The recoil was pounding him ferociously in the shoulder, but he retained control, spraying dozens of rounds into both of the men. Their bodies jerked violently in the hail of bullets before collapsing on the tracks. Thomas sent a few more rounds after their prone bodies, but most of them bounced off the rails and ricocheted violently with piercing shrieks. His gun clicked. "I'm out," he declared, looking in disbelief at what he'd done.

"Then run," Chuck said, sprinting and jumping over the motionless bodies and charging back towards the Fort. Barry was right on his heels. Thomas hesitated a moment, still held in the thrall of the carnage he'd created, and then he too leapt over the men and took off. It was my turn, and I ran and jumped just as the others had done, but I tripped and went down hard, smashing my chin on the tracks. I struggled to get back to my feet and keep moving, but I couldn't. My foot was caught on something. I rolled over onto my back, and found myself staring into the face of one of the men Thomas had just shot. His hand was wrapped vice-like around my ankle. I struggled to kick free, but he kept his grip with no discernable effort. Through my mounting panic I noticed he had a queer, nauseous smile on his face. His cheekbones were shuddering as well. Then, with a single horrific pop, his lower jaw dislocated and swung down, revealing two sets of curved, six-inch stainless steel fangs. That's when I started screaming.

I continued kicking and struggling to break free, but he paid me no mind. He was eyeing my leg hungrily, and he pulled me toward and underneath him until his head was above the top of my thigh. A passage from my tenth grade anatomy textbook flew through my mind.

The femoral artery, located within the thigh muscle, is one of the main passages through which blood is supplied to the lower body.

With a low hissing, he stretched his disjointed mouth even wider, to the point where he could've easily swallowed my entire head, or in this case, bitten completely through my thigh. I clenched my eyes and braced for it, but the bite didn't come. Rather, there was a resounding *whump*, and when I opened my eyes I saw Thomas standing above me, pulverizing the face of whatever this thing was with the butt of his gun. It took three more blows before he loosed his grip and I was able to kick him off of me. Thomas helped pull me to my feet, then, swinging his gun like a golf club, blasted my attacker on the crown of his skull with the pointed corner of the gunstock. We took off right away in pursuit of Chuck and Barry. After about five seconds or so, we'd built up an impressive amount of speed, and I chanced a look behind us to make sure we weren't being followed. We were. Both of the red glowing men were on their feet and running, at such speed that they would soon overtake us. The jaw of the one who'd attacked me was still dangling from his skull, bouncing obscenely as he ran.

"They're on us!" I cried to Thomas.

"I know."

"They'll get to us before we get to the Fort."

"I know."

"So what the hell do we do?!"

Thomas glanced over his shoulder and saw them swiftly gaining ground.

"I don't know."

We were now close enough to the fort that we were on the outside edge of the battle. Bodies were strewn about the dirt, which was damp and getting wetter. The tanks were still firing at each other, though they'd both retreated a bit. One of them was positioned to the right, only a few yards away from us if we slightly altered our course. It wasn't much, but it was the only form of protection we could possibly reach before they ran us down.

"The tank!" I shouted to Thomas. "Head for the tank!"

He nodded and began sloping right. We were barreling towards the tank as fast as we could, unable to slow down without making ourselves vulnerable. Unless we could jump up and onto the tank's neck-high platform, we were going to smash right into it. If we were fresh, we could've probably made it happen, but we had been running a long time at this point and I could feel lots of important muscles starting to cramp. This wasn't turning out to be the plan I'd hoped for.

We were only a few feet from the tank now, and closing fast, and I braced my muscles for what was almost assuredly going to be my last poorly planned decision on this earth, when Chuck and Barry popped up from the other side of the tank, assault rifles at the ready. We looked at each other in absolute shock, before Chuck bellowed "Get down!" and I tucked and rolled hard into the unforgiving side of the tank. Thomas did the same, and I was still dazed from the punishing blow when I heard the guns erupting above me. Chuck and Barry emptied their weapons into our pursuers, who went down just as they had before. I breathed a loud sigh of relief. I very much doubted they were dead, but now I had time for that rare luxury, a moment of peace on the battlefield. A moment was all it was, however, as almost immediately I felt the ground shake beneath me. The tank was thrumming, and when I looked at Thomas I saw he had his ears plugged, his eyes pinched shut, and his mouth wide open. I immediately did the same, not exactly sure why, but the second after I did the tank fired a thunderous round from its main cannon.

Thomas and I unplugged our ears and opened our eyes. My head was throbbing, and my ears were ringing, but I was still aware of my surroundings and able to think somewhat clearly. He quickly got up and ran around the tank to join Chuck and Barry, and I followed him. They didn't look good. Barry was sitting in the mud, next to the bodies of two dead and disarmed soldiers. His eyelids were drooping, and his mouth hung lazily open. He was gently rocking back and forth, like a sailor trying to reclaim his land legs. Chuck was on his feet, and had wandered several paces away from the tank. He stared blankly at the world through wide-open eyes. It looked a bit like he was trying to do long division in his head. They had been caught off-guard by the discharge of the tank's cannon, and were badly shell-shocked. Thomas was already on his knees and tending to Barry, so I went to help Chuck.

I approached him calmly, careful not to make any sudden moves, making sure I stayed in what I guessed was his line of vision at all times. He didn't react to my appearance at all. With great reticence,

I put my hands on his shoulders and shook him gently. "Chuck? Are you alright?"

"FIRE!" he calmly yelled in my face. "THEY DON'T LIKE FIRE!" He looked a bit stunned when I recoiled from the noise. Deafened by the blast, it was clear he didn't realize how loud he was being.

"Can you hear me? Can you hear me at all?!"

"FIRE DOES THE TRICK!" he screamed, and the ringing in my ears grew higher and more insistent. I slapped him in the face. His eyes focused on me for the first time, and he stared at me in stunned disbelief. I slapped him again. Hard. His lips bent into a sneer, and he grabbed me by the arm and began dragging me deeper into the battle, towards the burning guard tower. I was amazed once again at just how strong and fast he was, and how bravely or ignorantly he trooped through the line of fire as bullets flew before us and behind us. Over my shoulder, I saw Thomas had gotten Barry to his feet and was pulling him in his wake much like Chuck was pulling me. The storm of bullets intensified, and I could see a hint of fear on his face, but he admirably fought it and continued his advance. Barry remained blissfully unaware, though at least now he'd opened his eyes.

"Where are you going?" he shouted ahead at me. This time it was my turn not to know.

By now I could feel the heat of the fire on my face, and the ground was so swampy it threatened to swallow my shoes. The men who'd been working the fire hose had all been killed, but the hose was still on, uselessly spewing water directly into the soil. Chuck kicked open the door to the guard tower and pulled me inside. It was unbearably hot. Up to this point I had been too busy dodging bullets to have time to question Chuck's judgment, but now I suspected the tank blast had disoriented him to the point that he didn't know what he was doing. A second later Thomas and Barry came stomping in. Barry regarded the inside of the burning building with an almost comic serenity. "Iz hot," he drawled. Thomas looked seriously pissed.

"Why the hell did we come here?!" he demanded.

He got his answer a moment later when the red men burst through the door. The one with the gaping jaw looked furious, but his companion actually looked a bit nervous. They were both bleeding from their multiple gunshot wounds, but not nearly as much as they should have been. I drew my pistol and quickly fired twice, scoring two headshots. Despite my impending fiery death, I felt a surge of adolescent joy. I had rarely fired the gun since I bought it several years ago, and only then at stumps and tin cans, and most of the time I'd missed. I was actually a decent shot when I had to be. Chuck cocked an eyebrow and smiled. He was impressed. It shouldn't have meant much, but somehow, it did.

The red men crumpled to the floor, their heads still somehow bafflingly intact. Only a few seconds later, their limbs started twitching again, and they began slowly pulling themselves to their feet. My excitement instantly deflated. It was hopeless. These things were fucking unkillable. That's when I noticed Chuck holding a grenade in his fist. He must have taken it from one of the soldiers behind the tank. He pulled the pin and pelted it at the red men. He shouted "GET OUT!" and dove through the side wall of the tower, which was mostly ash at this point. Thomas flung Barry through the hole Chuck had created, then the both of us fled through it as well. On the outside, Chuck was already on his feet and slogging away from the tower as fast he could move. Barry had somehow grasped the seriousness of the situation and had crawled behind a concrete partition some of the firemen had been using for cover, and curled up in a ball. This time, he plugged his ears. Thomas and I were running as fast as we could, which wasn't all that fast, as the ground had become more or less a bog at this point. I tripped and went down face first in the mud. This was as far as I was going to get, so I covered my head, plugged my ears, and waited for the blast.

The force of the explosion was pummeling. I literally felt myself driven down about an inch into the mud. A few seconds later I felt the flaming ash and debris coming down like hot snow on the back of my neck. I rolled over and sat up, wiping the mud from my eyes. The destruction was spectacular and complete. Where the tower had once stood now remained only a smoldering heap being gradually swallowed by the wet earth. I warily regarded the tower's remains, expecting those things to come crawling out of the rubble unscathed to continue chasing us. They didn't. The tower simply continued smoking and sinking in peace. For the first time I realized just how silent the world had become. In disbelief, I snapped my fingers next to my ears to make sure I hadn't gone deaf. I could still hear alright, but there were no more bullets, no more tank rounds, no more sounds of men fighting. With the demolition of the guard tower, the battle had ended decisively, though it didn't look like anybody had actually won much of anything. I pulled myself out of the mud and went to check on the others. Barry was sitting on top of his jersey barrier, watching the tower disappear. He looked fine to me. Thomas was standing several feet in front of me, brushing the ash out of his hair with his hands. When he saw me looking at him, he shot me a halfhearted thumbs-up. He looked so tired, and looking at him made me realize just how exhausted I was myself. Of the four of us, Chuck had managed to get the farthest away from the tower, and he too was on his feet, staring emptily into the haze. What I didn't realize, until it was too late, was that this time he was actually looking at something. It was a large black pickup truck, with chains on the tires, spraying mud all over the place as it sped up beside us. There were two very dark-skinned men in the bed, covered with mud, pointing machine guns at us. We raised our hands in submission, and the two men jumped out of the bed and menacingly trooped towards us. One would keep his gun trained on the others while his partner handcuffed us one by one and put us in the bed of the truck. Once all six of us were set up in the back, one of the men with guns signaled the driver, and the truck sped off the way it'd come.

"Where are you taking us?" I asked.

"Away from here," the other man said with a thick, foreign accent, possibly African of some sort. "You're safe now. No need to worry."

"Seeing as how I've just been handcuffed and thrown in the back of a truck by strangers with guns, I'd say my worry is pretty well justified," Thomas said.

"We apologize for that. It's just the way things are done, for everyone's safety. I give you my word, we will not harm you. You look thirsty. Drink this." The man unbuckled a large canteen from his belt, unscrewed the cap, and poured water into Thomas's mouth. He swallowed it greedily.

"*Damn*, that's really good."

The man held out the canteen to the rest of us. "Anybody else?"

Of course, we all drank from it. Thomas was right. It was pretty much warm tap water, but sufficient desperation adds flavor to any food or drink. After drinking the water, I allowed myself to completely and truly relax for the first time I could remember. I laid back against the back of the truck and closed my eyes. It's feasible that I had been drugged by something in the water, but I think it's more likely that after a day and night of stress, beatings, combat, and exhaustion, my body had simply reached its limit and needed a break. So I went to sleep.

Chapter 9: The Coalition for Third-World Ascendancy

"The big cities of America are becoming Third World countries."
-Nora Ephron

When I woke up, I was indoors, seated in an office chair. My hands were still cuffed, but now I was also tied to the chair itself. As my eyes came back to life, I saw I was seated at a small desk. I heard a woman's voice from behind me.

"He's waking up. Hold him down; keep his eyes closed."

Two pairs of hands latched onto my shoulders and pushed me down face-first onto the desk, nearly tipping the chair over. Somebody else's hand turned my head to the side and held it against the table while another hand pressed itself against my eyes, blocking my vision. The hands on my head and face were covered with latex gloves. I felt something scribbling on my forehead.

"All done," the woman said. "Let him up."

The gloved hands let go and the other men pulled me off the table and returned me to my original position. Seated across from me on the other side of the table was a black woman, with short curly hair and a lab coat. Her face was hard. She held a mirror in one hand, facing me. "Tell me what you see," she demanded.

I looked into the mirror, and all I saw was myself. The taser burns on my neck had healed, and my face had been washed. "I see me," I told her, not sure what she was getting at. She sighed and bit her lip, exasperated.

"What do you see on your forehead?"

I looked in the mirror again. This time, I knew what she wanted me to see. There was a red triangle scrawled on my head in thick magic marker. "A triangle?"

"What sort of triangle?"

I chewed my tongue thoughtfully, stretching my mind all the way back to geometry. "Um, isosceles?"

A slight smile crossed her face, but she quickly returned to her stoic expression. "And what color?"

"Red."

She put the mirror back down on the desk and fully unleashed her smile. Her face had softened and grown warmer in an instant. She was rather pretty, actually.

"Ok, let him loose. He's clean." The men who had been holding me against the table moments ago were now untying me and freeing my hands. "You know, you're the very first person who's ever answered the triangle question mathematically. Most of the time they'll say its red, or small, or my personal favorite, 'Pointy.' You strike me as the analytical type. I like that."

"Well, thanks," I said cautiously, stretching my wrists and elbows. "But...I've got some questions."

"I knew you would," she said eagerly, beginning to rock back and forth in her padded leather chair. "Let's hear them."

"I suppose we'll start with why you tied me up and drew a triangle on my face."

She looked a little embarrassed. "I do apologize for that. I hope we weren't unduly aggressive with you, but we had to be cautious. We've been fooled in the past."

"By who?"

"Other vampires."

Swiveling in my chair, I saw that the three men who'd held me down were still watching me intently, but their postures and expressions betrayed curiosity, not aggression.

"So you know," I said neutrally, still prepared to jump up to fight or run at a moments notice.

"We do," she replied.

"And you're not going to kill me."

"Well, you passed the mirror test, so no, we are not going to kill you. As long as you don't try to hurt any of us, things will remain peaceful."

"Glad to hear it. So what was the deal with the whole mirror thing anyway?"

"Humans like us can't see whether or not a vampire like you has the Stain. However, we *do* know that a vampire with the Stain can't see his own reflection. So whenever we bring one in, we draw something on his forehead and hold up a mirror. If he's not Stained, like yourself, he can see what we've drawn on him, and we know he can probably be trusted, on a probationary level at least. If he can't tell us what we've drawn on him, then we know he's Stained, and we take...appropriate measures. It's pretty low-tech, I know, but it works better than anything else we've tried."

"What exactly is all this Stain business about? I've heard bits and pieces, but it seems important, and I'd really like to know more." She smiled. "I see Marcus still informs his boys on a need to know basis."

"Wait...*Marcus?*"

"You...don't know Marcus?"

"I don't think so."

"Hmmm." She absently scratched her head, deep in thought. "I don't see how that's possible. You came in on the same truck. He said you were with him."

Suddenly it dawned on me. "Does Marcus have long black hair, an old leather jacket, and scars all over his body?" I asked.

"Yeah, that's him." Then something dawned on her. "Ohhh, I see. He's not using his real name with you. Don't take it personally. We're the only ones he uses it consistently with."

"Marcus." It just sounded weird.

"Yeah." We looked at each other silently across the desk. "What name did he give you?"

"Chuck."

"Chuck." She tried to lighten the mood. "He's always been a monosyllabic kinda guy." I smiled sheepishly. It was an awkward conversation.

"But enough about...Marcus. I want to know about the Stain."

"Fair enough." She looked relieved that the subject had been changed, and regained her previous enthusiasm. It was easy to see she was the kind of person who loved answering questions. "Do you want to hear the myth, or the science behind it?"

"Both," I answered. "Let's start with the myth."

"Excellent choice." She flipped through a stack of papers in front of her and began to read.

"A long time ago, a widower lived in a small village with his two sons. His sister lived alone, in the same neighborhood, in a house that backed up to a river. The widower was a merchant, and frequently traveled to other nearby villages to sell what he could to support his family. Whenever he went on a long trip, he left his sons in the care of his sister. One day, in late spring, he left his children at his sister's and went on another trip, following the river to the next town. Just as he was making camp on the first night of his journey, he was attacked by thieves who robbed him, beat him to death, and threw his body in the river. That night, the river carried his corpse home, until it was trapped underneath a beaver dam only a few yards away from his sister's home. Early the next morning, she went to the river behind her house, and not seeing her brother's body under the dam, had her morning drink. Without knowing what she was doing, she ingested a small amount of his blood. A woman's consumption of her brother's blood is actually an ancient pagan ritual that provokes possession by a female demon. Surely enough, she was possessed that night, and became the world's first vampire.

"Possession is just as taxing for a demon as it is for a human, so the first thing the demon did upon entering the woman's body was go looking for a meal. She didn't have to go far. The dead merchant's children were sleeping in the next room. She drank their blood, killing them, and turning them into vampires as well. When the woman regained some control of her mind and body the next morning, she saw what she'd done to her nephews, and, in hysterics, ran outside and set herself on fire. Strengthened by the previous night's blood meal, the demon was able to evacuate the woman's body and jump into what remained of her brother. He was reanimated, and he climbed out of the river, and went to see his sons. He told them what they had become, and instructed them to carry on the demon's legacy, killing and feeding upon whomever they chose. There was only one rule they had to obey; they could harm anyone on earth, but not each other, as he had died providing for their welfare, and did not want his death to have been in vain. This was not a problem for the brothers, as they had always gotten along quite well. Their father said goodbye, and walked back into the river to decompose.

"That night, the boys, in their early teens, went door to door killing everyone in their village. They gorged themselves on all the blood they could hold, then went to sleep as the sun was rising. When they woke up three days later, they were hungry again, and went out once more to feed, but everyone in their village had either been drained, or eaten by scavengers, or rotted in the sun. They agreed to split up, and go looking for travelers on the outskirts of the village. In truth, they had a different plan. Each boy remembered there was one more survivor in town; the oldest man in their village, who rarely left his home. They hadn't killed him on their previous hunt; caught up in their newfound power, they'd forgotten the old man even existed. Now, he was the only thing left to eat. The boys split up, then each of them circled back around and snuck over to the old man's house. They both arrived at the same time, and each realizing what the other had done, and was now planning on doing, they began fighting. Furious and desperate with hunger, they fought viciously, until the younger brother ripped out his older brother's throat. Snapped back to reality, and covered in his brother's blood, the boy panicked, remembering the one rule his father had imposed upon him. He dumped the body in the river, and hid in his father's house. The next night, his father's voice called to him from the river.

"Where is your brother?" he asked

"I am not my brother's keeper," the boy answered.

"Surely, you are not. Rather, you are his killer. He is down here with me. You have broken the one rule I gave you, and as punishment, the blood of your brother shall foul the air around you for the rest of your life. Those that are like you shall see it, and know your guilt, and be free to kill you without incurring the Stain of Fratricide."

"It was an accident!" the boy cried.

"I do not care. You are more dead to me than the brother that you killed."

At that moment, all of the villagers the brothers had drained returned to life, and laid siege upon the house that the boy was hiding in. He narrowly escaped, and fled to the nearest town, where he began the lifestyle of vagrancy and murder familiar to all vampires. And to this day, the rules and penalties handed down by the father are still in effect. Vampires may harm humans however they wish, as it is in their nature and necessary to their survival, but they may not kill other vampires, as they are all brothers and sisters, descended from the same line. If they do, they will be marked by the blood of their victims, and other vampires may kill them with impunity."

"So? What did you think?"

"It was interesting. Violent. Didn't make a whole lot of sense."

"I know! It's very Old Testament. We understand a lot more about vampirism now than people did in the Middle Ages. Vampires, for all the fright and horror they've inspired over the ages, are simply regular people with a metabolic disorder. A fast acting blood-borne virus causes genetic mutations throughout the body, essentially putting it into constant overdrive. The body, upon awakening from what we call a vampiric coma, often mistaken for death, becomes stronger and faster, with extremely heightened sensory perception as well as healing ability. In order to sustain such demanding abilities, the body requires nearly constant blood transfusions, which it obtains through, uh, you know. As it's evolved through the centuries, the virus developed the ability to cause drastic physical changes very quickly. The growth of true "vampire fangs," as it were, is a fairly recent development, only a few centuries old. Before that, the afflicted had to just chew up their victims with normal teeth, then swallow the blood. Hollow fangs make the job much more efficient, and a lot less messy.

"For all the ways in which the virus makes its hosts' stronger, it also makes them very susceptible to other things. Sunlight, for example. The virus reacts very violently to Vitamin D, which the body produces in response to the sun's rays. It causes massive, instant cell damage that turns the host's soft tissues into something resembling carbon-based ash. Also, for some reason, the mutations caused by the virus are always accompanied by an allergy to wood. If wood gets into the blood stream, say, from splinters thrown off by a stake in the heart, death comes very quickly as well."

"Makes sense. So how does science account for the Stain?"

"Well, that's something we're working on. We know that the blood-borne viruses that cause vampirism are all about 90% the same. That last 10% determines things like just how sensitive the host will to be to sunlight, or wood, or which of his senses will be enhanced and to what degree. In order to develop the Stain, a vampire must be exposed to the blood of another. We believe the Stain itself is a result of what happens when the second vampire virus comes into contact with the first virus, the one that initially caused all the genetic changes, and starts trying to rewrite the host's DNA for a second time. We think the red glowing effect is caused by all the caloric energy the body must burn in order to sustain and stabilize the two competing viruses. The added metabolic demands don't enhance the vampire's abilities at all, as far as we can tell. They do, however, require Stained vampires to feed nearly twice as often as the non-Stained. They spend their typically short lives constantly hunting for food, looking over their shoulders for other vampires. Eventually they get weak from hunger, then another vampire comes along to finish the job. It's a nasty, brutal way to live and die. The reason you can see the Stain and we can't is because with your improved vision, you can see parts of the light spectrum we can't. That's the theory anyway. I've never seen the Stain myself, much as I'd like to. Us humans have to get by on the illustrations of other vampires. As for why Stained vampires can't see their own reflection, that's something we're only beginning to study. Could be a mutation of the optic nerve, or a psychosomatic symptom of guilt at having killed a fellow vampire and been made an outcast."

"And if a non-Stained vampire kills one that is, it doesn't transmit to the killer?"

"No. The DNA in Stained blood is so unstable it can't survive outside the host's body at all. It breaks down instantly. Also, the other vampire doesn't have to die for his blood to Stain you. If you were to punch a vampire in the face, and his nose bled onto your fist, you'd get Stained even if he didn't die. All it takes is blood-to-skin contact; it only takes a tiny amount of the virus, absorbed through the skin and into the blood, to cause the change." Suddenly, I understood why Chuck and the vampire in the first train depot hadn't fought each other, and why Chuck was so strict about prohibiting the four of us from having contact with each other's blood.

"How do you know all of this?"

"We've been doing research for a very long time. Unfortunately, we don't get many Reds passing through this part of the country anymore, and the few that do get snapped up by Bulwark right away. That's why we typically kill Stained vampires after studying them. It sounds awful, but it's done out of mercy. It's better they die quietly here than fall into the hands of those who run Bulwark."

"What do they do to them?" I asked.

"They weaponize them," she answered.

"We call them the Anaikolra. That's Tamil for 'Anaconda.' We don't know what they call themselves. In four years here, we've captured three, and we couldn't get one of them to say a single word. Then again, maybe they can't talk at all."

"What do they look like?"

"You tell me. Word on the street is you and your friends managed to kill two of them."

"So those things *were* vampires."

"That's how they started out, yes. Once they get done with them at Bulwark, they're practically a new species."

"The one I fought could open his mouth wide enough to swallow my head."

"The surgeons do that to them. They break their jaws and reset them with a pneumatic hinge. That was the hissing you probably heard. They also get new fangs, made from an incredibly durable steel alloy. The same pneumatic hinge that enables them to dislocate their jaws creates a vacuum inside the hollow fangs that can entirely drain an average adult male in less than three seconds. It also powers the jaw when biting, enabling them to bite with nearly 1,000 pounds of pressure per square inch, equal to that of a hyena. They can bite a human in half, no problem."

"Jesus."

"The way they use it certainly brings up some ethical issues, but it's one of the most impressive pieces of technology I've ever seen. But they don't just enhance them mechanically; they do it biologically, too. They inject steroids into just about everything, including the part of the prefrontal cortex that controls aggression. It makes them incredibly powerful, determined fighters, but it also drives them insane. They're also incredibly persistent. We have documented cases of them pursuing other vampires over 200 miles on foot, presumably just for the fun of killing them.

"Their defensive modifications are equally impressive. There's something like a chain mail ribcage enveloping the heart that protects it from puncture wounds. The same steel their fangs are made of is used to reinforce both the skull and the spine, which all but eliminates the options of neck-snapping or beheading."

"All of this information begs the question, how do we kill them?"

"Exposure to sunlight is always a winner. They're even more susceptible to it than regular vampires, but of course they know this, and so getting them out into the sun is all but impossible. Your other choices are A), blow them to pieces with an explosion of some sort, or B), set them on fire. Soft tissue is soft tissue, and they'll go up in flames just like you or I would."

"How many of them are there?"

"It's all but impossible to say. Bulwark keeps a very close eye on them, preferring to use them only in special situations or emergencies. As you can imagine, they're hard to control, especially in large groups, but the scientists are getting better at that. They aren't much good with sensitive, tactical operations, but if you need a high, indiscriminate body count fast, they're a dream come true. We rarely see them in groups of more than two or three. There could be as few as nine, or as many as 60. Like I said before, there aren't as many vampires coming through this area any more. There were a lot more of them two years ago, so we could observe much more of the Anaikolra's behavior back then. They eat humans too, but for whatever reason, they seem to prefer hunting vampires."

"What happened two years ago?"

"We don't know. All of a sudden, there was just...*less*. Of everything. Less people, less vampires, less resources, even less wildlife.

Our theory is that even though America fell almost a decade ago, there was still enough surplus, enough infrastructure in place that life could still go on, albeit a lot less comfortably. But now I think we're finally at the point where the last of the old is giving way. There's been talk of "Rebuilding America" since the week after the collapse, but you can't really rebuild around the remains of the previous version. You've got to wait for all that to burn or rot away, and start with a clean state. I think we're finally there. The only question left to answer is who's going to do the rebuilding; Fort Bulwark, or us?"

"And who, might I ask, is us?"

"We," she began, and for the first time I noticed the logo on the front pocket of her lab coat. Three globes formed a triangle; the two on the bottom were embroidered in black, one slightly larger than the other. The globe that formed the top of the triangle was the smallest of the three, and was stitched in a shiny gold thread that brilliantly reflected light. "Are the Coalition for Third World Ascendancy. And we are currently sitting in the capital, New Ethiopia."

"I…I thought we were in Kansas, roughly."

"And what exactly is Kansas, Ethan? Who decides what does and does not fall under the geographic subheading of Kansas? If we were to ask all, oh, what is it now…*eleven* presidents of the United States where Kansas begins and ends, would they all have the same answer?"

I didn't really know what to say to that.

"I don't need to tell you that the world is a very different place these days than it used to be. The American landmass still exists, but the nation is gone. Everybody's dead, or soon will be, but the land isn't. It's alive. The Yukon Flu came through and wiped out the human population, but the grass and the trees and the bushes keep growing, especially here, in your Midwest. Do you know how many people in Africa were dying of hunger, while hundreds of miles of farmland sat neglected? I couldn't tell you, and I was a doctor. I got too sad to count. One day, white men came down in helicopters and asked us how we felt about getting the hell out of Africa and eating three meals a day. *Everyday*. Everyone was sold at that point, it didn't even matter what they wanted from us. Turned out they wanted us to get on a big boat and wait for new instructions upon reaching land. The last time we did something like that, it didn't work out so great, but that's how desperate we were. A week later, we arrived in what used to be Texas via the Gulf of Mexico. And ours wasn't the only boat. There were hundreds of them, bursting with the citizens of the poorest countries of the world. The next day, they handed out gear. Some of us got tools, some of us got shovels, and some of us got farming equipment. And we started building our new home. New people came in off the boats almost every day. Once we had a community developed and stabilized, some stayed behind, and the more ambitious had the chance to move up the line and develop the next area in exchange for more authority, better food, luxury goods. I was one of the ambitious ones. Doctors were in very short supply, and I never wanted for work. As I kept moving north, along with the front line, the types of injuries I was treating began to change. There were fewer farming and construction accidents, and more gunshot victims. I had been working on the front for three years straight, and was privy to much more knowledge than the average citizen. I was told that we were being attacked by the remains of the U.S. military, which had set up headquarters in a Kansas fort. They considered us an invading force, and shot at us on sight. We weren't really invaders at that time, squatters on a grand scale, perhaps, but not invaders. But as the death toll rose, that's what we became. They stopped sending us tractors and backhoes and started sending guns and bombs. Most of the colonists became soldiers. We kept the farms running, of course, mostly to feed the army, but it became very clear that our No. 1 priority had shifted from construction to destruction. I hated it, but not as much as I hated Africa. That seemed to be the general consensus. If nothing else, death comes faster in an American battlefield than in an African village."

I was floored. "Why didn't you just retreat? Pull back into Oklahoma, or start developing east or west instead of north?"

"Because," she said, smiling bitterly, "Our bosses wouldn't let us. This was the plan all along. We thought we had come to build a farming community to feed the world's hungry, but that was just a cover. The Bosses wanted a massive army willing to fight and die for corn and potatoes, and that's exactly what they got. Maybe once we finish off Bulwark we can go back to recolonizing America, but it wouldn't surprise me in the least if we all got shipped off somewhere else to fight whatever god-forsaken war-du-jour is going on at that moment."

"Who are the Bosses?"

"Nobody knows. Everyone's got theories. My guess is the Soviets supply the weapons, with financial backing from a few faceless multinational corporations. Whoever they are, they have lots of money and guns. Back when we were just building and farming, some of them would occasionally come out and oversee things for a few days. We haven't actually seen any of them in person since the fighting started."

"Couldn't you just tell them you're not going to fight anymore?"

"One town did. New Bolivia. They bombed it with a plane."

I didn't know what to say again.

"None of our options are great. That's nothing new for these people. So we take the best one we've got; destroy Bulwark, and hope that's the end of the fighting. If you don't think about it too much, it's not so bad. For the first time in my life, I have my own research lab. Of course, I never thought I'd be researching how to kill souped-up vampires, but life's funny like that, isn't it?"

"Yeah," I answered. "Life's funny like that."

"Well, I've yakked at you long enough," she said, getting up from her chair. "You'd probably like to get back to your friends now."

"That'd be nice," I told her. "But there's one more thing I wanted to ask you."

"Certainly."

"When we were talking earlier, about vampires, you said that after they're bitten, they go into a coma, or something like that?"

"Almost exactly like that. Respiration slows, muscles are paralyzed, body temperature falls, heart rate drops to 20 bpm. With the body almost shut down, the virus is able to take hold much faster. But, contrary to popular belief, you don't die. You wake up confused and nauseated, with memory loss and what I'm told is a killer headache, but like I said, you're never dead. There are a few documented cases where the virus has actually reanimated the recently deceased, assuming the body died of a fairly non-traumatic cause, but those are the exception as opposed to the rule."

"I see."

"Kinda kills some of the mystique, doesn't it?"

"Yeah. Among other things." For the first time, I felt real guilt about the people I'd killed, the slaughter at the tavern especially. That night I had thought I was some supernatural, resurrected being, above the laws of mortal man, but now that the mysteries of vampirism had been laid bare, I realized just how foolish and vicious my behavior had been.

"For all the good it does, we pay a heavy price for science. It ruins the mystery. Do you want some fresh clothes?"

"Please."

"Wait here and I'll get you some." She left the room with the three men who'd held me, and came back a minute later with black cargo pants, a black t shirt, and boots. It looked like the civilian version of what the men in the pickup truck had worn. She stepped outside while I changed, then opened the door again and beckoned me out into the hallway. The floor was tiled in white, and the walls and ceiling were painted to match. It looked very industrial and clean. Four doors down we entered another room, also white and windowless, with a large round table in the center. Barry, Chuck, and Thomas were seated there, wearing the same clothes as me, drinking bottled water. They all had designs on their foreheads too; Chuck, a black X, Thomas, a blue circle, Barry, a green square. With washed faces and clean clothes, they looked so respectable as to be barely recognizable. Looking at us, a stranger wouldn't have suspected us of being anything other than four normal guys with similar taste in fashion. Barry had lost the tie, and Thomas the orange jumpsuit. Only Chuck retained his signature jacket. I took an empty seat at the table.

"Hey Ethan. How're you feeling?" Barry asked.

"Good, good. Glad to get into some clean clothes."

The doctor I'd been speaking with disappeared into the hall again, and returned a moment later with a bottle of water and four packets of blood, like we'd taken out of the freezer in the hospital. We tore them open and fed while she addressed us.

"First of all, I want to thank you for being so patient and tolerant of our security measures. I used washable marker on your foreheads, so it'll come off in a day or so. Marcus has brought me up to speed on your current situation regarding transport, and we're having a jeep prepared for you now. If you leave tonight, you should be able to catch up with your train."

"I…don't see how we'll be able to return it," Thomas said.

"Don't worry about it," she replied. "We'll just write it up in the inventory as having been lost in the battle. It's the least we can do after you brought down the guard tower and took the two Anaikolra with it."

"What do your jeeps run on?" I asked.

"Uh, gasoline," she answered, like she was stating the obvious. Then she remembered the gas shortage and elaborated. "The world hit peak oil almost a decade ago, but there's definitely still gas out there. You just have to know the right people. The Bosses, for instance. They resupply us once a month."

"We were told the gas supply was completely exhausted. All over the world."

"Well, I don't know what to tell you. You were told wrong. When the government started collapsing in the wake of the Yukon Flu, the oil companies stopped sending gas to the U.S. altogether. They didn't trust that your government would be around long enough to pay them"

I remembered something that had happened to me a few years ago. The Yukon Flu was still prevalent, but enough people had died that it wasn't able to spread as rapidly as it had at first. We hadn't yet been told that the nation was "Out" of gas, but reliable sources had it that severe rationing was going to be implemented within the next month. I decided to be reckless and fill up the car to make one last trip to California, back to the neighborhood I'd grown up in, to see who was still alive and who wasn't. I stayed less than a day. There weren't many people left to see. Three blocks had red quarantine seals on every single door. Nobody had cut their grass in some time. The air had a strange smell I couldn't identify. I got back on the interstate that afternoon to head home, and got stuck in a traffic jam. Sitting in the long line of vehicles, I saw an ambulance pulling up in the rearview mirror, driving on the shoulder. I hadn't even heard it coming. Sirens had become such a normal part of everyday background noise that half the time they went unnoticed. This ambulance had all the lights and sirens on, but I could see it slowing down as it approached me. It eased to a stop about four cars in front of me, and just sat there for a minute.

Then the sirens cut out, and two angry looking men got out of the cab and ran around into the back. They pulled the gurney out and started pushing it up the shoulder. The ambulance had run out of gas. That was something I had never expected to see. About two minutes later, I saw them turn around and start pushing the gurney back towards the stranded ambulance. They looked even angrier than they had before. Both of them were wearing latex gloves and clear hazmat hoods. One man grabbed a duffel bag out of the ambulance cab, while another yanked the body off the stretcher. Even from where I was sitting, I could see the man on the stretcher was dead. He had bled out through the orifices in his face. You wouldn't think so, but he was one of the lucky ones. Face-bleeders, or blushers, died the fastest. The two men from the ambulance walked down the road, dragging the body by the arms. They stopped at the van sitting in front of me, and pressed the dead man's face hard up against the passenger-side window. The driver got out and took off running. He didn't have a hazmat hood. The paramedics gracelessly dropped the body by the ambulance, climbed into the van, pulled onto the shoulder, and sped off. It took a moment to process what had just happened. *I'd been one vehicle away from being carjacked with a dead body.* That was the last time I ever drove on the interstate.

"I see," was all I could think to say. "We really appreciate your doing this."

"You're very welcome," she told me. "We have a small but loyal presence in New York, you know. If you need any help finding Deutchner, look them up. Most of them work border patrol." Chuck shifted in his seat at the mention of the dead man's name. I was tempted to call him on it, but he seemed to be held in high regard here, and I didn't want to jeopardize our chances of getting a vehicle.

"We'll be sure to do that," Chuck said, getting up from the table. His speaking voice had returned to normal. He walked over to the doctor, and actually hugged her, with surprising tenderness. "It was good to see you again Akili. Hopefully next time it'll only be a social visit."

"I very much doubt that," she said, "But it's a nice thought. The garage is where it's always been. Your jeep should be ready by now. Good luck, and be careful."

"You too," he replied, and they let go of each other. He turned around and headed for the door. "C'mon guys, we've gotta move."

The three of us got up and followed him towards the door. I was the last one out of the room. Before closing the door, I turned and waved quickly at Akili. She smiled shyly and waved back. Then I was out the door and back in the hallway.

Chuck was walking swiftly down the hall, looking straight ahead. "I'm sure you've all got questions," he said to no one in particular. "I'll answer them, but not until we're out of here with the jeep. Just keep quiet for another five minutes, and everything will be fine."

At the end of the hallway, Chuck pushed open the last door on the right and we stepped out into a massive, indoor car park. There were at least two dozen black jeeps lined up facing the main gate. One of the guards saw us come in and waved with his pinkie and ring fingers extended. Chuck waved back with his index finger. The guard smiled and beckoned us over.

"It's all gassed up and ready to go, Mr. Marcus," he said, opening the driver's side door. "It's manual transmission, just as you like it." He held out the keys.

"You're the man, Kele," Chuck said, shaking his hand and pulling away with the keys. Thomas took the other front seat; Barry and I climbed in the back.

Kele grinned affably. "There are two handguns in the glove box, just in case you need them. And don't scratch the paint. It's hell finding a body shop out here."

"Kele, you are never going to see this jeep again."

"Oh. In that case, scratch whatever you like." He walked to the left side of the gate and pulled a large red lever, and it swung open. Chuck started the jeep, tapped the horn, and sped past Kele into the darkness.

Chapter 10: Justifiable Homicide

"Dictators always look good until the last minutes."
- Tomas G. Masaryk

We rode in silence for the first twenty minutes or so. I had no idea where we were, and if Chuck didn't either, he hid it well. We kept the headlights off, just in case anyone from Bulwark was out looking for us. All of us, Chuck included, breathed a heavy sigh of relief when we crested a hill and saw the train tracks again.

"Well, that's the hard part," he said. "Now we just follow these to back to the train, preferably before sunrise."

"Think we'll make it?" Thomas asked.

"I sure hope so. If there's no sign of it an hour before dawn, we'll start looking for shelter, then get back on the road that night."

It was quiet again, the only sound that of the jeep's engine. We hadn't seen a single living thing since the guard at the car park. This was probably what driving on the moon was like, but with more vegetation.

I decided I'd be the one to break the silence. "So, should we call you Marcus now?" I asked from the backseat.

"What?" Chuck said.

"They told me your real name was Marcus."

"As far as they're concerned, it is."

"So Chuck *is* your real name?"

"As far as you're concerned, it is." I could only see the back of his head, but I could tell he was smirking.

"Well, what does it say on your driver's license?"

"Don't have one," he answered, and as if to prove his point, he accelerated into a sharp turn that carried the tracks up the side of a tall, narrow hill and back down again. I felt our weight shifting hard to the right, and the wheels on the left side of the jeep may or may not have risen off the ground for an instant, but we leveled out at the bottom of the hill and kept flying along the train tracks. It was probably best for me to leave the issue of Chuck's true identity alone for the time being.

"How did you know all of those people?" Barry asked.

"I've been going back and forth across the country for some time now," he began. "On the very first trip, my party and I were ambushed by Anaikolra, not too far from here. They killed the other three, and were going to kill me too, but one of the Third-Worlder's jeeps passed me on a patrol and got me out of there. They brought me back and took me to Akili, and I got the same briefing I'd imagine all of you got tonight. I spent the day there, and was getting ready to leave that night when the first Anaikolra they'd ever captured escaped from one of the labs. It tried to kill Akili, but I killed it first. Whenever I'm in the neighborhood, I stop by to see her. We help each other with our respective missions whenever circumstances allow." He stopped speaking momentarily to shift the jeep up another gear. "If she hadn't sent that truck for us when she did, Bulwark would've found us, and we'd all be on operating tables right now being fitted for detachable jaws or some shit like that. A few years ago, I bombed the medical/scientific wing of Bulwark, where they manufacture those things, but apparently I didn't bring enough bombs. That night was the first time I made it into the Archives, but I didn't have enough time to find anything useful. It was one of those nights where things only go half-right. I did manage to kill their entire surgical team, which was fun, but it looks like they've found some replacements. Sometimes you just can't catch a break."

The jeep had a radio, but it only picked up static. We drove quietly the rest of the night, until 4:30, when the first pink hint of sunrise spilled over the horizon.

"Goddammit," Chuck spat. "We aren't gonna find it tonight. Keep your eyes out for a place to stop." That's what I'd been doing since three, but to no avail. We hadn't passed a single structure in hours. We were deep into the plains, and the only sign that the human race had ever set foot here was the railway we were following and the occasional discarded beer bottle, the label long ago bleached into oblivion by the sun. Our litter survives us, I thought to myself. Seems only fitting.

The sun continued its unstoppable march into the sky, the light pink gradually melting into a neon orange. I could feel the hairs on my arms and neck standing at attention, like they were planning to make a run for it before their home caught fire. They didn't like where the situation was going any more than I did.

"Wait! Stop!" Thomas shouted, and Chuck slammed on the breaks. "On the left, below the hill. See it?"

I did. At the bottom of a gently sloping hill on the driver's side of the tracks was a junkyard, filled with hulking pieces of scrap and burned out, unidentifiable metal husks. I could see the remains of two or three steam engines poking out of the rusty debris, but it was easy to see what the landfill's main ingredient was; cars. Cars of all shapes and sizes; vans, minibuses, sedans, and closer to the surface, convertibles, muscle cars, and other luxury vehicles. When the gas ran out, the poor had been the first to hock their cars to pay for food, or rent, or the funerals of their loved ones. It was only at the end, when the realization finally sank in that the lifeblood of their prized possessions was gone for good, that the well-to-do and the car enthusiast finally parted ways with their beloved. By that time, there was almost nobody left to sell to, and the people who were buying already had more junked automobiles than they knew what to do with. They got less money for their Cadillacs than the common men had gotten for their Oldsmobiles. I had a neighbor, about 30 years old, unmarried, who owned the most desirable car I'd ever seen; a cherry red '66 Mustang. It had been his dad's, before he died of cancer. Not a dry weekend went by that he wasn't out in the driveway washing and waxing it, or rotating the tires, or tinkering under the hood. He finally sold it for scrap in '76, to pay for his little brother's funeral. They paid him $245. When a man in a tow truck came to haul it away on a Monday morning, I saw him cry for the first and only time. Less than a year later, he was dead. There wasn't anything left to sell to bury him, much less anyone to do the selling on his behalf. He went to the incinerator on Clark Street, where the drive-in used to be.

The junkyard was remarkable for two reasons; 1), it was a manmade structure, and 2), it had a four-car garage affixed to the eastern edge of the property. We had found our accommodations for the day.

Miraculously, the dirt path leading to the garage was unobstructed by garbage of any sort, and the entrance had been left unlocked. We drove up to the door, opened it, and went in on foot. It was completely abandoned, save for a few desks and a ceiling fan that, to no one's surprise, didn't work. Once we'd moved the desks to the back wall, we pulled in the jeep and shut the door. There were four small windows on the garage door itself that would need to be obstructed somehow. Under the driver's seat we found a giant blackout tarp. It wouldn't have surprised me if we searched the jeep and found milk and homemade chocolate chip cookies. Akili certainly knew how to pack for the itinerant vampire. We hung the tarp over the windows, tucking it into the space where the garage door met the roof. The seal was immaculate. We all felt the sunrise together, like we always did, but there was no longer any need to panic. We crawled under the desks and settled in for a long, much-needed rest.

For the first time, all four of us slept through the sunset that night. It was a little past ten when I woke up and crawled out from under my desk; everyone else was still asleep. Part of me wanted to wake everybody up and hustle them into the jeep, to set out and make the most of the rest of the night, but I decided to let them sleep. I figured they deserved it. To tell the truth, I was mostly basking in the glow of the fact that for the first time since I'd woken up in a new world with a mouthful of fangs I was inside of a non-moving structure, not worried about killing someone or someone killing me. I was neither chasing something nor being chased. It felt cozy, almost. Well, not exactly. The closest I can get to the word I'm looking for is…stable. Yeah, stable is close enough.

I sat against the jeep, and did something I'd long intended to do, but never had the time for; I pulled the sketch pad and pencils out of my cargo pants and began to draw.

At first I didn't even realize what I was drawing. I simply untethered my mind and soaked in the joy of a graphite tip gently imposing its will on the blank page. When I was a kid, I could spend hours doing that, and it didn't matter where I was; in the backyard, on the school bus, at the beach, it didn't matter. As I got older, I shifted my attention to painting, which wasn't as portable a medium, but even then, I always kept a small pad and pencil in my pocket.

Allowing my eyes to review my handiwork, I could already tell what I was drawing. It was the Chrysler Building. I drew it often. Not obsessively, mind you, but enough that it could generously be called a recurring motif in my work. My family went to New York for a weekend when I was 12. I can't recall what we did the first day, only that on the second day we were scheduled to take a tour of the building. At the end of the first night, we got a call that my grandmother had fallen and broken her leg. We flew back to California first thing in the morning. No matter how hard I squinted out the window of the plane, I couldn't see the Chrysler Building. To this day, I never have. Not in person, at least. If I'd never seen it, I wouldn't be able to draw it. I had pictures of it hanging on the wall in my bedroom, cut-outs from posters, books, travel magazines, brochures, etc. The first painting I ever did was of the Chrysler Building, actually. I think it's packed up in the attic right now. That, or the basement.

I had the base of the building more or less done. Later I could go back and put in more windows (there are always more windows, 3,862, to be exact), if I felt like it. Right now I wanted to get started on the spire. That was always my favorite part.

"What are you doing?" Chuck asked. He was in the driver's seat, looking down at me over the edge of the jeep's door as I drew.

"Drawing."

"Drawing what?"

"The Chrysler Building."

He leaned out further over the edge and squinted at the picture. "Chrysler Building doesn't look like that," he said dismissively.

"Yes it does."

"No, it doesn't."

"Have you ever even seen the Chrysler Building?"

"I've been to New York lots of times," he said. "That's not what the Chrysler Building looks like. At all," he added.

"I tell you what, Chuck. How's about we make a pit stop in Chicago, dig Deutchner out of his grave, shake all the worms out of his skull, and have him be the deciding vote?"

"You're an asshole."

"I hate you."

"We're leaving in ten minutes. If you're not ready, so much the better."

"Fine."

"Fine."

I went to go wake up Barry and Thomas. Chuck pulled down the blackout tarp and repacked it under the seat. We made the ten-minute deadline easily. Thomas opened the garage door, and Chuck started the jeep and coaxed it out onto the dirt road. While Chuck was shifting into second gear, Thomas ran back and hopped into the passenger seat. Barry yelled "Stop!" and Chuck's hand slid off the stick, stalling the jeep out. He cursed and demanded to know what Barry's problem was. Barry just pointed.

Situated on the southern border of the junkyard was the corpse of an old train. We had all seen it when we pulled in the previous night, but there was something different about it now. After a moment's thought, I figured out what had changed; there were now two cars vertically upended, their bumpers supported on the side of the train. The steam engine and two cars comprised the walls of what could best be described as an industrial lean-to. I could glimpse the embers of a dying fire in a crack between the two walls. Truth be told, it was an impressive, ingenious shelter. But who had built it? And when? Most puzzling of all, how had they moved so much steel without waking us up?

A humanoid figure walked briskly past the fire, casting a long shadow over the mechanical graveyard. All of us jumped.

"I don't care who that is, how he built that, or why," Chuck told us, gripping the stick with white knuckles. "We're getting out of here." He shifted into second and sped up the dirt road. A minute later we were back on top of the hill, following the train tracks east, leaving whoever had set up camp next to us in the junkyard to his own mysterious business.

It was another long and quiet drive. The radio had nothing to say. I was on the verge of falling back to sleep when Chuck called our attention to something in the sky. It was a thick plume of black smoke, wavering in the air above the horizon. The Yukon Glory was near, and based on the way the smoke was settling, it was currently stopped. We were close. Chuck shifted up another gear and we went to reclaim our prize.

Twenty minutes later, we were approaching the rail yard. From a distance, it looked abandoned. The Yukon Glory was nowhere to be seen. The main gate that separated the road from the train yard was shut. Chuck left the jeep idling and got out to open it. When it swung open, a pile of tin cans fell from the top, crashing loudly to the asphalt below. A blast from a shotgun rang out, and the windshield of the jeep exploded. I saw Chuck hit the ground, and I propelled myself over the door and outside the jeep. My gun fell out of my pants in doing so, and when I bent to pick it up, the second shot went off, shredding the front left tire, only a few feet in front of my head. I frantically fired a shot blindly into the night, if only to show our attackers that we were still alive and returning fire. Immediately after my shot, the third blast came, but I didn't hear it hit anything. I stood up cautiously, using the jeep as cover, and saw three men on the other side of the gate, running away from behind a stack of oil drums. One of them was still fumbling with a shotgun as he ran; the other two had abandoned their weapons. Taking hold of my pistol firmly with both hands I set my sights on the man closest to me. I had only just thrown the hammer on my gun when I heard three more shots go off in rapid succession, and all three men crumpled to the ground. Looking up, I saw Thomas standing on the passenger's seat, bleeding profusely from his forehead, with a smoking gun from the glove box in each hand. He wiped blood and sweat from his eyes and intensely scanned his surroundings. "Looks clear," he announced, dropping one of his guns over the side of the jeep. I heard Chuck catch it and cock it on the other side of the vehicle. Barry got up from the floor of the jeep and hopped out on my side. Thomas jumped from the passenger seat directly to the ground outside and signaled us to join him behind the jeep. We all crowded around back, kneeling behind the disabled vehicle like a bunker. Thomas was picking at his forehead and wincing. "Everybody alright?" he asked. We all were. "Good. Anybody have any theories as to just what the hell that was?"

"An ambush," Chuck said. "I should've seen the cans. Goddamnit."

"Do you think there'll be others with guns inside the depot?" I asked.

"No idea," Chuck answered. "I would assume so. Also, they definitely know we're here now, and they'll be pissed that we killed their friends."

"Could we drive through in the jeep?" Thomas queried.

"No," I replied. "They shot out one of the tires. If we're going in there, we're going on foot."

"Can I have a gun?" Barry asked. Everybody stared at him. "Seriously guys, I never get a weapon, and I'm always stuck hiding behind one of you or crouched in the back of the jeep hoping I don't die. I want to fight this time. I want a gun."

"Don't make me regret this." Chuck tossed him the gun Thomas had given him. Barry almost caught it, fumbled it in his hands, then finally clutched it to his chest, upside down. Chuck let out a quick sigh and slid the scissor out of his pocket. "Save your bullets for the ones who have guns. Finish the others with your hands. Kill as many as you need to, but remember, we're here to get back on the train and get it moving."

Still crouched behind the jeep, the four of us turned to face the depot and chanced a look over the bed. Through the blown-out windshield, it still looked deserted. Then, as if on cue, fire sprang out of one of the many trashcans, then another, then another, then another still. When they were finished, at least three dozen cans were burning like fetid torches. We ducked behind the safety of the jeep once again.

"How many bullets do we have?" Chuck asked tersely.

I checked my pistol. "Three."

"Seven," Thomas answered.

"Uh, how do you figure that out?" Barry asked sheepishly. The three of us slapped our foreheads. Thomas did a little subtraction in his head.

"Six, Barry. You have six bullets."

"Got it," he replied confidently.

"Let's see how eager they are to shoot," Chuck told us. "Everybody stay down." We did. Chuck held his arm up above the cover of the jeep and briskly waved it back and forth before pulling it down. There was no response from the other side of the gate. This time Chuck stood upright, making himself vulnerable from the waist up, counted to three, then dropped back down. Once again, nothing. Now he ran out around the jeep, up to the main gate, and kicked it hard. It rattled loudly in its hinges as Chuck dashed back to safety. This time we could hear some scurrying behind the cans, but again, no gunfire. Chuck brazenly walked out into the open and shouted "Hey! We're right here! Do something, Goddammit!" A small rock sailed over the gate and hit the jeep's hood with an impotent *ping*. He strutted back to where we were sheltered behind the bumper, no longer making any effort to conceal himself. "Rocks," he chuckled. "Assholes are throwing rocks at us. They used up all their firepower in the trap." He got up and strolled back to the gate, opening it with a flourish. "Let's get started, shall we?"

The four of us left the disabled jeep behind and entered the depot. It was telling that Chuck had made himself so vulnerable, and all they'd done was launch a rock, but still, I thought he was being a little cavalier about the whole situation. I kept my gun drawn regardless. Chuck walked confidently up to the nearest trashcan and kicked it over, exposing two emaciated homeless men crouching behind it. He grabbed them by their throats and threw them backwards, and they tumbled into another can, which fell to the ground with an impressive clatter. That's when everybody came out of their hiding places. Roughly 36 trashcans, at two people per can, came out to 72 opponents, not to mention the uncountable masses pouring out of the depot sheds and other buildings inside the rail yard. A few of them had knives, or forks, and I saw the occasional shovel in the crowd, but most of them had only rocks, sticks, or their bare hands. They weren't well armed, but they were desperate, and clearly didn't have much to lose. We regarded each other silently, until another gun shot went off. My first instinct was that we were screwed, that they'd baited us inside the rail yard in order to get a clear shot, but then I realized that Barry had shot a man holding a nail-riddled 2x4 in the head. That's when they rushed us, and the fighting began.

The battle was chaotic, to say the least. No matter where I swung, I made contact with at least three people, but there was always another wave coming to take their place. They were gaunt and scraggly from hunger and exposure, and many of them smelled strongly of alcohol. It was more like fighting a swarm of mosquitoes than men. I kicked one of the flaming trashcans into the group, and heard the anonymous crowd shriek and recoil from the scalding metal. Even so, they recovered quickly and kept up the pressure. I was becoming fatigued, and my knuckles were tender and splitting from the exertion. In a burst of creativity, I took out my gun once more and began using the butt as a surrogate fist. This rested my hands, and made a satisfying sound, but it slowed me considerably, and before long the steady waves of assailants blended into a single onslaught that crushed from all sides. It was imperative that I stayed on my feet. If I went down, I'd be trampled, or they'd dog pile on me and tear me to bits. One of them landed a jarring surprise blow just above my ear, and I involuntarily dropped to one knee. I could feel the pressure of the crowd weighing me down, pressing on my chest and shoulders, trying to force me to the earth. That's when I heard five shots go off in rapid succession, and the rushing mass of my attackers stopped, then reversed course and ran. When the dust had settled, I saw Barry standing to my left, his eyes tightly shut and his face contorted, still frantically squeezing the trigger. "Thanks Barry," I said, returning to my feet and brushing the dust off of me. "Impeccable timing."

He eased off the trigger, relaxed his face, and finally opened his eyes. "Is it over?" he asked tentatively.

"No," I answered, watching the mob flee in terror. Barry's well-timed outburst had sent not only my attackers, but the entire population of the rail yard into a full-on retreat. "But it soon will be. Hungry much?"

The entire scenario had changed in an instant from a gang beating to something more resembling the running of the bulls, and we were the bulls. We picked off the stragglers at our leisure. Invariably, the ones who tripped and fell or couldn't keep up were the drunkest of the lot, and as we drank them their giddy sense of intoxication was transferred to us. Lightheaded and warm, but with no loss of coordination, we loosened up and began enjoying ourselves. We herded them through the yard, swatting at the backs of their heads for sport, until we reached the end of the depot, where the dilapidated shacks and patchy asphalt gave way to bare dirt and trees, when we found what we'd come for; the Yukon Glory herself. She was stopped a few feet before a stout concrete barrier that had been lowered onto the tracks with a crude pulley system. The conductor was nowhere to be seen.

"Do you think they killed him?" Thomas asked.

"We'd better hope not," Chuck replied. "Let's clear the tracks, then start searching the sheds. Maybe he's hiding somewhere."

We didn't even bother fooling with the pulley system. All we had to do was coordinate our pushing, and in a few moments the barricade had been flipped over, opening an escape route for the train. It wasn't as heavy as it first appeared. All of the homeless men who could still move had fled into the woods, leaving us alone in the empty rail yard with the deserted engine. With that task taken care of, we split up and started kicking in shed doors. The first few yielded only filthy bunks, cigarette butts and empty bottles. Thomas was the first to find anything of interest. He'd uncovered a massive case of vodka bottles hidden underneath a blanket. None of them had been opened yet. We loaded them into our boxcar, just in case. The next few sheds were empty, but then Barry stomped open a door and called out "I found him! He's alive!"

The conductor recognized us immediately. He was tied to a chair, and sporting a nasty black eye. "Oh, perfect," he wheezed as we entered the shed. "You're here to finish the job. Just make it quick, you bastards."

"Relax, old man," Chuck commanded, cutting the ropes that bound him. "We've come to get you and your train out of here. All we ask is free passage for the rest of the trip. Letting us stow away is much better than being left here to die, isn't it?"

"I suppose so."

"Good. How soon can you have the train moving again?"

"Ten minutes. Less than that if I have someone to help shovel the coal."

"Barry, get him back to the train and help him however he needs it. We'll be along shortly." Barry helped the old man up and went with him to go start the train.

"Why aren't we going with them?" I asked.

"Might as well see if there's anything else worth taking here. The vodka was a good find. Maybe we'll get lucky again."

The three of us split up to scour the rest of the depot. I worked the structures on the left, and Chuck handled the right. Thomas went back to the main gate to see if there was anything worthwhile there. All of Chuck's sheds were empty, and so were mine, until I kicked in the second to last door. There were three men sitting in a circle, with belts tied off around their arms. One had just finished injecting himself, and was passing the needle to the next man, whose hands were shaking in anticipation. My nose flooded with the hot, chemical smell, and I felt the old appetites resurrecting in me. The two men who hadn't yet used leapt to their feet and started dragging their friend out of the shed with them. I could have stopped them all then, but I decided to give them a head start. This would be more fun if I worked up a little sweat first.

They made it out of the shed and onto the main drag, and right into Chuck's arms. He grabbed the one they'd been dragging out of the others' hands, and they fled into the woods where the others had gone. Chuck sniffed his catch appraisingly, then his face lit up with mischievous realization. Staring me right in the eyes the entire time, he bit the man's neck and quickly drained him. Nothing happened at first, but a few seconds later his eyes widened, his pupils dilated, and he took a shuddering step back, his arms swaying limply.

"Oh…oh wow, Ethan" he stuttered, rocking on the balls of his feet. "I can see why you care for this stuff so much." I didn't say anything. "Come on man, don't be like that," he taunted. "What, did you have dibs or something?"

It was about this time I turned off my brain and let the rage take over. Silently, I rushed Chuck, kneeing him savagely in the gut. He doubled over in shock. When I saw the handle of his scissor poking out of his pocket, I grabbed it, too angry to consider what that action might lead to. I grabbed a handful of his greasy hair tightly in my left hand, clearly exposing the back of his neck. He turned his face up to look at me. It wore no emotion I could discern at the time. In hindsight, there may have been a hint of resignation, or even a perverse, muted sense of gratitude. I think we both knew it was going to come to this, had known it without consciously knowing, for some time. I got the unmistakable feeling he'd been waiting for this moment for a while, for centuries even. His quest for redemption was over. He would taste his own steel, then peace, for the first time in ages.

Looking up at me, he gasped something that I couldn't hear. Based on the way his lips moved, he either said "Fuck you," or "Thank you." I've been kept awake many days trying to figure out which it was. I haven't yet, and I doubt I ever will.

I took his head off in one clean stroke. The arterial spray was nauseating in its intensity. Hot blood covered my hands and forearms as his body went limp in the dirt. I wiped the scissor clean and put it in the pocket opposite my sketchbook. I really don't know why. The knowledge of what I'd done didn't truly sink in until I looked up and saw Thomas staring at me. How much had he seen? I realized it didn't really matter. The aftermath was telling enough.

"So you finally did it," he said neutrally.

"I had to," I told him. I didn't want to sound like I was pleading for his approval, but I'm pretty sure that's how it came out. "Somebody had to."

"And that somebody was you?"

"Were you going to do it?" I shot back.

"I'm not saying he didn't deserve to die. He did." Relief washed over my insides. "But did he deserve to die over that?"

It was a good point, but I wasn't about to concede that with blood all over my hands. "He had to die for a lot of reasons. You saw what he did to Marty. You're *living* what he did to us. I lost my temper. So what? The bottom line is I did what needed to be done, and he got what he deserved. He'll never hurt anybody else again."

"That's true." He tossed me the blackout tarp from the jeep and half a bottle of water. "Clean yourself up." I did so to the best of my ability, and left the tarp and empty bottle on the ground. Thomas and

I both smelled smoke at the same time; the Yukon Glory was coming back to life. We made our way back to the boxcar and climbed in. Barry was waiting for us.

"Where's Chuck?" he asked.

"He's dead. I killed him."

"Oh…I see."

A few moments later the train began to move again. The three of us didn't say a word to each other. It wasn't that there was nothing to say, but rather, too much. The boxcar felt smaller than it had before, even though it held one less passenger than it used to. We all fell asleep a few hours before sunrise.

Chapter 11: The Stain

"In nature there are neither rewards nor punishments-there are consequences."

~Robert G. Ingersoll

"Ethan. Ethan, wake up. How do you feel?" I opened my eyes and saw Thomas looming over me, looking concerned.

"I'm alright," I answered groggily. "Why do you ask?"

"Do you feel…different? At all?"

"What are you getting at?"

"You're glowing."

I looked down at my hands, my forearms. As far as I could tell, I was no more luminous than I'd been before going to sleep. "I am not."

"Barry, is he glowing?"

"He's glowing," Barry said. He was regarding me from across the boxcar with curious fascination.

"You guys are full of it."

"Look at this." Thomas went back to the case of vodka and grabbed a bottle. It had a reflective silver label. He held it up to my face. "Can you see yourself?"

I couldn't. It was just…empty space. Where I should've been. Where I *was*. Bloody hell. "When did you notice this?"

"About ten minutes ago. You were asleep, and then all of a sudden, you just lit up. Like those things we blew up in the guard tower. We didn't know if we should wake you or not."

They wouldn't stop staring at me.

"So what?!" I snapped. "So what, do you kill me now? Is that it?! You can't catch it from me, you know. You get a free pass. If that's how it's gonna be, then fine, I can deal with that, but if not, quit staring at me and let me go back to sleep."

"I'm glad you did it," Barry said quietly, after some time had passed. "I hated him."

"Thank you," I said, more harshly than I meant to.

"He was insane," Thomas said matter-of-factly. "I think we all knew that. I'd been thinking about how to deal with him for some time. There really wasn't a good solution to be had. He was crazy, but he was also our best shot at making it to New York alive. If I'd known you were serious about doing it yourself, you could've told me. We could've made a plan about it, the three of us."

"Goddammit Thomas, I didn't *plan* it! It just *happened!* Do you know what that's like, to lose your cool and act on an impulse, or do you just sit there with your fucking fists in front of your mouth and watch it all like it's a movie?"

He just stared, inscrutable as ever.

"I still think you were right," Barry offered. "We used to need him, but not now. Not anymore. The three of us can make it the rest of the way together. Still, I'm sorry about what happened to you. I wish there was something we could do."

"Thanks Barry," I told him. I really meant it. "I'm gonna be alright."

"Do you ever think about all the people we've killed?" he continued. "The people we had to kill, to stay alive, because of what he did to us? When I went out to the train yard that night, there was only one person I intended to kill. I've definitely surpassed that goal now."

I wasn't sure how to proceed. "Yourself?" I asked with trepidation.

He smiled ruefully. "No, that wasn't the plan at all. When I was 20 years old, I got a job at Werther's Inc., a small insurance firm. I worked in Accounts Receivable for 15 years. Eventually, I ran it. The only thing that distinguishes Werther's from the thousands of other companies like it was a unique form of coverage that only we sold. In addition to the standard car, house, and life, we had another plan; pandemic insurance. Financial compensation in the event of an infectious, nationwide health crisis. As you can imagine, that got to be a very popular plan about eight years ago. My boss, Mark Palomino, had been a good friend of mine for the past decade. He put me in charge of handling the pandemic claims. It was enough paperwork to literally crush a man, but I said yes. I didn't want to, but I did anyway. I didn't want to let him down. My wife had been complaining about how much I'd been working lately, when all of a sudden, she stopped. It didn't bother her anymore. Like a fool, I thought this was a good thing. When they stop talking, that's when you know something's gone seriously wrong. Two weeks before I killed myself, I came home from another 14 hour day and found a note in the kitchen. It was one hell of a note, I'll tell you that. She had left me. She had left me for Mark. Mark had sent a private plane to pick her up that morning and take her to his other house, in New York, near corporate headquarters. Also, I was fired. I had 24 hours to clean out my desk and be escorted out by security. You know what the killer was, the real killer? They signed it together. With 'Love.' 'Love, Allison and Mark.' Can you believe that? The balls it took to rob me of my life, in 50 words or less, and sign it 'Love?'

"So I drank. I drank for five days straight. And when I sobered up, I knew what I had to do. I had to kill Mark. So I went and bought some arsenic. A guy eight blocks down had a meth lab in his basement, and access to all sorts of chemicals. Now that I had the poison, I had to get to New York. This would be difficult, since there was no more gas and I didn't have a private plane to go flying around the world destroying people's lives with. I did some brainstorming, and remembered that trains ran on coal, not gasoline. So I went to the rail yard, planning to hop a train east, and just rough it for a week or so. I waited six hours for an east-bound train. Six hours, with a bottle of arsenic in my pocket, waiting for a train. When it finally came, I tried to jump it, fell off, and twisted my ankle. It's a lot harder than it looks in the movies. And as I laid there in the dirt, foot throbbing, watching my train steam out over the horizon, I realized the truth, and the truth was simple; I'd been beaten. Completely and thoroughly, I had been beaten. So I took the arsenic myself, and waited for it to end. It didn't take very long. That is, of course, until I woke up with you guys. Now it looks like I just might make it to New York after all. And all I had to do was die once and kill dozens to get there. Not such a bad deal, huh?" he spat sardonically.

"Holy shit, man. I'm sorry. I had no idea."

"Don't sweat it. You had no idea because I didn't tell you. Not your fault. I don't want any pity or sympathy. I just want this to be over."

"If you don't mind my asking, why would you kill your boss, but not your wife? Isn't she just as guilty as he is, if not more so?"

"Because," he said, through another anguished smile, "That wasn't part of 'The Plan.' 'The Plan' was to kill Mark, bring her home, and make her love me again. Fix everything, 1-2-3. You have to realize, I'd been drinking for five straight days when the Gods of inspiration blessed me with 'The Plan'.

"Honestly, I just want to go back. Go back to the way things were. I know that's impossible, especially now, but hell, I can want whatever I want to, can't I?

"That's what the weaker half of me wants, anyway. The stronger half says kill them both, slowly, then leave the country and start all over again. Not make the same mistakes, not take so many damn orders, not show up to work at 6am on a Saturday while my boss is stepping out with my wife. Funny thing is, the weaker half ends up overpowering the stronger half. That's how it is with most people, I think."

"Barry," I asked. "That first night we went hunting together, at the tavern, when you killed that girl, why'd you do it? Why'd you do it the way you did?"

"I was scared, and I was hungry, and I was angry, and that girl had Allison's eyes, and my nose. That's what our kid would've looked like. And I just lost it. I'm not proud of it, in fact I'm sick as hell over it, every day I wake up. I can regret it, but I can't take it back, as much as I'd like to. It wasn't her fault she looked the way she did. If it's any comfort to you, I killed her right away. Everything else I did to her was after she'd died. It's not much comfort to me, but I thought you should know. I've never done anything like that before in my life, and I swear to God I'll never do it again."

"What if you make it to New York, and find Allison and Mark together?"

He sat quietly. "I think," he said finally, "I'll ask God to look away for a moment."

When the train stopped that night, we were still in the Midwest. I wasn't sure if we'd yet crossed the border into Missouri, or were still in the margins of Kansas. It was so deserted there wasn't even a train depot to stop at. The conductor just hit the brakes, put up his feet, and went to sleep. Outside, there was thick fog and no moon. No sign that anyone had been here for sometime. We should've gone back to the boxcar and taken the night off, but I was hungry, and besides, this was our first hunt without Chuck. This was our chance to prove we didn't need him after all.

The three of us walked the plains aimlessly. There was neither sight nor smell of any living thing at all, much less anything human. After a time we came upon another classic sloping Midwestern hill, and situated at the top of that hill was the first man-made structure we'd seen all night. I couldn't tell what it was, but it wasn't in very good shape. We were standing downwind of it, and the only smell the breeze carried was that of rotting wood, with a slightly acidic undertone that may have been termites. We weren't going to find any people in there, but we'd been cooped up in a boxcar all day and decided to explore regardless.

As it so happens, the building was a church, or had been at one time. The small steeple had collapsed in through the back half of the building. Only one stained glass window had endured the elements successfully; a portrait of Cain, standing victoriously over the corpse of Able. It was ugly, unskillfully rendered. I had half a mind to break it myself.

It had a signboard, in much the same condition as the church itself. The sign identified this particular place of worship as home to the Flagellant Brothers of The Cross. The top of the sign read "Bible Study," but the placard establishing the time of said Bible study was nowhere to be seen. Below that, instead of a witty message, or even the movable letters required to spell it, was a simple whitewashed wooden canvas. Painted upon it in dark red letters was the phrase "WE DESERVED THIS". Underneath that, in small black pencil barely large enough to be read, somebody else had come along to vandalize the sign. "the MAN-EATING PRESBYTERIANS killed my brother on the connetikitt turnpike".

Thomas regarded the message board in disgust. "Cryptic, self-loathing bastards," he mumbled, and kicked the sign in half.

The church was situated on the highest hill in the area. We had a clear view of the region from all sides. There was nothing to be seen but tall weeds and overgrown grass. We walked around a little more, in the interest of stretching our legs as opposed to catching something. It was obvious that wasn't going to happen. Our predatory career minus Chuck was off to a rather inauspicious start.

When we smelled the Yukon Glory start smoking back to life, it was a big relief for all of us. Nobody wanted to be the one to admit this was pointless. With the train getting ready to leave early, we could blame our lack of success on a lack of time. That would make it easier to sleep the next day.

The conductor was standing outside the train, waiting for us. When he saw us, he waved. We waved back. And with that, he climbed back inside and prepared to leave. I was still brooding over our failed hunt when Thomas opened the door to the boxcar, and a glowing red hand thrust out of the darkness and clenched itself around his throat. I knew right away it was an Anaikolra, but more importantly than that, I knew I had to save Thomas.

I jumped into the boxcar with Barry in hot pursuit. The Anaikolra kicked me in the head as I got to my feet, but he hadn't seen Barry go in, and Barry came from behind and ground his forearm into its throat. I made it to my feet and started raining fists into his face. It was like punching a stone, and my barely-healed knuckles burst open on contact, but I kept drilling him. This one looked almost exactly like the other two we'd fought, same clothes and hair, only shorter and stouter. I saw his jaw muscles beginning to vibrate, and I redoubled my efforts to punch straight through his damned face. There was no way I was going to let this one get his mouth open.

Thomas was still held firmly in the things' grasp, but he was clutching frantically at my right hip. I was clueless as to what he was trying to accomplish. Each time, he came up a few inches short. I trusted him, and in between blows I took a long shuffling step towards him. His thrust his hand down my pocket, and pulled out Chuck's scissor. Brilliant. Even without oxygen, he'd been the only one with the presence of mind to go for a weapon.

The train shuddered to life and began rolling down the track once more. All four of us stumbled a step to the left, but stayed on our feet. Thomas pulled back the scissor and slashed the thing's face, drawing a thin curtain of blood. It finally let go of him, clutching at its cheek, and Barry kicked him hard in the small of the back, ejecting him from the train. He tumbled out to the ground below and rolled over several times before coming to a stop. The train was picking up speed now, but I'd seen these things run, and if he got to his feet he could still give chase. Of course, that's exactly what he did. I waited until he was only two cars behind us, then I laid down on the floor, leaning half of my body out of the boxcar. Thomas grabbed my ankles to keep me from being sucked out of the car by speed. The Anaikolra was less than one car away from us now, and I could see him preparing to make a leap at us. I waited until his heels left the ground, then I shot him. I had meant to get him in the chest, but he jumped a little sooner than I anticipated, and the bullet sailed cleanly into the center of his stomach. He let out a hacking gasp of breath and went down face first, nearly bouncing underneath one of the oncoming cars. By the time he'd pulled himself back to his feet, the train was running at full speed, and he was too far away to catch us, and he knew it. Thomas pulled me back into the boxcar, and we shut the door tightly, collapsing to the floor, redolent of spent adrenaline and relief.

When the three of us had regained our breath, it was time to figure out just how this could've happened.

"Where do you think it came from?" I asked.

"It's gotta be Bulwark," Barry answered. "That's only place that makes those things, as far as we know. And if they did have an external plant producing those, it wouldn't be here. We were on top of the hill; we saw how deserted this place is."

Thomas was chewing his lip in concentration. "It must've been following us then." He returned the scissor to me, and I pocketed it.

"And making damn good time. We have a train; as far as I know, that guy was only moving on foot."

"Do you think he was alone?"

"I don't know, probably. If he had a partner, it doesn't make sense that he would've attacked us alone."

"There's no way he could've caught up with the train on foot," Barry said. "No way. They're fast as hell, certainly, but they couldn't run like that all night, or move around in the sunlight. It doesn't add up."

"I don't like this," Thomas said softly. "I don't like this at all."

"Neither do I," I answered, "But the important thing to remember is we handled it. We're on the train, getting closer to New York every minute, and he isn't. We'll keep our guard up for the next few days, and we'll be in the clear. Let's just try and get some rest." At first, sleep was elusive, kept at bay by hunger and paranoia, but the rhythmic rolling of the train soothed our troubled minds, and we finally fell asleep.

Chapter 12: The Locusts, Part 1

"When he opened the Abyss, smoke rose from it like the smoke of a gigantic furnace. The sun and sky were darkened by the smoke from the Abyss. And out of the smoke, locusts came down upon the earth."

-Revelation 9:2

When we woke up, somebody on the outside was opening the door to the boxcar. It was mid afternoon; the sun hadn't set, which meant the train had stopped early. Something had gone wrong. The door slid open, and the three of us scurried like cockroaches to the other side of the car, fleeing the sun's wrath. But it didn't come. Outside the boxcar, there was a hazy, dusk-like ozone the sun couldn't penetrate. A man stepped inside the car, and I grabbed him by the sleeve, pulling him into the darker side of the car. "Why are you following us?!" I screamed, putting my gun to his head.

"Jesus fucking Christ!" he gasped, and as my eyes adjusted to the new half-light, I saw he wasn't an Anaikolra, but rather the old train conductor. I sheepishly let go of his arm and put the gun away. "Sorry, I...I thought you were someone, uh, something-"

"I'll tell ya what I think ya are, I think yer' fucking crazy, is what I think!" He pointedly jerked away from me, and squinted at the three of us. "Wasn't there another one with you?"

"He...he got off," I stammered. The conductor stared into me with cataract-stained eyes. He knew I wasn't being entirely truthful.

"Well, it's nunna my concern," he said, turning around and stepping out of the boxcar. "You all come out here, I wanna show you something."

The three of us looked at each other, unsure of how to proceed. Barry tentatively stuck his hand out into the gray pseudolight leaking into the car. He wiggled his fingers, then stuck his whole arm out. "I think it's safe guys," he reported. "It tickles a little, but it's safe." With that, he boldly stepped into the light and hopped out of the car. Thomas and I followed him. The light felt a bit like pins and needles, or a sunburn in progress, but it wasn't harmful to us. I stepped out of the boxcar smiling. I never thought I'd get to take an afternoon walk again.

The world waiting for us outside of the car looked like a ghost-town in hell. Thick black clouds marred the entire sky, eclipsing the sun. You could still see its faint outline, if you looked hard enough, but barely any of its light could penetrate that dark wall. It was perpetual twilight. On the horizon, we could see the burned out corpse of a city. Only the tallest buildings still stood, their walls dyed black from soot. When the wind blew, thick clouds of ash rose from the ground and lifted into the air, slowly sinking back once the breeze vanished. Looking at my feet, I saw the grass was dead, crunchy, also dark. Ash had stained the whole world a funereal black.

"That," the conductor announced, pointing at the desolate cityscape in the distance, "Used to be Chicago. We're in the Dead Zone now. Things are going to be a lot different from here on out."

"How…how did this happen?" I asked.

"Locusts," the conductor replied casually.

"Bugs?"

"People. That's just what we call them. They're more like bugs than people these days anyway."

"I don't think I understand."

"After America collapsed, people just sorta lost their minds. Not very prudent, but understandable, I suppose, given the circumstances. They panicked and started looting and rioting and when they were done, burning anything that would catch fire. At first there were only a few isolated pockets of this, but nobody could stop them, and all the different riots blended into one another until it was just one great wall moving westward, razing everything in its path. The western wave is there, inside Chicago. There's one more wave behind it. In order to get to New York, we have to go through both of them. It's dangerous as hell, but we've come too far to turn back now, so here's where you boys earn your passage. I need one of you up front in the train with me. If they kill me, good luck getting this thing moving again. I need another one of you shoveling coal into the furnace the entire time. The more coal we burn, the faster we break through the Locusts, and the less time there is for something to go wrong. The third man needs to protect the one shoveling the coal. If the coal man dies, the train stops, and we all die soon after. From what I've seen, Barry's damn fast with a shovel; I'd suggest we put him on coal duty. Who's gonna watch his back?" Thomas volunteered. "Good deal." He slapped me on the shoulder. "Guess that means you're riding with me. Don't let me die, or swear to God I will haunt the motherfucking hell out of you." He grinned mischievously, and I had the feeling that even though he was older than dirt, and we were vampires, there was enough spit and vinegar in his bones that he'd outlive us all.

"Are you guys ready to do this?" We nodded. "Good. Let's get to going."

The four of us reported to the conductor's cab at the very front of the train. Barry got a shovel, a lighter, and a gas can; Thomas, a baseball bat and a rusty can of mace. They disappeared into the coal car. Once the conductor and I were inside the cab, he produced a long, thick chain and secured one end around his waist, the other around mine. Then he used a second, shorter chain to link the one that connected us to a stout iron bar I suspected was the locomotive equivalent of a steering column. We had enough slack to move freely around the cab, but not enough to be dragged out of it. It was an ingenious idea, and I told him so. He just laughed. You learn these things because you have to, he said.

Smoke began belching from the stack atop the coal car, leaking upwards into the black sky. The conductor let the engine warm up for a few minutes, then he pulled a lever and the train lurched to life. He handed me a baseball bat, and grabbed one for himself. I was watching the left opening of the cab; he was covering the right. As the train began picking up speed, I called over my shoulder and asked if he had any advice. "Swing hard," he said.

As we neared Chicago, he shouted over the roar of the engine that the track didn't run through the center of the city anymore, so we'd be skirting the edge of the south side. I didn't see how that was relevant, but it gave me something to think about besides the nerves bouncing around the pit of my stomach, and the subtle tremble of the bat in my hands, so I listened attentively. The train was nearly at full speed now, and I could make out more details of the ruined cityscape as we approached. Broken windows, rotting shacks, piles of ash that shifted like sand dunes. Still, I couldn't see any people. "Steady now," the conductor warned me. "Here they come."

I squinted into the horizon, and panic leapt through my bones like an electric charge. I still couldn't see them; rather, I saw their *movement.* Like everything else, they were dyed black from the omnipresent ash, and they blended perfectly into the background of the Windy City's corpse. Their movement gave them away though. It was a gentle undulation, a living, breathing ripple. As the train advanced, they spotted us, and began rippling our way. I was now close enough to see their raised fists, to hear them crying out to the black godless sky, a shrill, wavering call, mournful and furious and devoid of all humanity. Now I knew why they were called Locusts. It didn't seem right to call them people. The ripple crescendoed into a stampede, and I choked up on my bat as they ran up to meet us. We steamrolled headlong into the mob, and we did battle, to the soundtrack of war cries and steel grinding bone.

They were packed so tightly that I wasn't swinging at a person; I was swinging at a writhing, multi-part organism too large to be seen all at once. Each time I pounded my bat into the wall of flesh, a thick cloud of ash blew back into my face. It was like beating a living rug. Underneath the soot, their skin was sunburned and cracked, their hair matted to their skulls in a muddy, sweaty paste. Their teeth were yellowed from age and neglect. I looked at all of these things, but not their eyes. I learned quickly that their eyes were the singular trait that maintained their humanity; capable of showing fear, pain, sadness, even individuality. As a group, they were Locusts; as individuals, they had simply been born in the wrong place at the wrong time, and were now doing what was necessary to survive. A lifetime ago, they had been fathers and sons, mothers and daughters, brothers and sisters, friends, neighbors, dentists, stockbrokers, teachers, clergymen. I could banish these thoughts from my mind, temporarily, at least, as long as I didn't look at their eyes. I let my vision go out of focus and kept swinging. It was impossible to miss.

As I continued clubbing, the conductor and I fell into a rhythm, passing the beat back and forth. He swung, I swung, he swung, I swung. It became automatic, and my mind wandered to other things. The train for example. Had it stopped? No, but it had slowed considerably. The cow catcher in front kept most of them from getting caught under the wheels, but there were just *so goddamned many* of them they put up powerful resistance through sheer number alone. With a shuddering groan, the train stopped. I was caught off balance, and stumbled left. An anonymous hand reached out of the chaos and grabbed my ankle. I bludgeoned it off with the bat. "What happened?" I shouted to the conductor, clubbing at the throng as fast as I could.

"Little busy here!" he yelled back. Our rhythm was gone. With a muffled roar, the train began moving again. I was thrown off balance for the second time, and would've stumbled out of the cab if not for the chain around my waist anchoring me to safety. My arms were exhausted. I had no idea how the old conductor was still swinging. There was a second roar, louder this time. The cab rocked violently, and both the conductor and I fell flat on our asses. An instant later, the train was flying again, and the faceless writhing monster outside was left in our wake, its screaming fading into the distance. We'd broken through the first wave. The conductor and I dropped our weapons and fell to our backs, our heads landing a few inches from each other on the corrugated steel floor. Breathing heavily, I thrust my right hand straight up in the air, palm facing him. He reached up with his own hand and slapped it victoriously. We caught our breath in silent celebration.

A few seconds later, Barry and Thomas came running into the cab, over the railed bridge that connected us to the coal car. Barry was as black as the blackest of the Locusts, and wispy ash trailed his movements like Pigpen from the Peanuts comics. Thomas wore a much thinner black cloak, but his was heavily accented with blood.

I couldn't tell whether it belonged to him or the Locusts. Probably a mixture of the two

"Everyone ok up here?" Thomas asked. The conductor and I, still lying on the floor, flashed him a lazy thumbs up.

Barry coughed, and a small cloud of soot burst from his lips. Even his tongue was black. "That…sucked," he declared emphatically, and began slapping the ash from his body. He had a lot of work in front of him.

"Barry was a goddamn champ," Thomas declared, slapping him heartily on the back, releasing another dusty cloud from his body. "Three of them made it past me into the furnace, and Barry took them all out with the shovel, Bam! Bam! Bam!, then went right back to work like nothing happened. You got it done, man."

"Was nothing," he said humbly, brushing soot from his forearms. "How'd things go up here?"

"Good, good," I told him, sitting up. "You should've seen, uh… what's your name?"

"Zachariah," the conductor answered, still sprawled on his back. "You boys can call me Zack."

"Zack, gotcha. Anyway, Zack's got a hell of a swing. You'd think he was a ball player."

"I *was*," Zack interjected proudly. "Shortstop, not too far from here actually. Hell of a long time ago though. But as you can see, I've still got it."

I gave him a hand getting to his feet. "No argument here." I untied the chain from around his waist, and he returned the favor. He pulled a folding chair off the wall and sat down in front of his controls. "Now that all that's over with, things should be quiet for awhile. If you guys wanna go back to your car and get some rest, that's fine by me. I've got a few sandwiches, if you all want some dinner."

"That's very kind of you," Thomas said, "But we brought our own food."

Thomas, Barry, and myself crossed the bridge connecting the cab to the coal car, and shut the door behind us. In the corner of the room, opposite the furnace, the battered bodies of six Locusts were stacked on top of each other. "Second helpings tonight," Barry chuckled. "We damn sure earned it."

Satisfied like we hadn't been in days, we gingerly stepped from the coal car back to our boxcar. The connecting bridge led to a tiny auxiliary door, long ago rusted shut, so I kicked it open and the three of us crawled inside. We pulled a bottle of vodka from the case we'd stolen and passed it around. It was surprisingly good, much better than you'd expect to find in a ragtag camp of junkies and winos. We were soon drowsy and content. Ironically, we felt better inside the Dead Zone than we had for some time. Against my better judgment, when the others weren't looking, I grabbed the empty vodka bottle and stared intently into the reflective label. Nothing stared back. Oh well. You can't have it all. I decided my reflection was expendable. Still, I couldn't stop myself from continuing to gaze into the bottle. Such a weird trick. I had no idea how I was doing it. I doubted I'd ever get used to seeing a blank space where I should have been. When you peer into the abyss, the abyss peers into you. Was it Nietzsche who said that? It sounded more like something Yakov Smirnoff would say, in one of his more cerebral moods. I giggled. I was drunk. It was time to go to bed.

We woke up lazily the next night. Maybe it was late afternoon, I can't rightly say. The crepuscular gloom that had greeted us in Chicago hadn't lifted, making it hard to tell exactly what time it was. Thomas and Barry were still sleeping off the previous night's excess. I decided I'd go for a walk.

The place where we'd stopped for the night was entirely unremarkable. There were no structures of any kind, no identifying features. Just train tracks and ash clouds as far as the eye could see. I walked by the conductors cab to check on Zack. He was sleeping soundly in his folding chair, his feet crossed and resting atop something like a dashboard. It didn't look like a very comfortable position to me, but he smiled serenely in his sleep. I smiled too. I hoped I had half his spirit when I was his age. It was a bit of a ridiculous thought. If the fates were willing, I could live two or three times as long as him, yet never reach his age. I was stuck at 24. Lots of people would kill for that bargain, but I didn't really appreciate it. I'd never known anything but youth, and never would, and thusly didn't assign it the value that others did. It wasn't something to lionize, something to pine to recapture. It was, unnaturally, the natural state of things.

I heard the sounds of a scuffle in the boxcar. When I looked towards it, I saw the back half of an Anaikolra entering, with a second right behind him. Shit.

"Zack! ZACK!" I screamed. He woke with a start, nearly falling out of his chair.

"Whozat? Wuz'going on?" Zack called groggily.

"Start the train! It's an emergency!"

"What happened?" He was looking at me through bloodshot eyes from the cab.

"Zack, if you wanna live, start the train NOW!"

I didn't have time to argue with him anymore. Either he'd believe me, and start the train, or he wouldn't, and we'd all die. It was out of my hands. As I sprinted back to Thomas and Barry, I could hear shoveling in the coal car. That was a good sign.

I dove into the boxcar, with my gun in one hand and my blade in the other. Time and space dripped by in slow motion. Before I could make it to my feet, a crushing blow from a fist rocked the side of my head.

Don't go down. Don't drop your weapons.

With great difficulty, I was able to stay up on one knee. The Anaikolra swung again, but I ducked, and he nearly tripped over me. I thrust the scissor straight into the air and felt it tear into the meat of his stomach. Bloody satisfaction. I gave it a twist, for the sheer sadistic hell of it. I forced the scissor upward, trying to gut the bastard, but he got hold of my wrist and pushed down. The blade slid out, and I kicked him hard in the stomach. He toppled haplessly into the wall of the car. I jumped on top of him, and we wrestled for God knows how long, me trying to put the blade in him, him trying to avoid it. Eventually he took an arm off of me to punch me in the face. It hurt like hell, but this was what I'd been waiting for. He'd gotten in a good shot, but in doing so, exposed his neck. I was about to find out just how hard it was to take the heads off of these things, but the train jerked abruptly and began rolling again. I was thrown off balance, and missed his neck, driving the blade downward into the floor of the boxcar. Now it was his turn to have an opening, and he put his feet to my midsection and pushed me off of him. He flung me to my feet, and I tottered backward, until I crashed back-to back with the other Anaikolra. We spun on our heels, and recognized each other immediately.

This was the same one who'd attacked me at Bulwark, who'd dislocated his jaw and been inches from biting through my leg. The one who should've died in the explosion at the guard tower, but quite apparently had not. He was burned terribly, on his arms, his hands, his face, and probably a lot of other places obscured by his clothing. A ruddy patchwork of skin grafts had been applied over his milky flesh. He did not look happy to see me.

I thrust the scissor forward to stab him, but he swatted it from my hand, and it tinkered to the floor. Next I went for my gun, but he knocked that away too. His jaw began to quiver, hissing, and I froze.

Do something. Do everything. For the love of God, don't do nothing. On second thought...

I dropped flat to the floor. He looked down at me, unmistakably confused. His jaw was shaking so fast it blurred, but before it could drop, Thomas shot him three times. Twice in the back, once in the back of the head. He stumbled forward, and I wrapped one hand around his ankle, recovered the scissor with the other, reached behind his shin, and slit the tendons in his calf. Thomas grabbed him by the back of the shirt, and like a bouncer heaving a drunk into the alley, ejected him from the car. The train was nearing full speed, and from the open car door I watched him hit the ground, rolling and tumbling through the black grass. When he finally came to a stop, I watched him try to get up, and collapse. He tried again, with the same results. As badly as I knew he wanted to, he couldn't give chase with one leg. I was immensely proud of myself. Then I saw Barry.

He was on his back, on the floor, a few feet away from me. He'd been staked, cleanly, through the heart. Drool hung from his lips. His pupils were quickly fading to white. He wasn't even convulsing. He was obviously and completely dead.

I was startled from my shock by two more gun shots. Thomas had shot the remaining Anaikolra in each shin. He fell to his knees, grimacing. Thomas took hold of his shirt, preparing to throw this one out of the car like the last, when I stopped him. Keep the gun to his head, I told him. I'll be back.

I darted across the connecting bridge to the coal cart. Sweating profusely, Zack was shoveling coal into the furnace like a madman. I told him to run back to the cab, and bring me the big chain. He did as I asked him, with remarkable swiftness. Then he went back to loading the furnace as fast as he possibly could. I took the chain from him, and returned to the boxcar. Thomas had his gun jammed up underneath the Anaikolra's chin. He looked furious, but he knew he was in check. Swiftly darting behind him, I took hold of both his hands, and tied them together with the chain. Then I tied his feet together. Finally, looping the chain around itself, I tied the loop that held his hands to the one that held his feet, and doubled knotted it. He was securely hogtied. I kicked him in the head, and he toppled over on his side. I crouched down next to him, and looked him straight in the eyes.

"I don't know what the slowest, most painful way of killing you is," I told him, "But I'm going to find out."

"The facts are as follows," I began, closing the boxcar door. I was pacing the car in front of him, twirling the scissor around my finger. Given the violent death of my friend mere moments ago, I was surprisingly calm. To be honest, I didn't even feel like I was really myself. It felt more like a movie than real life. "You, are going to die. It is going to hurt. It is going to take a long time. You cannot change this. However, you do have some control over how long it takes, and how much it hurts. The sooner you tell me what I want to know, the sooner it ends. Believe me, you'll want it to end."

"Ethan…I…" Thomas collapsed on the floor behind me. His hands were clutching the wooden stake protruding from his chest.

Oh God, no. Thomas.

I pulled him up to a sitting position again the wall. He was wrestling with the stake, but he couldn't get it out. "Hold my shoulders," he gasped. "Push me against the wall." I did what he asked me to. His entire face twisted, and he jerked the stake out of his body. It was gnarled and broken at the tip. He examined it briefly, then tossed it to the floor. "Thanks," he said.

"How do you feel?" I asked, panic shaking my voice and my body and my soul.

"Not great," he answered. "But better, now that that's out of me." He was sweating and shaking, but I didn't know if that was from shock, or a sign of something far worse. I simply did not know what to do. He smiled at me, applying pressure to the hole in his chest with his hands. "I think they missed the heart," he told me. "I twitched before they got it in, just like Chuck did. It was in for less than a minute. I'll be fine." He smiled again, weakly. I looked back at the Anaikolra tied up on the other side of the boxcar. He was smiling too. I got up and kicked him in the face, as hard as I could. It didn't make me feel any better, but I did it again anyway.

"Three questions," I told him. "Where did you come, how are you following us, and why won't you and your friends just leave us the fuck alone?"

He stared back at me dumbly. "I figured as much," I said, moving behind him.

"Those things can't talk," said Thomas, hoarsely. "Akili said so."

"Akili said she'd never *heard* them talk," I replied. "There's a difference."

"You think she never tried torturing them?"

"What I think is that Akili was never as pissed off at them as I am at this one." I took the scissor and slit the webbing between all of his fingers on both hands. "Feel like talking yet?" He looked back at me stoically. "More? Happy to." I pulled off his boots and did the same between his toes. He still wouldn't talk. He wouldn't even react. I didn't want to keep going. I felt sick all over at the things I was doing. Badly, I wanted to stop, but I couldn't. I owed it to Thomas. I owed it to Barry.

"Where did you come from?" I barked. No answer. I sliced a long stripe down the right side of his face, slowly.

"How are you following us?" No answer. Another stripe.

"Why are you doing this?" Still silent. One more stripe.

"TALK, GODDAMN YOU!" I screamed, and slashed randomly at his face and torso until I was exhausted. When my rage fizzled out, I sat heavily on the floor.

"She was right. You were right," I admitted. "He can't talk."

"Duhzn't hurrrrrt," rasped the Anaikolra. I scuttled back in shock. Thomas's eyes were wide. "Duhzn't hurrrrt," he repeated. His voice was horrible. He sounded like a snake who'd had a back-alley tracheotomy.

"You…you can talk?" I stammered.

He nodded gravely. "When I wan-to."

"What…what doesn't hurt?" I asked, thinking I already knew the answer.

He smiled. "When they make you like me. Duhzn't hurrrt.

"You are al-ready Stained," he croaked. "One friend dead. Other die sssoon. Then, you come home with uzzzz."

We stared at each other a long time. The red glow from his skin flickered in the air. It looked positively evil. I hoped I didn't look like that, but I'm pretty sure I did. Without saying another word, I got up and walked to Barry's body. I went through his pockets until I'd found the lighter Zack had given him. Then I grabbed a bottle of vodka from the case. I poured it all over him, in his mouth, in his hair, underneath his clothes. Then I pulled open the boxcar door, lit him on fire, and kicked him out of it. Still bound and burning like a torch, he hit the ground and rolled awkwardly like a misshaped log. When he finally stopped rolling, I was pleased to see that the fire hadn't gone out. After shutting the door, I walked into the coal car, where Zack was still shoveling like a machine.

"You don't have to do that anymore," I told him. "We can coast from here on out."

"What was the problem?" Zack asked.

"Locusts," I lied. "Some of them followed us. They killed Barry."

Sadness and shock swept over his face. "I'm sorry."

"Me too."

"Are they gone now?"

"Yeah, but we should put some distance between us, just to be safe."

"Yeah. Did they…did they get his body?"

"No. We've still got it."

"Good. We should bury him. We can't do much more than that, I'm afraid, but he deserves it."

"He does. We'll do it tonight."

Chapter 13: The Funeral

"Why is it that we rejoice at a birth and grieve at a funeral? It is because we are not the person involved."

-Mark Twain

When the train stopped that night, we were in Indiana, or so Zack told us. I had more faith in his sense of direction than my own. Thomas had spent the rest of the day sleeping, while I tried to get Barry cleaned up for the burial. Without water or clean clothing, there wasn't a whole lot I could do. The train slowed to a halt, and Zack walked into the boxcar. He was wearing clean overalls and a black fedora. Paying his respects as best he could, under the circumstances.

The land around the train was featureless and desolate, like it always was these days. I carried Barry's body; Zack helped support Thomas as he walked. Thomas had clearly seen better days, but at least he was stable for the time being. We stopped a few yards away from the tracks. There was nothing significant about this place, nothing that I could identify, at least. It just felt like the place to stop.

Thomas handed me the shovel from the coal room, which he'd been using as a cane. I dug quickly, making the grave a little longer than his body, perhaps three or four feet deep. When I was done, I placed Barry inside as gently as I could. His glasses were crooked. I fixed them. Then I climbed back out of the hole and began replacing the earth I'd moved. When it was full, I patted it flat with the back of the shovel. It was done.

Nobody was sure what to do next. We'd given him the best burial we could, but it seemed wrong to just turn around and leave him there.

Don't they usually have priests at these things? A priest would know what to do.

"I remember when you guys sprung me from that camp," Zack began, "And sent me an' Barry back to start the train. I tried to kill him. I thought you all were gonna kill me anyway, and I at least wanted to go down swinging. So I waited until he was shoveling coal, and I left the cab, and snuck around to the back of the coal car. I came up behind him, tried to choke him, but he pulled my arms off, and held me by the wrists. He could've brained me with the shovel, or wiped the floor of the coal car with me, but he didn't. He just held me by the wrists and told me to calm down, until I did. He told me that you all weren't going to hurt me, gave me his word you all were just trying to get to New York. He said that he and you guys weren't as bad a bunch as you looked, that you'd look out for me. So I trusted him, and it turned out he was right. I didn't know him that long, but I'm not gonna forget him."

Thomas went next. "I'm not gonna forget that day we rode through Chicago, through the Locusts. They were climbing all over the coal car, screaming and fighting, and I was running back and forth knocking them off with the bat. Barry just blocked it all out, kept on feeding the furnace, like nothing was going on at all. I don't think I could've kept my cool like that. Then, three of them made it into the coal car, made it past me, and Barry turned around, knocked them all out, and went right back to work. It was the damndest thing. I was…I was proud of him." He looked at me. "You remember what he was like when we first met him?"

I laughed and nodded. "I thought he was a square because of his tie."

Now Thomas was laughing. "Oh man, I'd forgotten about that tie. That ugly, ugly tie. If you had told me on that first day what Barry was gonna do to get us through Chicago, I wouldn't have believed you." The smile left his face, replaced with a mask of solemnity. "He changed so much. My God, did he change."

It was my turn. "Do you remember when the train first stopped at Bulwark, and we stalled them for a whole day, but then we finally had to give ourselves up?"

"I was scared out of my mind," Thomas said.

"I was too. But Barry wasn't. We were gonna get our asses kicked, and he knew it, but he just accepted it. He knew it had to get done, so he got ready to do it. I wouldn't have had the balls to go through with it if not for him. I think that's real courage, going into a fight you know you're going to lose, because it's what has to be done. He had courage, all right. Courage like you wouldn't believe."

"He saved my life," said Thomas. His eyes were wet. "When they came in the boxcar, he took the time to wake me up. That's what got him killed. He took the time to wake me up."

Nobody said anything for a while. Then Zack said the Lord's Prayer, and we all bowed our heads. It still didn't feel quite right to leave after that, but it definitely felt less wrong. Thomas was getting short of breath, and shivering, though it wasn't really that cold outside. We went back to the train and slept for a long time.

When I woke up the next day, I didn't feel much better. The loss of Barry hadn't yet fully sunk in, but it was beginning to. Maybe I would go out hunting. Odds were I wasn't going to catch anything, but it would give me something to take my mind off of just how empty the boxcar felt. Bitterly, I realized that the train was still moving; I would be trapped inside a while longer yet. I went to go check on Thomas. He was in bad shape; his breathing was fast and shallow, and he was sweating buckets. I pushed on his shoulder to wake him up, and when he didn't respond, my heart skipped a beat. I tried again, harder this time, but he still wouldn't respond. Finally, desperately, I slapped him in the face, hard. Slowly, he opened his eyes and blinked at me. To my horror, I saw the usual brilliant green of his pupils was fading to gray, being swallowed by the whites in his eyes. It was obvious he was dying. "Hey," he said weakly.

"Hey," I replied, consciously steadying my voice. "How do you feel?"

"I'm dying," he confessed. His bluntness rattled me.

"Don't say that."

"It's true."

"No it's not."

"I'm glad I met you Ethan," he wheezed. "You were…a friend."

"Shut up. Shut up," I said, getting up from beside him. I couldn't deal with this. I couldn't lose him.

"Get to New York," he whispered, and was seized by a coughing fit. When it had passed, he continued. "One of us has to make it. Get to New York. Don't forget me."

"Just shut up, ok! I can't think with you talking!"

But there was nothing to think about, other than the inevitability of my having the boxcar all to myself, and that wasn't a thought I cared to entertain. I sat down, soaked in defeat. Something sharp poked me in the thigh, and I jumped. I had sat on Chuck's scissor, and suddenly, I had a very bad idea that just might save Thomas's life.

Moving quickly, I grabbed two bottles of vodka from the case and sat down next to Thomas. I had to slap him again to wake him up.

"Drink this," I told him.

"Not thirsty."

"Too bad." I poured it down his throat. After a ten minute break, I made him drink the second bottle. He was fading in and out. An agonizing ten minutes later, I asked him how felt.

"Derunk," he slurred.

"Perfect."

I pulled his shirt off over his head. The wound in his chest was deep, and rusty with dried blood. Then I turned his filthy shirt inside out and cut the sleeves off. I hastily braided the two sleeves into a fat roll of cloth.

"Bite this," I commanded.

"Don'wanna. You can'tell me-" I shoved it into his mouth. It shut him up nicely. I climbed on top of him, and peered into his wound. Visibility was poor. There would be merciless trial and error.

"Thomas," I began, opening a third bottle of alcohol and pouring it on my hands and the scissor. "I want you to think happy thoughts, and remember, this will be over soon." His eyes sparked with realization; he finally knew what was coming, but couldn't cry out with the gag in place. I shook the excess liquid from my hands and the blade.

"Sorry, mate." I plunged the scissor deeply into him, just to the left of the wound, and excised a sizeable fraction of his chest.

He was bucking and twitching and attempting to cry out. There was a lot more life in him than I'd expected. "Hold still," I commanded. "Hold still, Goddamn you!" It took all of my energy to keep him in place. I hoped he'd tire himself out soon, or this would drag on a lot longer than either of us wanted it to. He paused for breath, and I was able to get a good look at the incision I'd made. No heart. No splinter. I'd have to try again.

I made another cut, half an inch over. His squirming resumed in earnest. I wrestled him into motionlessness, and looked at the newest cut. Jesus Christ, still nothing. All at once I deeply regretted having killed the only person I knew of who'd performed this procedure successfully.

Cut number three. This time I went a little higher, instead of to the left. Thomas shook the gag out of his mouth and began screaming bloody murder. It was rather distracting. I managed to look into the latest opening, and heaved a sigh of relief. Jackpot. I could see a small cork of wood, throbbing rhythmically with his heartbeat, which I would estimate was about 180 beats per minute at this point. I reached in, yanked the splinter out, and looked around for any others I might've missed. There was a small wooden satellite floating in his chest cavity, which I also removed, but other than that, I'd gotten the last of it. I frantically set about putting his chest back together, then tightly bound it in place, wrapping the body of his t-shirt around his torso like a tourniquet. He lay backward and sprawled onto the floor. I wiped my hands on my shirt and collapsed to the floor myself. His breathing had slowed considerably. That was a good sign.

He addressed me on the verge of consciousness. "Ethan?"

"Yeah?"

"Thanks dude."

"Anytime."

Chapter 14: Thomas's Story, or My Failure of Courage

"The most important things are the hardest to say. They are the things you get ashamed of, because words diminish them-words shrink things that seemed limitless when they were in your head to no more than living size when they're brought out. But it's more than that, isn't it? The most important things lie too close to wherever your secret heart is buried, like landmarks to a treasure your enemies would love to steal away. And you may make revelations that cost you dearly only to have people look at you in a funny way, not understanding what you've said at all, or why you thought it was so important that you almost cried while you were saying it. That's the worst, I think. When the secret stays locked within not for want of a teller but for want of an understanding ear."

-Stephen King, The Body

I woke up early the next day and went to check on Thomas immediately. He was sitting up against the wall of the boxcar, already awake.

"How do you feel?"

"My chest hurts a little. Must have heartburn or something." I wasn't amused, but he was. "Seriously though, I feel better. Not great, but better."

I moved in closer to look at his eyes. They weren't as green as they'd once been, but they were definitely heading that way. I felt enormous relief.

"I think you're gonna be ok," I told him.

"Yeah," replied Thomas. "I think so too."

I sat down next to him, and we listened to the train rolling across the countryside for a few minutes.

"Do you ever wonder why this kind of stuff keeps happening to us?" I asked him.

"What kind of stuff?"

"You know, being turned into vampires, getting captured by the military, being stalked by murderous super-vampires, having to do surgery to each other, things like that?"

He didn't say anything.

"It just seems a little, I don't know...unfair. I don't mean to whine or anything, it just puzzles me a little bit. I mean, maybe we weren't the best people on earth before all of this started, but we certainly weren't the worst, were we?"

"No," he finally answered, "We weren't."

"We got a bad hand," I told him. "We didn't deserve this."

"'Deserve' has nothing to do with it," he replied. "Things just happen, regardless of your individual behavior. Sometimes they're good, sometimes they're bad. Most of the time, they're bad. It's not the sort of thing that can be changed; ergo, it's not the sort of thing that's worth thinking about."

I asked Thomas the question I'd wanted to ask him since the first time I saw him. "Why did you get sent to jail?"

He smiled ruefully. "I was wondering when you'd get around to asking that. I went to jail for something I didn't do. It's a cliché, I know, but it's also the truth. In my case, anyway."

"Well then, what did they charge you with?"

"It's a bit of a long story. Got time?" I assured him that I did.

"A very long time ago, when I was, I'm guessing, a little bit younger than yourself, I graduated from high school. I didn't care for it much. It was easy, but God, was it boring. I did rather well, not as well as I could've done, but well enough for me. I applied to all the usual colleges, state schools, things like that, but that wasn't enough for my dad. He made me send out all sorts of long-shot applications; Brown, Princeton, Yale, etc. I thought it was a waste of time, money, and office supplies, but he wouldn't hear any of it. So I did it to make him happy. I loved my dad, and even though I knew I was just setting him up for disappointment, I filled out every application he left on my bed.

"A few months later, the rejection letters came pouring in. It didn't sting too badly, because I'd already gotten into all of the state schools I'd applied to, and that was good enough for me. None of the long-shots came through. Except for one; Harvard. Harvard Fucking University. It made no sense at all. My grades were good, but not Harvard good. My dad just smiled. 'Sometimes,' he said, 'Good things just happen.'

"We didn't have a lot of money, but you don't get into a school like Harvard when you have no business getting into a school like Harvard and say 'No thanks.' So I took out an unspeakable amount of student loans, packed my bags, and reported to class that fall.

"I loved it. I absolutely loved it. Great roommate, great teachers, great classes, hell, even the food was great. For the first time since 6th grade, I applied myself to doing well in school, and that's exactly what I did. I hadn't picked a major yet, but it was only first semester; I had plenty of time. I was so happy, and I had so much time.

"The week before finals, I got a phone call from my sister. Dad had pancreatic cancer, stage 4, metastasized. She had just had a baby, and mom had died years ago, and he was in bad shape and had no one to take care of him. I left Harvard the next day. Didn't stick around for finals. Failed all my classes. Flunked out. Didn't care. Dad was gonna die. I wouldn't let him die alone.

"Dad was in bad shape. Three months after I got home, the cancer spread to his brain. He was different after that. Angry. Paranoid. Didn't recognize me most days. That didn't stop the mortgage bill from coming every month though, so I got the only job you could get in my hometown; construction. I built apartment complexes ten hours a day. It wasn't enough to pay all the bills, but it was enough to pay some of them. Then, the student loan bills started coming. I'd failed out, and they wanted their money back now. I was drowning in debt, dad was losing his life and his mind, and every night I went to bed with a sore back that only felt worse in the morning.

"I was paralyzed. Given the situation, there was just nothing that could be done. I had no idea what my next move would be. It turned out I didn't have to know; somebody else was about to make that decision for me.

"The news broke that somebody had been embezzling money from the construction company I worked at. A lot of money. Somebody called in with an anonymous tip and said it was me. It couldn't possibly have been me; I'd never worked in the office, never done any accounting of any sort. But who had been working there the shortest amount of time? Me. Who needed lots of money, the sooner the better? Me. I was the perfect fall guy.

"I got the maximum penalty. 20 years. I had no prior record, but the man who owned the construction company was rather fond of his money, and had no shortage of connections in the legal system. So 20 years it was. They put my dad in a home. That's all they told me; 'We put him in a home.' Didn't tell me where. I couldn't even write to him, but he was so far gone at the time he probably wouldn't have been able to read my letters anyway. Of course he's dead by now, but I don't know when it happened, where it happened, how it happened, how much he suffered. I'll never know. I threw my life away to make sure he didn't die alone, but he did. I couldn't stop it.

"I did 10 of my 20 years while the world was apparently falling apart on the outside. We had no idea. We had no newspapers, no tv, no contact with the outside world at all. But gradually, guards and other staff members stopped showing up to work. Then, other prisoners started disappearing. Whether the staff all died, or abandoned us to make a run for it, I don't know. All I know is I saw an opening, so I took it. I got out. For the first time in a decade, I was free. I headed for the local rail yard to put as much space between me and the prison as possible, and that was the night I met Chuck. The next morning, I met you. And that about brings us up to the present day."

I was speechless. Thomas stared at me neutrally. "Questions? Comments?"

"You got screwed," I told him. "Jesus Christ, you got screwed."

"I did." He shrugged. "It happens."

"That's it? That's all you can say? 'It happens?'"

"Well, what else is there to say?" The temperature of his voice was rising. "That there was a point? That there was a purpose? That I *learned something?* I shared a cell with a priest, a priest who killed a little boy, for a year and a half, and do you know what he used to say to me? He used to say there *was* a purpose. That the Lord worked in mysterious ways. That we were born wicked, born in sin. That he gave us trials to make us stronger. That he punished us because he loved us. What does that sound like to you? To me, it sounds like a battered woman making excuses for her husband. 'It was my fault. I deserved it. He did it because he loves me.' Tell me this Ethan, which thought is more comforting, which thought helps you sleep at night; That we're all alone, stumbling through the world blindly, with no one to guide us, that this is it, in the most literal sense, *this is IT,* or that we're all pawns in whatever sick game the great cosmic wifebeater happens to be playing at the moment?"

"I don't like either of those options," I told him.

"Neither do I," he answered. "Neither do I."

He grabbed two bottles of vodka from the case, and handed me one. "We," he said, opening his bottle, "Are going to get stupendously drunk, and never speak of this again."

That's exactly what we did.

Getting really drunk and not waking up with a hangover is pretty much the best thing ever. I was mellow and well rested. Thomas's eyes were as green as they'd ever been. All was right with the world.

"We're getting close," said Thomas.

"What?"

"To New York. We're getting close. Right now we're in Ohio. Once we go through Pennsylvania, we're there."

"How do you know we're in Ohio?"

"Zack told me. He came by while you were still asleep. Brought me a new shirt"

"Gotcha."

"One state away Ethan; one state away."

"It's hard to believe it."

"I know, but that doesn't mean it's not true. What are you gonna do when we get there?"

"I…I don't know. Until recently, I'd planned on Nazi hunting, but it doesn't look like that's going to pan out. I guess I'll just see what happens when I get there. How about you?"

"I'm not gonna stay too long. I'm leaving for Canada as soon as I can. Ontario. My dad and I used to go camping there in the summer. I always loved it there."

I had to choose my words carefully. "I'll go with you," I told him. "That is, if you want me to."

"You really mean it?" he asked. "You want to come with me?"

"Yeah. Yeah, I do."

He smiled broadly. "Alright. It's a plan then. We'll go to Ontario, just you and me. Start over again."

"I'm really looking forward to it."

"I am too," he replied.

That was as close as I ever came to telling him how I really felt about him.

Chapter 15: The Locusts, Part 2

"Never before had there been such a plague of locusts, nor will there ever be again."

~Exodus 10:14

A little bit later, Zack came back to talk to us.

"Don't get me wrong, I do rather enjoy your visits," I told him, "But while you're back here talking to us, who's steering the train?"

Zack laughed. "There's actually not much steering to be done, as far as trains go. I'm mainly up there in case something goes wrong. But as long as the terrain's not bad, and the track is more or less straight, she just steers herself."

"Interesting," said Thomas.

His face grew serious. "We have a bit of a situation," he told us. "We're coming up on the second wave of the Locusts. Once we break through, then it's clear sailing all the way to New York. But breaking through isn't going to be as easy as last time.

"For one thing, there'll be a lot more of them. Second, they'll be nastier this time. The bunch we broke through before was the more civilized group."

"You're joking."

"No, I'm not. That group keeps moving westward, trying to sustain itself. Maybe one day they'll get lucky, find a city that's still more or less in tact, some land to grow food on, and stabilize themselves. Work their way back to being an actual society. I'm not saying it'll happen, I'm just saying it's a possibility.

"This group, however, doesn't think like that. They've given up. They just wallow in the shithole they created, content with doing cruel things to one another until they all do the planet a favor and die. Life means nothing to them. They'll kill themselves trying to kill us, just to have something to do.

"Finally, with Barry gone, we're short handed. We need someone working the furnace, someone manning the cab, and someone else to protect each of those someone's. But there's only three of us. Any ideas?"

Nobody had any ideas. "It'd be a different story if we had weapons," Zack mused. "I don't think the bats and the mace are going to cut it this time."

Weapons.

"I have an idea," I said.

Half an hour later, I was sitting on top of the coal car with the case of vodka, slicing my t-shirt into thin strips of cloth with the scissor. It was dark as night outside. Although my internal clock had been thrown off by the absence of sun, I guessed it was early evening. It was surprisingly warm for late October. Indian summer.

Zack was stationed in the conductor's cab, chained to the steering column, bat in hand, waiting. Thankfully, he had had an extra chain.

Thomas was underneath me in the coal car, standing at attention with the shovel. He swore up and down that he was healthy enough to feed the furnace, so Zack and I backed off and let him do it. We were rolling towards Pennsylvania, and for the time being, we were alone.

I had gotten about three dozen solid strips of cloth from my shirt. Working carefully, precisely, I opened the vodka bottles, stuffed the cloth down the neck, quickly turned them upside down, and put them back in the case. I took Zack's lighter out of my pocket, fingered it nervously, flicking it on and off. Now it was my turn to wait.

The plan was as follows: Thomas would feed the furnace. Zack would man the cab. I would stand on top of the coal car and rain Molotov cocktails down on the Locusts, keeping them away from the train. It had sounded good in my head. Now, standing atop the coal car as we sprinted to make it out of the Dead Zone, with the lives of my only two friends in the world held unsurely in my hands, I was beginning to have doubts.

This wasn't my first experience with Molotov cocktails, or Booze Bombs, as my friends and I had called them. We'd drive out to the rock quarry and pitch them off the cliff. They made a nice explosion, and quickly burned out in the gravel. No harm, no foul. I'd never actually thrown one at a person before. As long as I didn't look this bunch in the eyes, I didn't think I'd have a problem doing it. For the sake of Thomas and Zack, I'd better hope I didn't.

Being on top of the coal car, I was the first one to spot them. I clicked on the lighter and grabbed my first bottle. "Here they come!" I shouted, unsure if anyone could actually hear me or not. This group didn't rush out to meet us; they let us come to them. We smashed into them like a bowling ball thundering down its lane into a crowd of pins, and it had begun.

From my bird's eye vantage point, I could see much more than I wanted to. This wave was thick, thicker than the last one, thicker by two or three times. These Locusts were stained an even darker black than the last ones. I wouldn't have been surprised to find out that the ash had seeped under their skin, like a tattoo, permanently branding them. They were all naked, skeletal with hunger. A few were dragging others around by chains fixed around their necks, like pets. They were almost uniformly male. The few women I saw had almost no teeth, and their eyes were swollen shut from the punches the men used to herd them back and forth through the crowd. I didn't see a single person that didn't have at least one bite mark-shaped scar, human bite marks. A few of them had chunks of flesh bitten clean off of their bodies. I saw no children. This truly was mankind at its lowest. I would enjoy burning it out of existence.

They were swarming around the train now, swarming on all sides. I lit the first bottle and threw it to the left of the coal car. I threw the first one a few feet out, because I wasn't sure how big the explosion would be. If the coal car caught fire, it would be disastrous. The bottle shattered, and flame roared upward. The explosion wasn't as loud as I was expecting, but the speed with which the fire spread was truly impressive. Those who'd been caught in the blast shrieked and ran away from the train, frantically trying to put themselves out. Nobody tried to assist them. I wasn't surprised.

I sent the next bottle to the right of the coal car, with equally impressive results. There was now a ten foot berth between the Locusts and the car. This was going better than I'd hoped. Then I noticed that although they were now avoiding the coal car, they were doubling up on the conductor cab, crawling over top of each other to get inside. I lit another bottle and flung it overhand, to the left. It landed dangerously close to the cab itself, burned a wide swath through the Locusts and gave Zack some breathing room. After throwing another bottle on the opposite side, Zack was enjoying the same level of personal space that Thomas and I were. The train was still chugging through the mob, bringing us closer to freedom. I couldn't believe it; this was actually going to work. We were going to make it.

I felt the coal car rocking violently back and forth beneath my feet. The case of vodka nearly slid off the roof. I had to dive to catch it before it fell over the edge. The Locusts had turned their attention to the coal car again, trying to tip it over. I frantically pulled another bottle from the case, but it slid through my shaking fingers and shattered uselessly at my feet.

Steady now. Don't get angry.

I took a deep breath, turned around, and reached for a new bottle. Looking behind me, I saw somebody crawling out of the fifth and final boxcar attached to the Yukon Glory. That car was a tiny, rusty thing, too small for the four of us, we'd decided, at the beginning of our journey. The Anaikolra, however, felt differently. Two more were crawling out onto the roof now, then another, then another. The last one to crawl out was wearing a fresh bandage around his right shin. His inflamed skin grafts clashed harshly with the black sky. It was the one from the guard tower, the one who'd killed Barry, the one who was now staring at me from across the divide, flanked by seven of his men, their sinister glows melting together behind him. He looked me squarely in the eye as he dislocated his jaw. I clutched the bottle tightly and flicked on the lighter. I knew I was almost certainly not going to survive this. I was ok with that. Just as long as I got to kill him first.

They were running at me now, charging like bulls, leaping over the chasms between the cars.

So that's how they followed us. They stowed away in the back car. They did the same thing we did.

They were closer now, two cars away, one car away.

And the burned one? After I cut his tendons? He was probably crazy enough to chase us on foot, as painful as that would've been, catching up with us when we stopped, then waiting, waiting with the others. Waiting for the right time.

The right time was now.

I lit the bottle and threw it at them, threw it right in their fucking faces. The burned one, the one I wanted, ducked, and I saw glass smash and fire explode into the face of the one behind him. Hissing, clutching his face, he stumbled off of the boxcar and into the hands of the Locusts below. I saw him disappear under the black roiling undertow of arms and legs, and he didn't come back up.

The Anaikolra froze in their tracks. I already had another bottle in my hand, two more at my feet ready to go. We were each daring the other to make the first move. The Locusts on the ground were finished with the Anaikolra, and had resumed their efforts to tip over the coal car. I lit the bottle I was holding and pegged it at the side nearest me. They screamed and backed off. The Anaikolra made like they were preparing to make the last jump onto the coal car roof, but I was too quick on the draw, and had another bottle up and ready to go before they had the chance. They froze again, stymied. For the first time ever in my dealings with the Anaikolra, I was on the offensive. It was a feeling I could get used to.

Before I knew what was happening, they jumped. Not onto the roof of the coal car like I'd expected, but down, down below me, onto the small bridge that connected our boxcar to the coal car. Down where I couldn't hit them without blowing up the train. Down to where Thomas was alone.

Underneath my feet, beyond my range of vision, I heard hissing, and the door to the coal car being opened. The hissing grew louder, and I heard the sounds of a shovel clattering against flesh. Looking down, in shock, I saw the Anaikolra reemerge. They were retreating. A moment later, I saw Thomas step onto the connecting bridge, clutching the shovel, covered in soot, blood and drool and furious vengeance leaking from his body. The Locusts grabbed at their ankles as they crossed the bridge, but Thomas and the Anaikolra ignored them. This was bigger than them. I saw one Locust manage to claw his way onto the bridge, behind Thomas, who was still beating back the Anaikolra with the shovel. I dropped the lighter in my pocket, pulled out my gun, and shot the Locust with my last bullet. He crumpled off of the bridge, dead. Thomas didn't even flinch at the sound of the shot.

The Locusts were more of an annoyance than anything else at this point. I hastily lit and threw two more bottles, one on each side of the coal car, to stop the rocking once more. The first Anaikolra to retreat was now at the end of the bridge, and he carefully stepped off onto the narrow platform that circled our boxcar. He opened the large sliding door, and stepped inside. The others followed him. When the last one, the one with the skin grafts, had made it inside, he slammed the door shut. Thomas lowered the shovel, turned around, and motioned for me to join him on the bridge. I stuffed two bottles into my pockets and jumped. As soon as I landed, a Locust reached out and grabbed my leg. Thomas brought the shovel down on his head, and he relented. The blade of the shovel was nearly bent in half from all of the beatings.

"How the hell did you fight off seven of them?" I asked.

He shrugged. "I got pissed."

"You are unbelievable."

"Thanks." He smiled winningly. I was shaking all over.

"What do we do now?" I asked.

He pulled a bottle from my pocket. "Light it, open the door, throw it in?"

"Sounds good to me."

I lit our bottles. Thomas pulled open the door. When he did so, a hand shot out, grabbed him by the neck, and yanked him inside. They tried to shut the door again, but I stuck out my foot and blocked it. The pain was terrible; I'd broken at least three toes. I swung the door open, and saw the seven remaining Anaikolra huddled together. The one with the skin grafts stood in front. He was facing me, holding Thomas from behind, using him like a shield. His jaw still hung open. He had a hand wrapped around Thomas's neck. "You move, he diezzz," he rasped.

I was paralyzed with shock. It was a fake retreat. They'd planned this. We'd done exactly what they wanted us to. Now they had Thomas, and by extension, myself.

Thomas, inexplicably, was smiling. He looked me in the eyes, winked, then quickly glanced down at his stomach. He'd hidden the bottle underneath his shirt, which was beginning to smoke a little where it touched the fuse. He waved slightly with his free hand.

"Goodbye," he said. He dropped the bottle and stomped it.

Flames shot upward, engulfing him, his captor, and three others standing behind him. The boxcar filled with chaotic, frenzied hissing. Thomas didn't scream. He broke free of the one who'd held him by the throat, the one who wouldn't die, and punched him right between the eyes. The smile on his face was brighter than the flames surrounding him.

I felt something burning my thumb. Looking down, I saw the fuse on my own bottle was moments away from reaching the vodka. Thomas turned around to face me.

"Throw it!" he yelled. "Throw it!" Then one of the Anaikolra who'd escaped the first explosion tackled him to the floor.

I threw the bottle, and fire erupted inside the boxcar again. It was too bright to see anything. I slammed the door shut. A few seconds later, against my better judgment, I put my ear to the door. No hissing, no screaming. No sound at all. When I opened the door again, a thick cloud of pungent smoke wafted out. There was nothing inside but a few puddles of flame, some bones, and metal parts that I supposed were the Anaikolra's iron enhancements. They were dead.

Thomas.

Thomas was dead.

I limped back across the bridge, dragging my wounded foot, and lugged myself onto the roof of the coal car. Zack was standing on top of the conductor's cab, bewildered, swinging his bat at anything that moved. I apathetically lobbed a few bottles his way, thinning the mob. He beat the last of them back, tipped his hat to me, and swung himself through a window back into the cab. Good for him.

I grabbed another four bottles, lit them, and pitched them off the roof. I didn't really care where they landed. I didn't really care in general. I grabbed the vodka case under my arm, climbed down, and shut myself inside the coal car. The furnace was still roaring; the train was still moving. I let myself collapse onto the floor. I could hear the Locusts outside shrieking, moaning, pounding on the side of the car, trying to dismantle it.

Go for it. Tear shit up. You want to destroy the world so bad, do it. Do us all a favor. You have my blessing.

I opened the vodka case. There were 12 unused Molotov cocktails inside. I pulled the fuse out of one and drank it. I finished it, and did it again, then I did it one more time after that. I passed out. Whenever I woke up, I interpreted that as a sign that I should start drinking again. That's what I did for the next three days, until the train stopped, and Zack walked inside and told me we'd made it to New York.

Epilogue: February 11th, 1980

"Scar tissue is stronger than regular tissue.
Realize the strength; move on."

-Henry Rollins

I've been in New York for about four months now. I like it. It's civilized. I'd forgotten what civilization was like. I read the newspaper every day. I pay for goods and services with cash. If something catches on fire, the fire department comes and puts it out. Those things make a big difference.

Zack sold the Yukon Glory for scrap the night we got here. I don't know how much he got for it, but it wasn't much. He says we barely made it through the last wave of Locusts. He was sad Thomas didn't make it. He asked if we still had the body, if we were gonna do a burial. I told him we didn't, so we couldn't. He told me he was very sorry. Then he went back to Canada. He decided he didn't want to go to England after all. Getting across the Canadian border isn't as hard these days as it used to be. He offered to take me with him, and I thought about it, but I respectfully declined. When I think about all the things I went through to get to New York, it just seemed like it would be disrespectful for me to leave so quickly.

I still have Chuck's scissor. I keep it in a desk in my apartment. I hope I never have to touch it again.

I finally saw the Chrysler Building. It looked like it did in all the pictures. I know that sentence conveys a sense of disappointment, which isn't entirely fair. It's a beautiful building, I just think I built it up a little too much in my mind to the point that nothing could've lived up to my expectations. Still, I saw it. I touched it. I stood in its shadow. One more item crossed off the list of things to do before I die.

I called my parents once. Yes, you can still make phone calls to the west coast, but only at certain times, and it's really expensive, and you have to know the right people, but you can do it. They thought I was dead. My mom wouldn't stop crying. It was uncomfortable. They asked how I got to New York, and I told them I took a train. I wouldn't elaborate any further than that. When they asked why I left, I told them I didn't know, I just felt like it. They didn't press. I told them I loved them. They told me they loved me. I hung up. I'll probably never see them again.

I'm spending more time on my art these days. I still have the sketchbook and pencils from the trip, but at the moment I'm more into painting. I found an amazing easel at a pawn shop in the Bronx. Expensive as hell, but worth it. Haven't sold anything yet; there's nowhere to sell it to. Assuming I stick around here long enough to make some money, I'd like to open a gallery. That'd be pretty cool.

I still do heroin sometimes when I'm bored. Mostly out of habit. I'm immortal, or as close to it as you can get, so my health isn't really at stake. All the same, I probably should quit, but hell, you know how that stuff goes.

I still see Thomas in crowds. The first time it happened, three days after I got here, I totally flipped out, chased the guy down. Once I got close enough, I saw it wasn't him. Just looked like him. Not really, but enough, I guess. It used to happen three or four times a week. Eventually, I stopped chasing them, stopped getting close enough to make sure. I just let them keep walking. Now, I only see him once or twice a month. I'm pretty sure that's how it's gonna be from now on.

They have a border patrol here in New York, along the southern border. They kill Locusts who get too close, occasionally go into outlying areas, looking for supplies, refugees, etc. I went and talked to them, told them I knew Akili. That got me a job right away, but I told them I could only work nights. They got suspicious. They asked why, and I said I was just a night person. They told me to open my mouth, and I said why, and they said it didn't make any difference to them, they don't discriminate, but at the same time, they needed to know. I opened my mouth and showed them my fangs. I got a job working nights.

There are other vampires who work the night shift. 12 of them. We keep people on the border safe at night, and get to eat all the Locusts we want, along with a place to live and a little cash every week. I'm not very close with the others. I'm the only one who's Stained, and they don't quite know what to make of me. In the four months I've been there, everybody has saved everybody else's life at least twice. They know I have no desire to hurt them. Still, they don't really know how to act around me.

My favorite part of the border patrol is finding refugees. People who come along after the Locusts have moved through, and quietly start rebuilding, start having families. Those people give me hope. Since I started working with the border patrol, I've saved 36 refugees, gotten them into New York, set up with the Recolonization Commission. I'm actually getting to do some good with myself after all.

Things are pretty quiet right now. I sleep during the day and work nights. When I have a night off, I go out walking around the city, exploring. Sometimes I just ride the subway all night. You can't quit trains cold turkey, or at least I can't. I'm getting used to things, used to my new life. There are good days and bad days. I'm just doing the best I can to get through them, to try to make them mean something, just like anybody else. Just like you.

Special Thanks

The families Ziemba, Whysong, Harris, Waggoner, Hume, and Sink, including but not limited to; Steve Ziemba, Zack Ziemba, Gene Harris, Christie Harris, Nate Waggoner, John Waggoner, Evan Hume, Justin Sink, and Paul Krumholz. Tatyana Worthy, Mike Emanuel, Noni Ackman, Lisa Cook, Paige Peck, Dr. Dan, Dr. Richard Childs. Connie Casserly and Susan Braaten. Bob Lawson, Amanda Long, Gonzi Aida, and Christie Blouir. Sir Arthur C. Clarke, Stephen King, Peter Straub, Joss Whedon, Henry Rollins, Ray Bradbury, Neil Peart, Richard Matheson, Ernest Hemingway, Johnny Cash, Al Gore, Stephen Hawking, and you, the reader.

Printed in the United States
203266BV00004B/55-102/P

9 781604 811124